Forbidden Planets

BOOKS BY MARVIN KAYE

The Amorous Umbrella
Bullets for Macbeth
A Cold Blue Light (with Parke Godwin)
Fantastique
Ghosts of Night and Morning
The Country Music Murders
The Incredible Umbrella
The Last Christmas of Ebenezer Scrooge
The Laurel & Hardy Murders
A Lively Game of Death
The Masters of Solitude (with Parke Godwin)
My Son the Druggist
The Soap Opera Slaughters
Wintermind (with Parke Godwin)

ANTHOLOGIES EDITED BY MARVIN KAYE

Angels of Darkness
Devils and Demons
Don't Open This Book!
The Dragon Quintet
The Fair Folk
Forbidden Planets
Ghosts
Haunted America
Lovers and Other Monsters
Masterpieces of Terror and the Supernatural
Masterpieces of Terror and the Unknown
13 Plays of Ghosts and the Supernatural
The Vampire Sextette
Weird Tales
Witches and Warlocks

Forbidden Planets

Edited by
Marvin Kaye

SCIENCE
FICTION

First Science Fiction Book Club printing May 2006

Book design by Christos Peterson

Published by Science Fiction Book Club, 501 Franklin Avenue, New York, New York 11530.

Visit the SF Book Club online at www.sfbc.com

ISBN: 1-58288-211-8
978-1-58288-211-6

Printed in the United States of America

Contents

Introduction

The Fantastic Power of "No-No"

❧❧❧❧

SINCE 1970 I have edited twenty-seven anthologies, mostly for the Science Fiction Book Club. A few of the exceptions are theatre collections, a trio is devoted to Sherlock Holmes, but most of them are chiefly concerned with fantasy literature. *Forbidden Planets* is my first anthology to consist exclusively of science fiction.

I am surprised it took me so long. When I was a teenager, science fiction changed my reading life. The transfiguring moment occurred in 1950 when I bought one of the first books I ever shelled out scarce capital for: the Bantam Books paperback edition of Ray Bradbury's *The Martian Chronicles.* Not the Brothers Grimm, not *Alice in Wonderland,* not even L. Frank Baum's wonderful Oz books stirred my imagination and touched my heart as deeply as Ray's poetic prose. His poignant writing woke in me a love for language's power to enrich, astound, and transform the human spirit.

"O brave new world!" If this was science fiction, I wanted *more*! In my impassioned search for comparable SF authors, I became one of the first members of the Science Fiction Book Club. What a thrilling time, discovering Isaac Asimov, Alfred Bester, James Blish, Fredric Brown, Arthur C. Clarke, L. Sprague de Camp, *and* Fletcher Pratt, Robert Heinlein, Eric Frank Russell, Olaf Staple-

don, and space opera's Grand Master Jack Williamson! (Though I'm a fan of *Star Wars*, George Lucas has never come close to the special effects potential of Williamson's *The Legion of Space!*)

But for all the pleasure science fiction afforded me, I soon realized that no one affected me as powerfully and consistently as Ray Bradbury. Eventually I saw that Bradbury, despite the many stories he set on Mars and a few other planets, was primarily writing fantasy that employed space travel as its metaphor.

In other words, I got hooked on fantasy, and today, though I regard fantasy as the principal speculative genre, I believe its boundaries are vast enough to encompass science fiction. Thus, *Forbidden Planets* is not so much a foray into new territory for me as it is a long-overdue broadening of my editorial parameters.

So off we go . . . but why to **Forbidden** *Planets?*

As I was trying to come up with an idea for a new anthology, a task that grows more difficult with each passing decade, I began "browsing" my old friend (both the person and the book) *Leonard Maltin's 2005 Movie Guide* seeking films that might tweak my overworked imagination. Soon I found myself rereading Leonard's (or a member of his staff's) description of the landmark SF film *Forbidden Planet*, which I had the good fortune to see during its first run in 1956, the year I graduated high school.

During the '50s and early '60s, I'd seen most of the then new spate of science fiction movies, classics such as *The Day the Earth Stood Still, The Thing from Another World* (NOT John Carpenter's!), *Village of the Damned*, and the Tom Cruise-less *War of the Worlds*; near-greats like *The Day of the Triffids, Invasion of the Body Snatchers, It Came from Outer Space, When Worlds Collide*; and the duds, some of them now wildly overpraised, e.g., *Invaders from Mars*, and some of them at least laughable, such as *Fire Maidens from Outer Space* and, of course, Ed Wood's *Plan 9 from Outer Space*.

Note that every one of these movies was a science-fictional variation on the old horror formula: if we don't understand it, be afraid of it! Even the 3-D film *It Came from Outer Space*, a compassionate and original idea from Ray Bradbury, still set up an atmosphere of ethnocentric fearfulness for much of its length (as did the more recent great SF film *Close Encounters of the Third Kind*).

Fear of science, of course, was a constant element of many of the horror films of an earlier decade, especially *Frankenstein* (which one may reasonably label as early medical science fiction). The essential theme of these films, often declared just before *The End* flashed on the screen, was that "There are some things mankind must not meddle with."

Though *Forbidden Planet* explored the same thematic territory, this time it was not the people of Earth who were at risk, but the pre-*Star Trek* spacemen who set down on a world loosely patterned on Shakespeare's *The Tempest*, complete with Prospero (Walter Pidgeon), his innocent daughter Miranda (Anne Francis), and an invisible monster more or less analogous to Caliban. The film's ultimate revelations concern advanced but woefully misused technology. Thus, *Forbidden Planet* is very much about the quality the Greek tragedians might have called *hubris*: that overweening pride that causes great heroes and kings to overleap their place and bring disaster down upon themselves and their loved ones.

Let's put it another way: "There are some things mankind was not meant to meddle with."

Now Goethe (and Disney!) invoked this idea in "The Sorcerer's Apprentice," but it is actually much older, it is surely our culture's most venerable caveat: the snake tempting Eve to tempt Adam to eat the apple. Ah, but which apple? Not the one plucked from the Tree of Life, as Lord Byron mourns in his unproduceably splendid drama *Manfred* . . . it is the Tree of Knowledge that we are supposed to stay away from.

Q: What is one of the first words we learn as infants?

A: No. No-No. Not. Non. Nein. Nyet.

Now I suspect the next opinion will vary depending on the color of the state you live in (both emotionally and geographically), but unfortunately, or fortunately, depending on said viewpoint, human nature is psychologically constructed to test boundaries, defy rules, flout authority, overstep boundaries. In the words of Nobel Prize–winner Juan Ramón Jiménez (cited by Ray Bradbury in *Fahrenheit 451*):

"If they give you ruled paper, write the other way."

So the idea of worlds off-limits to the likes of our species calls up visions of dangerous places that we fear to set foot upon—BUT that also ought to stir up the desire to challenge the status quo, i.e., the "No-No." So whether we are Adam or Eve or just plain us, it does appear that our nature is to venture "where angels fear to tread" . . .

Which is as wholly human as the dread of "off-limits" worlds with their potential to stir our collective fears of the unknown.

—Marvin Kaye
New York City
August 2005

Forbidden Planets

analyzed before it can be taken. The indigenous human inhabitants, the descendants of those who survived the crash of the old off-course colony ship that ended up here, are all on the other side of the planet." Marston struggled to retain his composure. "The occasional Commonwealth science party that visits them necessarily sticks to one minimally invasive site located on the other hemisphere."

"That's what the prep files said," Urbinski agreed. "Nobody comes over here, nobody checks over here."

"There's a good reason for that, which is the point I'm trying to make." Marston was calming down some. "Without an indigenous human to provide guidance and assistance, nobody can survive down in the forest for more than a day. Since the company surreptitiously established the outpost on this mountaintop, I've lost a dozen people in there. Good people; well-trained, experienced, and careful." He shook his head dolefully. "There isn't a scientist on staff who wouldn't give a month's pay to have the assistance of an indigenous guide for one week."

Urbinski sniffed ever so diffidently. "Evidently despite what you say, your own people are not well-trained, experienced, or careful enough."

Marston's face flushed anew, but he held his temper. "My job is to supervise company activities and keep this place viable with the equipment and talent I'm supplied by the company. I don't hire people." Turning, he gazed moodily out the port. "Olin was the best xenobotanist in the place. Research on biopharmaceuticals almost came to a dead stop when he went missing. It's just now getting back up to speed, but the section will never achieve full potential without his knowledge and experience."

"I know." Urbinski was patient. "The company knows. That's why I'm here."

All the bluster and defiance seemed to go out of Marston as he slumped low in the chair behind his desk. The anger, though subdued, remained. "Olin of all people should have known better than to go into the forest on a solo collecting run. Idiot."

"You see?" Urbinski considered lighting another stimstick, decided to hold off until the meeting had been concluded. "We don't

disagree on everything. Thom Olin went AWOL." His eyes
flashed. "My people and I will bring him back." As a conciliatory
sop he added, "Any advice you can give me and my team will of
course be appreciated."

Taking a deep breath, Marston sat up in his chair, the back of
which promptly followed him forward in order to continue providing proper support. "Don't do it."

Urbinski almost laughed out loud. "Any *other* advice?"

"I'm sure you've been 'briefed.' As much good as a formal
briefing, no matter how in-depth, can do to prepare someone for
this place. I suppose there isn't much else I could add." He gestured over his shoulder in the direction of the rest of the sprawling,
modest, heavily armored, and highly illegal research complex.
"One thing I can tell you for certain: you won't be able to talk any
of the resident technicians or their assistants into going with you.
They've all been traumatized by the deaths of colleagues who tried
similar outings. Nobody even goes outside any more unless they
have no other choice.

"Except for the oceans and other large bodies of exposed water, this ball of impenetrable foliage is covered with dense alien
rainforest that tops out at about a thousand meters in height. The
skies are full of flying predators, some of whom would make sushi
of eagles. According to the native humans, whose oral records the
company has managed to swipe from restricted Commonwealth
science sources, there are seven distinct levels to the world-forest.
Every one of them is swarming with lifeforms; plant, animal, and
otherwise, that can and will macerate a wandering human at the
slightest opportunity. The resultant pulp might be spit out instead
of consumed, but that's pretty small consolation to the macerated."

"It is also," an unimpressed Urbinski pointed out, "lush with all
manner of unique, potentially extractable biochemical agents." He
indicated their heavily shielded surroundings. "Hence the considerable risk and expense the company has gone to in order to establish and maintain this outpost."

"You know," Marston murmured as he studied his folded
hands, "there are fragmentary records of another such installation
here, set up by a different company, that precedes this one. On the

Mid-Death

by *Alan Dean Foster*

---

*Here is a brand-new story that takes place on Midworld, a planet so full
of dangerous life-forms that no one in her or his right mind would ever
venture to explore it; unfortunately, the space folk in "Mid-Death" don't
have much choice in the matter.*

*The prolific Alan Dean Foster has written more than one hundred
award-winning science fiction, fantasy, detective, western, historical,
and contemporary books—including novelizations of* Star Wars, *the first
three* Alien *films,* Alien Nation, *and other movies—plus excellent shorter
fiction, a personal favorite of mine being "Diesel Dream," which appears
in my earlier GuildAmerica anthology* Angels of Darkness.

*Foster's love of the exotic has led him to travel both extensively and
riskily. "My wife JoAnn and I have been through Asia and the Pacific, in
addition to exploring the back roads of Tanzania and Kenya. I've camped
out in the 'Green Hell' of the southeastern Peruvian jungle, photograph-
ing army ants and pan-frying piranha (lots of small bones; tastes a lot
like trout)."*

*Foster's real-life adventures powerfully flavor "Mid-Death," whose
setting was used in two novels of his Commonwealth cycle,* Midworld
(1975) and Mid-Flinx *(1995). "In the Commonwealth," he explains,
"Midworld is a planet Under Edict, which means visitation is not al-*

lowed under any circumstances. The theme of this anthology made the
idea of setting a new tale on Midworld come very naturally, though this
new novella reads quite independently of the novels that precede it."

–I–

MARSTON REGARDED THE man standing before him as if he was
fully certifiable. "Are you out of your mind? Have you taken leave
of your senses? You can't go down in there." The station supervisor
took a deep breath. "I thought this was to be a robotic expedition,
conducted from a distance. Nobody actually goes down deep into
the forest. Nobody. Thom Olin did, and nobody's seen him since."
His tone hardened. "And you've only been here a couple of days."

Urbinski stubbed out the end of the stimstick he'd been puffing
and smiled. He was used to people, both within the company and
outside of it, underestimating his abilities. They, and his complete
self-confidence, had allowed him to rise high within the former
and take revenge on the latter. He decided to be patient with
Marston. The supervisor knew nothing of his official visitor's history, and therefore could be excused his ire. For a little while.

"Company wants Olin back. They want him back very badly
indeed." Urbinski's eyes, which were small and dark and missed
nothing, glittered. "Since your people appear to be too unskilled to
go after him, or too afraid, I was instructed to come here and bail
you out."

Marston's face had been getting redder from the start of the
meeting. Now it threatened to turn quite maroon. "Look, I've got
enough trouble trying to keep this place from being overgrown
and overrun without being lectured by either the home office or
know-it-all neophytes."

Urbinski bristled, but restrained himself. He had shot men for
lesser remarks. Such unfortunate encounters did not usually, however, involve fellow employees. He allowed the outpost supervisor
to continue.

"Operating an illegal installation on a planet like Midworld
that's Under Edict means every action has to be analyzed and re-

other side, where the indigenous colonial descendants have survived. Apparently that station, and every one of its employees, vanished."

"Poor preparation. Lack of understanding. Insufficient research. Inadequate funding and incompetent staffing." Urbinski remained unfazed. "The company is determined not to repeat that mistake. For one thing, there are no colonial survivors here to be concerned about. For another, this site, like the Commonwealth station on the other side of the planet, is located on the peak of a mountain above the treeline. One is safe here from any occasional wandering nuisances posed by the denizens of the forest."

Marston couldn't help himself. He burst out laughing.

Urbinski was not amused. "Excuse me. I don't recall saying anything particularly funny."

The unit supervisor wiped his eyes. "Yes, you did. You referred to the lifeforms that call this forest home as 'nuisances.'" Having dried his tears, he eyed his visitor with sudden intensity. "I hope your professional abilities match your gift for understatement."

Seeing there was nothing else useful to be learned from the bureaucrat seated across from him, Urbinski rose. "Thank you for your help," he said coolly.

"Hey, don't get me wrong." Marston also stood. "We may disagree on prospects, but we're on the same team here. No one would like to see Thom Olin back in camp any more than I would. I promise that my people and I will do everything in our power to help you accomplish that."

Urbinski thawed, slightly, and nodded. "I'll be sure to make a note of that in my report." He looked toward the single window. Triple-paned and made of reinforced single-poured plexalloy, it showed a view across the bare rock of the mountaintop. Swathed in cloud, stretching toward the horizon, a solid line of gray and green was just visible below the first ridge line. The edge of the jungle. "My team and I will start out tomorrow. Though we have our trackers, it would be helpful to have someone to point us in the general direction Olin took when he went out on this last collecting trip."

"I'll show you myself." Marston came out from behind the desk.

Urbinski was pleased. "That's the kind of individual commitment that makes my job and that of my people a lot easier."

Pausing at the vacuum-worthy portal that led from the office
back out into the pedestrian passageway, Marston looked back at
his guest. "Personal commitment doesn't have a damn thing to do
with it. No one else will do it, and as senior supervisor on site, I'm
stuck with the job."

−II−

Never one to waste company time or his own, Urbinski intended
to start out as early as possible the following day. Marston wouldn't
hear of it.

"Too many aerial predators active that early. Better to wait until midday, when it's hotter, but before it starts raining."

Urbinski could only shake his head in disgust. "My people
aren't afraid of a few alien birds."

The supervisor offered a wan smile by way of reply. "Indulge
me this one time. It'll be the last time you'll have to do so. Once
you're in the forest and beyond the outpost perimeter, you'll be on
your own."

Urbinski shrugged. As impatient as the team was to get going,
he acceded to Marston's request. They would wait around and kill
another few hours checking out gear. As the supervisor said, they
would be rid of his hesitancy soon enough.

By the time Marston agreed to go outside with them, everyone
on the team was itching to get moving. The sooner they did so, the
sooner they would find Olin and bring him back, the sooner they
could leave this forbidden horticulturist's nightmare, and the
sooner their appropriate bonus slips would be deposited to their
respective individual accounts.

The mountaintop was a small island in an ocean of festering
green. Even the sunlight, diffused by clouds and mist, had a faint
greenish cast to it. Few of the billions of local plant forms had
found a way to establish a foothold on the rough outcropping of
broken, shattered bare granite. Those that did were kept under

continual pressure by the company's maintenance professionals. The talents of two of Marston's best people were applied around the clock to ensure that the rock stayed clear of creeping, insinuating, feverish growth.

The supervisor was waiting for them in the south airlock. While the atmosphere outside was perfectly breathable—exhilarating, even, given all the oxygen being continuously pumped out by the endless rainforest—many of the spores and seeds and other vegetable matter that rode its humid updrafts and occasional breezes were not. One of the omnipresent fears that afflicted those doing work at the outpost centered around the possibility of inadvertently inhaling the wrong spore, which would then settle down to mature inside that unfortunate person's lungs. The airlock and the outpost's extensive network of internal filters were not viewed as luxuries by those who lived and labored behind them.

Urbinski had to struggle to keep from laughing when he and his team met up with Marston at the lock. The supervisor wore a full environment suit that rendered his person as constricted and clumsy and mechanically overwrought as if he was preparing to step out of a ship into empty space. Urbinski had to shush his own people. They all worked for the same company, he reminded them, and there was nothing to be gained by publicly disrespecting the supervisor.

"Ready?" Marston peered past him, checking out the rest of the team leader's personnel.

"Sure we are." Behind his team leader, Bernard had to stifle a chuckle. "How about you?" Next to him, Alesha giggled. Stoic as always, even the hulking Temura was hard-pressed to muffle a guffaw.

"I wish there were more than four of you going out." Marston's concern, Urbinski felt, was touching but misplaced.

"We'll be fine. In fact, I was thinking of letting Bernard stay behind. But that's not what he's getting paid for." Urbinski nodded toward the airlock door. "Let's go." In a nod to the supervisor's excess of caution, he could not keep from adding, "We've lost half a day already."

None of them had to cradle a weapon. Heavier ordnance traveled slung across their backs. Sliders strapped to left arms could provide instant firepower without the operator having to reach to unholster or unlimber a gun. All four team members were clad in color-coded spilk suits. Internally cooled, the two-piece, overlapping outfits were fashioned of the lightest, most comfortable, most durable body armor that contemporary materials science could devise and company money could buy. Hardened, narrow-brimmed caps fashioned of the same material were equipped with powerful built-in illuminators for night-vision. Flip-down lenses enabled a wearer to view his or her surroundings in visible, infrared, or ultraviolet light. Duty belts and packs contained everything necessary to support a well-trained search and locate team for weeks out in the field.

In fact, Urbinski knew, they were actually going to able to travel lighter than usual, since frequent potable rain and the presence everywhere of water-storing bromeliads made it unnecessary to carry more than a day's worth of water. Not having to haul the usual water-weight rendered the team members downright jaunty. Compared to work on desert or cold-weather worlds, this promised to be a cakewalk, albeit one where you had to watch your step lest you slip off the tree branch on which you happened to be walking. Such branches and vines, linking together the thousand-meter tall trees, provided the only access to the interior of the interminable jungle. The dense web of growth rendered the use of skimmers—or, as Marston had apparently thought, robotic recovery vehicles—impracticable.

Halfway to where the first small branches extending outward from the tops of trees began to probe bare rock, Marston halted. "This is as far as I go. You've locked on the signal?"

Taking his own tracker from his belt, Urbinski first made certain it was synchronized with those of his three companions. Reassuringly, the relevant indicator showed solid on all four units. The modern powerpaks utilized by explorers and researchers at the outpost were designed to emit an intermittent, extremely low-level locator signal even when the device they powered was "completely" run down or turned off. The one Olin had carried was no exception.

Urbinski turned to the supervisor. "I still don't understand why, if you know his position, you haven't gone in after him?"

Marston looked uncomfortable. As well he should, Urbinski thought. "Olin broke the rules. He knew the boundaries. He went beyond them, and kept going." A suited hand waved at the outpost looming behind them, a series of corridor-linked smooth-faced mounds pimpling the crest of the mountain. "Everyone who works here knows the parameters. If you're going into the forest, you don't exceed them. Do so, and you're on your own." With his other hand, he indicated Urbinski's tracker. "Olin not only exceeded the specified parameters, he went way, way beyond them. Despite that, I asked for volunteers to go after him." There was a slight pause, or maybe it was a choke, in the supervisor's voice. "No one spoke up. I didn't expect them to."

"Which is why I am here." Urbinski coughed into a closed fist, then took a deep, deliberate breath, as if challenging the surrounding forest to take offense. Nothing did. All that emerged from the surrounding treetops was a steady susurration of alien cries and squalls. He turned to his team.

"You've all had plenty of time to go over the prep on the way out here, and commit to memory the most critical portions. To review: don't touch anything, don't smell anything, don't pick the flowers. Don't be lulled by appearances. Assume everything you see, no matter how harmless-looking or innocent or pretty, is faster than you are and potentially lethal. Stay together at all times. If something looks suspicious, notify your buddies immediately. If something starts toward you, or even seems like it might start toward you, and you can't positively ID it as harmless from the prep, fry it first and ask me about it afterwards. Now, let's get this over with." Unlimbering climbing gear, he started toward the first treetops. His team followed.

Alesha was last to disappear into the verdure. As she prepared to drop down behind Temura, she looked back long enough to smile briefly at the watching supervisor. "Thanks for the 'help.' See you in a week or so."

Marston nodded, raised a hand in farewell, and nodded slowly. "I'll pray for you."

Alesha, who had done difficult work on a dozen different worlds, just sighed and turned away. How a wimp like Marston had ever been put in charge of such an important, clandestine company project she could not begin to imagine.

–III–

It was magnificent in the forest. As they descended from the tree-tops (the region the original colonists' surviving descendants quaintly referred to as the Upper Hell), the team soon found itself immersed in the eruption of perfervid life that characterized the Edicted planet. Identified on restricted Commonwealth navigational schematics simply as "Midworld," the innocuous name gave no hint of the botanical wonders that were to be found thereon. For profusion and variety of plant life, for sheer rampant biodiversity, no other discovered world, not even Fluva, came close. But Fluva was a recognized, known world, open to authorized study and development by various branches of the Commonwealth government as well as its two dominant local sentient species. Research, exploration, and potential exploitation were legal there.

This Midworld was Under Edict. That meant even casual visitation was officially forbidden, the tiny scientific outpost on the other side of the planet notwithstanding. It also meant that whatever company or great family House could get in first, could potentially get out with research worth untold wealth. Hence the risk the company was taking in establishing its tiny, covert, mountain-top outpost.

It was an expensive as well as risky proposition. The company did not suffer losses lightly. Senior xenobotanist Thom Olin was not one such loss to be easily written off, hence Urbinski's assignment to bring him back. If he and his team could just recover the absent researcher's knowledge, that would have satisfied the company. Unfortunately, such an extraction was not possible. They would have to bring back the rest of the man as well.

Ten minutes in, they stopped for a quick check. Everyone was feeling fine, everyone's equipment was functioning optimally, and the signal from the missing scientist's power unit remained weak but unmistakable.

"A week. Week and a half at most," Temura grunted as he methodically scanned the green envelope that had closed in around them. " 'Nother week to bring him out. Maybe two if he's injured."

"Must be," Alesha observed. "Otherwise he would've come back by now on his own."

"Not necessarily." Urbinski wiped a bead of sweat from his forehead. Neither his suit nor his cap could completely dry and cool those areas of exposed skin that were not covered by either. "If there's one thing I've learned about scientists in the course of working for the company, it's that when they're deeply immersed in their work, everything else tends to shut down. They can forget all about time. They can forget to eat, forget to sleep, until their body screams at them to do both. Even then, they're as likely as not to just keel over from exhaustion or lack of nourishment." Raising an arm, he pointed ahead and down the length of the two-meter-wide branch they were standing on.

"If this Olin thinks he's onto something important, I wouldn't be surprised to find out that he's just forgotten to check back in. Especially if like the supervisor says, he's gone beyond authorized limits. Again, being a scientist, he might not even be aware of how far he's strayed."

"Do you think that's why he hasn't responded to requests for callback?" Bernard asked. " 'Course, he could be dead, too."

Urbinski dipped his head slightly to one side. "Possible. But the record of readings taken at the outpost indicate a steadiness of signal within a very limited range. If he was dead, it's likely weather or something else would have shifted the location or caused the signal to alter at least slightly by now. If some animal had carried off the communicator, or him with it, it would be moving around a lot more. The signal's steadiness suggests his communicator is being kept within a specifically circumscribed area, such as a campsite. So I don't think our boy is deceased.

"My own feeling is that when we reach him, we'll find that there's a good chance his unit has suffered a malfunction. *That* I can see someone like him overlooking. If he's that into his work, he'll have forgotten to let his associates know that he's okay. Or if he's not into verbal backchat and his communit is on the blink, he might even think that he's been complying with regs and checking in automatically as required." Urbinski grinned. "The company will probably dock him for the cost of sending us out here to fetch him. Absentmindedness can get expensive."

"Might not worry him if he's found something special," Alesha pointed out.

Turning away from her, the team leader resumed walking carefully along the wide, reasonably flat top of the branch. "Let's hope for his sake, and that of his bank account, that he has."

Advancing in single file, they moved deeper into the forest. It was possible, Urbinski knew, to walk completely around the planet without ever leaving the all-pervasive jungle and without ever coming within a hundred meters of its actual surface. The few available records that the company's researchers had been able to access through the judicious use of outright theft and shrewd bribery stated that there were no names for various regions of the planet because there were no various regions. Except for the open seas it was all one, contiguous forest. A lumberman's dream, he decided, careful to look to left and right as well as straight ahead and beneath his feet as he contemplated possibilities. How much exploitable old-growth alien wood could a modern facility extract from a single tree a thousand meters tall and wider around at the base than some starships?

As he pondered the prospect, certain leaves in his immediate vicinity quivered. A vine or two shifted position ever so slightly. Moisture, heat, and rising air could manipulate vegetation in peculiar ways.

Throwing up a spilk-gloved hand, he brought the team to a halt. Behind him, a trio of sleek sliders flicked effortlessly into firing position. Temura started to reach for the rifle slung against his back.

Bernard strained to see past his superior, frowned. "What?" he muttered tersely.

Lowering the warning hand, Urbinski pointed with it. "Straight ahead. Right in front of us."

Alesha crowded closer, straining for a better look. Behind her, Temura held his natural curiosity in check. His job was to stay alert for threats on their tail, not those in front. If an immediate threat loomed before them, his colleagues would fill him in on any necessary details soon enough.

"I don't see anything." Her slider was aimed straight along the line of the branch they were presently utilizing for a footpath through the trees. Braced by her free right hand, her left arm was as steady as any of the pillar-like trunks rising around them.

Urbinski sucked air and jabbed his pointing hand at the object of his attention. Directly before them lay a shallow hollow in the branch that was filled with collected rainwater. It was Bernard's turn to strain to see.

"Something in the pool?"

"You could say that." Turning, Urbinski began hunting among the long, rippling leaves of a nearby epiphyte. Spotting something, he reached in, his hand striking like the head of a snake, to extract what looked like a ten-centimeter long pink finger. Its underside sported dozens of wildly writhing blue legs. It immediately began stabbing at him with the pair of tiny, forward-curving, horn-like appendages that protruded from its head. With each thrust a drop of a clear liquid was forced from the tip of each horn. The horns could not penetrate the spilk and the droplets they oozed slid harmlessly off his gloved fingers.

"I believe, if I recall my prep work correctly, that this is a representative of just one of several dozen families that have been classified as mx-arthropods until a proper local taxonomy can be constructed. The venom you see running off my fingers causes disseminated intravascular coagulation. All the body's blood-clotting defenses are used up at one point while the rest of the tissues bleed to death."

"Adorable." Bernard leaned forward to examine the squirming, azure-limbed little monster.

Turning and taking careful aim, Urbinski tossed his writhing prisoner. It landed in the middle of the two-meter-long puddle of water. The water erupted.

The jaws that emerged from below (or rather, within) the pool were perhaps a meter in length and lined with three-centimeter-long teeth that interlocked like the spines of a zipper. In the case of the unfortunate crawler Urbinski had designated a visual aid, they were hardly needed. It vanished unbitten within the depths of the exposed, upthrust maw.

In a matter of seconds the clashing jaws had fallen back out of sight. In a matter of minutes, the water that concealed the camouflaged carnivore's presence had settled. Its surface once more was as still and smooth as a mirror.

"First lesson." Jumping across to another branch that paralleled the one they were on but was devoid of threatening standing liquid, Urbinski gave the water-hunter a respectful berth. "Don't step in any puddles. Some hide predators. Some are filled with highly corrosive acids that just look like water." As he resumed forward march, he nodded skyward. "It rains frequently enough that we don't have to resort to filling containers from any standing pool."

His explication was unnecessary. They had all done their homework prior to arrival. They were a tightly knit, highly professional team. Still, it was always useful to see dry, collated, filed information illustrated by examples from reality. Only a couple of hours walk from the outpost and they had already been treated to the killing methods of not one but two very different examples of the local fauna. As the days passed they would undoubtedly be exposed to more of the same. They were not overly concerned. Alesha and Temura, at least, felt they had done work on and survived planetary environments far more lethal than this one.

Of course, they were only a couple of hours out.

They made even better time than Urbinski had set aside for the first day's hike. It did not rain, so they were able to keep the integrated sensor spikes that lined the soles of their boots at minimum height, sacrificing stability for additional speed. Nothing leaped out at them from among the dense tangle of vines and lianas, creepers and branches. The farther and deeper they went, the wider and easier to negotiate became the branches that served as their walkways. Two hundred meters below the treetops, they started to lose some sunlight, but not enough to affect their progress. Ranging the missing xenobotanist's locator signal indicated it was holding unchanged at an altitude of between six hundred and six-fifty meters above the dark, unseen surface.

Mid-level on Midworld, Urbinski thought as the team prepared to settle down for the night. The light down there would be muted, but far from absent. At noon, local time, it ought to be nearly as bright as at the outpost, and perfectly adequate during the remainder of the daylight hours. The various species of mirrorvines that carried sunlight even to the depths of the forest would make up for the loss of direct sunlight. They had to, or below a certain level there could be no photosynthesis.

Compared to some expeditions he had led, this one had so far been a walk in the absurdly luxuriant park, the presence of water-camouflaged carnivores and toxic quasi-caterpillars notwithstanding. He valued such assignments. They were always interesting and invariably instructive. No doubt tomorrow would bring forth an equally enlightening encounter or two.

Temura and Bernard set up the shelter while he and Alesha kept watch. Working smoothly and efficiently together, they had the structure and its accessories up and functioning well before sunset. It was Alesha who chose the location. Nestled in a crook between two branches, it was so wide at the junction with the tree's trunk that there was ample room in all directions to expand the range of the team's defensive electronic sweeper. Generated by a compact projector, the fine-tuned, softly beeping device sent out a rotating signal that completely circled the encampment every couple of seconds. Intercepted by anything bigger than a perambulating worm, it would sound an alarm. Once activated, it was also capable of delivering a mild electric shock to any potential intruder.

They wouldn't rely on the sweeper and their other integrated alert gear to look out for them, Urbinski knew. In addition, they would sleep shifts: four hours on, four off, two at a time, one team member stationed on either side of the shelter while always remaining within sight of the other save for those occasional infrequent moments when private functions required attention. He himself had always slept soundly while out in the field, secure in the knowledge that both his equipment and his personnel were the absolute best the company could procure.

That first night away from the outpost was no different. He and Alesha took their turns on sentry duty while Bernard and Temura

dozed peacefully inside the shelter. Nightfall brought with it a sym-
phony of alien screeches, screams, shrieks, wails, hums, and buzzes
that were completely different from those that haunted the day-
time. In spite of the noise, and the occasional deeper bellow or
howl, when they broke camp the following morning everyone was
rested, alert, and more confident than ever.

Especially when Bernard, taking over point from Urbinski for
a while, threw up a hand to call a halt to their descent down a gentle, winding, two-meter-wide branch. Festooned with epiphytes
and bromeliads, fungi and other parasitic plant life, it was a
wooden artery leading deep into the forest and to the next major
trees on their route. It was also alive with hundreds of hallucina-
tory growths for which the team leader had no name. This was not
because of a lack of pre-expedition study on his part. He could not
name them because they had yet to be given names and, in many
cases, even classified into families.

The others crowded close behind the point scout—but not so
close that their freedom of movement, or range of fire, was inhib-
ited. "See something?" Like his companions, Temura had his slider
out, armed, and ready.

Reaching up, Bernard tapped the lenses that hung down from
the brim of his field cap. "Go to UV." Extending an arm, he
pointed. "Four meters straight ahead. Section of branch."

Urbinski had been peering through the polarizing lens. Switching to ultraviolet, the source of Bernard's concern was immediately
apparent. Directly ahead of them, a distinct section of the thick
branch beneath their feet showed a pale greenish-blue when
viewed in UV. He flipped up the lens. In normal light, there was no
visible difference between the selected couple of meters and the
rest of the branch. It appeared as solid and imposing as any other
section of the great tree limb. In UV, however, its spongy internal
structure was immediately apparent.

"I don't get it." Coming forward, Temura twisted his cap to one
side and squinted.

"It's a sham step." Urbinski was nodding thoughtfully to himself. "Anything substantial that puts weight on that section breaks
through. It's wood-ribbed, not wood-solid."

Having moved to the edge of the branch, Alesha was leaning out and peering down. The potential drop did not concern her. As unafraid of heights as her companions, the fact that the ground lay hundreds of meters below her and completely out of sight did not unsettle her stance. Besides, between her and the unseen surface thousands of branches, vines, and other representatives of the local vegetation formed an interlocking web of brown and green that would break any fall.

"Have a look."

While Urbinski and Bernard complied, Temura kept watch. At no time until they returned to the outpost would all four of them focus their attention on any one object, or in any one direction. Someone would always be looking behind.

The branch that thrust outward and curled away beneath the one on which they were walking was about half its diameter. It was similarly lush with alien foliage. One especially large clump immediately drew Urbinski and Bernard's attention, just as it had Alesha's. Lying in the middle of the clump of dark green was a lumpy shape covered in fur that was only slightly lighter in color and marked with black and brown streaks. Instead of being positioned on the end of a neck, the cow-sized head and trio of limpid, half-shut brown eyes protruded from the middle of the creature's dorsal side. Whether they grew from there naturally or had migrated up and over like the eyes of a flounder was an interesting question they would have to leave for those of a more formal biological bent. The team members just thought it was ugly. Ugly, but well designed for its purpose.

Urbinski said as much. "I'm guessing there's some kind of symbiotic or parasitic relationship between the plant matter that imitates the overhead branch structure and this thing underneath. It lies in wait, hiding in the bush that its fur matches almost perfectly. Something comes walking along this branch that doesn't see into the UV. It steps on the weakened section, breaks through, and becomes lunch. The predator doesn't even have to leave his leaves."

"Neat," Alesha agreed.

"Nasty." Bernard tapped the rim of the UV lens suspended

from the brim of his cap. "Never would have noticed the weak spot without these."

Urbinski turned away from the sight, nodding. It was amazing, he mused, how limited was human vision. So much plant life pressed in so tightly on all sides as well as above and below that it was hard to believe they were standing and talking hundreds of meters above the ground. On a tree branch, no less. Pity they couldn't relax and soak up the sights. Do that, and you very well might get soaked up *by* the sights. They could enjoy the sounds, however, as the alien cacophony swelled and fell all around them. And the smells—everything from high perfume to low stink.

As they used climbing gear to switch over to a parallel branch that boasted no deceptive sections, he found himself trying to visualize the local equivalent of a monkey. The scientific records that had been illicitly obtained by the company made mention of a large, bulky, minimally intelligent omnivore called a furcot that had been domesticated by the colonial survivors on the other side of the planet. Did he and his people risk encountering one here? If so, he doubted that any kind of conversation was likely to ensue. No furcot on this hemisphere had ever seen a human. Where large, powerful, sharp-tusked fauna was concerned, he preferred to shoot first and debate ethics of intelligence afterwards.

He was spared having to back up the decision he had already made. They saw no furcots. Three days in and they had yet to see anything bigger than a pack of dog-sized herbivores that scattered at their approach. The bright pink and black-blotched nibblers took off as soon as the first of them spotted the approaching humans. Utilizing the four tentacles that protruded from their backs, they bolted into the tangle of creepers and lianas that bound the forest together, emitting little more than frantic faint squeaks as they fled.

This panic at their appearance in no wise persuaded the team members to relax their constant vigil. Just because they had not encountered anything big and dangerous did not mean it wasn't out there, watching them. In fact, it was logical to assume that something was.

"Too much prey for there not to be any predators," Temura murmured as he strolled down the branch just behind Alesha.

"There was that ambush creature," she reminded him.

The big man grunted. "I mean active carnivores. Evolutionary pressures plus the availability of so much food practically screams the presence of active predation."

Looking back, she grinned at him. "As soon as something appropriately ravenous announces its presence, I'll step aside so you can be the first to confirm your hypothesis."

In the lead again, Urbinski smiled to himself. Truly, his people were the best. Why trust your life to anything less? Alesha's tease was just one more sign of how relaxed they were. Idly pulling his tracker, he once more checked the signal being put out by Olin's powerpak. Boosted by appropriate algorithms in the tracker, the signal was now strong and easy to read.

Temura had been conservative, back at the outpost, when he had voiced his estimate of how long this trek was going to take. They'd walk in on the absent researcher in a week, if not less. Urbinski glanced skyward. Or rather, up into the luxuriant roof of branches and creepers. They had not been able to see the sky since they had left the outpost. Rate of travel through the forest depended on the rain. A serious deluge could render even the widest and most stable branch slippery beneath their special boots. Daily downpours might add a whole day or two to the journey. But it would not stop them. Nothing would stop them.

He looked forward to seeing the look on that nannying Marston's face when they reappeared atop the rocky rise on which the outpost was situated with a chastened Thom Olin in tow and ready for official debriefing.

He had almost begun to relax, to believe that the number of paragraphs in the prep file that had been red-lined constituted a bureaucratic as well as biological exaggeration of the worst kind, when on the fourth night away from the outpost they nearly lost Temura to beauty.

–IV–

"Oh!"

Fighting back the dark of night and the perfume of alien blooms, Temura turned in the direction of his partner's unexpected exclamation. It was after midnight, local time. There was no moon. Or rather, there might have been a moon, but they were unable to see it. Forest and foliage shut out the night sky as effectively as it did the sun during the day.

Within their individual, linked-together portable shelters, Urbinski and Bernard slumbered on. Alesha's vocalization had been muted as well as sudden. Before moving toward her, Temura instinctively ran a quick locality check. The circle swept by the sweeper projector that watched over them and this entire stretch of branch had not been violated. No alarm had been sounded, and the steady, muted beep of the device indicated it was functioning normally. His clothing was clean. No unusual noises had been recorded by his suit's instrumentation. Visual, UV, and IR scans revealed small things moving through the trees and the parasitic growths that grew upon them, but nothing coming toward the encampment.

All this verification took less than a minute, by which time he was moving toward his colleague. What he saw when he stepped around to the other side of the shelter did not take his breath away, but it certainly gave him pause.

She was standing and staring at the creature before her. She had also, thoughtfully, unlimbered her rifle and held it aimed directly at the being's midsection. It might be beautiful, spectacular, amazing even, but like the good and experienced expedition member she was, Alesha was taking no chances.

"Wow," he murmured even as he continued to carescan the damp, oxygen-rich darkness that surrounded them.

"Yeah. Wow." Without taking her eyes off the nocturnal camp caller, she gestured with the point of her rifle. "It hasn't given any indication of trying to come any closer than where it is right now. If it does, glorious or not, I'm gonna have to shatter it."

Since she had her rifle leveled, he saw no reason to mess with his own, and settled for letting his slider slip effortlessly into the palm of his left hand. Tightening his grip on the weapon, he approached slowly, not wanting to frighten their extravagant visitor away. Automatically, a cam mounted on top of the gun saved images of whatever its muzzle happened to be pointed at. There would be a record of the encounter. The company researchers back at the outpost would be pleased.

It had six wings, all sprouting from the same two ridgelines on either side of its arm-length body. Each pair of wings radiated in a different sequence of colors. These were not a consequence of reflected light. The intense luminescence was the product of internally generated phosphorescence due to the presence of the enzyme luciferase or some native alien equivalent. Except for the light they produced, the fast-beating sextuple wings were transparent. It was as if the big-eyed night-flyer was being held aloft by flashes of tinted flame. Yellow, crimson, gold, royal lavender, electric blue—there seemed no end to the combination of colors the wings could produce. Behind the wings, the slender candy-striped body tapered to a whip-like tail. Each of the three tri-lensed eyes that formed a line across the front of the head glittered iridescent in the beams sent forth by Temura and Alesha's cap lights.

It did not flap its wings, like a bird or a bat. Instead, they swept forward and back, forward and back, rotating like those of a hummingbird, only far more slowly. It was unquestionably the most beautiful exemplar of alien fauna either of them had ever set eyes upon.

While allowing themselves to soak up the vision of the exotic beauty, neither team member neglected their gear. The continuously updated readouts broadcast by their instruments were unequivocal. The circle guarded by the sweeper had not been violated. Standing inside its perimeter, he and Alesha did not set it off.

Drifting just beyond its reach, neither did the hovering rainforest entity.

Leaning slowly and slightly to her right, Alesha whispered to her colleague while never taking the leading edge of her rifle off the example of silent, drifting, multi-winged splendor. "It's just floating there, like a skimmer."

Temura grunted softly. "Maybe it thinks *we're* beautiful."

"Make a great specimen." Visions of a sizable bonus danced in her head.

It was a thought that also occurred to Temura. Given a moment to simmer, it passed of its own accord. "Not our responsibility," he replied. In a whisper, so as not to startle the vision drifting before them. "Our job's to collect the collector and bring him back."

"It's too big and too fragile to shove into a boot." She was visibly disappointed. "If it's not restricted, maybe I can wangle a hard-copy off the visuals that we can reproduce out later and sell."

"Don't count on it." Finding himself fascinated by the near-hypnotic splendor of those silently beating, chromatically hued wings, he made sure to periodically turn and check the space behind them. They were still alone. Within the shelter, Urbinski and Bernard slept on in silence. "This world being Under Edict and the company's outpost being one that's wholly circumscribed, I don't think . . ." He broke off in mid-admonition.

Not yet alarmed, she pulled her gaze away from the object of fascination to frown at her partner. In response, the organism that was more striking than a thousand birdwing butterflies drifted with her, almost as if it was visually clamoring for her attention.

"Temura? You all right?"

He blinked. "I'm fine. Fine. Just a little dizzy there for a momen . . . for a mo . . ."

Later, she was unable to remember what had shocked her more. The way his eyes rolled back in his head, or how he simply toppled backward like a fashion mannequin that had been indifferently knocked aside by a speeding delivery platform.

"Temura!"

From within the shelter came the sound of confused voices rapidly returning to coherency and the rush of those trying to find where they had laid important accoutrements in the dark.

She started to bend over him. Only a passing glance from her cap beam caught the curve of the narrow vine. The same color as the bark of the tree on which they had made camp, its leaves the same shape and texture, it could have fooled any experienced xenobotanist. It would have passed Alesha's notice except for one small, crucial detail that she noted right away.

One end of it was sticking out of the heel of the fallen man's boot.

She started to reach for it, stopped herself at the last moment. Adding to the confusion, alarms were going off within the shelter as the oversized butterfly-thing swept inward. It did not attack Alesha as she bent worriedly over the fallen Temura. It had nothing to attack *with*. No claws, no teeth, no stinger, not even a clearly discernible mouth. Only beauty, which it employed by frantically darting back and forth in front of Alesha's face in a frenzied effort to attract her attention and draw it away from the now unconscious team member lying motionless on the branch before her.

Urbinski and Bernard came piling out of the shelter; beams flashing, sliders in hand. The team leader was in front.

"Alesha, what the . . . ?" He drew up sharply. "What the devil is that?"

"A deceptively beautiful one." Straightening, she whirled around and, with a single blast of her rifle, reduced the exquisite night-flyer to its component parts. A few fragments of transparent wing, devoid of color now, sifted down to settle on the surface of the wide branch like so many slivered icicles.

"Deity." An anxious Bernard regarded his insensible buddy. "Ah, shit." Taking careful aim, and before either Urbinski or Alesha could stop him, he took aim with his slider and fired.

It parted the creeper halfway between the place where it emerged from the body of the branch and where it entered the bottom of Temura's boot. The amputated length of woody material did not react like a vine. Instead, blood spurted from the severed end that proceeded to flop around wildly, repeatedly smacking into the branch. After a couple of mad, mindless thrashings, it withdrew back down into the solid wood. The hole from which it had emerged was barely visible even though they knew right where to look.

Urbinski had bolted for the shelter. Now he returned, carrying the expedition's main medkit. "Bernard, get his damn boot off! Now!" He glared over at Alesha. "Maintain sentry. Anything comes within clear vision, flash-fry it! I don't care if it's the sexiest member of the home species you ever set eyes on. Nothing comes closer than twice the diameter of the sweeper's perimeter."

"We didn't see anything." Her usually rock-steady voice was uncharacteristically shaky. "We were just standing and watching the colors. They distracted us so that we couldn't . . ."

Ripping furiously into the medkit, Urbinski growled back at her. "Of course you were distracted. That's what foul beauty is designed to do. It distracts the prey, the prey stands in one place gaping, and while its brain is on beauty-idle, this ugly sucker sneaks up from underneath and starts siphoning the life out of you." One curse followed another as Bernard finally got his colleague's boot off and Urbinski set to work with tools and antiseptic.

"Pretty slick," Bernard observed dispassionately. Working together, he and Urbinski gradually extracted the severed length of alien worm from the bottom of their colleague's foot. It made a wet, sucking sound as it was pulled out of the insensible man's flesh. The bloody business end was tipped with a trio of pointed, razor-sharp, silicaceous teeth. These had drilled through the sole of the preoccupied Temura's boot and, while simultaneously excreting some as yet unknown combination of nerve-numbing proteins and anticoagulants, had proceeded to feast on his bodily fluids to the point where he had lost so much blood that the loss had caused him to pass out.

Alesha dared a quick glance away from her sentry work. "That's filthy."

"Filthy clever, I say." Eyeing the ugly wound with clinical detachment, Bernard methodically passed Urbinski whatever bit of medical kit the team leader requested.

The first task was to patch the lesion and stop the bleeding. Sprayskin closed the perfectly round hole. That was the easy part. It didn't stop the bleeding that, thanks to the presence of a hefty dose of alien anticoagulant in the unconscious man's bloodstream, threatened to cause other problems. Urbinski countered this with appropriate medication. There was, thankfully, no evidence of congruent toxicity. A transfusion utilizing all-purpose dehydrated serum restored some of what the alien bloodsucker had leeched away. Bubbles began to form on Temura's lips as he struggled to speak. Urbinski rose and wiped his forehead with the back of one hand. The spilksuit struggled to wick away the unusual volume of body sweat.

"Let's get him inside." He shot the sole female member of the team a murderous glance. "You stay on watch. Remember: nothing comes inside the perimeter. Nothing! No matter how harmless it looks and—no matter how 'pretty.' "

She just nodded, turning a glum expression on her partner. "He gonna be okay?"

"I think so. No sign of any poisoning." The team leader glanced over to where the shattered wings were the only remaining physical evidence of the butterfly-thing's presence. "Stripper distracts the johns while her partner picks their pockets. Only, this is the lethal version. The Midworld version. I wonder how the two such different species go about sharing the eventual spoils. Does the worm regurgitate ingested blood for the butterfly to drink? Does it modify or adjust the necessary proteins somehow?"

Alesha's expression showed that she was less than enthusiastic about pursuing this particular line of scientific reasoning, however relevant.

Bending, Urbinski got his hands under the now moaning Temura's lower legs while Bernard hefted their injured partner beneath his arms. Together, they wrestled him into the shelter. After a while, Bernard emerged, rifle in hand, to join Alesha on look-out. They would be awake and on sentry for the remainder of the night.

Until daylight supplied by a hidden sun began to illuminate the surrounding verdure and the ominous, eerie cries of the night gave way to the brighter, crisper calls of the forest's diurnal inhabitants, neither of them said so much as a word to the other.

–V–

They had no choice but to sit out a full day waiting for Temura's foot to begin to heal. Even with the judicious application of mod-

ern analgesics, it was simply too painful to stand on. Urbinski
fumed at the delay, but not overly. Time- and travel-wise they were
still ahead of estimates. There was no need to push the team un-
necessarily hard, and the time might come when Temura would
need to be able to put weight on his punctured heel without having
to waste time worrying about possible consequences.

So they stayed where they were, and killed time, and amused
themselves watching all manner and type of outrageous alien creatures both large and small as they fought and sang and hunted and
gamboled through the kilometer-high jungle.

Temura was sitting in front of the entrance to the shelter; back
straight, legs crossed, the bandages on his unshod right foot prominent. Urbinski had changed them at first light, and the new ones
showed only a minimal amount of red stain.

"Never felt a thing," he was murmuring for the tenth (or was it
the eleventh?) time. "Standing there watching the beautiful flyer
one minute, then a second or two of dizziness, and the next thing I
know I'm waking up inside the shelter." He looked over at Alesha,
who was seated nearby sipping the liquid half of her breakfast.
"Must have been a bit of a shock."

She looked up from the self-heating mug. "You damn near
scared me to death, you inconsiderate son-of-a-bitch."

Cradling his rifle, Bernard wandered over to join them. "You
lost a lot of blood in a real short period of time." His gaze shifted to
the surrounding, all-enveloping alien forest before coming to rest
on the shelter. "Can't beat a team leader who knows his medics."

Temura reached down and, grimacing, dragged his foot
around to where he could see the bottom of the bandages. "Won't
happen again. Until we're back at the outpost, you won't catch me
lingering in any one spot for more than a minute, unless it's inside
the shelter."

"Same here." Finishing the last of her breakfast, Alesha shook
out the dregs, rose, and moved toward the shelter to wash and ster-
ilize the empty cup.

Watching his people, Urbinski was not entirely displeased.
While the encounter had been life-threatening, thanks to modern
medicine Temura had come through with little more than a rapidly

healing hole in his foot. If the team hadn't been operating at maximum efficiency and awareness before, it certainly was now. The incident had cost them a day, spent allowing the injured Temura time to recuperate. They were already halfway to the missing researcher's location and still days ahead of schedule. If anything, they ought to make even better progress now.

Working their way downward as well as onward was akin to a slow descent into a fragrant green sea. The lower they went, the more massive became the boles of the gigantic trees. Some began to feature bark so thickly ribbed that they were able to advance by traversing directly from one trunk to another, much as mountain climbers could scoot sideways on a heavily fractured rock wall. At other times, especially when descending, they would make use of lianas from which brilliant flowers and huge leaves sprouted, the stems of the latter providing steps like the rungs of a ladder. Given the scale of the flora that surrounded them, stereotypical simian swinging was never required. They were able to continue on course by walking and climbing.

It was late on the afternoon of the following day when Temura paused in the middle of a paired branch that coiled in and around upon itself, blinked in confusion, and spat something to one side. Taking a purely professional interest in the sudden expectoration, Bernard leaned forward behind him. The flecks of spittle his colleague had splattered on the wood were a dull red, but were not blood.

"Hey buddy, you all right?"

Smacking his palate, Temura unlimbered the drinking coil of his slim condenser unit and sucked several mouthfuls of fresh water from the spigot. Wiping his lips with the back of his hand, he grinned and shrugged it off.

"Stomach's been twitching all day. Raced through breakfast too fast, I guess. That, and the humidity."

"Humidity? What humidity?" Alesha looked back and smiled. Her expression fell the instant she got a glimpse of her partner's face. "Hey, you don't look so good."

"Now what?" Walking point, a resigned Urbinski turned—just in time to see Temura go down.

Grabbing his gut, cheeks and eyes bulging, the biggest of the four team members collapsed in a contorted heap. Reaching out to help, both Bernard and Alesha had to draw their hands back lest they be covered with the red foam that was frothing from their colleague's mouth. And his ears. And other orifices.

"Dammit!" Bernard tried to find an unfoamed place to grab his friend so he could roll him over. By the time he was able to reach in and get a grip on his colleague's lower right arm, the other man was dead.

Medkit at the ready, Urbinski was bending over him. Leaning down for a closer look, he hastily drew back. The foam was still active.

The kit's magnifier supplied an explanation. Within the foam, thousands of tiny hair-like shapes were writhing and twisting violently. Even as the team looked on, these dark curlicues began to burrow themselves into the wood of the branch, or spill over the sides to spread themselves to other sites below. Looking on, clutching their useless weapons, neither Bernard nor Alesha heaved. But both wanted to.

Urbinski was as angry as he was revolted. "This shouldn't have happened. I dosed him with enough general xenobiotics to kill anything in his system." He looked up at his surviving associates. "Little bastards must be armored against it."

Swallowing hard, Alesha forced herself to look closely at the foam that was still bubbling out of the dead man's mouth and ears. The flow had slowed considerably from the initial outpouring. "Larval . . . larval state of the bloodsucker that went into his foot?"

Urbinski stepped back. There was nothing they could do for Temura. Not even bury him, lest they risk contact with the bloodsucker's swarming offspring. "Reasonable assumption."

"At least he went pretty quick." Bernard was retreating along the two entwined branches. "No real pain. Just an upset stomach." Saying it brought to mind a vision of what his former friend's insides must have been like just before the thousands of tiny larva foamed their way forth. He turned away, sick.

Having no choice and no time to spare to wait until the filthy larvae had fully dispersed, they left Temura where he had fallen.

Urbinski did so secure in the knowledge that even if they somehow retraced their route exactly, any trace of the body would be gone before they came back this way. In Midworld's monumental forest, nothing organic would go to waste. Within days, scavengers and fungi would have broken down and carried away any sign of the corpus.

All the more reason, he felt, to accelerate their pace, pick up Olin, and hie it back to the outpost.

As they resumed their advance, they found that their perspectives had undergone a measurable change. The immense forest was still beautiful, its smells still beguiling, its sounds as alien and exotically intriguing as before. Only now, that beauty had been tarnished by a deadly dose of reality. Temura's training hadn't saved him, nor had his methodical prep work, his superb physical conditioning, his state-of-the-art expeditionary equipment, or the lithe and lethal weaponry he had carried. More critical to their continued survival than any of those things, the surviving three members of the team realized, were their own senses and the speed with which they responded to them.

Urbinski was determined to find the researcher, pack him up, bring him back, and get out without losing anyone else. Aside from the fact that he had known all three members of his present team for many years, losing people in the field was bad for one's reputation. Among other things, it had a determinedly detrimental effect on recruiting.

They had no trouble the next day, or the day after that. Their trackers showed they were two days away from shaking hands with Thom Olin; three at the most. Urbinski allowed himself to unwind, a little. Or more accurately, his level of concern dwindled from the overwhelming to the merely excessive.

It did not subside entirely when they came upon the glade, but their spirits were undeniably heightened as they took in their unexpected surroundings.

Preparations for the mission suggested they were likely to encounter magnificence as well as danger. During the preceding days, Temura's unfortunate death notwithstanding, they had certainly seen a good deal of the former—but nothing like this. Nothing could have prepared them for it, because no cautious, tentative scientist from the outpost had ever encountered or recorded anything like it. The sight was so exquisite that for a moment even Urbinski gaped in amazement and found himself taken off guard. But only for a moment.

Half the size of the outpost, the glade consisted of silken strands that had been laid down in an intricate weft between the boles and branches of two massive gray-streaked trees. Possessed of the color and gleam of spun gold, thicker strands supported the entire communal structure above a fifty-meter drop devoid of branches or vines. Within the sausage-shaped bower, individual nests had been woven of strands that were thinner but no less glimmering than the larger structural cables.

The entities who had constructed the glade were no less wonderful to look upon than the product of their exertions. Slightly less than a meter tall, they sported intricately combed and colored feathered crests atop narrow, down-curving skulls. Wide eyes and a fetch of small, slowly rippling tentacles completed the heads, each batch of feeding and web-weaving facial appendages a riot of bright color.

In contrast, their short-furred, fuzzy bodies were a comparatively dull yellow or beige, save for the six flexible limbs each employed to move about within and outside the shimmering bower. These shared the same colors as the flourish of facial tentacles.

"Elfin elephants." Alesha was entranced, but not to the point of letting her guard lapse. Not after Temura.

"More like a cross between a squid and a chicken," Bernard suggested more prosaically.

Urbinski just shook his head. "Humans always have to terrestrialize everything. They don't look like anything except what they are, whatever that is."

"I'll tell you what it is." Alesha gestured with one hand. "It's freakin' spectacular. An alien ballet inside an egg made of spun gold."

The team leader squinted at her. "Ballet?"

She didn't flinch. "Good for maintaining flexibility. Helps with high kicks."

They expended a few more moments staring, utterly enthralled, drinking in the wondrous scene. It was just as they were turning to depart and continue on their way that Hell arrived.

Ululating excitedly, it arrived so fast none of them was able to make an accurate estimate of its length. Forest green with black stripes that ran the entire length of its body, it looked like a huge, flexible cigar that had been thrust through a gigantic ball of string. It was the dozens of "string" ends that enabled it to travel through the forest at such a high rate of speed. Each of them acted as a leg or tentacle, gripping and grabbing at branches and lianas above, below, and on all sides of the creature.

The outside of the slightly tapering head was lined with long, triangular teeth. Or they might have been spines. From the center of the cranial terminus, a single tube-like mouth occasionally thrust outward to snap at one of the web weavers and suck it down. It was able to do so because the head rotated sharply back and forth on what must have been a uniquely designed ball-and-socket joint. This spun the teeth-spines like a circular saw that shredded the sticky gold strands. As first one web denizen and then another disappeared down that extruding throat, it appeared to Urbinski and his companions that the bower community had no defense against such an overwhelming assailant except flight.

They were wrong.

First one web dweller and then another flung themselves against their far larger and stronger attacker. It seemed a suicidal effort, perhaps an attempt at a diversion to let the younger inhabitants of the bower escape. Gripping the sides of the slithering attacker with all six limbs and their smaller facial appendages, they hung on tightly.

Then, one by one, they began to burst into flame.

Slicing and sucking, the intruder's moan of pleasure rose to a howl of pain as it twisted and contorted, trying to throw off the hurtful burning beings that had fastened themselves to its body. The combusting web dwellers hung on, having securely attached themselves to their assailant. Their efforts were indeed suicidal, but not futile. Bernard was reminded of bees sacrificing themselves for the sake of the hive, each one stinging and then dying as a consequence.

"Pyrotics." Like his companions, Urbinski was taken back by the utter alienness of the scene unfolding before them. "Only seen the like once before, on Tipendemos, and they were much smaller creatures. Beetle-sized."

Alesha gestured with her slider, which she had snapped out and held at the ready as a precaution. "I can't even tell if the damn thing that's attacking is an animal or motile flora."

"Could be a bit of both." The team leader continued to stare. Half the attacking creature was now enveloped in flame as the glade dwellers continued to swarm it and immolate themselves for the sake of their community. "You remember the prep. For every described species on this world, they estimate there's a million more waiting to be discovered."

"Oh, crap," Bernard muttered as he swung his rifle around and off his back. His sentiment, if not his exclamation, was shared by his colleagues.

Still trying to throw off the burning entities that were roasting it alive, the knife-headed predator was swinging its way clear of the golden strands—and heading straight for the branch on which the team was standing.

There was no time to distinguish between it and those strand-spinning pyrotics clinging to its back and sides. More powerful than sliders, rifles were brought sharply into play. Three shots from three muzzles seared the moist air, leaving in their wake the sharp actinic stink of ozone. The bursts ripped into the writhing, howling carnivore. One shot, probably Alesha's, tore away the head. Still on fire, the badly damaged corpse lost its multiple grip on the sur-rounding, supporting verdure and went tumbling, spinning, and bouncing down into the deep green depths until it was finally lost from sight. Its flaming corpse would not spread fire, Urbinski knew. The forest was too damp, too wet. Too green.

As they reslung their long guns, each of them felt a little better. Not because they had inadvertently helped to save the remainder of the striking community of golden strands, but because they now had concrete instead of theoretical proof of the effectiveness of their weapons against at least one powerful and voracious local lifeform. Unable to do anything to prevent the death of the unfortunate Temura, it felt good to deal out a little retribution. Not an entirely rational reaction, perhaps, but one that left their spirits boosted nonetheless.

Ducking slightly to one side as the creature had come their way, Alesha had bumped into the tree trunk and suffered a slight facial scrape. Bernard took extra time to make sure it was completely cleaned out, dosing it twice to eliminate the slightest possibility that so much as a single alien microbe might survive within the wound.

Reflecting on an encounter that had started out inexpressibly beautiful only to turn unexpectedly violent, Urbinski realized that it had been nothing less than typical of this world. In a forest of superlatives, it was only expected that they would encounter extremes. Traditional prep work notwithstanding, Temura clearly hadn't been ready for it. The team leader glanced back at his surviving associates. If they had not been adequately prepared before, the recent encounter ensured that they certainly were now. If anything, the reaction of the communal web-weaving pyrotics had been more of a wake-up call to this world's deadly potential than had the monster that had attacked them.

Nothing materialized to trouble or confront them all the rest of that day. The next proved to be as tranquil as its predecessor had been intense, with only the lightest of cozy, warm drizzles to obstruct their vision and only the most colorful of flora and fauna to distract it.

They were feeling much better as they went about the business of making that night's camp. Displaying only minute variations in their respective readouts, all three trackers indicated they were less than two days away from the meeting with the absentee researcher. If the weather held and they encountered no further delays, they might even be chatting amiably with their quarry by tomorrow night.

Down one team member, Urbinski was required to make a decision regarding sentry duty. Despite his qualms, having one sleep while two stood watch seemed counterproductive. He decided they would compensate by going to shorter shifts. One person would stand guard while the other two slept, but they would change to three-hour breaks. Each of them would stand one shift, allowing his or her companions six hours of proper sleep.

Setting an example, he took the middle shift, the most awkward one, himself.

Alesha drew first watch. When she woke him, it was with an expression of near contentment.

"No trouble," she told him as she stepped past him on the branch, heading for the shelter. "Not even any loud noises."

He nodded, cradling his rifle. "Sleep well. With luck, we'll have our boy in hand tomorrow and be on our way back the following morning."

Nothing tested the perimeter while he was on watch. Secure inside the softly beeping sweeper field, he was able to enjoy the sounds of the immense jungle. Occasionally, something phosphorescent and glittering could be seen flitting among the branches and creepers. Though individual colors and patterns differed, he was sure they all belonged to various predators, striving with their lights to attract potential prey. Nocturnal herbivores tended not to advertise their presence.

The campsite was unusual in that it sat beneath a small but unmistakable circle of sky. Like a green-lined shaft, the atypical opening permitted them to see all the way to the top of the forest and beyond. They had encountered such isolated gaps in the canopy before, but never in places or at times that had allowed them to linger and enjoy the sight. On top of that, it did not rain on his watch. For a while at least, the cloud cover had cleared.

It was good to be able to see the stars. To be reassured of the reality that waited to welcome them back. The first place he was going to go as soon as this trip had been successfully wrapped was any world that was highly urbanized. One where the only green he would have to look at would be in the color of the clothing draping expensive women.

With wondrous sights and intriguing sounds aplenty to occupy his attention, the three hours of his shift passed quickly. Stepping into the shelter, he took care to avoid waking the softly slumbering Alesha as he shook Bernard awake. It took only a touch. Like anyone trained for this kind of work, the other man was a light sleeper.

A nod, a terse exchange of perfunctory whispers, and the two men went about switching places. By now familiar with the sights and sounds of the planetary rainforest at night, there was much to occupy but little to surprise Bernard as he took up his position beyond the shelter's entrance. Like Urbinski, he found the opportunity to occasionally tilt back his head and for the first time in days catch a glimpse of the stars both reassuring and comforting.

Even the small group of stellar pinpoints that was visible served to remind him of distant civilizations and the promise that he and his companions would soon be able to return to more salubrious climes. He called up memories of clubs and beautiful beaches, good food and fine drink, all the activities and wonders that were open to someone with a positive cred balance. His was soon to be boosted by the bonus awaiting the team that came back with Thom Olin. For now it was enough to dream of what he was going to do with the money and whom besides himself he was going to lavish it upon. Of how he was going to lose himself in a dreamy whirl of pleasure and relaxation, in places and times where threats were intermittent and only of the irritating human variety. One blissful rejuvenating dream followed close upon another, as the stars themselves seemed to be coming closer and closer . . .

–VI–

Alesha's screams woke Urbinski instantly. First, because they had the timbre of pure visceral horror, and second, because Alesha never screamed. She was as tough and resourceful as any member of the specially selected team. For something to cause her to lose control to the point where it resulted in a scream had to be something gruesome indeed.

Half-dressed, he burst out of the shelter, slider in hand. He saw Alesha immediately. She was fully clad, having risen before him to start in on the morning meal. Her rifle was slung across her back. Her hands, instead of holding and supporting her slider, were pressed to her face. He could not see her eyes, but did not have to.

Lying on the branch before her was Bernard. Or rather, what was left of the third member of the team. A putty Bernard. The sunken, oozing, liquefied remnant of what Bernard had once been. Covering the lower half of the glutinous, mushy shape was what at first glance looked like nothing more than a black velvet blanket. Looking closer, Urbinski saw that its center and forepart were moving, slowly heaving up and down. It was not shielding Bernard from the elements or keeping him warm.

It was feeding.

He ought to have lit into Alesha for not reacting to the sight in a more professional manner. He should have smacked her upside the head for not doing anything but standing and staring and screaming. But he was too angry, and not a little nauseous. Stepping up alongside her, he raised the muzzle of his slider. His action was deliberate and without hesitation. There was no need to worry about hitting Bernard. Their companion was already dead. If any additional proof was needed beyond the general condition of the body, the fact that the contents of his skull were leaking out his ears and mouth was the kind of confirmation that was as absolute as it was sickening. He fired.

It jolted Alesha out of her paralysis. Within seconds, her slider had joined his in ripping into the black blanket. As the flattened, almost manta-like shape was struck, it rose into the air and attempted to flutter away. A single slender proboscis extended downward from the leading edge of the hapless creature. The feeding organ was dark with blood, liquefied flesh, and dissolved organs.

They fired more than was necessary to bring it down, but neither chided the other. They kept on firing until the creature was not merely dead but shredded. Only when the remnants of its unmoving form lay draped in pieces over smaller branches and epiphytes did they swallow the gorge that was rising in their throats and slowly approach the ruination that had been their partner and companion.

Urbinski had done company work on hard worlds; first as a general employee, then as a reservist, finally as a team leader. He had borne witness to death dealt by a variety of alien predators and diseases. This was the first time he had seen a human being

melted by something other than excessive heat. As he and Alesha
looked on, one of Bernard's legs, with the femur disarticulated
from the ileum, oozed over the side of the branch, its passage lu-
bricated by the gelatinous remnants of the muscle and tendons that
had once supported it. Experienced or not, tough or otherwise,
Alesha finally turned away and stopped trying not to throw up.
Urbinski offered no comment on her reaction. Instead, he bent to
examine the body more closely. He could not quite, however,
bring himself to touch it. He rationalized the lack of physical contact by telling himself it might not be safe. And besides, there was
no need.

A quick instrument check indicated that the sweeper was still
working perfectly. "The thing must have slipped inside the perimeter between pulses. It's possible it could detect the electrical output. A number of animals have that capability. If it could get close,
it could inject an anesthetizing agent, and then begin to feed. What
I don't understand is how it could get right on top of Bernard without him noticing anything." Straightening, he turned toward the
fragments of alien. "Bernard had good reactions, good instincts."

Taking a mouthful of water Alesha swirled it around, spat it
out, sucked up another. When the inside of her mouth was clean,
she started toward the largest piece of alien. Urbinski joined her.

Surprisingly, the black skin was soft to the touch. Not leathery
at all. A possible explanation for the apparent ease with which it
had overcome their companion was revealed when she gripped
the large fragment with both hands and turned it over. The underside was a perfect representation of the night sky, complete to stars
and wisps of cloud. Urbinski envisioned a scenario: the creature
slipping inside the electronic perimeter and slowly taking up a position above Bernard's head. Lowering itself carefully, carefully toward its intended prey. Freezing whenever Bernard chanced to
look up and, in doing so, saw only a section of night sky no different from any other. Descending until it was right on top of their
dead associate and then injecting him with some subtle soporific.
Wrapping him up in its black night wings and . . .

He didn't need to visualize the rest. It was lying spread out before him. Perhaps the creature was even able to adjust the size and

brightness of the "stars" that camouflaged its underside, much as
Terran cephalopods could alter their color and shape through ad-
justment of the chromatophores in their skin. For the first time, he
began to understand why the indigenous survivors of the original
lost colonists referred to the region above the treetops of this world
as the Upper Hell. Here, even the night sky was potentially lethal.

From now on, they would take care not to camp anywhere it
was visible.

Bernard fared better than the unlucky Temura. After repeatedly scanning and testing the deep hollow in a nearby branch to
make sure it was unoccupied, and not an innocent-appearing
stalking horse for some unimaginable new alien horror, they
made themselves haul the remnants of their liquefied colleague
over to the depression and dump them inside. In the absence of a
sufficiency of epiphytic soil, they used leaves and branches to
bury him as best they could. Urbinski murmured a few words
over the makeshift arboreal grave while Alesha muttered under
her breath, cursing the entire loathsome green globe in terms as
eloquent as they were bitter. Splitting the most useful elements of
the dead man's gear between them, they moved on, without looking back.

Despite taking turns on sentry and assuring themselves they
would be okay, neither of them slept that night. They tried, but
they couldn't. They carried medication for sleeplessness, but the
last thing either of them wanted to do was lessen their ability to react quickly to anything that might emerge from the vegetation surrounding them. So when morning finally came, it found both of
them sleep-deprived, irritable, and frustrated.

"It'll be all right," Urbinski observed, as much to himself as to
Alesha as they packed up. "With just the two of us, we'll push it so
we make Olin's camp by nightfall. We can sleep there."

His surviving companion just nodded. She was more than
tired. He could see it in her face. Not resigned, exactly. But the
confidence and enthusiasm she had shown on departure from the
outpost were absent. He couldn't really blame her, and said nothing. Now was not the time to criticize. All that mattered was getting
to the missing researcher's encampment. Not just Temura and

Bernard's deaths, but the manner of their demise, had sucked some of the life out of her.

He frowned. It was a bad choice of words, even if unspoken.

The casual conversation that had characterized the expedition since it had first set out from the outpost was missing as they pushed on. Grim-faced, speaking only when necessary, they set a pace that was as blistering as the heat. Once, their path along a chosen branch was blocked by something foot-sized, yellow-green, and displaying a double column of spinal fronds. Like most of the creatures they had encountered, it had three eyes and six legs. Whipping out her slider, Alesha blew it clean off the branch before they had a chance to determine whether it was aggressive or harmless. Urbinski threw her a wordless glance.

She shrugged, utterly indifferent to his reaction or to the animal's nature or intentions. "It was in the way."

Her apathy did not extend to her reactions. If they were going to link up with Olin before nightfall, they had to move as fast as humanly possible. Not wanting to spend another night in the endless forest by themselves, they lengthened their respective strides as much as was safely possible. Urbinski's being longer than hers, he found himself having to pause several times to wait for her to catch up. Each time she said nothing, just nodded acquiescence and kept moving. As a consequence of her shorter legs, they did not travel as fast as he could have by himself, but near enough that he was satisfied with their progress.

In the course of their near run through the trees they passed enough new and striking species to keep a brace of botanists busy classifying and analyzing for the rest of their natural lives. When something really extraordinary presented itself and all but demanded a moment of their attention, they paused briefly to look, but did not linger long enough to make a formal record of so much as a single exotic liana.

There was the seething cluster of tiny swimmers, hundreds of them, dwelling in apparent contentment inside a single bromeliad. And the walking vines. And the bark borers whose intricate chambers resembled miniature cathedrals hewn from the enormously thick interior of a single massive emergent.

And the glass flowers. Alternately transparent, translucent, and opaque, the variations doubtless having to do with the amount of pigment in each, the spectacular blossoms of a new parasitic plant completely covered the branches of the tree they had to cross to continue on their chosen course. The alternative meant breaking out the climbing gear to go up or down in search of a new path. Unwilling to waste time on even a minor detour, they elected to push straight through.

No toxins irritated the exposed skin of their faces as they made their way through the mass of two-meter-high blooms. No thorns probed their spilk armor. No hidden tentacular creepers tried to wrap around their feet and hold them back. The enormous, glistening corollas that blocked their route resisted their presence with some stiffness but in every instance were easily pushed aside.

Clinging to the edge of one towering, glistening petal was a fist-sized crimson crawler with shimmering gold spots and sapphire-blue legs. Wholly iridescent, it sparkled like a living jewel when it moved. Alesha paused a moment to lean forward and study it. Every time it took a step up the edge of the petal, the integuments of its body briefly flashed a deep, intense purple. Doubtless it was acrid to the taste, if not outright poisonous, or it could never have gotten away with such an explosively colorful display. For a moment, she considered collecting it, then decided that without knowing anything about what kind and manner of defenses it might possess, it would be better to leave it alone. Turning away, she resumed striding through the flowers and along the branch.

She had been walking for several minutes when she realized that she was still surrounded by the massive blossoms. Her pace ought to have carried her through the last of them and on into the next, flowerless tree. Worse, she could not see Urbinski in his usual position just ahead of her. Raising her voice, she shouted. Her cries were largely drowned out by the persistent volume of animal calls and shrieks. With a sigh, she started off again. Either she would catch up to the team leader in a few moments, or he would stop and wait for her.

Having crossed into the next tree, that was devoid of the huge blooms, Urbinski had already realized that Alesha was no longer behind him. He reacted exactly as she expected he would, by stopping and waiting. As important as he knew it was to keep moving, he was secretly glad of the chance to take a short breather. Settling himself down on a couch-sized burl, he waited for her to rejoin him.

It took several minutes of plowing through the flowers before Alesha realized that none of them were transparent any longer. Nor were they translucent. Every one of them had gone opaque, resulting in a profusion of perfectly mirror-like surfaces. Every direction she turned, everywhere she looked, Alesha Rogov found herself looking back at—herself.

House of flowers, she thought wildly. House of mirrors. The blossoms had not gone mirror-opaque by accident, or by coincidence. It had to be deliberate. That implied an awareness of something in their midst. Something they wanted to keep among them.

Easy, she told herself. No panic. As soon as he realizes that you're not coming out, Urbinski will come looking for you. Meanwhile, she had no intention of waiting until the team leader came riding, or in this case stomping, in to rescue her. Even the anticipation of the potential embarrassment was demoralizing.

Around her, on the branches above and presumably also below her, there were only more of the flowers. Exquisite, gleaming, remarkable, ominous. There were no landmarks and the sun was hidden high above, beyond clouds and hundreds of meters of intervening greenery. Well, she didn't need any of them. Pulling her tracker, she headed for the location of the missing researcher's camp. Before long, she emerged from the last of the flowers.

Only to find herself on the end of a branch, with a vast, open gap stretching out before her. Her climbing gear was not sufficient to bridge the green chasm. Gritting her teeth, she turned and plunged back into the thicket of reflective flowers. All she had to do was find her original position and then follow the tracker's directive from there. And meanwhile, where the hell was Urbinski?

This was ridiculous. She would just have to suffer the humiliation. Halting in the midst of the flowers, she pulled out her communit. It immediately came to life.

"Where are you?" came the team leader's stern but reassuring voice.

She relaxed. If for some unimaginable reason the communit had failed to function . . . but communits were simple devices and designed to be fail-safe. Hers, and Urbinski's, worked perfectly.

"Damn flower petals all went mirror on me," she replied. "I'm still on the same level, on the same tree. But every time I try to get back to where I last saw you, I find that I've somehow been doubled back."

"Stay there. I'll come get you."

She hesitated. "Then we're both liable to find ourselves in the same situation."

"This time I'll burn a path. Let's see some flowers try mirroring *that.*"

She nodded, even though there was no one present to observe the reaction. "Thanks. Sorry, Urbinski."

"Don't be. Not in this place. I've crossed to the next tree complex. Might take me a few minutes to get back."

She wasn't worried. Their communits would keep track of increasing proximity. Just as Thom Olin's unit allowed them to pinpoint his location, so hers would allow Urbinski to come straight to her. Looking around, she found that she was going to enjoy cutting a wider path on the way off this particular growth. It was stupid to have allowed herself to be distracted, and subsequently disoriented, no matter how stunning the alien crawler she had been observing. She vowed it wouldn't happen again.

Slider out and utilizing the steady signal from her tracker, she started forward, intending to meet Urbinski at least halfway. When one of the giant blooms threatened to sidetrack her by offering up a mirror image of a different path, she simply blew it out of her way. Around her, lustrous corollas rustled and fluttered. Anywhere else she would have considered it an unnatural reaction. But not here. Not on this world. Her imminent escape from their midst was combining with her aggressive reaction to unsettle the flora that had intended to trap her. She found herself grinning. In its own way the mirror thicket was very clever—for a bunch of plants. But it was still only a bunch of plants; nothing more than an oversized, if unusually shiny, bouquet.

She exploded another stunning, deceiving blossom directly in front of her. It made no sound as shards of petals rained down in all directions. Stepping over the smoking ruins, she glanced down to see bits and pieces of severed stem shrinking away down into the wood of the branch from which the plant itself sprang.

The next growth in her way was older than most, a number of its aged petals lying flat on the supporting wood. Slider aimed resolutely forward, she continued her relentless march through the thicket. Another couple of minutes and she would be reunited with Urbinski. Another couple of hours and, with luck, they would be standing and chatting with the missing researcher. There would only be two and not four of them, but better than zero.

Her right foot came down on a prone petal—and contacted nothingness. Her attention focused forward, she was unable to catch herself in time. The burst from her slider did nothing to break her fall as she plunged downward—through the mirror-image of solidity that had been reflected by the thin section of flower.

Surrounded by a forest of mirroring blossoms, it was difficult to say exactly how far she fell. Far enough, in any event, to break her back. Conscious but unable to move, she lay on the branch that finally halted her plunge. Her slider had been knocked from one hand, the tracker from the other. Technologically as well as personally, she was all alone.

Incapable of breaking her fall, and in any case not inclined to do so, the petals of the flowers all around her began, slowly and inexorably, to bend forward.

"Alesha?" High above, methodically burning his way through the luxuriant blossoms, Urbinski called into his communit. No reply. When he checked it again, the readout brought him up short.

His partner's signal had shifted. Suddenly, and vertically. The difference implied a sudden, sickening fall instead of a gradual climb-down. Cursing under his breath, he swiftly and methodically began to unlimber climbing gear.

Two hundred meters below, in a gathering, threatening darkness that was not entirely the result of oncoming night, he finally located her tracker. It was battered but still functioning. Of his remaining companion there was no sign. She must have dropped it, he realized, or else it had been knocked free from her belt, or her hand. Though exceedingly tired, he retraced his descent. Every ten meters, he paused to survey the surrounding verdure, scanning, calling out, and occasionally even firing a burst from his slider.

He never found the body. Which, after seeing what had happened to Temura and then Bernard, was perhaps a good thing.

–VII–

He spent the night huddled up against the building-sized bulk of a tree with rippling, vertically ribbed bark, crowding himself as far back into one gently curving groove as he could, not even bothering to set up the shelter or the sweeper. Though fearful of falling asleep, his lack of rest the night before was too much even for his trained determination to overcome.

Waking with a start, he immediately realized three things: he had slept through most of the night, it was already mid-morning, and he was not dead.

A quick check revealed, insofar as hand inspection and a swift scan with his personal medkit could, that his body had not been invaded during the night by some indescribably awful alien parasite or virus. A look at his tracker was enough to get him moving. He was very close to Olin's signal source. Though the thought of food threatened to make him sick, he forced himself to eat on the march. He knew his body needed the energy, the fuel.

The calories made him feel a little better, as did the energy drink he mixed into his condenser. When exhaustion threatened to slow him, a renewed burst of fury served as a suitable pick-me-up. He was a team leader, the best the company had on offer, and he would not be denied by any world—far less one dominated only by a bunch of plants.

Olin's encampment, when he stumbled into it sometime after noon, was techno-basic but had been modified and enlarged by the use of cut wood. The portable shelter that differed little from those carried by the team had been enhanced through the addition of a crude but serviceable hewn roof and underfloor. There was also a separate covered kitchen and ablution area plus a platform/blind from which to observe the surrounding forest. He found the scientist's tracker flickering away inside the shelter, neatly attached to one wall. Everything bespoke care, good science, and a knowledge of woodsmanship. Nothing appeared upset or disturbed.

But there was no sign of Thom Olin.

Urbinski began as simply as possible—by shouting. When no response was forthcoming, he set his own extraneous gear aside and commenced a formal search, starting with the shelter and exploring those massive branches that were on the same level as the camp. It was still a possibility that the researcher had been carried off by some unimaginable local carnivore, but the team leader continued to doubt it. For one thing, Olin's slider and rifle were neatly laid out inside his shelter. Urbinski could not envision a scenario where a scientist knowledgeable about the hazards of this world would go outside his shelter without weapons and tracker, not even for a quick snack or to attend to necessary bodily functions.

Yet while both guns remained inside the shelter, there was no sign of their owner. Nor had he found any evidence of violence.

His spirits were falling in tandem with evening when he found the ladder.

Having spent the arduous hours before sunset scouring the branches on the same level as the scientist's encampment, Urbinski was not surprised that he had overlooked it. Flexible, compact, lightweight, and tinted brown, it snaked down the trunk of the tree. Its coloration was clearly designed to camouflage it, doubtless so its lengthy alien appearance would not startle any creatures who came this way.

Still, he hesitated. It would be dark soon. He promised himself that he would only follow the ladder as far as its terminus, then climb back up. Though curiosity and anxiety raged within him in equal measure, nothing would make him continue the search for the missing researcher in the dark. Not on this world.

It was good that he decided to descend the ladder. It allowed him to find Thom Olin.

The researcher looked very relaxed. More than relaxed. Content. Or perhaps sedated would have been a better description. Becoming aware of the team leader's presence, his eyelids fluttered and drew back.

"Oh . . . hello." A faint smile flickered across his face. "Company. Company company, I presume."

Urbinski did not reply. He couldn't. He could only stare. After the first moment, he began biting the knuckles of his left hand. The pain helped to keep his mind clear and focused.

Thom Olin lay not in a bed of vines, but of them. They ran into and through every limb, every part of his body—and out again. Only a few tattered remnants of clothing clung to the reclining botanist. His flesh had gone a pale but unmistakable green. His lower abdomen was bloated, his arms and legs shriveled, his eyes glazed ceramic. He was not so far gone, however, that he was unable to recognize the expression that had come over the face of his visitor.

"There's no pain, you know. Some kind of numbing agent. Very considerate, when you think about it. Why should the forest care if I'm in pain?" His eyelids trembled anew but did not close. "Strange sensations, peculiar feelings. Entirely new ones, from time to time." Turning his head with a visible effort, he eyed his upraised right hand. Woody shoots emerged from each of the fingertips. "Odd. You'd think there'd be pain . . ."

His eyes closed. Drool began to dribble from his open mouth. Wide-eyed and wordless, Urbinski just kept staring, staring at him. There was something curling, coiling out of the researcher's left ear. It was small, bright, ivory-yellow in color, and immediately recognizable. A flower.

The scientist was immersed in his work, all right.

Urbinski wasn't sure if he screamed or not as he fired the slider. One shot was enough to put an end to whatever it was that the missing researcher had become. Other blasts severed vines and lianas. They recoiled back upon themselves, perishing soundlessly. He kept firing until the slider's powerpak was empty. Only then did he scramble, or more properly, flee, back up the ladder.

Somehow, he held onto enough sense and sanity to wait until

morning before starting back. The homing signal that would lead him back to the outpost was understated enough to avoid detection from above but strong enough so that the instrumentation he carried would not lose it.

His tracker was still working weeks later when a reluctant but resigned Marston began to compose the official report. Despite the strength of the persistent, lonely signal far out in the great forest, the outpost supervisor did not try to send anyone from the company station to search for either it or its owner. He knew it would have been useless in any case to issue such an order.

None of his people would have gone.

Walking Star

by Allen M. Steele

*"Walking Star," a rough-and-tumble science-fictional riff on the Old West, is set on the same world as the critically acclaimed Coyote trilogy of novels (*Coyote, Coyote Rising, *and* Coyote Frontier*). Coyote is a world that, though not strictly forbidden, is no place for dudes, milquetoasts, or gentlefolk.*

Allen M. Steele is the author of twelve novels and four collections of short fiction. His work has received several major awards, including the Hugo, Locus, and Seiun awards, and has been translated worldwide. Born and raised in Nashville, Tennessee, he now lives in western Massachusetts with his wife and their two dogs. He has served on the Board of Advisors for both the Space Frontier Foundation and the Science Fiction and Fantasy Writers of America, and is a former member of the SFWA Board of Directors. In April 2001, he testified before the U.S. House of Representatives in hearings on the future of space exploration.

WE GROW UP believing that our minds are our citadels, unassailable fortresses behind whose walls our thoughts are protected, unknowable to all save when we choose to open the gates of our mouths, our eyes, our hearts. Certain that ours is a separate reality, we spend our lives creating inner worlds, ones whose relationship to the true nature of things is tangential at best. We see the same things, but we perceive them differently; all we have in common, really, is a universe that we've agreed upon by consensus.

At least, this is what I once thought. Then I met Joseph Walking Star Cassidy, and nothing was ever the same again.

By the time I returned to Leeport on the last day of the third week of Asmodel, the first signs of early spring had come to Coyote. The rainy season hadn't yet begun, so there were still patches of snow on the ground and ice on the banks of the West Channel. I'd spent the last week in the southern half of New Florida, in the savannahs of the Alabama River; three wealthy German businessmen had come to Coyote to hunt boid, and they'd hired me to be their guide. It hadn't been an easy trip; my clients had more money than sense, and none of them had ever fired a gun at anything more threatening than a hologram on a Berlin rifle range. So when I tried to keep them from tipping over our canoes or show them how and where to set up their tents, I was also worrying whether a boid would kill them instead of vice versa.

Yet we got along well enough, and on the morning of the fifth day I'd managed to track down a boid just northwest of Miller Creek, in the equatorial grasslands where boids were known to migrate for the winter. It was only a young male, no taller than my head, yet nonetheless ferocious enough to give my clients their money's worth. The Germans opened fire as soon as the creature charged us from the high grass; although most of their bullets went wild, enough struck home to bring it down; once I was sure that the boid was mortally wounded, I allowed Herr Heinz, the group's leader, to approach the giant avian close enough to deliver a coup de grâce to the narrow skull behind its enormous beak. After we dragged the carcass to the nearest blackwood and strung it up from a lower branch, I took the pictures that would give them bragging rights once they returned to Berlin, then we cut the boid down and everyone got feathers as souvenirs before I butchered it. Boid meat is actually rather gamey—those of us who live here eat it only when we're desperate—but it was all part of their vacation, and once I broke out another jug of bearshine they didn't mind the taste so much.

The other two Germans wanted to stay longer, perhaps hoping they'd bag a creek cat, but I knew we were pushing our luck; where there's one boid, there's bound to be more, and the last thing I wanted was to be surrounded by a pack with any of these gringos at my back. So I used my satphone to call for a gyro pickup–another C500 fee, not including my own surcharge–and by early evening we'd been airlifted northeast to Liberty. I settled the bill with my clients at the upscale B&B where I'd first met them, then let them take me to Lou's Cantina for some serious drinking. Truth to be told, by then I was sick and tired of their company, but experience had taught me that a little indulgence goes a long way; once they'd put away a few pints of ale, the three of them emptied their wallets and put another C300 on the table. And they even paid the bar tab.

The next morning, once I returned the canoes to the outfitter from which I'd rented them, I hitched a ride home on a shag-team wagon hauling a load of Midland iron from Liberty to Leeport. I was exhausted by the time we rolled into town late that afternoon, but with C5,000 deposited to my account at the First Bank of Liberty–minus expenses, it came to C3,000 that I could call my own–and another C300 cash in my pocket that the Ministry of Revenue didn't have to know about, I was solvent for another month or so. Not rich, by any means, but with luck I wouldn't have to get a real job any time soon, so long as I didn't do something stupid like blowing a wad at the poker table.

My place was a two-room flat on Wharf Street, above a ceramics shop where I had the benefit of hot air carried up through vents from their kiln. Once I put away my gear, I pumped some water into the tub and lit the heating coil. While the bath warmed up, I hid my cash within a knothole in the wall behind the dresser, then peeled off my filthy clothes. A long soak in the tub with a glass of bearshine, then I dried off, pulled on a robe, and went to bed. I was asleep before I remembered to check my comp for messages.

I woke up later that evening, hungry and restless. So I shaved, put on some clean clothes, and hit the town in search of a decent meal. Leeport was still a small settlement in those days–a dozen or so wood-frame and adobe buildings on either side of three muddy streets, a waterfront with tugboats and barges lined up at the piers—so this time of night there was little question where I was going to find dinner and a mug of cold ale.

Not surprisingly, the Captain's Lady was only half full; it was Orifiel night, after all, and Leeport was a workingman's town. Tomorrow morning the barges would be back on the channel, the wharf lined with wagons. A handful of boatmen sitting around the hearth, warming their feet by the fire; a few more locals gathered around a nearby table, cards in hand and a modest pile of chips between them. The usual familiar faces; a few of them looked up as I shut the door behind me, and I nodded back as I hung up my jacket, then sauntered to the other side of the room. The bartender saw me coming; Hurricane Dave had already pushed a mug beneath the middle spigot on the wall by the time I reached the roughbark bar where he spent his evenings.

"Welcome back," he said, favoring me with a seldom-seen smile. "How was the trip?"

"Good 'nuff. Where's the chief?"

"Off for the night. Town business." He topped off the mug, passed it to me. "On the house. Good hunting?"

"Okay." I lifted a hand, waved it back and forth. "A little one. Made the tourists happy." The porter was black as coal, bitter as a lie; the Lady's ale came straight from the brewpots down in the cellar, which Dave tended as lovingly as if they were his own children. "Thanks, I've been waiting for this. What's on the menu tonight . . . the usual?"

"Got a fresh batch in the kitchen. Want some?"

"Only if I have to pay for it." I dug a couple of wooden dollars out of my vest pocket and dropped them on the counter. "Cornbread, too, if you've got it."

"Sure, we've got some left, I think." Yet Dave didn't leave the bar. Instead, he picked up a rag and, making a pretense of wiping down the counter, moved a little closer. "Expecting trouble?" he murmured.

Dave was a big guy, a giant even in a town full of men with a lot of muscle. His boss didn't tolerate troublemakers in her establishment, and neither did he; firearms were surrendered at the bar, and anyone caught with a knife larger than those used to clean a redfish was evicted at once. So if Hurricane Dave sensed a problem, it was worth taking seriously. "Not really," I said quietly. "Why do you ask?"

"Two guys, at the table behind you to your left." Dave kept his voice low, didn't look in their direction. "Came in a couple of days ago. Took a room upstairs, paid for it a week in advance. Been asking questions about you."

"Uh-huh." I felt the hair on the back of my neck begin to rise. There wasn't a mirror behind the bar; otherwise I might have been able to sneak a peek at them. "What sort of questions?"

"Where you've been, mainly . . . also if you're reliable." Dave continued to swab the deck. "Dana's done most of the talking. She told them that you're a good guide, if that's what they're asking, and that you're out of town and she didn't know when you were getting back. Didn't let 'em know where you live, just that you drop in now and then."

"I see." Good old Dana, always looking out for my back. "Anything else?"

"Sure. Two more things. They wanted to know if you and her were . . . y'know. Related."

Once again, I felt my face tingle. An old question, yet one I still hadn't become used to, even after all these years. "I hope she set 'em straight," I muttered, and when Dave raised an eyebrow I knew she hadn't. Crap. "Aw, hell . . . so what's the other?"

"One of them's coming over now." Dave backed away from the counter. "White chili and cornbread," he said aloud, scooping up the coins I'd just put down. "Anything else, sir?"

I might have asked for the stunner he kept under the bar, just so I could have it in case this was someone's jealous husband, yet that was out of the question. Dana Monroe wasn't only the proprietor of the Captain's Lady, but also Leeport's mayor, not to mention one its founders. So while she and I were close—perhaps even closer than I was willing to admit—a brawl was the last thing she wanted in her place of business. Not good for either commerce or politics.

"No," I said, "thanks anyway." Dave nodded and headed for

the kitchen. I picked up my mug and took another sip of ale while I waited for someone to ask my name.

"Pardon me, sir," a deep voice said a moment later, "are you Sawyer Lee?" And that's how it all began.

The guy who'd come up behind me was only slightly smaller than Hurricane Dave, with long blond hair pulled back in a ponytail and a thick beard. I wondered how I could have missed seeing him; perhaps I was more tired than I thought.

"You've found him," I said. "May I help you?"

"Yes, sir, you can." His voice was surprisingly mild; despite his size, there was nothing menacing about him. "I have someone with me who'd like to speak to you, if you don't mind."

"Sure." I nodded toward the beaded curtain through which Dave had just disappeared. "I just ordered dinner. If your friend wants to come over here . . ."

"He'd like to speak to you alone, please. At our table." He paused. "If that's inconvenient just now, we'll gladly wait until you've finished your meal."

Jealous husbands are never so polite, and this bloke could have easily wrenched my arm behind my back and frog-marched me wherever he pleased. Instead, he was giving me the option of eating in peace before attending to whatever business his friend had in mind. Not only that, but apparently these guys had been patiently waiting for me to reappear in Leeport, to the point of renting an upstairs room and staking out the tavern for the last two nights. And Dana's accommodations don't come cheap; she provides soap with a bath, and even washes the bedsheets once a week.

I decided to take a chance. "No, no . . . I can have dinner over there just as well as over here, Mister . . . um?"

"Kennedy." A dour nod. "If you'll follow me, please . . . ?"

As he led me across the room to his table, a few people I knew in the place gave me curious looks. One of them was George Waite, a tugboat operator who'd carried me and my clients as passengers on more than one occasion. He was having a drink with his nephew, Donny; the boy ignored us, yet I couldn't help but notice the cautious expression on George's face. I gave him a brief nod, and he reciprocated with one of his own, and in this way a silent understanding was reached: if there was trouble, he'd back me up. That's the way things are, out on the frontier; friends look out for each other, particularly when strangers are involved.

The other man seated at the table had his back turned to the room. Despite the warmth of the nearby fireplace, he wore a dark blue cloak, its hood pulled up over his head. Clearly he didn't want his face to be seen. He stood up as we approached, and I saw that he was a small man, no taller than my shoulder, middle-aged and thickset. Yet it wasn't until he pushed back his hood that I recognized him.

"Mr. Lee?" he said quietly, holding out his hand. "Good evening. I'm Morgan Goldstein."

If St. Nicholas had suddenly appeared in the Captain's Lady, I wouldn't have been more surprised.

There was no one on Coyote who didn't know his name. The founder and CEO of Janus Ltd., Morgan Goldstein had been one of the richest men on Earth even before his company managed to negotiate a near-monopoly on hyperspace shipping rights to 47 Ursae Majoris; since then, he'd become even more wealthy, if that was possible. Over the last couple of years, he'd relocated his business from North America to Coyote, where he'd established a sizable estate on Albion just outside New Brighton. Yet Goldstein hadn't been content with merely having more money than anyone else; two years ago, he'd run for president of the Coyote Federation. His defeat by the incumbent, Wendy Gunther, in an unprecedented second-term bid for office, apparently settled his political ambitions; after that, he'd retired to his ranch, where he contented himself with raising horses and underwriting expeditions to the unexplored regions of the planet. Although he occasionally emerged for one public event or another, lately he'd become something of a recluse. We heard a lot about him, but no one ever saw his face.

And now, here he was, nursing a mug of ale in a beat-up cantina halfway between somewhere and nowhere. It took me a moment to unglue my tongue. "Pleased to meet you, Mr. . . ."

"Roth." He lowered his voice as I grasped his hand. "So far as anyone here knows, my name's Irving Roth." He grinned as he sat down again. "I like this town. Everyone minds their own business."

"It's a nice place." I took a chair across the table from him. Kennedy moved behind me to take the chair between us. "I understand you've been looking for me."

Goldstein raised an eyebrow. "How did you . . . ?"

"Pardon me." Unnoticed until this moment, Hurricane Dave placed a bowl of white chili and a plate of cornbread on the table in front of me. "That it? Want another drink?"

"No, thanks." I pointed to Goldstein, then Kennedy. "You? How about you?" Goldstein had already raised his hood again, and Kennedy silently shook his head. "We're fine, Dave. Thanks."

"What is that stuff?" Goldstein peered at my meal. "I saw it on the chalkboard, but I didn't ask . . ."

"White chili. Made from chicken, not beef." I picked up a spoon, stirred the grated onions and goat cheese on top. "Try it. House specialty. So what brings you here, Mr. Roth?"

"A job." Goldstein settled back in his chair, clasped his hands together in his lap. "But first things first. I understand you're a professional wilderness guide, Mr. Lee . . ."

"Uh-huh. Best in the business." Not to mention almost the only one in the business. True, Susan Gunther and Jonathan Parson had their Coyote Expeditions outfit in Clarksburg, but they specialized in camera safaris, and refused to take hunters. I liked them well enough, and Susan and I shared a certain remote kinship, but nonetheless we had a certain difference of opinion. They saw boids as an endangered species, while I saw any creature that can disembowel me with one swipe of its claws as a danger only to myself and my clients. So if you wanted to take pictures of a boid from the safety of an armored skimmer, you hired Sue and Jon; if you wanted to take home its head, I was the man you wanted to see.

"So I've heard." Goldstein watched while I dipped my spoon into the chili. "I've also heard that you've gone north . . . across the Highland Channel, up to Medsylvania."

"A couple of years ago." The chili was hot and spicy, just the way I liked it. I reached for my ale. "I once led a survey group from the University up there. We spent a week or so mapping the southern peninsula."

"Find anything interesting?"

"Not really. Mainly forest. The trees are a bit taller . . . different species of roughbark, with faux birch as the understory. Other than that . . ." I shrugged. "Swamp. Ball-plants. Creek cats and swampers. Seen one, seen 'em all."

"Uh-huh." Goldstein smiled. "You don't sound very impressed, considering . . ."

"Considering what?"

"From what you've told me, you've seen a part of this world no one has ever seen before, yet it seems to have no more of an impression on you than . . . well, the compost heap out back."

"It's my business. After a while, it all begins to look the same." It wasn't quite true; there were places, like the view of Mt. Bonestell from the Gillis Range, or the giant massifs of the Meridian Archipelago, that still took my breath away. But the people who usually hired me as a guide never wanted to see these beauties; more often than not, I found myself babysitting rich tourists who just wanted to shoot a boid or a creek cat. For them, it was a rich man's thrill; for me, it was something that paid the bills and kept me in ale without demanding that I find honest work.

"Uh-huh. Of course." Goldstein sipped his beer. He remained quiet for a minute or so, giving me a chance to eat. I welcomed the silence; no one made chili like Dave. I was working my way to the bottom of the bowl when he spoke up again. "I understand you're related to Captain Lee . . . are you?"

I hated it whenever someone mentioned this. Captain Robert E. Lee—himself a descendant of the Confederate Army general of the American Civil War—was nearly as famous as his namesake for being the commanding officer of the URSS *Alabama,* the first starship to reach the 47 Uma. There's a life-size statue of him in front of Government House in Liberty that looks nothing like me.

"So I'm told," I said, putting down my spoon and reaching for a napkin. "I don't know if it's true. There's a lot of people back on Earth who claim they're related to Captain Lee . . . or General Lee, for that matter."

"Aren't you curious?" Goldstein raised an eyebrow. "If you're a descendant, I mean."

"Not really." I wiped my mouth, tossed the napkin on top of the bowl. "He was before my time. So far as I know, we've got nothing in common, except maybe a gene or two here and there."

Not entirely true, either. Once I immigrated to Coyote aboard one of the first ships to carry passengers through the starbridge, it wasn't long before I made my way to Leeport. My first night here, I met Dana Monroe; I was trying to gamble my way to passage aboard a boat bound for Great Dakota, and made the mistake of trying to hide an ace of spades within my boot. Another guy at the table caught me, and that was when I learned that card-cheats weren't tolerated in Leeport. Dana saved my ass; using her authority as mayor, she hauled me into the kitchen and put me to work washing dishes until I earned enough money to cover my civil fine, and in the meantime discovered that I may or may not be distant kin to Captain Lee.

That was when I discovered why this place was called the Captain's Lady. Dana Monroe had been the Chief Engineer aboard the *Alabama*; indeed, there was a torn piece of metal mounted above the fireplace that once belonged to the ship, recovered from its wreckage on Hammerhead. But it went further than that; Chief Monroe was Captain Lee's partner in the last years of his life, and although they'd never been formally married, she still carried a torch for her man.

So here I was, some guy from Earth so down on his luck that he'd try to cheat at poker just to buy his way aboard a tugboat to a place where he might get a job at a sawmill, only to have his fortune change when he met a woman who'd been the former lover of a legend. A legend with whom I shared questionable heritage. One of the great regrets of Dana's life was that she and Captain Lee never had any children; although she never came right out and said so, I became the son she didn't have. I was almost the right age, after all, and . . .

So this was how I came to live in Leeport, and why the Captain's Lady was a second home to me. I never called Dana my mother, and she never called me her son, but the relationship was

nearly the same. And once I became a safari guide, willing to escort visitors into the wilderness for a fee, I discovered that sharing
the last name of Coyote's most famous figure worked to my advantage. It helped attract clients, and I couldn't fool myself by believing that the reason why I had an extra *C*300 in my cubbyhole
tonight wasn't because three guys could go home to Germany and
claim that they'd gone boid-hunting with the descendant of Captain Lee.

But this sort of secondhand fame can also be a curse. As I
looked across the table at Morgan Goldstein, I saw from the look
in his eyes that he was expecting more than I could deliver. And although I didn't yet know what he wanted from me, Morgan Goldstein wasn't some rube looking for a stuffed boid head to hang
above his fireplace.

"Perhaps. Perhaps not. Mike . . . ?" He pointed to my half-
empty mug, then made a gesture to Kennedy. Without a word,
his aide—or maybe he was Goldstein's bodyguard—left us, marching across the room to the bar. "Regardless, I have great need of
an experienced guide. Someone who can take me to Medsylvania."

"Hunting?"

"Yes . . . but not for animals. For a person." A pause. "A
friend, to be exact. His name's Joe Cassidy . . . Joseph Walking
Star Cassidy."

Kennedy returned to the table with two fresh mugs of porter. Goldstein took a drink, smiled. "One nice thing about coming all the
way out here . . . best ale on Coyote." I nodded, hoping that he
didn't like it so much that he got it in his mind to buy the place.
Noting my impatience, he put down his mug. "Joe came with me
from Earth, where he'd worked for me for many years as my
equerry." I raised an eyebrow, and he added, "Stable master.
Someone who takes care of horses."

"Gotcha." One of the first things that brought Goldstein to the
attention of everyone on Coyote was his gift to the colonies of his
private collection of horses. Forty-eight in all, everything from Ara-
bians and Percherons to quarter horses and donkeys: breeding

stock, possibly the last herd of this size left in existence. He'd given most of the horses to the different settlements, with the stipulation that they would be treated well and allowed to have offspring. Horses had become nearly extinct on Earth, and it was Morgan's intent that, by introducing them to Coyote, they'd have a chance to survive; yet he'd reserved a half-dozen or so for himself, which he continued to raise on his Albion estate. "Go on," I said.

"Joe was . . . is . . . an employee, but . . ." Morgan hesitated. "Well, over the years I've come to consider him a friend. He's something of the last of the breed himself. Full-blooded Navajo, and a shaman at that. His people were scattered when climate change caused the reservation to become uninhabitable, and Joe made his way up to New England. I was looking for someone to take care of my horses, and . . ."

He shrugged. "I suppose we were meant to find each other. Neither of us ever had much in the way of families, and Joe always made it clear to me that he didn't give a damn how much money I had, it was the fact that I cared so much about horses that mattered. So I took crap from him that I would have fired anyone else for saying, and he let me know when he thought I was wrong about something, and . . . well, I guess you can figure out the rest."

And indeed I did. In my line of work, I'd seen my share of rich and powerful men, enough to know that extreme wealth bears a curse of its own: you never know for certain who's really your friend and who's just kissing your butt so that they can keep their seat on the gravy train. If Cassidy was as sincere as Morgan Goldstein made him out to be, then he was as rare as the horses that he tended.

"And you say he's missing," I said. "Why do you think he went . . . ?"

"Let me finish." Goldstein lifted one finger from the handle of his mug, a subtle yet imperious gesture that had probably intimidated entire boardrooms. "As I said, Joe has a mystical streak in him. Now, I don't know for sure if what he told me about himself is true . . . that he comes from a long line of Navajo medicine men, that he talks to the spirits and they talk back to him . . . and I've never had much use for religion of any kind, but he believes it, and that's been fine with me. When we had the estate in Massachusetts, he built a log hogan on the property and from time to time he'd go there to have a sweat, commune with the gods, that sort of thing. I tried to talk to him about it, but that was one part of himself that he always kept closed to me. And I let him, because . . ."

"Because it was none of your business."

"Exactly." Morgan picked up his mug again, took another sip. "I even knew that he'd cultivated peyote, in flowerpots in a corner of the greenhouse where my gardener raised roses. Duncan was rather upset when he found them, and wanted to rip them up, but I forbade him from doing so, because I knew that they belonged to Joe and that he used them for . . . y'know, spiritual reasons."

"That's interesting, but I don't know why . . ."

"Let me continue, please." Again, a cold stare. Goldstein was obviously someone who didn't tolerate interruption. "When we relocated the estate to New Brighton, I let Joe build another hogan so that he could continue his practices. I think he might have brought some peyote seeds with him . . . in fact, I'm sure he did . . . but something happened, and he was unable to cultivate any plants."

I wasn't surprised. Although most of the crops humankind had attempted to introduce to this world had been successful, there had also been notable failures. Coyote's long seasons had much to do with it; although our springs and summers collectively lasted for a year and half by Earth reckoning, so did our autumns and winters. Corn and bamboo did well, for instance, but tubers like carrots and potatoes were notoriously finicky, and tomatoes could only be raised in greenhouses. The hardier strains of apples and peaches were able to withstand cold snaps, but citrus fruits like oranges and grapefruit were nearly impossible to grow even in the equatorial regions. Native predators and plant diseases also took their toll; grasshoarders loved turnips and soybeans, while it was very difficult to keep strawberries clean of fungus.

"But Joe needed something to assist him in his meditation," Goldstein continued, "so he began to look around." He sighed, started to pick up his mug again, then put it down without taking a drink. "He found . . ."

"Sting." For the first time since he'd approached me at the bar,

Mike Kennedy spoke up. I'd almost forgotten he was there; he sat between me and Goldstein, and although his expression was as stoical as before, his eyes were glacial. "He started using sting."

Goldstein glared at him. "Mike . . ."

"C'mon, boss. I knew about it before you did." The bodyguard reached for a piece of cornbread on my plate. "So did everyone else. He got into that stuff like there was no . . ."

"I know that," Goldstein said angrily. "But what I still don't understand is why didn't you tell me."

Kennedy shrugged and said nothing, looking away as if this was some minor detail he'd neglected to mention to his employer. Yet I knew exactly where he was coming from. He and Joe Cassidy had one thing in common; they both drew their paychecks from the same source. And only a fink rats out the other guy to the head guy, particularly when it comes to drugs.

And sting was pretty powerful stuff. It was derived from the venom of pseudo-wasps, large flying insects that nested within ball-plants, large spherical plants that grew in abundance in grasslands and marshes across most of Coyote's western hemisphere. Indeed, ball-plants and pseudo-wasps formed part of an interesting three-way symbiosis. Swampers, the ferret-like creatures that inhabited those same areas, hibernated within the ball-plants during the winter; the weak and old that perished during that period decomposed within the plant's hollow core, and thus supplied nutrients to the plant. Pseudo-wasps built their nests within the plant's tough outer shell; they protected the swampers by attacking potential predators who might try to get an easy meal by ripping open the inner cell, and in return the insects pollinated the plants.

Pseudo-wasp venom wasn't fatal. Containing a natural form of lysergic acid, it made animals like creek cats and boids so confused that they simply forgot what they were doing and wandered off; lower forms of insects were so paralyzed that the pseudo-wasps were able to feed upon them while they were still alive. For humans, though, the effect was more pronounced; the original *Alabama* colonists stung by pseudo-wasps staggered around like happy drunks, and some experienced hallucinations. After that, they learned to avoid ball-plants, particularly during the autumn and spring seasons when the pseudo-wasps tended to be most active.

Yet once more settlers arrived on Coyote aboard the Western Hemisphere Union ships that followed the *Alabama,* someone discovered how to trap pseudo-wasps by dropping a sticky-net, like those used by Union Guard troops, over the ball-plants. Once the insects exhausted themselves and died, it was possible to extract them from the nets and, with careful use of a pair of surgical forceps, crush their bodies until the venom seeped from their sacs. It was a slow and painstaking process, to be sure, but it yielded a quarter-centimeter or two of fluid that, once diluted with a little water, gave whoever put it on their tongue a cheap high that would last for hours.

That was sting, as it was commonly called. It had been made illegal long before I came to Coyote, but that never stopped it from being sold or bartered on the black market. I'd tried it once, for the bloody hell of it, but didn't like it very much; when an old girlfriend stuck her head up from the ground and asked if I wanted to come down there and screw, that was enough fun for one night. Yet there were stingheads all over Coyote; the stuff wasn't supposed to be addictive, yet you can't tell me it wasn't habit-forming . . . and there was nothing worse than seeing some poor fool clawing at the walls and screaming that his mother is coming for him with a knife between her teeth.

"Never mind." Goldstein looked away from his bodyguard, turned his attention back to me. "Fact is, Joe started using sting. I don't think he meant to use it as . . . as dope, I mean . . . but rather as a substitute for peyote. All the same, though . . ."

"He got whacked on the stuff." Kennedy didn't try to hide his contempt. "He dropped it whenever he could . . ."

"Mike . . ." Again, there was a note of warning in Goldstein's voice. Kennedy shut up, and his boss went on. "I didn't know what was happening at first, but when I did . . ."

He absently ran a hand across his bare scalp. "I told him that I couldn't have someone on my staff who was abusing drugs. He argued, of course, that his reasons for using it were spiritual, that he wasn't doing it just to get high, but I couldn't accept that. There was too much evidence that he was taking sting whenever possible . . ."

"Such as?"

"I first realized that he was using it when people I'd never met before started coming to the estate. Friends of his, whom he'd met in New Brighton. One or two of them were suppliers, others were just . . ." He sighed. "Lowlifes. Scum. Immigrants who'd come here without any plans, just trying to get by however they could."

I bristled a bit when I heard this, for he was describing guys like me. One thing that frequently ticks me off about the wealthy is that they often don't realize that not everyone has a burning ambition to acquire money and material possessions. Ever since the starbridge had been opened, more people were arriving every month; most were simply trying to flee their ruined homelands on Earth, and didn't have any plans other than getting by as best as they could, one day at a time. The rich don't understand this; unless someone has made it their mission in life to die with more toys than anyone else, then he or she is a deadbeat.

Goldstein didn't notice that he'd just insulted me, but Kennedy did. His face remained stolid, yet his eyes briefly rolled upward. "Anyway," Goldstein went on, "Joe and I had a long talk, and we eventually agreed that he needed to take some time off. I knew that the Colonial University medical school had recently started a drug treatment program, so I told him that I'd put money in his account to pay for him to travel to Shuttlefield and get help. Joe said he'd do this, and a few days later he caught a gyro-shuttle to New Florida."

He ran a fingertip around the rim of his mug. "When a few weeks went by and I hadn't heard anything from him, I called the university, and that's when I discovered that Joe had never checked in. So I called the bank, and found out that he'd dissolved his account at the branch in Liberty, taking out all the money I'd put in, plus his own earnings."

"I imagine you were rather upset."

"To put it mildly, yes." The lines of his face tightened. "But more than that, I was concerned about what he was doing to himself. Understand, I like Joe. As I said before, I've always regarded

him as being more of a friend than an employee . . . and from what
I could tell, he was in trouble."

"When did all this happen?"

"Last Barchiel . . . about a month and half ago." Like everyone
else born and bred on Earth, I mentally made the conversion from
Gregorian to LeMarean calendars. Approximately one hundred
and sixty days, give or take a couple of weeks: the middle of Coyote's winter. "To make a long story short, I put some people I knew
on Joe's trail, and found that he met up with several people in Liberty . . . some of whom were the same guys he'd met earlier in New
Brighton . . . and together they'd hired a boat to take them to New
Boston."

"All the way up there?" That surprised me. New Boston was
the most remote colony of the Coyote Federation, located on the
northern coast of Midland. No one went there in mid-winter unless
they absolutely had to do so. "Why?"

"From what I've learned, Joe and his friends stayed there just
long enough to buy food and supplies, then they hired a boat to
carry them across the Medsylvania Channel." Goldstein picked up
his mug again, took another sip without any of his previous pleasure. "After that, the trail goes cold."

"So I take it that you want me to go up there and find him."

"No. I want you to take me up there so I can find him." He
gave a sidelong glance at Kennedy. "My associate will only be going part of the way, assuming that our first stop will be New
Boston. Apparently he has no desire to assure himself that his colleague is alive and well."

"Sorry, boss," Kennedy rumbled. "My job description doesn't
cover chasing junkies."

Not very sympathetic, although I wasn't sure that I blamed
him. People like Joe Cassidy made disappearing acts like that all
the time on Coyote. Most were would-be frontiersmen, harboring
ill-conceived fantasies of going into the wilderness with little more
than a backpack, a tent, and a hand-axe; sometimes they succeeded at homesteading, but more often than not they simply vanished, never to be seen again. Others were holy fools, believing
that Coyote had some mystical powers that would bring enlighten-

ment. A gravesite just below the summit of Mt. Shaw on Midland held the bones of the members of the Church of Universalist Transformation, who went cannibal when they were trapped on the mountain during a winter storm.

I didn't know if either fate had befallen Joe Cassidy and his friends, nor was I eager to find out. In fact, I was still getting over my last trip. But clients like Morgan Goldstein don't fall from the sky; if I played my cards right, I could stand to make enough money to last me until the beginning of summer.

"Five grand up front," I said, "and another three grand for expenses . . . not including a gyro ride to New Boston."

Goldstein didn't even blink. "Fair enough . . . but no gyro. I want to go by boat, all the way." He caught the puzzled look on my face. "Not many gyros fly to New Boston, I'm told . . . and if Joe's just across the channel, he'd see one coming. I don't want him to be expecting me."

"If you say so." I turned my head to look at George Waite. As I expected, he'd leaned back in his chair, pretending not to eavesdrop but doing so nonetheless. George caught my eye, gave me a sly grin; he knew a lucrative deal when he saw it coming. I turned back to Goldstein. "I think that can be arranged."

"I thought so." He hadn't missed the silent exchange between me and George. Goldstein picked up his mug, polished off the rest of his ale, then pushed back his chair. "See you here tomorrow morning, Mr. Lee," he said, reaching into his pocket to toss a handful of dollars on the table. "I hope your reputation for reliability is well-earned."

I hoped it was, too.

We left Leeport early the next morning, as passengers aboard the *Helen Waite.*

Before I met Goldstein and Kennedy again at the Captain's Lady, I went down to the wharf and negotiated passage with her captain. George was a buddy, so I held nothing back from him; I told him that my client was none other than Morgan Goldstein, and that although we were heading for New Boston our destination would be somewhere in Medsylvania. As it turned out, George had already intended to go to New Boston; three barges of coal were waiting for him up there, for shipment to Clarksburg further south. I wasn't surprised when he told that he'd recognized Goldstein, nor was I particularly shocked when he hit me up for a larger fee than usual. C1,000 for the three of us was steep, but George knew the money wasn't coming from my pocket; in return, he agreed to wait a few days for us in New Boston and continue to pretend that one of his passengers was named Irving Roth.

I'd packed equipment for both of us, but once I rendezvoused with Goldstein at the Captain's Lady, I discovered Goldstein had brought his own gear. Although I was pleased that he'd come prepared, some of his stuff was unnecessary; the brand-new solar tents and particle-beam rifles were fine, but I made him leave behind the portable hydrogen-cell stove, the infrared motion-detection system, and the seven-day supply of freeze-dried rations, telling him that, unless he wanted to carry all that junk on his back, he'd do just as well living off the land. He argued with me, of course, but I put my foot down, and he reluctantly agreed to put the extra equipment in storage at the Captain's Lady until we returned.

Just before we left, I linked my pad with his and downloaded C5,000 into my private account. George did the same, taking C1,000 for passage to New Boston. Goldstein performed the transactions with scarcely a blink: more evidence that the rich have different lives than mere mortals. Kennedy and I shared another glance–he was accustomed to this sort of free-spending, and was quietly amused that I wasn't–then I shepherded him and Goldstein aboard the *Helen Waite*. Donny untied us from the pier. George yanked twice on the cord of the steam whistle, then the tugboat chugged out of the Leeport harbor.

The journey to New Boston took two days. The first leg of the trip was spent traveling upstream along the West Channel to the northern tip of New Florida; we dropped anchor overnight at Red Point, the mouth of North Creek where, ten Coyote years ago, Carlos Montero led his team from Midland on the morning of Liberation Day. All had gone well until then, but the *Helen Waite* was meant more for hauling barges than passengers; its cabin had only three racks, and those were occupied by George, Donny, and Jose, the retarded man whose job it was to shovel coal into the tugboat's steam engines. It took a lot of talking for me to get it through to Goldstein that, as passengers, our accommodations were little more than a tarp stretched across the aft deck, and his money didn't cover anything more than this.

Goldstein grumbled about the arrangements, going so far as to try to bribe Jose into giving up his bunk. George put a stop to this, though, and he finally had to resign himself to sleeping out in the open. I did my best not to smile; it was time that Morgan Goldstein got used to the absence of luxury. Once we had dinner in the pilot-house, he retired to his sleeping bag, complaining to the moment that he finally fell asleep, while the rest of us stayed up for a while to share a bottle of wine and watch Bear rise to the east, its silver rings reflected upon the cold, black waters of the delta.

The following day we crossed the confluence of the West and East Channels and entered the Medsylvania Channel. To our left lay the northern coast of Midland, the lower steppes of the Gillis Range just visible on the southeastern horizon; to our right, on the far side of the broad channel, lay Medsylvania, its rocky shores and dense forests dark and forbidding. This far north, winter still lingered, yet with spring quickly approaching, the snow was beginning to melt. Boulder-sized chunks of ice, carried downstream from the Northern Circumpolar River, bobbed along the channel like miniature icebergs, making the passage treacherous. George hugged the Midland coast as much as possible, keeping the engines at one-third throttle; Donny stood at the bow, calling out to his uncle whenever the boat came too close to some ice, yet even so there were occasional bumps and scrapes as the hull collided with something that came up too fast for George to dodge.

It was slow going, and we didn't reach New Boston until almost twilight. I'd been there only a few times in the past, and never by choice. The most northern of Coyote's settlements, it was also the most remote; its closest neighbor on Midland was Defiance, nearly fifteen hundred miles away on the other side of the Gillis Range. Like Leeport, New Boston was a river town, a shipping port for the coal, nickel, and iron mines located further inland, yet even Leeport was a bustling metropolis compared to this lonely place. As the *Helen Waite* chugged into the shallow harbor, I saw lights gleaming within the windows of log houses and wood-frame buildings, heard the low gong of the lighthouse bell as the watchman signaled our arrival.

"Hope you have a place to stay." George twisted the wheel to follow the harbormaster's lamp to the nearest available slot on the pier. "Me and the boys are sleeping aboard."

"Uh-huh. I've always had good luck with the Revolution . . ."

"Why are you staying aboard?" Goldstein stood next to us in the pilot-house, leaning against the railing. "You said you were going to pick up coal . . . why not sleep in a decent bed while you're here?"

"No, thanks. We'll stay on the boat."

"I insist." Reaching into his jacket pocket, Goldstein produced a money clip stuffed with enough Colonials to plug a leak in the hull. "You've done well by us. Let me make it up to you."

Once again, George and I exchanged a glance: *oh, brother.* "Put that away, Mr. Roth," the captain said. "First, we're going ashore tonight just long enough to get a bite to eat. So far as accommodations are concerned . . . I appreciate the offer, but there's nothing in town much better than what we have here. Second, this isn't . . . shall we say, the safest place to be." He nodded toward Kennedy, who stood silently beside his boss. "If I were you," he added, "I'd keep your friends close, and your money even closer, if y'know what I mean."

"I . . ."

"Do what he says." I gave him a long, hard look. "You hired me to be your guide. So shut up and let me do my job, all right?"

"Of course. Certainly." The wad disappeared as suddenly as it had appeared. Kennedy handed him his cape; he pulled it on, tugging the hood over his head. Once again, Morgan Goldstein became Irving Roth, an anonymous traveler. Or so I hoped.

Once we tied up at the pier and George paid the harbormaster, we went into town, leaving Jose behind to watch the boat. Fish-oil lamps illuminated our way along the muddy main street; potholes covered by thin skeins of ice softly crunched beneath our boots.

The evening air was cool, warmed by the odor of fish and herbs, boiled meat and tobacco. Kiosks lined both sides of the street, their tables offering skins, handmade jewelry, liniments, secondhand electronics; prostitutes and hard-eyed men lingered in doorways, watching us as we passed by.

The Revolution Inn was located a couple of blocks from the waterfront, a ramshackle two-story building that looked as if it had been hammered together by a crew of drunk carpenters. Which probably wasn't far from the truth; despite the patriotic name, the Revolution was little more than a beat-up tavern, with sawdust on the floor and benches in front of a fireplace half-filled with ash and soot. Yet there were a few guest rooms upstairs, and although they were most commonly used by the local hookers, they'd do for the night.

Once I paid the bartender for two rooms, we parked ourselves at a vacant table in the corner. Dinner was goat stew, watery and undercooked; one bite, and Morgan pushed aside his plate, muttering that he'd rather go hungry. I distracted myself by studying the crowd. It was early evening, and already the place was full: fishermen, mill workers, a handful of loggers and miners who'd come down from the mountains for a night on the town. I polished off my stew—it was wretched, but since it was probably the last hot meal I'd have for a few days I made myself eat it—then left the table and wandered over to the bar, ostensibly to buy a drink but really to ferret out some information.

It didn't take long for me to find out what I needed to know. The bartender remembered Joe Cassidy, all right; he'd come through town about a month and a half ago, along with seven other people: four men and three women. They'd stayed in New Boston just long enough to buy supplies, then they hired a local boatman to ferry them across the channel to Medsylvania. As luck would have it, the same boatman was at a table on the other side of the room; at first he pretended not to recall who I was talking about, but the jug of bearshine I bought for him and his cronies helped restore his memory. Sure, he remembered those people . . . and for a modest fee of C200, he'd be happy to give me and my friend Mr. Roth a ride to the exact place where he'd dropped them off.

Something about me must have smelled like money. Either that, or I'd spent too much time lately with rich people. We dickered for a bit, and finally agreed that he'd get fifty bucks up front, and the rest once our feet touched dry land on the other side of the channel. I went back to my table and reported what I'd learned.

Goldstein wasn't happy with the arrangement. "Two hundred for a lift across the channel?" he muttered, glaring at me from across the table. "Hell, we could buy our own canoe for that kind of money."

"Sure, we can ... but what would we do with it?" I took a drink of ale. "This guy knows exactly where he put off Joe and his pals. Chances are, they're not far from that spot. Without knowing that, though, we could wander up and down the coast for weeks without finding them."

Goldstein considered this for a moment, then turned to George. "Mr. Waite, if you knew where to go ... that is, if we were to get directions from this fellow Sawyer just met ... ?"

"Not a chance." George shook his head. "Sorry, but I'm not about to risk my boat trying to make landfall on a shore that doesn't have a deep harbor. *Helen* draws too much water for that sort of thing."

"I'll pay you ..."

"Uh-uh." He picked up his mug. "Nice to make your acquaintance, Mr. Roth, but this is as far as I go." George looked at me again. "I'll wait until Camael"—by this he meant four days from now—"for you to do your business, but if I haven't heard from you by then, we're going to have to cut you loose. My people in Clarksburg are waiting for their coal, and every day I hang around here means that I lose money."

"I understand. Thanks for being willing to wait." I looked at Goldstein again. "So there it is, Morgan ... Mr. Roth, I mean." He blanched when I said his real name; George and Donny pretended not to notice. "Either we take our chances with that guy over there, or George carries us back home. Your call."

Goldstein scowled, then slowly let out his breath. "You know I don't have a choice," he said quietly. "Mike ... ?"

"I'll stay here." Kennedy was the only one at the table who

seemed to like goat stew; he was working on his second helping. Meeting Goldstein's gaze, he went on. "Look, chief, Joe and I never got along. That's a fact. If I go with you, he'll just get pissed off when he sees me. You've got a satphone. If you run into any trouble, you call me and I'll come to the rescue."

Goldstein seemed so hesitant that, for a moment, I thought he was going to kill the rest of the trip. This place had clearly given him the willies—not that I blamed him—and for the first time, I think, he'd come to realize exactly what it meant to leave behind even this rough excuse for civilization and venture into the wilderness. The temptation must have been great: abandon Cassidy to whatever uncertain fate had befallen him, pay George for return passage to Leeport, then retreat to the comforts of his ranch, where he could play with his horses and spend his free time making even more money.

Yet there was something within him that simply wouldn't let this go. For better or worse, he had to see this through. Joseph Walking Star Cassidy was his friend . . . perhaps his only friend. Like it or not, he couldn't give up now.

"We'll do it," he murmured. "Dammit, we'll do it."

Without another word, he pushed back his chair, stood up, and marched across the room to the stairs. He left so suddenly that it took Kennedy a moment to remember his duty; he quickly left the table, following his boss upstairs. I wondered if his job included tucking in the boss's bedsheets and singing him a lullaby.

George watched them go, then quietly shook his head. "Sawyer, I appreciate the work," he said, "and you won't hear me complain about the money . . . but if you ever bring aboard someone like that again . . ."

"I hear you, man." And indeed, I was beginning to have second thoughts about the entire business.

The boatman's name was Merle—no last name, or at least none that he was willing to give me; "Just call me Merle," he said—and his craft was a single-masted pirogue that he used to inspect the trotlines he'd rigged along the Midland side of the channel. Once

Goldstein and I loaded our gear aboard, we cast off from the dock, with the boatman and I using the oars until we were clear of the harbor, at which point he unfurled the sail and set out across the channel.

It had rained during the night; a dense fog lay low and thick upon the water, making it difficult to see more than a few dozen yards ahead. Yet the boatman knew the channel well; he steered between the ice floes, tacking against the cool morning breeze that drifted up the river. At first he said little to us, but after a while he began to ask questions: who were we, and why were we so interested in finding the guys he'd carried over to Medsylvania last Barchiel. I told Just-Call-Me-Merle that my name was Just-Call-Me-Sawyer and my friend was Just-Call-Me-Irving, and the rest was none of his business. He got the message, and shut up after that.

It took less than an hour to cross the channel, but much longer than that to reach the place where he'd dropped off Walking Star and his companions. This turned out to be the mouth of a narrow creek, about sixty miles southwest of New Boston; the *Helen Waite* had cruised by it only yesterday. Yet George wouldn't have been able to safely take his craft this way even if we'd known of its existence; as we glided closer, I caught sight of jagged rocks just beneath the pirogue's flat keel. The tugboat would have run aground.

Merle lowered the sail and unshipped the oars once more, and we paddled the rest of the way to shore. We beached the pirogue just above the creek; Merle remained in his boat, not lifting a finger to help us as Goldstein and I unloaded our backpacks, waded through the ice-cold water, hauled them to the rocky shore.

"You sure this is the right place?" I asked.

"Yessir. Right on this very spot, that's where I left 'em." Merle had produced a tobacco pouch from his jacket; as he spoke, he pulled out a chaw and tucked it into his right cheek. "Last time I saw 'em," he said, pointing to the tree line a few yards away, "they were headed ..." He hesitated, then grinned. "Y'know, I think I done forgot."

I glanced at Goldstein. He reached into his jacket, pulled out his money clip, and counted out C150. I coughed, and he scowled, and added another C50. "Yeah, I think I remember now," Merle said as he took the money. "Right thataway, through those trees." He pointed to the thicket of faux-birch that formed the tree line just a few yards from the riverbank. "That's as much as I know."

"Thanks." Wading ashore, I picked up my pack. "You got a sat-phone code in case we need a pickup?"

"Yup." Merle spit brown fluid into the river. "Nancy Oscar two-two-three-niner. If my ol' lady picks up, ask for me. Just call me . . ."

"Merle. Got it. Thanks for the ride."

"Think nothing of it." Merle thrust the handle of his oar into the water and shoved off, then backpaddled into the channel. "Good luck," he called back, then he j-stroked until the prow of his boat was pointed back the way we'd come.

"Think he was being honest with us?" Goldstein was seated on a nearby boulder; he'd taken off his boots and opened his pack, and was in the process of exchanging his waterlogged socks for a dry pair. "He could have dropped us off anywhere, you know."

"He could, but what's the point?" I didn't mind hiking in wet socks—they'd dry out soon enough—so I hoisted my pack and settled its straps upon my shoulders. "He knows better than to lie to us."

"Why . . . ?"

"Because people out here in the boonies play it straight, Mr. Goldstein. Word gets around that you're a liar, then no one trusts you any more . . . and when the chips are down, that kind of trust is more precious than all the money you've got in the bank." As I said this, I was scanning the tall grass between us and the tree line. "Of course, you already know that, don't you?"

He said nothing, only grunted as he relaced his boots. Once again, I doubted that Morgan Goldstein had seen much more of Coyote than what he'd seen from the cockpit of a gyro. After nearly forty Earth-years of human colonization, almost two-thirds of the planet was still unexplored; even Medsylvania had barely felt the human presence. The population was growing, but the world itself was still untamed. With any luck, it would remain that way for a long time to come.

"So which way do we go?" he asked.

"That way." By then, I'd spotted what I was looking for: a place

where it looked as if the frozen grass had been trampled and
pushed down, creating a narrow trail that led into the trees. Even
though months had gone by, the grass was only now beginning to
thaw; the trail still remained. Not by coincidence, it ran parallel to
the creek. Made sense: follow the creek, find the people.

Goldstein peered in the direction I indicated, yet he didn't see
the clues I'd spotted. "Whatever you say," he said, standing up and
hoisting his own pack. "You're the guide. Lead on." A moment of
hesitation. "How far do you think . . . ?"

"No idea." I picked up my rifle, checked its charge. "As far as it
took for your friend to find whatever he was looking for."

Goldstein gave me a sharp look. "You think he was looking for
something? What?"

"Don't know." Pulling the rifle strap across my left shoulder, I
led the way toward the trail. "Reckon we'll find out when we get
there."

We followed the trail into the forest. It hadn't been used in quite a
while, yet there was still enough snow on the ground, sheltered
from the sun by the faux-birch that rose around us, that I was able
to discern footprints here and there. As I figured, the trail ran parallel to the creek; if Cassidy and his people intended to set up
camp then it made sense for them to place it near a source of fresh
water.

The terrain was flat, but it didn't make the going any easier.
Faux-birch soon gave way to Medsylvania roughbark so tall that
we couldn't see the treetops. The trail had vanished by then, forcing us to rely upon the creek as our only guide; now and then I
stopped to pull nylon ribbons from my pack and tie them around
lower branches, a precaution I'd learned to take against getting
lost. Before long we found ourselves entering a low swamp.
Trudging through ankle-deep pools of brackish water, we used
our machetes to hack through thickets of clingberry and spider-
brush.

We were halfway through the swamp when my nose caught an
out-of-place odor among the mildew: wood smoke, as if carried
through the woods from a nearby campfire. Goldstein smelled it,

too. He looked around, then pointed toward a bright place between the trees where it seemed as if the sun had penetrated. "Over there, maybe?"

I stopped, peered more closely. Yes, it looked like a clearing; the creek seemed to lead in that direction. "Worth a try," I said, then I tied another ribbon around a branch to mark our location. "Let's go."

Morgan's guess turned out to be right. We left the swamp behind and went up a low rise, and suddenly came upon a broad natural clearing, a place where a lightning storm had long ago caused this part of the forest to burn, leaving behind only brush, rotting stumps and tall grass. And it was here that we found the camp.

A half-dozen dome tents, like blue-and-red-striped pimples, were arranged in a semicircle around a stone-ringed fire pit from which brown smoke tapered upward. The grass had been cleared away, but not recently; tufts of green rose here and there among untidy stacks of firewood and under sagging clotheslines strung from one tent to another. On the far side of the camp was a low, six-sided wooden structure, its windowless walls fashioned from crudely cut roughbark logs, its roof a thatchwork of tree limbs stuffed with lichen. As we came closer, we passed a small, tarp-covered shelter that reeked of urine and feces: a latrine, probably little more than a hole in the ground, with tarpaulins rigged around it for a modicum of privacy.

The camp was run-down and ill-kept, as if the people who lived here no longer cared about maintaining it. If, indeed, anyone was still here. No one was in sight; were it not for the smoke rising from the fire pit and the damp clothes hanging from the lines, I could have sworn the place was abandoned. Frost-covered grass crunched beneath the soles of our boots as we ventured closer; looking down, I realized that I'd unconsciously pulled my rifle off my shoulder and was holding it in my hands, my right forefinger an inch away from the safety.

"Oh, my god." Goldstein's eyes were wide with horror. "What the hell . . . what happened here?"

"I don't know. I . . . ." Then I glanced his way, and felt my heart skip a beat. "Morgan . . . freeze. Don't move a muscle."

"What are you . . . ?" Then he saw what I'd spotted, and went dead in his tracks. "Aw, crap."

No more than three yards to his right, half-hidden among the brush, lay a ball-plant. It wasn't very large, yet its shell was still closed; and the immature flowertop rising from its top showed that it was in early bloom. A bad time to be close to one of these things; the pseudo-wasps would be coming out of winter dormancy, ready to protect the plant while they pollinated it.

Yet that wasn't the worst of it. I looked around, saw another ball-plant to my left, a little farther away and yet just as menacing. Glancing to my right again, I spotted yet another, only a few feet past the one near Goldstein.

A chill went down my spine. The field was practically evil with ball-plants. Which only made sense, in ecological terms. Marsh-land nearby, affording shelter for hibernating swampers, yet with enough sunlight to allow for photosynthesis. And although these specimens were smaller than the ones closer to the equator, they weren't so close to the subarctic regions further north that they couldn't survive. I was no botanist, but if they could make it through winter here . . .

"Don't worry, Morgan," a voice called out. "Just back away, and everything will be fine."

A tall, muscular man stood at the edge of the campsite, arms folded across his broad chest, long black hair gathered in a braid behind his neck. Tough as a slab of Arizona sandstone; one look at him, and you knew that nothing could ever scratch him.

"Joe!" Goldstein looked around. "Thank God, I thought we'd never . . ." He stopped, remembering where he was. "What do you think you're doing, camping so close to these things?"

An amused expression appeared on Cassidy's face. "They're not so dangerous, once you know how to approach them," he said. "You'll only get swarmed if you come within six feet of them. Just back away, and you won't be harmed."

Goldstein was less confident than his friend, yet he took him at his word. He carefully walked backward, picking his way across the field until he'd joined Cassidy. I followed him, keeping a wary eye on the plants. Under different circumstances, I would have retreated to the safety of the woods . . . yet this was the person we'd come to find, so that wasn't an option.

"Good to see you again." Once Morgan was away from the ball-plants, he visibly relaxed. "You don't know how worried I've been about you. I mean, you just . . ."

"Disappeared, yes." Cassidy shook his head. "Sorry I didn't leave word where I was going, but this was something I just had to . . ."

"Don't give me that crap." Once again, the imperious tone crept into Goldstein's voice. "If there's something wrong, if there's something bothering you, you can come to me, we'll work it out . . ."

"There's nothing wrong. Really." An elusive smile crossed Cassidy's face. "I don't expect you to understand, but . . . everything's fine. You didn't have to hire a guide to find me."

How did he know who I was? Sure, it was probably a safe assumption, but . . .

"The name's Sawyer," I said. "Like your boss . . . like Mr. Goldstein says, he's been worried about you."

"Of course." Cassidy's eyes barely flickered in my direction. His expression darkened. "I appreciate your concern, but you shouldn't be here. This place isn't for you."

As he spoke, I gazed past him. People were crawling out of their tents, like nocturnal animals cautiously emerging into the light of day. Men and women, their hair unwashed and matted, their clothes threadbare and soiled. Shielding their eyes from the midday sun, they regarded us with silent curiosity, as if Morgan and I were mirages that would vanish as suddenly as we'd appeared.

"Maybe, but . . ." Goldstein's puzzlement gave way to stubborn resolve. "Joe, I've come a long way to find you. I'm not leaving until I get some answers."

"Mr. Goldstein . . ."

"Don't 'Mr. Goldstein' me." Morgan stepped closer. "That's all there is to it. Come clean, or so help me . . ."

"Okay, all right." Cassidy sighed, held up his hands. "Look, I'll make you a deal. If I let you know what I'm doing . . ."

All of a sudden, he stopped. An absent look appeared on his face. At first I thought that he'd simply lost his train of thought, yet there was a moment when his head cocked slightly to one side and his eyes shifted to the ground, that he seemed more like someone who was listening to a comment whispered in his ear. He could have been wearing a comlink implant, but . . .

"If I let you spend the night," Cassidy went on, looking straight at Goldstein once more, "and I show you that we're fine, will you leave? Leave and promise never to come back?"

"Joe, you know I can't . . ."

"Please . . ." Cassidy's voice became insistent, almost pleading. "It's the best I can do. If you'd only understand what I'm . . . what we're doing here . . ."

"What are you doing here?" Until then, I'd kept my mouth shut. "I'd like to know myself, if you don't mind."

Cassidy scowled at me. "I *do* mind, Mr. Lee . . . but you're here, so there's no avoiding that, is there?" Then he let out his breath, as if resigning to the inevitable. "All right, c'mon. Least I can do is offer lunch."

Already I was feeling uncomfortable about being there. There was something that wasn't right about this place. Yet it would have been rude to turn down our host's offer, however reluctantly it may have been made. I fell in behind Goldstein as Cassidy led us through the clearing to his camp . . .

And it didn't occur to me, at least just then, that he'd called me "Mr. Lee," even though I'd told him only my first name.

Lunch was rice and red beans, congealed and unappetizing, left over from dinner the night before. Cassidy told us that his group had been getting by on this ever since they'd made camp here; now and then, someone would go down to the creek, chop a hole in the ice, drop in a fishing line, and manage to pull out a brown-head or two. Otherwise their diet pretty much consisted of what they'd brought in twenty-pound bags they'd bought in New Boston.

We ate sitting on logs beside the fire pit. After a while, other residents of the camp wandered over to join us. It was obvious that they'd lost weight; their faces were gaunt, their clothes hanging off their slumped shoulders. There were open sores on their faces and hands; one or two of them looked as if they'd recently lost teeth and one man walked as though his knees hurt him—all classic signs of scurvy. They smelled bad; when a woman bent over me to offer another helping from a rusty pot, I had to hold my breath to keep from gagging. Cassidy was the healthiest of the bunch, yet even he looked malnourished.

No one spoke. That was the weirdest part. On occasion, they'd exchange a word or two, perhaps a gesture, but otherwise they remained silent. Yet despite their hunger and obvious ill-health, their eyes remained lively; they constantly glanced at one another, exchanging looks that might have been furtive except that they didn't bother to hide them from us. And between those looks, all the usual expressions—indifference, amusement, dissatisfaction, curiosity—that would normally accompany a conversation, except that now they came in the absence of speech.

Goldstein noticed none of this. He regarded the camp with horror, his gaze roving across the dilapidated tents, the unwashed plates and skillets piled beneath the tarp that served as a communal kitchen, the rubbish carelessly discarded here and there. He did his best to be polite, making small talk with Cassidy about how the horses were doing at his estate, yet when a young woman ambled over to a nearby patch of grass to lift her skirt, squat, and pee, he lost his patience.

"For God's sake, man," he whispered. "How can you live like this?"

"Like how?" Cassidy shrugged. "You've got a problem with this?"

"Do I have a . . . ?" Goldstein stared at him. "Look at yourself. You're living like an animal."

Cassidy studied him for a moment, not saying anything. A smirk inched its way across his mouth. "You'd rather see me back at the ranch. Sitting around the fireplace, feet propped up, glass of cognac in hand . . ."

Goldstein's face went red. "I didn't . . ."

"You know, you're right." Closing his eyes, Cassidy arched his back, his hands resting lightly upon his knees. "I can almost taste it now. And there's music . . . classic jazz, twentieth century. Dexter Gordon . . . no, wait, Miles Davis . . ."

"Don't make fun of me."

"I'm not." Opening his eyes again, Cassidy calmly gazed at his employer. "I miss those evenings, believe me. I wouldn't mind having more like them. But out here . . ." He let out his breath, gave an indifferent shrug. "It all seems so superficial, so . . . limited, really. A rich man at home with his toys, lonely now because no one will share them . . ."

"Pet." Standing nearby, the bowlegged man leaned upon his crutch, intently staring at Goldstein. "Nice doggy. Ruff-ruff . . ."

Goldstein's face went pale; there was shock in his eyes. Seeing this, Cassidy became angry, "Ash . . . out!" he snapped, glancing over his shoulder at him. "Go away!"

The other man winced, recoiling as if he'd been slapped, then he clumsily turned his back to us and hobbled away. Cassidy watched him go. "Sorry. That was uncalled for."

Morgan looked shaken. "Thanks . . . thank you," he stuttered. "I . . . I . . ."

"Ash knows who you are. He assumes too much." Yet there was a cool tone to his voice that had been absent before.

"Ash . . ." There was something about what Cassidy had called him that got my attention. "That's not his real name, is it?"

Again, the others gathered around the fire pit cast knowing looks at one another. Yet no one spoke until Cassidy did. "No," he said reluctantly. "That's only his tribal name, just as my original tribe gave me the name Walking Star. His is Ash, because it . . . well, because it fits him."

"Your tribe. I see." I glanced at the others; some glowered at me, others were defiant. "And the rest of these guys . . . ?"

"They'll tell you if they wish to do so." Ignoring me again, Walking Star picked up a stick, snapped it in half, and fed it into the smoldering fire. "You shouldn't have come here, Mr. Goldstein . . ."

"Morgan." Goldstein put down his plate, inched a little closer. "I told you, Joe. We know each other better than that."

"I know we do." Cassidy stared at the fire intently, as if closely examining every smoking ember. "Believe me, I do. But this is not the place for you, trust me . . ."

"How can I trust you?" Goldstein became insistent. "I gave you money, sent you to a doctor . . ."

"A doctor is the last person I want to see. What I want . . ." He paused. "What *we* want is be left alone. I appreciate your concern, but there's a reason why we've come out here."

Goldstein looked away, gazing toward the edge of the field where we'd encountered the ball-plants. "I think I can guess what it is," he said. "You and your . . . your tribe . . . have gotten hooked on sting. So much so that you've decided to go straight to the source. Why buy it on the street in Liberty when you can . . . ?"

His words trailed off as he became aware of the reaction of the people around us. For the first time since we'd entered the camp, they displayed some sort of emotion. A few concealed grins behind their hands, while others quietly giggled; some snorted back derisive laughter. Cassidy tried to remain respectful, but there was no hiding the smirk on his face.

"You think we're just a bunch of junkies. Is that it?" His voice was seasoned with contempt. "Sting may be many things, Morgan, but even a doctor would tell you that it's not addictive."

"Not physically, at least," I added.

Cassidy looked at me. "You're right. It can be habit-forming, at least in the psychological sense. But so is cannabis, and that's culti- vated in the colonies. If getting high was all this was about, we would've just as soon stayed home and taken jobs on hemp planta- tions." He turned back to Goldstein. "But you're half-right, boss. Yes, we came here because of the ball-plants. We needed to find a wild stand that hadn't been discovered, and the privacy in which to . . ." Again, he paused. "Shall we say, experiment."

"Experiment. Right . . ." Now it was Goldstein's turn to show contempt. Standing up, he raised a hand to encompass the run- down camp. "Look at this place. You're so far gone, you don't even realize how . . . how sick you've become."

"No." Cassidy pushed himself to his feet, stared Goldstein straight in the eye. "Not sick. In fact, we've become something you can't possibly imagine . . ."

"Don't say." This from the gap-toothed woman who'd served me earlier. Cassidy looked around, stared at her. A moment passed, then she seemed to wither, visibly recoiling from his dark brown eyes. Indeed, it seemed as if the others did the same, all at the same moment. Almost as if . . .

"Perhaps they should know," Cassidy said. "It's unfortunate, because I think we need more time to study this." Then he looked at Morgan again. "But I know you all too well, boss. You're tenacious. Once you learn about something, you don't give up easy. And I can't allow you to go home with misconceptions about what we're doing here."

Goldstein smiled with the confidence of a man so accustomed to winning that losing was no longer a possibility. "That's all I want. Just straight answers."

"Then you'll get them. Not now, though. This evening . . ."

"Joe . . ."

Cassidy nodded toward a vacant spot within the camp site. "Pitch your tents over there," he said. "Rest. Take a nap. Don't eat, and drink as little water as you can. Around sundown, go over there . . ." He pointed to the log hogan at the periphery of the camp. "We'll be waiting for you."

Goldstein studied the shack with suspicion. "Why can't you just tell me . . . ?"

"Because you'd never believe me. This is one of those things you have to experience yourself to know is true." Then he looked at me. "I don't expect you to attend. You can sit this out, if you wish."

"I'll . . . think it over." I was already considering the possibility of something going wrong. What, I didn't know. But it was comforting to know that I had a satphone in my pocket. If worse came to worst, I could always call Mike Kennedy, get him to bring in the cavalry.

"I'll leave it to your discretion, then. But . . ." He held out his hand. "One condition. I'll need your satphone, please."

I felt a touch of suspicion. "Why?"

"You'll get it back. Promise." A wry smile. "I just want to make sure that we're not interrupted."

Again, subdued laughter from those around us, as if Walking Star's tribe had caught a whispered joke I hadn't heard. I traded a glance with Morgan; he didn't know what was going on, either, yet he reluctantly nodded. I dug the satphone out of my jacket and handed it to Cassidy.

"Thank you, Mr. Lee . . . Sawyer, I mean." Then he turned away from us. "Tonight at bear-rise. See you then."

The last rays of sunset were filtering through the trees when Goldstein and I left our tents and walked across camp to the hogan. The evening was chill; we could see our breath before our faces. To the east, the leading edge of Bear's ring-plane was already rising above the forest, its silver bow bright against the twilight sky. Tall, slender torches had been lit on either side of the hogan, their flickering light illuminating the faces of the men and women waiting for us outside its open door.

"You don't have to do this, you know," Goldstein murmured as we approached them. I noticed his pensive expression. We'd spoken little that afternoon; once we'd erected our tents, we'd spent our time taking catnaps and . . . well, just waiting. I regretted having surrendered my satphone; at least I then could have called George, told him that we'd located Cassidy.

"Goes with the service," I replied, keeping my voice low. "Besides, I'm just as curious about this as you are."

He looked as if he was about to say something, but then Cassidy stepped forward. "You've accepted my invitation," he said. "I hope you've taken my advice not to eat anything." Goldstein nodded, and so did I. "Very well, then. Before we go in, though, you're going to need to do one more thing. If you'll please remove your jackets . . ."

"Joe, it's freezing out here." Goldstein stared at him in disbelief. "I can't see why . . ."

"I wouldn't ask you to do so if it wasn't important." Even as Cassidy spoke, the others were pulling off their jackets and serapes, neatly placing them on the ground just outside the hogan before entering one at a time, ducking their heads to pass through the low doorway. "Trust me, it'll be warm inside. But you've got to do it."

Goldstein hesitated, then reluctantly unzipped his fleece-lined, Earth-made parka and placed it outside the door, just a little apart from the others. The evening wind bit at me as I did the same; I wore a light sweater beneath my catskin jacket, and Cassidy paused to look me over. "Take that off, too," he said. "Loosen your collar and roll up your sleeves. It's important."

"Yeah, sure." I removed my sweater, noticing that he hadn't yet taken off his jacket. "Any reason why you're not . . . ?"

"No. Just waiting for you." Cassidy unbuttoned his jacket, carelessly tossed it aside. "After you, gentlemen."

One last, uncertain glance at each other, as if trying to decide who'd go first, then Goldstein lowered his head and, crouching almost double, entered the hogan. I was about to follow him when Cassidy stepped in front of me. He said nothing, yet it was plain that he wanted to be with his old boss. I waited until they disappeared through the door, then I followed them inside.

The hogan's interior was dark, almost pitch-black; torchlight seeped through thin cracks between the log walls, the only source of illumination. I smelled the dank odor of dirt, mildew, and roots, heard the faint scuffling sounds of a lot of people crowded into a small space. When I tried to stand erect, the back of my head connected with the ceiling; I snarled an obscenity, then someone grabbed the back of my shirt, and roughly hauled me down to a sitting position.

"Hush," Cassidy hissed at me. "Be quiet."

My eyes soon adjusted to the gloom. Ten men and women, Goldstein and myself included, seated in a circle within the hogan, so close to one another that our elbows and shoulders almost touched. To my left was Cassidy; to his left was Morgan. Almost directly behind me was the door; a woman to my right leaned over to pull it shut, and now we were all together in the suffocating darkness.

There was something in the middle of the room. A tall, rotund object, only half-seen yet so close that, if I'd leaned forward, I

could have touched it with my fingertips. My nose caught a faint
vegetable fragrance, the smell of something alive and growing.
Suddenly I began to suspect what was in the hogan with us . . .

"See," Cassidy whispered. "See and know."

Then he broke open a lightstick and tossed it on the floor, and
in the wan chemical glow we saw what grew from the center of the
hogan. A ball-plant, perhaps the largest I'd ever seen; nearly five
feet in diameter, it rose from the ground like a giant tumor, malig-
nant and obscene.

My immediate reaction was to shrink back in alarm. Yet even
as I did, I noticed that, despite its size, the plant was somehow retarded. By this time of the season, leaves should have sprouted
from its upper shell with the first flowerstalks beginning to blossom. Deprived of sunlight, though, it did neither; only the most
smallest, vestigial leaves had begun to appear, and those were
withered and stunted.

That's when it occurred to me what Cassidy and his people
had done. They'd found the largest ball-plant in this field and built
the hogan around it. I glanced up at the ceiling, spotted a circular
crack of light. A ceiling hatch, like a removable skylight; once a
day, I surmised, they'd open the hatch, allowing in just enough sun
and rain for the plant to remain alive, but not enough for pollina-
tion. In that way, they managed to keep the ball-plant a captive
specimen, contained within its own miniature greenhouse.

"Oh, for the love of . . ." Goldstein was just as horrified as I
was. "Joe, what are you . . . ?"

"You'll see." Then Cassidy raised his left foot and slammed his
heel down on the packed-earth floor.

The others did the same, stamping on the floor, causing the
plant to shake. When I realized what they were trying to do, my
first thought was to get out of there as fast as I could. Yet by then it
was too late; the door was shut, and there was no escape.

I couldn't see the pseudo-wasps when they emerged from their
nests within the shell; there wasn't enough light. Yet I heard an angry buzz from the plant, and for an instant it seemed as if the immature leaves parted just slightly.

Something small purred past my face, and I felt insect wings against my cheek. I reached up to swat it away, and a white-hot needle lanced into the back of my hand.

I yelped, and instinctively started to clamber to my knees. Cassidy grabbed my shoulder, forced me to sit down. "Just be calm," he said quietly. "It'll all be over in . . . *ah!*"

"Joe, for God's sake . . . *dammit!*" I heard Goldstein slap at something, then he cried out again in pain. "Holy . . . get 'em off! They're all over me!"

By then the air was alive with pseudo-wasps. They swarmed the hogan, buzzing all around us, stinging everyone with whom they came in contact. I tried to bat them away, but there were too many; I was stung again on my face, and when I leaned forward to put my head between my knees and cover the back of my neck with my arms, they attacked my wrists and shoulders.

Glancing up from my folded arms, I caught a glimpse of Cassidy. It almost seemed as if he was in meditation; seated beside me in lotus position, his eyes were shut, his body relaxed. Others had done the same; although they occasionally gasped in pain, they weren't bothering to fight off the insects. Goldstein was curled up on the floor, rolling this way and that, screaming in terror as he tried to ward off the insects. Then a pseudo-wasp alighted upon my face, just below my right eye. I managed to swat it away before it stung me, then I buried my head within my arms again.

It seemed to go on forever. Then I heard a wooden creak from somewhere above, felt a cool breeze. Hesitantly, I raised my head again. Someone had used a rope to move aside the ceiling hatch; bearlight streamed down through the opening, and I saw a thin cloud of insects fly upward, their wings appearing as tiny silver halos.

For a moment it seemed to me that they were miniature angels, vengeful yet innocent, spiraling upward into the night. Despite the pain, I found myself entranced by their beauty; I laughed out loud, and watched their ascent with fascination. Others chuckled, as if understanding what I'd seen. When I looked down again, I saw Cassidy gazing at me.

"There, see? The way has been prepared." He handed a catskin flask to me. "Drink. Relax."

The water in his flask was tepid and lukewarm, yet it tasted like wine. I drank a little, then passed it to the woman sitting beside me. A certain numbness was rapidly spreading through my body; the places where I'd been stung no longer burned, and although they itched for a few minutes, after a time even that sensation passed away. I was vaguely aware that Goldstein was on his hands and knees, violently retching, yet he was no longer my concern. All I knew was that the hogan was no longer as menacing as it'd once been; indeed, it was now as comfortable as my favorite table at the Captain's Lady, and all these people had become my friends.

Time lost meaning. I watched Bear slowly come into view through the skylight, its silver-blue radiance painting the log walls with colors I'd never seen before. Ash stared up at the stars, humming beneath his breath; the gap-toothed woman rocked gently back and forth on her haunches, muttering to herself as if carrying on a conversation with some invisible person. Across the room, a man and a woman pulled off each other's clothes and, oblivious to the presence of everyone else, started to have sex; I observed their fornication with disinterest, neither aroused nor offended. A skeeter, wandering in from the nearby marshes, flittered above the ball-plant, performing a delicate ballet just for me. It was as if a universe I'd never known to exist had opened before my eyes, and I was an astronomer seeing its hidden wonders for the very first time.

—Do you see . . . ?

At first, I thought Cassidy had spoken to me. When I looked at him, though, he was staring straight ahead.

"What?" I said. "Do I see what?"

—Do you see? . . . do you hear? . . . do you feel?

His lips never moved, and he didn't look my way. Yet I could hear his voice—no, more than that; I could sense his presence—as clearly as if he'd spoken in my ear.

"I . . . I can . . ."

His eyes shifted in my direction. *—No . . . don't speak . . . don't need to . . . open your mind . . . hear me with your thoughts . . .*

I stared at him. At first, it seemed as if there was a barrier between us, translucent as rice paper, solid as iron . . .

—Concentrate!

I squeezed my eyes shut, fought against the barrier. A sharp pain within my temples, almost like a migraine headache. Then, suddenly, an audible snap, as if someone had broken a twig within my head . . .

(The smell of horse manure, sour-sweet and ripe. A flash-image of a hand holding a brush, gently stroking a coarse brown mane. The horse raises its head, looks at me, love within its dark brown eyes . . .)

I snapped out of the trance. What the hell . . . ?

—You saw the horse, didn't you?

Again, I looked at Cassidy. A quiet smile played at the corners of his mouth, yet he continued to gaze straight ahead. "Yeah," I mumbled. "Yeah, I saw the . . ."

Then the shock of what had just happened swept through me, and with it an uncommon clarity. Looking away from Cassidy, I stared at the couple screwing on the other side of the hogan . . .

(Flesh moving across flesh, rough hands gripping smooth thighs, soft hands stroking back muscles. The sweet-sour odor of sweat, warm and close. Loins straining for release. The rapture of sex . . .)

I glanced away from them, saw Cassidy staring at me.

—Do you feel them?

Confused, I hastily looked away, only to find myself gazing at the woman with the missing teeth. All at once, I knew that her name was Alice Curnow, although she now preferred to be known as First Light of Day . . .

—Donald, I'm so sorry . . . so sorry . . . I never meant to hurt you, but . . . you asked too much of me, and I couldn't . . . Donald, I'm sorry, so sorry . . . please forgive me, I . . . sorry, so sorry . . .

Too much. Far too much. Within this hogan were places where I was never meant to be, secrets I was never meant to share. Sick at the pit of my stomach, feeling an overwhelming urge to vomit, I frantically crawled toward the door. A hard shove, and it fell away before me.

On hands and knees, I crawled out of the hogan. Cold air blasted me like an arctic wind; at once I was chilled to the bone. I managed to get a few feet from the hogan before my guts betrayed me. I vomited across grass that looked like a plain of emerald stone.

Then I passed out. Yet not before Cassidy's voice came to me one last time . . .

—I'm sorry, but you're not ready yet.

I awoke in the same place where I'd lost consciousness. It was early morning, the sun just beginning to rise above trees at the edge of the clearing. Someone had thrown my jacket over me, yet my clothes were damp with dew, my arms and legs stiff from sleeping on bare ground. My head throbbed with the worst headache I'd ever had; for a long time I simply lay there, feeling every ache and pain in my body.

If I could have, I would've gone back to sleep again, yet the sore places on my neck, arms, and hands where I'd been stung kept me awake, so I finally rolled over and sat up, and found Joe Cassidy staring at me.

He sat cross-legged upon the ground, a blanket wrapped around his shoulders. Behind him, the burned-out torches smoldered; a cool breeze caught wisps of acrid black smoke, caused them to drift past the hogan. Its door was shut once more. No one else was in sight.

Walking Star and I regarded each other for several long moments, neither of us saying anything. After a while, he closed his eyes, lowered his head slightly. A few seconds passed, then he raised his head again, opened his eyes.

"You didn't hear that, did you?" he asked. I started to shake my head, but it hurt too much, so I simply looked at him. "Didn't think you would," he added, a smile touching the corners of his lips. "It usually takes more than one session for . . ." he paused, as if groping for the right words ". . . the effect to become permanent."

"Permanent?" There was a copper taste in my mouth. I spit, saw my saliva was tinged red. Apparently I'd bit my tongue sometime during the night and not even realized it. "What effect?"

"You really have to ask?" He squinted at me, as if searching for something. "You know what happened. You just won't admit it to yourself."

All I knew for certain was that I was thirsty, although my stomach roiled at the very thought of food. Without my asking, Cassidy picked up a catskin flask from the ground beside him. "You probably won't want to eat for a while," he said, tossing the flask to me. "No one ever does."

A shiver ran down my back as I picked up the flask. "You can read minds, can't you?"

Cassidy gazed at the camp, motionless within the early morning haze, the silence disturbed only by the songs of grass-hoarders stirring within the field. "We all do, now," he said after a time. "Telepathy, you might call it, although I prefer to think of it as a form of mental gestalt . . . a joining of minds. After a while, you don't even need the pseudo-wasp venom. It just . . . happens, y'know?"

The water rinsed away the blood in my mouth. I spat out the first mouthful, swallowed the next. "I don't believe it. I think we were all just . . ."

"Hallucinating?" A wry smile. "Just a weird experience we all shared at the same time. That's what we thought, too, back when we first started using sting. I thought it was nothing more than peyote dreams. But then . . ."

He held out his hand, and I passed the flask back to him. "Well, it became obvious this wasn't just a drug thing, that we might actually be onto something. It would take a neurophysicist to explain it to you, but there's a theory that a small part of the brain . . . just a few cells, really . . . contains a certain potential for psychic ability. Sort of a throwback to primitive times, when our forebears had to rely upon their senses for survival. No one's ever been able to explain it, or at least test it to any reliable degree, but . . . well, it's there."

"And you think sting has something to do with this?"

"No." He took a drink of water. "Sting only gave us a hint. The stuff we found in the colonies was always diluted. Sometimes with water, more often with other drugs to make it more potent for guys who just wanted to get high." He shook his head. "That's not what we were after. We were . . . we *are* . . . searching for a more transcendental experience. A way to open the doorways of the mind."

Cassidy was persuasive, to be sure, yet there was something within me that remained unconvinced. "So you came all the way up here just to camp out in a field full of ball-plants, when there's plenty in New Florida and Midland . . ."

"Being wiped out as fast as they're found. Besides, we needed isolation for our experiments."

"Experiments. Right . . ." Tents on the verge of collapse, trash scattered here and there, a group of men and women suffering from malnutrition. "You're making a lot of progress."

Cassidy was quiet for a moment. "One of the drawbacks," he said after a moment. "You get to the point where you can easily read another person's thoughts and emotions, it's hard to be around them. Everyone here has their secrets, their hidden pain. We're still learning how to cope with that . . ."

"Sure. Okay." I sat up a little straighter, pulling the blanket around me. What I wouldn't have given for a bottle of aspirin just then . . . "So you decided to come straight to the source. Build a shack around the biggest ball-plant you could find, and crawl inside every night to get a mighty fix of . . ."

"Your full name is Sawyer Robert Edward Lee," Cassidy said, looking straight at me. "Your parents . . . Carl and Jessica . . . named you after your father's older brother, and added your middle names because the family believes they're descended from Captain R. E. Lee, the commanding officer of the *Alabama*. Although you have personal doubts about your ancestry, you didn't have many qualms about using your name to your advantage once you immigrated to Coyote."

I felt my face go pale. "How did you . . . ?"

"You've got a lifelong fear of reptiles," he went on, "which is lucky for you because there's none on this world. You prefer dark-haired women to blondes, unless they wear glasses, in which case you feel yourself drawn to them because the first girl who let you kiss her was a blonde-haired girl who wore glasses . . . that was when you were about nine or ten, right? You're good at poker, but you refuse to cheat, even though you know how to. You drink, but not too much, because your father was . . ."

"Shut up!" I hastily pulled on my jacket, yet I couldn't keep myself from trembling. "Just . . . shut up."

"Sorry. There was no other way. If there was any other way to make you believe . . ."

"Okay. All right. Just . . . no more, okay?" I shuddered, not willing to meet his eyes. "So . . . what is it that you want from me? Why are you telling me this?"

Walking Star slowly let out his breath. "From you, very little. So far as I can tell, you're just some guy caught up in all this." Then he rose to his feet, offering a hand to help me up. "But Morgan Goldstein . . . that's another issue entirely."

We found Morgan in his tent, in no better condition than I was. His face was haggard, and he slumped on his sleeping bag, clutching at the flask of water Ash had brought him. The other man quietly nodded as Cassidy and I came in, then left the tent without a word, leaving the three of us alone.

Or at least so it seemed. I noticed that several of Cassidy's friends were beginning to gather near the fire pit. They said nothing, only quietly observed us. I wondered if there was a limit to the distance for their newfound abilities. Did it even matter? If they now shared a mental gestalt, then there were no secrets among them . . . or, indeed, with anyone with whom they came in contact.

"So it's true, isn't it?" Goldstein stared at Cassidy with haunted eyes as he gently touched the side of his head. "I heard your voice in here last night, Joe. Goddamn it, I felt you walking around in my mind . . ."

"It's telepathy, Mr. Goldstein." Although he hadn't spoken to me, I felt as if he needed an explanation. "The pseudo-wasp venom, it's . . ."

"He knows." Cassidy folded his arms together, regarded him with implacable stoicism. "In fact, he's known all along. Just one more thing I found out about him last night."

Not believing this, I looked down at Goldstein. Unwilling to meet my gaze, he hastily averted his eyes. "I didn't know," he murmured. "At least not for sure . . ."

"Yet you suspected." Cassidy's gaze didn't waver from him.

Goldstein sharply looked away. "One of my people in New Florida reported to me that you were trying to . . . to do this. I didn't think it was possible, but . . ."

"But you had to find out for yourself, didn't you?" Cassidy squatted down to sit at the edge of Goldstein's sleeping bag. "Don't feel so abused, Sawyer. What he told you was true . . . somewhat, at least. He really was concerned for my well-being." A sardonic smile played upon his face. "And for that, at least, I'm grateful. So glad to know that I have a true friend."

"Go to hell, Joe." There was murder in Goldstein's eyes. "You've no right to . . ."

"Just as you had no right to intrude on our privacy." As with me, Cassidy was perpetually one step ahead of the conversation. "You should've left us alone. Yet you decided to seek us out, because you thought that, if your suspicions were true, just perhaps . . ."

"You could take advantage of this." Things were beginning to come clear to me; I didn't need to be a telepath to figure out the rest. "It'd be a real asset to have a mind reader on your payroll, wouldn't it? Awfully handy to have one for your next business deal . . ."

"Get out of here." Goldstein angrily gestured to the open flap of the tent. "Make yourself useful and find your satphone. Call Kennedy and tell him I want a gyro pickup in . . ."

"Find it yourself, bub. I want to see how this plays out." I looked at Cassidy. "Go ahead. Sorry for the interruption."

"No problem." Cassidy picked up the flask at Goldstein's feet, treated himself to a sip of water. "Let's get to the end of this, all right? Then we'll get you a ride out of here. First, I quit . . ."

"You can't . . . !" Goldstein stopped himself, then shrugged. "All right, go ahead. Sort of figured this was coming, anyway." He hesitated. "I'm going to miss you, Joe. We've been good friends."

"We still are." Joe recapped the flask, dropped it on the ground. "Maybe I won't be taking care of the horses any more, but that doesn't mean we can't be seeing each other." Then he smiled. "Because now that you know what we're doing here, you're going to help us."

Goldstein's expression became puzzled. "What? I don't . . ."

"Understand? Let me make it clear." Cassidy rested his elbows upon his knees, clasped his hands together. "You've already remarked upon the sorry condition of this camp. Well, you're going to make it better. Soon as you get home, you're going to hire a construction team to come up here and build permanent dwellings. Individual cabins, each with its own solar electrical systems and toilets. A community hall, too, complete with a kitchen." He paused, glancing up at the roof of the tent. "Artesian wells and water filtration systems," he went on, "satellite communication systems . . ."

"Like hell!"

"More like a retreat really . . . or perhaps a monastery." A sly grin appeared on Cassidy's face. "Come to think of it, I sort of like the sound of that. A monastery." He chuckled quietly, then went on. "The people you hire, of course, won't be told the purpose of this place, and you yourself will say nothing about it to anyone. Is that clear?"

"And you expect me to pay for this myself?" Goldstein was incredulous. When Cassidy nodded, he shook his head. "Forget it. There's no way you can expect me to . . ."

"You don't understand. This isn't a request." Cassidy stared straight at him. "I found out a lot of things about you last night, Morgan. Here's what I learned . . ."

Once again, he closed his eyes, lowered his head. Morgan was about to say something just then, yet in that instant his jaw went slack. Only a few seconds went by, yet in that brief time, I saw his eyes go wide, the color drain from his face.

What Cassidy revealed to him, I'd never learn. Perhaps it was just as well that I didn't. All the same, when the moment passed and Walking Star opened his eyes again, Morgan Goldstein looked as if someone had just told him the worst thing anyone could ever imagine. Which is what you might expect, if someone revealed your innermost darkest secrets to you.

"You . . . you'll have it," he said, very quietly.

"Thank you. I thought you'd see things our way." Cassidy pushed himself to his feet, then turned to me. "You can call Merle now," he said, reaching into his jacket pocket to produce the sat-phone. "He can pick you up the same place he left you yesterday."

He started to leave the tent, then he stopped, looked back at Morgan. "See you around, boss. Not too soon, I hope, but . . . see you around."

Goldstein said nothing. I left him in the tent, still staring at the ground, as I followed Cassidy outside. The others were still hover-ing near the fire pit. Cassidy started toward them, but stopped when I touched his shoulder.

"Just one more thing . . ." I began.

"You've got nothing to worry about." Walking Star didn't look back at me. "I'm not interested in your secrets. Just your inten-tions." He paused. "You're good with us. Just never come here again."

I let go of Cassidy's arm, slowly backed away. I didn't need to say anything, and he didn't need to ask. And meanwhile his tribe silently regarded me with eyes capable of unlocking the doorways of my mind.

A few hours later, Morgan Goldstein and I sat upon the shore of Medsylvania. It was early afternoon, the sunny warmth of an early spring day slowly baking away the cold memory of the night before. Across the waters lay the Midland coast; not far away, we could see a small white sail. Merle's pirogue was slowly making its way across the channel toward us. We'd found a large boulder upon which to wait for him; our backpacks lay next to us, our sleeping bags and tents rolled up and lashed to their frames.

Neither of us had spoken much since we'd left the camp. No one said farewell; we were guests who'd overstayed our welcome, and our hosts were only too happy to see us leave. There'd been little conversation between Morgan and me as we followed the creek back through the forest, this time sidestepping the marshes.

The ribbons I'd tied around trees on the way in helped make it easier to find our way back to the trail. On the way out, though, whenever I found one of them, I used my knife to carefully cut it loose and shove it in my pocket. Morgan noticed me doing this, but didn't say anything about it. Not until then, at least.

"Think you're ever coming back here?" he suddenly asked.

I looked around at him; he was idly picking up pebbles and tossing them into the shallows. I didn't know if he was genuinely curious, or just making small talk.

I found a small, flat stone. A flick of the wrist made it skip across the still blue waters. "I doubt it," I said, then decided to be honest. "No. If anyone ever tries to hire me as a guide again, I'll say no. At least not as far as this place is concerned."

"Can't say I blame you." He picked up a piece of loose shale, tried the same trick. It sank as soon as it hit the water. "What would you tell 'em?"

"I'll tell them there's dangerous creatures up here." Realizing what I'd just said, I smiled. "Not too far from the truth, really."

"No . . . no, it's not." Morgan tried again with another rock; this time he managed to make it skip twice. He learned fast. "What if I asked you?"

I looked at him again. He continued to peer at the channel; no expression on his face, and his thoughts were unreadable. By me, at least.

"I'd still say no," I replied. "Why? You think you're coming back?"

He glanced over his shoulder at the woods behind us. Almost as if he was expecting to see someone standing there, studying us from the shadows of the tall roughbark that lined the shore.

"No . . . no, I don't think so," he said at last, looking back at the channel again. "You're right. There's too many dangerous creatures here."

The pirogue was closer now, near enough that we could see Merle sitting in its stern. Mike Kennedy was with him; he raised a hand in greeting, and I raised mine in return. "That's probably wise," I said quietly.

"Uh-huh." Morgan skipped another rock, then hoisted himself to his feet. "Not that it matters."

"Come again?"

Morgan was quiet for a moment as he leaned down to pick up his pack. "Joe's not going to stay here forever," he said at last. "We're going to see him again . . . him and the rest of his tribe. Oh, they'll stay here as long as it takes for them to learn how to control what they've learned to do. But when they're ready . . ."

He fell silent. He didn't need to finish his thoughts. Nonetheless, I felt a chill despite the warmth of the midday sun. He was right. Sooner or later, we'd see Walking Star and his people among us.

And when we did, we'd never again be alone with our thoughts.

JQ211F, and Holding

by Nancy Kress

⬤⬤⬤⬤

"Death by misadventure in a hostile environment" is a verdict that might be rendered on any one of the planets in this book, but there are even worse things waiting for the hapless scientific team that investigates JQ211F. In spite of this tale's core of utterly hard science, it stirred recollections in me of Cordwainer Smith's story, "A Planet Named Shayol," a Dante-influenced Hell-world, as well as the similarly inclined Walt Disney film The Black Hole.

Nancy Kress is the author of eleven SF and three fantasy novels, two thrillers, three collections of short stories, one YA novel, and three books on writing fiction. She is perhaps best known for the Sleepless trilogy that began with Beggars in Spain *and continued with* Beggars and Choosers *and* Beggars Ride. *In 1996 Kress temporarily switched genres to write* Oaths and Miracles, *a thriller about Mafia penetration of the biotech industry. Her most recent books are* Nothing Human *(2003), which concerns the long-term consequences of global warming, and the "duology"* Crossfire and Crucible *(2003; 2004).*

In addition to writing fiction, Kress teaches regularly at various places, including the East (Michigan State) and West (Seattle) locations of the Clarion Science Fiction & Fantasy Writers' Workshop. She is the monthly "Fiction" columnist for Writer's Digest *magazine. She lives in Rochester, New York.*

"MY GOD, LOOK at it," Captain McAuliffe said. "Just *look* at it."

It was a naïve thing to say, but then the captain was not a scientist. We all stared at the planet below, devoured it with our eyes. Serena looked as if she wanted to eat it. It isn't every working day that one sees a planet that does not exist.

"How soon until we go down?" Serena demanded.

McAuliffe said, "No one is going down."

"I am," she said, and now her gaze did leave the planet to lock angrily with his. I had to look away; sometimes her intensity scares me a little, although it is one of the things I love about her.

"Paul," she said over her shoulder to me, "you're going down with me, aren't you?"

I looked from Serena Wambugu—no one had ever looked less "serene"—to Captain McAuliffe, and a small part of my mind noticed, yet again, how well they matched physically. Well, that was to be expected. They were the only two of the ten aboard the *Feynmann* who were genemod. Serena and McAuliffe dazzled, and the rest of us crept carefully through their luminous shadows. Which was only fitting, since Captain Robert McAuliffe commanded the *Feynmann* and Dr. Serena Wambugu led the scientific team that was the ship's reason for being here.

I, of course, had another reason for being dazzled.

I shifted from one foot to the other, gazing around the bridge, playing for time. The *Feynmann,* a Solidariat United Space Navy non-combat ship, was grudgingly on special assignment for the Science Academy. Small and tidy, she had no wasted space. Nine people were a tight fit on the compact bridge, and my left elbow almost touched one of the two dozen display screens, visual and data, that the crew monitored so efficiently.

"Paul?" Serena demanded. "Aren't we going down?"

I chose the safe answer, opposing neither of them. "I think the protocol is to send a second probe." I hoped I had the words in the right order; English was not my first language. It wasn't Serena's, either, but then she spoke five fluently.

"A second probe?" she said impatiently. "Why, when we obtained no data from the first one?"

"Since you got no data from the first probe," Captain McAuliffe said dryly, "the destruction of a second one makes no sense. Nor does the destruction of your scientific team, Dr. Wambugu. Not even you could wish that."

"I don't wish it," she snapped back. "I wish for answers! The greatest scientific discovery since space tunnels and you 'wish' to just *look* at it? The military mind at work!"

If Serena got started on her version of "the military mind," Captain McAuliffe wouldn't let anyone go anywhere. Usually she was more cautious around him, since as commander he made the ultimate decisions on ship's movements, and she on scientific matters. Both were jealous of their turf. This had led to a very strained trip out, although in the beginning they had at least been polite.

Once more I slipped between them as a buffer. "We certainly do need answers, including what happened to the first probe. But at least now we know the planet exists. Why does it register on the ship's sensors now when it didn't before?"

McAuliffe smiled at me. He knew exactly what I was doing. But he spoke to Carin. "That's your area, isn't it, Dr. Dziwalski? You're the physicist. I suggest you retire with your team to discuss it. The wardroom is at your disposal."

The tips of Carin Dziwalski's ears reddened. I knew what she was thinking: "her" team! This was Serena's team, completely, even if my own work was the reason we had come here. Neither Carin nor I could ever have gotten funding from the Academy. But Serena didn't like any undermining of her authority. I felt my stomach tighten, and Carin's plain features creased painfully.

However, Serena surprised me, as she often does. She said coolly, "A good suggestion. Carin, get the print-outs and join Paul and me in the wardroom. I don't think Captain McAuliffe would be able to follow our discussions, anyway." She swept out.

Carin scurried to obey. I followed Serena to the wardroom after one last look at the planet on the bridge's real-time display.

It had as yet no catalogue designation but was informally called "JQ211F," a bloodless name for the most important place in the galaxy. About one-third the size of Terra but denser, it had just enough mass to hold an atmosphere. Thick dark clouds covered the entire globe, but I knew from the sensor data what we would find below: poisonous atmosphere high in methane and hydrogen sulfide, acid seas, enormous volcanic and lightning activity. A young world in the throes of early, one-celled life.

Which, according to my calculations, was older than any other planet in the galaxy.

∞

"Let's go over it again," Serena said, "just to be sure we haven't missed anything. Paul? Does anything we've learned so far affect your initial calculations?"

The three of us sat alone in the wardroom. The largest continually pressurized area aboard ship, it looked as if it belonged on a different, much larger vessel. The *Feynmann*, Carin had told me, occasionally ferried dignitaries and diplomats. The wardroom served as state reception area, conference room, dining room, and off-duty lounge for officers. It was luxurious, even ceremonial, with dark paneling on the bulkheads, dark green plush chairs, and an enormous polished table of real wood. Finely detailed holoscapes of half a dozen planets glowed on the walls.

But despite the size of the table, we three scientists had managed to fill it with print-outs—or maybe it was Serena's outsize presence that filled the room. Six feet tall, full-breasted, with smooth skin the color of caramels, she wore one of her long, flame-colored robes. Her black eyes gleamed with excitement barely restrained by a scientist's disciplined intelligence. Beside her, in gray tunic and pants, drab Carin Dziwalski looked like a squirrel scampering to keep up with a tiger.

I said, "Nothing we've learned so far affects my initial calculations. This is the place where life originated in the galaxy."

Serena smiled at me. "I like your certainty."

"I am certain," I said, not only to please her—Serena liked certainty, always—but because it was true. I had spent six years gathering and analyzing data on every life-bearing planet that humanity had discovered since the Perkins-Valachev equations had first given us access to the stars through space tunnels. Some planets, like Terra, had evolved advanced sentients. Some had gotten only as far as non-flowering plants; some had evolved multicellular sea life; some merely had proto-cells. All were DNA-based. And my math was clear: graphing complexity levels against spore-dispersal mechanisms pointed indisputably to panspermia, drifting clouds of spores originating here, at the nexus. Here, on this planet orbiting an undistinguished yellow sun. Here, on this oldest of all planets.

Which somehow displayed all the characteristics of a young planet orbiting a fourth-generation star.

Carin said timidly, "We need to know what happened to the probe."

"We need to know more than that," Serena said. "Why didn't the planet register on ship's sensors until we parked ourselves in orbit? And the probe—it *should* have reached the surface, no matter how noxious or acidic the atmosphere. Of course, it might have just malfunctioned. They do that. Carin, any specific reasons you can think of why the probe might have failed?"

Carin licked her lips. "Well . . . its instruments could have been wiped out on entry by an electromagnetic impulse of some sort. There's a lot of lightning activity going on down there. A burst of several million volts in the upper atmosphere just as the probe entered, that could do it. Lightning discharges like that also create temporary gamma-ray bursts when stray electrons get propelled upward at almost c. If an electron then hits a heavier particle, the kinetic energy of the electron's sudden deceleration is cast off as a photon. If that's happening a lot, a strong gamma-ray burst could have destroyed the probe's telemetry."

Serena nodded. "But that sort of coincidence probably wouldn't happen twice. If we sent a second probe, we'd get real data. That cloud cover is just too particle-dense for anything but the most basic data."

Carin ventured, "Captain McAuliffe—"

"Does not make probe decisions. *I* do. But if we can explain to him—in terms even he can understand—just why the first probe failed, that it was a chance occurrence unlikely to happen again,

then he'd be obligated to allow shuttle descent. I want to *look* at
what's down there."

Carin said, "But–"

"Put together some probability figures showing that what happened to the probe is statistically unlikely to destroy the shuttle."

"I can't be positive that–"

"Of course you can't be positive. I said 'probability figures.' I'll
present them to our tin tyrant."

"Serena," I said gently, "I think it would be a good idea to send
down the second probe before we go down in the shuttle."

Her black eyes opened very wide. She did that, too, at the moment of orgasm, and it was disconcerting to see it now. "Paul, is this
your area?"

"I–"

"Carin is the team physicist and I'm chief scientist."

It was said quietly, but clearly. I heard the unspoken corollary:
And you, Paul Cho, are secondary xenobiologist. Secondary.

I gave way. "It's not my area, Serena."

"No. Put together the probability figures, Carin." Serena
smiled at her, then at me. "And we'll use them to make a decision
about the second probe."

●●●

Serena and I lay naked in my narrow bunk. I ran a hand over her
smooth, supple thigh. Her long black hair, unbound now from its
usual knot, lay over my chest in ropes and coils. I said, "You have
the most beautiful skin in the galaxy."

She raised herself on one elbow, her breasts swelling beside
my chest, her face teasing. "Yes? And by what standard are you
measuring? I doubt you've seen all the females in the galaxy, let
alone *all* their skin, so your statement is inaccurate. 'Measurement
defines reality,' you know." It was what Carin often said; Serena
had even captured Carin's fussy, pedantic tone.

"My statement is not inaccurate," I said, drawing her closer. "If
measurement defines reality, then *my* measurements define *my* reality, and you have the most beautiful skin in the galaxy because *I*
define 'most beautiful' as you."

"Sounds circular to me."

"I'll give you something circular."

I knew she liked me like this: masterful. It was a sham, of course; we both knew who was master here. But I would do anything that would make her look at me as she did now, sideways from her glittering dark eyes, the lids heavy with lust. So we made love again, and again I marveled that, against all odds, she had chosen me.

At the start of the voyage, I had thought it would be Robert McAuliffe. He was so genemod handsome, black hair and blue eyes and a body like a warm Greek statue. I've seen those statues, in Athens. I grew up on Terra, one of the teeming and hopeless urban poor who escaped only because I whipped my intelligence day and night like an overworked donkey. I don't know if Serena knew that this was my first trip into deep space, as well as my one chance to make a name for myself in scientific circles. Certainly McAuliffe knew; he was a thorough, competent captain who checked everything. Whereas Serena—

Even in my besotted state, I knew Serena wasn't perfect. Her work in xenobiology was actually not very distinguished, nor very original. She could be sloppy and hasty, and she wasn't above claiming credit for work built on others' ideas. But she made amazing presentations, she filled a room with scientific excitement, she could visualize and describe in glowing words the larger picture. Those were the things that secured both reputation and funding. Without Serena, without Serena's promoting and championing my ideas, this expedition would never have happened.

And then she had chosen me. Not Captain McAuliffe, nor the dashing shuttle pilot, Vlad Cowen. Me, Paul Cho, who reached only up to her ear and had narrow shoulders, a potbelly, and a presence so thin that people often forgot I was in the room. Yes, she had chosen me for my work, but that was all right, too. I was my work.

"Yummm," Serena said, sated and content. We lay quiet for several minutes, and then she rose. "I have to get dressed before I fall asleep."

"Don't go. Fall asleep here."

But that she would never do even at night, let alone in the middle of the afternoon. She slept alone in her own bunk, always. I watched her dress, the only color in my drab, tiny quarters. Somewhere on the *Feynmann* there must be V.I.P. cabins, but we scientists were housed as Navy officers, and I had not bothered to hang anything decorative on my gray bulkheads. Nor were there any personal items on my table or bunk. I had left my old personal life behind me on Terra, and I wanted no reminders.

After Serena left, I was drifting into a post-coital doze when a knock came on my door. Serena changing her mind? Instantly I was awake again. "Yes?"

"Paul? Can I see you for a moment?"

Carin Dziwalski. I pulled on pants and tunic and opened the door.

"I'm sorry to wake you," she said, averting her eyes as if I were still naked. "I just wanted to ask you something . . . I'll wait in the wardroom. Although the captain is there with his—"

"Come in," I said. She made me feel as calm and in control as Serena made me feel the opposite. Watching her perch on the edge of my one chair, I felt sorry for Carin, for any woman who had to exist beside Serena. And yet Carin was a good physicist, with a solid if not stellar reputation. "Is it about the probability figures for the probe?"

"No. I finished those and I just gave them to Serena. The chance of a second probe being destroyed by lightning, pulse field, gamma-ray flash, or anything else I can think of, based on the data I have, is less than .5 percent. But that's only based on the data I have, which isn't much."

"It's enough to justify a second probe, if not the shuttle." Serena would want the shuttle. But that decision was Captain McAuliffe's.

"Yes. But I didn't come here to ask about the probe or the shuttle."

"What, then?"

She was silent so long that I had a sudden fear that her question might be personal. Even that she might . . . but that was silly. It was true that I had occasionally caught her looking at me in a shyly interested way, but that was at the very start of the expedition. And although I had, months ago, returned those shy gazes, that was before Serena had exploded into my cabin, changing everything.

When Carin finally did speak, her words startled me. "You know I'm a Christian."

I hadn't. There were so few Christians left, and mostly they kept to two or three colonies, and almost exclusively to themselves. I was surprised that one had chosen to become a physicist. I didn't know much about Christianity except that they believed in a God who had created the universe, who directed it personally, who had "died" for its sins, and who sorted the good from the bad in some sort of supernatural afterlife. How could a rational physicist believe all that?

"I didn't know," I said, when I had to say something. Carin sat twisting her fingers together in her lap.

"Yes. And I want to ask you something. When you first mapped the point from which panspermic clouds must have drifted, was it *before* you knew there was even a star system in that piece of space, or *after*?"

"Before. I plotted the life distribution, created the drift algorithms, and then checked the star maps. That's when I found out that there was a G-1 here, but no known planets."

"And no spectral analysis ever revealed a planet?"

"No. You know that, Carin. But the planet is small and it didn't occlude the star enough to show any spectral or gravitational variation."

"I do know. I did the measurements or, rather, the non-measurements. Although we should have received *some* data before we did. But what I'm asking now is if you, personally, did any other measurements of the star or planet at any time, or had any other definitive, non-recorded data about its existence before we arrived."

"No, I recorded everything I surveyed. But I knew from the panspermic drift that the planet *had* to be here. And it is. Why? What's this about—does it matter what I knew when? I got no answers."

"Probably it doesn't matter." She tried a wobbly smile. "It's just a speculation I have. Probably it won't amount to anything. No data, and without measurements it—"

Another knock on the door, followed immediately by its bursting open. "Paul! McAuliffe has the probability data, and we're sending the second probe down right away! If it transmits anything reasonable at all, we're going downstairs!"

Serena bounded away. I don't think she'd even noticed Carin.

" 'Reasonable,' " Carin said, as if trying the word out aloud, as if she'd never heard it before.

∞

Probes are not very expensive, but no expedition likes to lose one. Serena, particularly, felt it as a personal affront. She'd been enormously frustrated when the first probe failed, as if it had deliberately flouted her command. So I held my breath as we crowded onto the bridge for our second attempt.

"Set probe for launch," Captain McAuliffe said.

"Probe set for launch," said the helmsman. Serena rolled her eyes. The elaborate military protocol for the *Feynmann*'s small crew alternately amused and exasperated her.

"Prepare to launch probe on three."

"Prepared to launch on three."

"One . . . two . . . three . . . launch probe."

"Probe launched. Trajectory on course . . . approaching atmosphere . . . entering atmosphere . . ."

"There!" Serena interrupted. "It's sending!"

The displays lit up with data. Carin's fingers flew over her hand-held. I leaned forward, interpreting what I could, waiting for her to run the equations that would give us the rest. But instead of atmospheric composition or temperature, Carin said a strange thing, in a strange voice.

"There. We've finally measured it."

Serena snorted. "That's what we came here for, isn't it?"

We waited for the probe to clear the cloud cover and send visuals. When it finally did, after what seemed a much longer time than actually elapsed, Serena said, "Well, it could be worse, I suppose."

But not much worse. The disappointment in Serena's voice was mirrored, I suspected, on my own face. An expedition down to JQ211F was going to be difficult, if McAuliffe allowed his shuttle down at all.

The images told the story. Speeding toward us was a landscape of fiery lakes, volcanic mountains, rivers of glowing lava. Everything looked black and red. The closer the probe got to landfall, the more daunting the terrain. Burning rocks—I knew without checking that they had to be sulfur—floated on a lake hurtling toward us at enormous speed. I actually saw the helmsman cringe backward. The probe's rockets fired, slowing it, and the nightmare land approached more slowly, allowing longer but no more reassuring views. Then the probe hit the surface of the water and all images disappeared.

No one spoke until First Officer Drina Parker said, "A hostile environment, to say the least."

"No one is going down there," the captain said, and Serena turned on him. "This is a scientific expedition of inestimable importance, *Captain.* Without a landing—"

"No one goes down there," McAuliffe repeated. "I'm not risking either my shuttle or my crew."

Serena's face distorted. But she had just enough self-control to turn silently and walk off the bridge. I took a step to follow her, then stopped. I wanted to see whatever data we'd gotten. I wanted to console Serena. I wanted—

"Better let her calm down first, Dr. Cho," Captain McAuliffe said, and I heard, or thought I heard, satisfaction in his voice. It angered me—we'd come so far and worked so hard to organize this expedition. So much depended on it, especially for me. But, of course, I didn't show my anger, although my reasons differed from Serena's.

Carin said, "Atmosphere predominately CO_2, CO, nitrogen, hydrogen chloride, with water vapor present. Surface temperature ninety degrees Celsius. Atmospheric breakdown by percentage—"

I went after Serena.

Uncharacteristically, she sat quietly on the edge of her bunk. I had expected storming and screaming. But she sat as if carved from stone, every muscle rigid. As I knelt beside her, her dark eyes focused on my face.

"You're going to convince him, Paul. Not me—there's no way he'll listen to me now. But he might listen to you, if you can just get his respect. Don't look so . . . so humble when you ask for a meeting. Try to–don't look like that, for God's sake, or nobody would respect anything you say!"

I didn't know how I had looked. Her anger, turned now on me, hurt. I rose to my feet. "I don't think I can persuade the captain to let us go down."

"But you'll try? You'll really try? Fuck it, scientific knowledge shouldn't be held captive by a third-rate tin soldier!"

"I don't think he's that," I said, before I thought. But she didn't turn on me for contradicting her. Instead she reached for my hand, looking up at me beseechingly from that beautiful face, almost humble. Serena humble . . . I could not have imagined it. In some deep part of my mind, I suspected that she was acting, manipulating me. That was all right. Serena could knead me any way she wished, as long as the touch was hers.

"You'll try?" she said again. "You'll try to convince him? You and Carin?"

"I'll try."

◉◉◉

I decided to wait a day before sitting down with McAuliffe, and I told Serena to stay out of his way for the rest of the afternoon and evening. It felt odd to be giving her orders. But she agreed to stay in her bunk and work with the data that Carin and I fed to her hand-held.

It was pretty skimpy data. The probe had lasted less than five minutes before hitting that burning lake, and none of our information looked likely to convince McAuliffe to risk his shuttle and pilot. But just after dinner, and for perhaps the first time on this expedition, we caught a break.

Carin and I sat on the bridge, which was lightly crewed now that we were in orbit. Lieutenant Parker had the conn. The helmsman said, "Ma'am, object drifting thirteen degrees starboard . . . belay that. Not an object, ma'am. It's a cloud of some kind . . . scanning now."

"A cloud?" Lieutenant Parker walked toward the main screen. Carin and I looked up from our data.

"Yes, ma'am. Registering very small discreet particles . . . enhancing visual . . . there."

The screen was filled with a loose, slowly drifting mass of tiny particles, backlit against the reflected light from the planetary clouds below. I said urgently, "Lieutenant, we need to capture a few of those! I think they're panspermic spores!"

"Is there a chance they might be toxic?"

"I doubt it. But we're prepared to examine them in biohazard alpha conditions." The lieutenant already knew this. She just wanted a documented record of her caution.

"All right. Mr. Silverstone, deploy robotic arm to sample that cloud."

"Deploying robotic arm."

Panspermic spores. I could barely wait to tell Serena.

❧❧❧

She and I suited up and squeezed ourselves into the tiny biohazard lab. It had been converted from some other use of ship's space and consisted of two chambers, the lab itself, and Decontamination. The robotic arm connected directly to the lab from outside the ship, so our samples awaited us in its sealed cache. Even the suits weren't really necessary; the spores would stay in a sealed chamber, worked on by lasers and tiny nano-robotic fingers that Serena and I directed from the outside. But the suits, like DeCon, represented another layer of military caution.

My fingers trembled as I took the console controls.

The back wall of the sealed chamber contained a magnified visual of our prize, which in turn was magnified hugely on a second display in the lab. We had sixty-four tiny particles. I inserted one under the nanoscope and watched the scope adjust itself.

"A cell wall," Serena breathed.

We set to work.

Two hours later we knew everything possible about our tiny life-giver. It was indeed that: a spore theoretically capable of giving rise to life. A tough, desiccated membrane surrounded a carbon-based string of thirty-two protein-like molecules that were, or could be, precursors to amino acids.

"There's enough here for a primitive self-replicator," Serena said. "At least enough to give rise to simple metabolic pathways. And formaldehyde! That could lead to adenine."

"But there's no evidence yet that it has, or will."

"Oh, Paul, don't be so stuffy. Look at it! It's life!"

Not yet. But I didn't say any more to discourage her; I was too eager myself.

The basic problem with natural selection is, has always been, that you must have something to select *from*. Life's biggest mystery is its first: How did that first self-replicator arise from the havoc of pre-life chemicals? Metabolic pathways are complex, and they do not seem to be reducible. Nothing simpler will work, and life must have developed complicated strings of chemical reactions all at once—seemingly an impossible task in a mess of billions of particles that could interact in billions of different ways. I still didn't know how that first enormous leap of evolution had happened. But now I was looking at where.

Our next step was to put the spores into an environment that would encourage them to emerge from dormancy and germinate. Of course, we had no idea what that environment should be.

Panspermia posits that these spores drifted through the galaxy, landing on many different kinds of planets, germinating and growing on at least some. To do that, they had to be primitive enough— and these were very primitive—to adapt to a variety of conditions. But it was unlikely that all spores could grow in all conditions. What did these need?

Water, of course. No life had ever been found, anywhere, that didn't require water. Beyond that, we didn't know. We set up a variety of growth media in a variety of atmospheres, each sealed within a separate tiny chamber, and varied the wavelengths and intensity of light. Sixty different mini-environments. By the time we were done, I suddenly realized that I was famished, and so tired my knees shook.

"Serena—it's ten o'clock."

"Is that all?"

"Ten o'clock in the morning. We've been in here fifteen hours."

"My God. Really?"

"Come on out, love. We need to eat and sleep."

She nodded, her face all but obscured behind her biohazard mask. She must be exhausted, or she would have reacted to that "love" that had just slipped out. Ordinarily Serena hated endearments.

We went through DeCon, me first at her insistence. When I emerged, Carin Dziwalski sat slumped on the deck outside the De-Con door.

"Carin! Is anything wrong?"

She raised her face and I was shocked. She looked a wreck, as if she hadn't slept all night. Neither had Serena, but Serena was strong as a rock. Carin's thin, pinched face sagged and she seemed about to faint. She seldom ate much, but now she had the hollow-cheeked look of a naturally thin person who had starved for days.

"No, Paul, nothing's wrong. I just want to know what you found."

"What we found? But, Carin, you had access to all the data as we recorded it, plus the visuals from the lab."

"I know. But I wanted to hear it from you. Are the spores alive?"

I peered down at her. It's always hard to tell just how much biology physicists actually know. Still, Serena and I had been chattering for the entire expedition. Carin should already know the answer to her question. Something wasn't right here.

I said gently, "Spores aren't ever alive. Nor dead. They're more like viruses—potential life. These contain a string of thirty-two molecules, a sort of peptide, that might well be able to self-replicate. We're germinating the spores and we'll see what happens."

She said, almost musingly, "Neither dead nor alive. Like Schrödinger's cat."

"Well, no," I said. The famous physics parable about quantum mechanics had nothing to do with spores, which depended on nutrients and energy rather than on the Uncertainty Principle.

"Well, yes," Carin said. And then, "Do you know what day it is?"

She seemed stranger and stranger. I said, "It's, um, Day 803, 2287."

"It's Ash Wednesday." She dragged herself to her feet and started, slumped from her thin shoulders, toward the bridge.

I didn't know what she meant, and I didn't care. I staggered the other way, to my bunk. All at once I was so tired I could barely lift each foot off the floor. I didn't even wait for Serena to emerge from DeCon, and a man who wouldn't wait for Serena was halfway to being dead.

●●●

I slept for ten hours. When I woke, my first thought was of the spores. Scrambling from my bunk, I reached for my pants, but before I'd so much as pulled them on, Serena burst in. Instead of her usual flowing robe she wore neat dark-red tunic and pants, but her hair was an uncombed mass of wild ropes and her face radiated panic.

"Paul! I just woke up and—"

"Did you check the spores?"

"No, McAuliffe woke me, he called to say we're leaving orbit!"

"Leaving orbit? Why? We can't!"

"I know, I know, but he says"—her face moved from panic to anger—"that since we're not going downstairs and we have plenty of spores, the mission here is done. Done!"

I sank back onto my bunk, pants falling to the floor. And yet, I could see the captain's point of view. To his knowledge, the scientists had done everything possible, and chances are he had never wanted to captain this minor, non-military expedition in the first place. It was a tiny detour on his own career path; he had fulfilled his assignment; he wanted to move on. Nor had Serena's disdain moved him toward being helpful.

"This is my fault," I said. "I counseled you to wait a day before explaining everything to him. Maybe if I had sat down with him yesterday—"

"Yes, it is your fault. So you fix it—go sit down with him right now. Convince him, Paul! We need to go down there!"

I gazed at her helplessly, loving her fire, disliking her complete inability to see her own part in McAuliffe's decision. And someone like McAuliffe was not going to listen to someone like me.

Maybe Serena thought the same thing. Her attention focused on me, me as a physical object, and I realized once again how I must look to her: scrawny, pale body slumped on my bunk, my trousers puddled around my ankles.

I said, "I'll take Carin with me to talk to McAuliffe."

"Well, all right . . . but Carin's been acting pretty weird lately."

So I wasn't the only one who'd noticed. "Serena—what's 'Ash Wednesday'?"

"I haven't any idea. Are you going to talk to the Tin Soldier or not? He's preparing to leave orbit!" She said to the small screen on my bulkhead, "On. Priority One call to Captain McAuliffe."

"Serena, don't say it's a Priority One because he—"

"Dr. Cho? What's wrong?" McAuliffe's baritone, accompanied by his frowning image on the bridge.

"Nothing's wrong, Captain, I—"

"If nothing's wrong, what the hell are you doing sending a Priority One?"

"I'm sorry, I . . . Captain, I very much need to talk to you. Now, before we leave orbit. Please. It's essential to this expedition, and we've already come so far from . . . please."

Serena scowled, undoubtedly at the subservience in my tone. But the captain said, "Well . . . all right. Wardroom in five minutes, Dr. Cho."

Serena knelt by my bunk and threw her arms around me. Her warm, generous body pressed into mine. "Thank you, Paul, thank you . . . and don't blow it."

Five minutes. I yanked up my pants, reached for my tunic, and said to the screen, "On. Priority One to Carin Dziwalski. Carin, we have to talk to McAuliffe in the wardroom now. It's our only chance. Meet me there immediately."

"All right." Her tone was subdued. My screen showed her in the corridor outside the biolab. What was she doing there?

No time to wonder. I yanked on shoes. I wouldn't have minded going barefoot, but nothing was more likely to disgust McAuliffe. For the same reason, I actually took twenty seconds to run a comb through my hair and to tie it back. Then I was running toward the wardroom, hoping to arrive before the captain.

No such luck. He was already seated at one end of the table, his face impassive, his outsize masculine presence crowding the room. Carin slipped quietly in through another door and took a seat as far away from McAuliffe as possible.

"Come sit there, Carin," I said, trying to sound authoritative, pointing to a seat beside the captain. Slowly she moved along the huge, gleaming table, and I sat on his other side. He showed no reaction to these probably pathetic maneuvers. The rich brown-and-green luxury of the wardroom oppressed me, despite the colorful holoscapes. I felt dwarfed.

McAuliffe said, "Please begin, Dr. Cho. What is so 'essential to this expedition'?"

"That we not leave orbit just yet, and that you authorize a trip down to JQ211F. Please, Captain, hear me out. There's additional information you need to make a completely informed decision." Was this meeting being recorded? Of course it was. That would help, wouldn't it? If anyone ever reviewed the records, McAuliffe would want his superiors to know his decision had been made with full understanding of all aspects of the situation.

"Begin, Dr. Cho."

I clenched my fist in my lap, below the table, and plunged in. "If part of your decision to leave orbit is based on a belief that life cannot exist on the planet below, then I have to start with why I believe there *is* life downstairs, and life worth investigating. If I explain things you already understand, please forgive me. I'm not used to talking to non-biologists. Micro-organisms can exist under all kinds of conditions, including what we saw. Lithotrops can derive nutrients from rock—in fact, we already know of bacteria that flourish on just volcanic rock. We've found micros living at over 120 degrees Celsius. They're enormously versatile chemical feeders, able to extract or fix carbon from methane, methanol, ether, formic acid, hydrogen sulfide, ammonia . . . There's absolutely no reason to think there's no life below."

"That belief was never part of my decision," McAuliffe said. Did he look bored?

I raced on. "The long-held theory of life's beginnings on Terra was that it started in a sort of primordial soup. That chemicals in the warm, shallow seas were stimulated by lightning to eventually form simple molecules that became proto-replicators. The problem was that in a few centuries of increasingly sophisticated lab experiments, nobody has *ever* been able to generate anything close to a self-replicating molecule. Not one. All you get when you try— no matter how you try, with what ingredients or with what energy sources—all you get is a kind of organic tar. Muck. Scum. Crud. *Always.*"

"Ummmm," McAuliffe said.

"Proto-cells are just too complex to create that way, so eventually panspermia became the favored theory for the origin of life." I could see from his face that I was losing him, but I didn't know what else to do and so went on lecturing.

"Panspermia has never been supported by physical evidence. But now we have these *spores*! They came from the planet, proof of life down there, and all my data and calculations show that this planet was the starting point for all spores that fanned out to seed the galaxy. Or what we know of the galaxy, anyway. These spores are the most important scientific discovery in five hundred years." Too much, too much—a non-biologist would certainly not see it that extravagantly. "Or one of the most important, anyway. Investigating their source is tremendously important. They may be the original source of *all life in the galaxy.*"

"So I gathered," McAuliffe said dryly.

"And a trip downstairs to verify that, to take samples, would aid biology beyond what we can even imagine now. I know the planet looks dangerous, but xenobiologic expeditions have landed in volcanic environments before and everyone survived. The shuttle needn't stay long, just time enough to grab samples, and of course the landing party would all be in s-suits and of course an s-suit can withstand those temperatures for as much as an hour and—" I had tipped over into babbling.

McAuliffe shifted his massive shoulders in the plush chair. "Dr. Cho, the safety of this expedition is my responsibility. You haven't convinced me that the benefits here outweigh the risk. What biological benefits would you obtain from these 'samples'? Medicines? Life-prolonging drugs? Usable genes?"

He didn't see it, wasn't touched by science for its own sake. I should have known, should have taken another approach. What other approach? There wasn't any. Desperate, I began repeating myself. "The planet is unique, it's the origin of life in this galaxy, it's the start, the alpha, the genesis of—"

"It's Hell," Carin said.

"Carin, don't—"

"What did you say?" McAuliffe said.

"Paul is right," Carin said, so low she was almost inaudible. "The planet down there is *not* just another planet in the throes of early geological upheaval. That planet is the source of biological life, the Genesis." From the way she said the word, I would swear it was capitalized. "And it's Hell. Fire, brimstone—'brimstone' is the archaic word for sulfur, you know—burning on the water. Great burning mountains, scorching all with great heat, the smoke rising up from the pit forever. Lakes of fire, tormenting the damned. The scarlet beast. Hell."

McAuliffe stared at her. I was about to protest when I saw something move behind his eyes, and I realized that I, Paul Cho, scientist who had spent ten years coordinating panspermic data, cross-checking meticulously, verifying and researching—I had not done my homework. Unlike Carin, I had never researched Robert McAuliffe, Lieutenant Commander in the Solidariat United Space Navy.

McAuliffe was a Christian.

●●●

That wasn't, of course, the official source of his decision. It couldn't be. He asked me to once more go over the scientific gains from going down to JQ211F, and he asked Carin for reams of data on planets of this particular type. She was a physicist, not a geologist, but she got him the information from ship's deebees. He asked his first officer, Lieutenant Parker, to draw up a list of similar planetary expeditions over the last decade, with methods of contact, outcomes for personnel and equipment, and best practices. McAuliffe was thorough, complete, and Navy. But I knew he had made his decision at the moment Carin said, "Hell."

I sensed something else, too. Carin was holding back. After McAuliffe finally gave us permission to shuttle downstairs, I cornered her in the corridor outside her quarters.

"What is it, Carin?"

"What is what?"

"Whatever you weren't telling the captain."

"Nothing, Paul."

"I don't believe you."

She raised her eyes to mine, astonished at my tone. I was pretty surprised at it myself. But after a moment all Carin said was, "I have . . . reservations about what we might find below. But nothing that contradicts anything I said to the captain, and nothing that would in any way compromise the safety of the expedition downstairs."

"I believe you," I said, because I did. But I grabbed her arm, hard. "But then why won't you tell me what your reservations are? And why do you look like your best friend just died?"

"None of your business!" She jerked her arm away from my grip. Appalled at my own bullying, I dropped my hand. But before I could even say, "Carin, I'm sorry," Serena flew around the corner.

"You did it! You did it! Oh, Paul—" She enveloped me in a hug. Her perfume filled my lungs. Had she been listening to the meeting with McAuliffe? Yes, of course, it was on the official record.

A little embarrassed by her embrace in front of Carin, I gently loosened Serena's arms and stepped back. "I thought you were in the lab." I would have been.

"Not yet. We'll go now, together. You did it!"

Carin had disappeared into her own quarters.

I followed Serena to the biolab. Eagerly we examined each of the sixty cultures designed to germinate the spores. Not one of the widely varying environments had worked. Every single spore remained dormant, suspended in the inert state between life and death.

∞∞∞

We didn't tell McAuliffe about the spores, and he didn't ask. I wouldn't have known what to say, anyway. There was no explanation. Every spore I had ever heard of germinated as soon as favorable conditions existed, wasting no time in propagating life. And we had provided sixty different sets of possibly favorable conditions.

The three of us attended another wardroom meeting, this time to plan the trip downstairs. I was coming to dislike the wardroom, that opulent sterile luxury that was the scene of so much strife.

"The shuttle seats four," Captain McAuliffe said. "My pilot and Gunner's Mate Telin Eyer will go down. That's a military decision. That leaves two scientists. Which scientists go is your decision, Dr. Wambugu."

Serena said, "Paul and I will go."

McAuliffe frowned. "Does it make sense for both biologists to take the risk?"

It didn't, of course. But Serena set her lips. "Dr. Cho and I will go."

"No," Carin said. "I'm going."

Everyone turned to look at her. And well they might. Carin wore an expression I had never before seen on her face, or on anyone's. Her thin lips pulled back over her teeth; she almost seemed to be snarling. Yet her eyes darted around the wardroom in what struck me, viscerally, as the most abject fear. What was she afraid of? Serena? We were all a little afraid of Serena—but not like that.

Serena said, each word distinct, "I beg your pardon?"

"I'm going down to the planet," Carin said, and now her voice was steadier, steelier, than I would have thought possible. "Look at our grant from the Academy, Serena. It says that unless circumstances warrant otherwise, a physicist shall accompany the expedition to assess planetary conditions."

"You *have* assessed planetary conditions," Serena said, too levelly. "You just gave us your assessment of the probability of landing safely, of the physical characteristics of the planet, and of its energy parameters. You accompanied us here, you assessed, and no circumstances warrant otherwise than my choosing my scientific team. Paul and I are going down."

"There's more down there than you think," Carin said, and

now her desperation began to break through her voice. "My assessment is not complete. I need to go down."

"If you have a theory about additional physics findings relevant to JQ211F, then tell us now." Serena's voice, if anything, had grown quieter, but I caught myself pulling away from her side.

"I can't," Carin said.

"' *Can't*'? You have data that you are not sharing with this expedition?"

"It's not data. It's not even a theory. It's . . . you wouldn't understand."

I could have told Carin how dangerous it was to say that to Serena. She never accepted that there was anything she couldn't understand. Serena's dark eyes snapped and I felt, rather than saw, her body tighten along its entire impressive length. But before she could rip Carin apart, Captain McAuliffe spoke.

"Dr. Dziwalski will be one of the two scientists on the shuttle downstairs."

"That's not your decision!" With the air of pulling a sword from one enemy to turn on another, Serena swung her gaze to McAuliffe. Two dark splotches appeared high on her cheekbones.

"Yes, it is my decision, if I have reason to think that the safety of the shuttle party is at risk," McAuliffe said. "And I do. Dr. Dziwalski, as the expedition physicist, has stated that there are additional, unassessed characteristics of the environment below. These characteristics fall into the realm of the physical sciences, not the biological ones, making her the person most likely to gauge their impact on the shuttle. Therefore, I order Dr. Dziwalski to be included in the landing party."

"You can't do that!" Serena cried.

"I just did. Decide, Dr. Wambugu, who the other scientist will be, and I will have my crew begin preparations for shuttle launch."

I thought Serena's gaze might bore a hole through McAuliffe. But he merely returned her look with a small smile, and I thought: *He's enjoying this.*

Evidently Serena decided to not give him that satisfaction. She rose to her full height and said with a good imitation of calm, "The other scientist will be me. When can you launch?"

"All pre-launch procedures must be completed first."

"Fine. You complete your little procedures. I'll be in my cabin, and you can–"

"Wait," I said. No one heard me, so I said again, louder, "*Wait*."

"Yes, Paul?" Serena looked down on me. The edge of her orange robe brushed across my shoulder, searing me like flame.

"I . . . I want to be the other scientist on the shuttle."

Serena's face looked absolutely blank. It was as if she suddenly didn't comprehend English. A part of my wildly agitated mind thought: *I wish I could say it in New Swahili.*

No, that would be worse.

"I don't understand," Serena said.

"I want to go down to JQ211F with Carin and send the data back up here to you."

Now the blankness on Serena's face dissolved. I had to look away. "*Paul–*"

McAuliffe said, not even troubling to hide his amusement, "Dr. Wambugu?"

This was my only chance. I had to do it publicly because in private there would be no chance at all. I could never stand out against her. "Serena, I spent six years on this data. It's my lifework and if . . . if anything happens to me down there, you could still present the work better than anyone I know. I want you safe so that you can be the inheritor and presenter of my work!"

It sounded lame even to me. That it was true, or partially true, made no difference. I did feel a laughable masculine protectiveness toward her–as if *I* could ever protect someone like Serena! But I also felt an intense, not-to-be-denied need to go down myself to the planet, and an unexpected resentment that she stood in the way, and half a dozen other things. I saw that Serena, gazing at me as if at a cockroach, knew everything I felt. It had no effect whatsoever on her decision but, I saw, an apocalyptic effect on her affections. I had betrayed her by even asking.

"Dr. Dziwalski and I will go downstairs in the shuttle," she said in a clear, dispassionate tone. "Captain, how soon can we leave?"

"I've already told you—as soon as all pre-landing procedures have been satisfied."

"Fine. I'll be in my quarters." She prepared to sweep out, but McAuliffe's words stopped her.

"Then Lieutenant Vollmueller will examine you there."

Serena turned. "Examine me?"

"Lieutenant Vollmueller is, as you may remember, ship's physician. Part of pre-landing procedure is a complete physical, Dr. Wambugu. A shuttle ride is not the equivalent of a cruise in space. You'll be pulling gees. A medical certification must be on file."

"I was medically certified at the start of the expedition!"

"And you'll be medically certified again," McAuliffe said. He was the only person I had ever seen dominate Serena, but I was too wretched to be impressed. I had just lost everything. I was not going down on the shuttle, and Serena was going to discard me.

"Fine. In my quarters," Serena said, and swept off the bridge. I scrambled to follow her. If I could explain, if I could just touch her while I talked—

A small hand grasped the bottom hem of my tunic. "Not now," Carin whispered. "Let her go for now."

She was right, of course. But everything in me roiled. My breath pounded in my lungs, I couldn't get enough air, there was a rushing noise in my ears, and—

"Just for now," Carin said, and pulled me again to sit down, while McAuliffe looked on with contempt.

∞∞∞

I tried to see Serena. She wouldn't talk to me. First she was closeted with Lieutenant Vollmueller, and then I was, impatiently enduring being poked, imaged, and sampled. "Thirty-six hours to culture blood and tissue for pathogens," the doctor said crisply. I barely heard her, merely enduring until I could go to Serena.

She wouldn't even open her door, which was locked. She

wouldn't answer a call. I wanted to sit in the corridor outside her quarters and waylay her, but that would have looked too ridiculous even for me. So I waited in the lab, the one place I was sure she would come eventually, in an agony of longing and frustration.

The thirty-six hours dragged by. Serena did not come. And none of the spores germinated.

Why not? It made no sense. Surely, from sixty varied and carefully chosen growing conditions, one should have proved favorable for germination?

Part of the time I slept, a fitful dozing on the bare deck that I knew wasn't the best physical preparation for the trip downstairs. Periodically a sailor brought me food that I didn't eat. I should have been getting rest, nutrition, briefing. I wanted none of it. I wanted Serena. I wanted the spores to sprout. I wanted–

"Paul," Serena said, bending over me, and my arms reached up and closed gratefully around her. But it wasn't Serena; it was Carin.

"Paul," she said, freeing herself, her face mottled with an unbecoming blush. "You have to get up. The captain wants you in the wardroom."

"The . . ."

"The *wardroom.* Come on, Paul, get up. Here." She handed me a cup of steaming coffee.

I staggered to my feet and gulped the hot coffee. Carin produced a comb from somewhere in her tunic and, still blushing, wordlessly ran it through my hair and retied my queue. I nodded gratitude, all the while wondering: Where was Serena?

"What does McAuliffe want now? Are you going down?" I couldn't see, even in my exhausted anguish, why that would make McAuliffe summon me. I wasn't going downstairs.

"I don't know what he wants. The spores, have they–"

"Nothing. All still dormant, or dead. I don't understand it."

I didn't understand anything.

"Dead," Carin repeated, and at her tone I finally broke out of my self-absorption to genuinely look at her. Eyes so bloodshot they resembled lava pools. Face so haggard she looked fifteen years older than she was. Her right hand trembled.

"Carin–"

"Let's go," she said, and I wasn't steady enough, or kind enough, to probe further.

Captain McAuliffe, First Officer Parker, and Gunner's Mate Telin Eyer waited in the wardroom, all three of them upright as statues on the plush green seats. Eyer was a big, solidly muscled man who looked as if he could take on an entire human division. I suspected that he, too, was genemod, but that not even his official Navy records would say for what. McAuliffe said briskly, "Dr. Cho, you are to prepare for the shuttle trip planet-side."

I felt my mouth fall open, and somehow I couldn't shut it.

"Dr. Wambugu's blood tests show an unidentified pathogen, something not in the deebees. It may or may not have resulted from exposure to the spores captured by this ship. Your biologic samples show no such unidentified contamination. Therefore, you will make the trip downstairs and Dr. Wambugu will remain aboard the *Feynmann.*"

"Unidentified . . . but Serena wore a biohazard suit! And the lab is shielded! And the spores didn't even germinate, none of them!"

I had blurted out that last without thinking. Something shifted behind McAuliffe's eyes. He was not a biologist, but he was intelligent and well-read; he must know that at least a few of the spores should have shed dormancy. But all he said was, "Military regulations specify that no personnel with any unidentified medical conditions may land on virgin planets. Lieutenant Vollmueller tells me that Dr. Wambugu most likely harbors a harmless retrovirus that has just happened to flare up at the moment. On my ship, however, we follow regs. The shuttle launches at 1100 hours. Are you going to be on it?"

"Yes," I said, and a small part of my mind noted that, treacherously and for the first time since I'd met her, I was glad that Serena was not by my side.

●●●

The shuttle screamed uneventfully through the atmosphere and then we were down.

"Permission to leave ship," Telin Eyer said to the shuttle pilot, Lieutenant Cowen, and even I felt slightly impatient with this formal military protocol. We were four people, three of them already in s-suits, jammed into an airlock the size of a supply closet and facing a landscape seemingly empty of life. Yet Cowen kept a laser-like gaze on the displays that monitored the outside, and Gunner's Mate Telin Eyer carried in his hand and on his suit enough weaponry to blow up a small city. What did the Navy do for first landings on planets with actual predators?

Not that there wasn't danger enough outside. But it was not going to respond to either barked orders or technological threats.

"Permission granted," Lieutenant Cowen said. And then, with a change of tone, "Good luck, Tel." I saw then what I had overlooked before: the danger of this mission to more than just Carin and myself. Scientists are no less self-absorbed than anyone else. Maybe more so.

The inner airlock door slid closed, the lock depressurized, and the outer door opened. We stepped, our military escort first, onto the surface of the planet that Carin had called "Hell."

Cowen had set the shuttle down on the most stable place he could find, a rocky and fairly level plateau ringed with active volcanic mountains. They smoked and belched, their sides glowing with molten lava, or streaked pale yellow with sulfur sprayed during previous eruptions. Through air thick with ash, I could see a small lake a few hundred meters to my left. Chunks of sulfur, some of it burning, floated on the water, undoubtedly releasing fumes of sulfur dioxide. The lake would be noxiously acidic and the air, could I have smelled it, foul and poisonous. Beneath my feet the ground rocked gently: subterranean quake. In the near distance a geyser suddenly erupted, an explosive outcasting of superheated steam where seeping rain water met hot magma below. The whole scene was lit, through the thick ash, by dim sunlight tinged with sickly red. My suit said the external temperature was ninety-six degrees Celsius.

"Fucking gods," Eyer breathed into his commlink, and I saw Carin glance at him sharply.

I said, "We need to spend as little time here as possible, so let's split up and I'll—"

"No, sir," Eyer said definitively. "My orders are that this landing party stays together."

"But don't you see that—all right." It was not the place or time to argue.

What place or time *was* it? More than the probe readings, actually standing on the surface of JQ211F convinced me that this was a young planet. It looked not unlike Terra must have looked once, over three billion years ago. A young planet that had somehow sent out all the spores leading to galactic life everywhere, after slow drifts through space that themselves would have taken a few billion years. It made no sense.

Carin said, her voice high and strained even through the commlink, "The lake first, Paul?"

"Yes."

We lumbered toward it, Telin Eyer sticking close. To do what? The gun in his hand looked fantastic, ridiculous, in that setting. Then I forgot the gun and everything else in my fascination with the lake. *Measurements make realities and different measurements make different realities,* Carin the physicist often said. I wanted to make sure we measured the right thing.

Fortunately, the water's edge was well defined here, roiling a foot or so below a lip of solid rock. I knelt and filled beakers, each one fitted with internal sensors and made of an alloy more indestructible than even that rock. It would take days to analyze everything in the scalding water, but the preliminary readings, displayed on the beaker's outer screen, were what I had expected: a high concentration of sulfuric acid. This was hopeful. Many thermophilic microbes can breath or eat sulfur or its compounds, and many of those generate sulfuric acid as a by-product.

I took scrapings from the side of the rocks under the water level, snatching back my hand when a chunk of burning sulfur floated too close. Everything we did, of course, was transmitted back to the *Feynmann* over cameras mounted on our helmets. Was Serena watching?

Of course she was.

Carin was busy with her own instruments. With her head bent over them, I couldn't see her face. I shouted, over a sudden noise like the clap of thunder, "I want samples from the geyser!"

She nodded, and the three of us set off toward it. Telin Eyer glanced every few seconds at his suit display. I knew he was looking for any excuse to pull us in, any rise in temperature or change in pressure. For some reason, this gave me a sudden rush of courage so great it almost felt like contempt for his military caution. I said on commlink, "Eyer, it's only sulfur. Your body carries over two hundred grams of it and it hasn't killed you yet!"

Through his faceplate he gave me the look that this stupid bravado deserved. But my irrational elation continued. We were doing it. We were proving my theory. This planet was the source of all life, and I stood on it, and I had actual samples from it! If this wonderful sense of triumph was merely a rush of adrenaline from fear, or a mental counter-reaction to my anguish over Serena, or a predictable response to too little sleep and no food—well, I didn't want to know it. For that moment, on the surface of Hell, I was invincible, omnipotent, god-like.

We took samples from the geyser, from a pool of stagnant water, from random cracks in the rock. Some bacteria, let alone pre-bacterial microbes, can survive on a diet of volcanic ash. We took rocks themselves. And then all three of us got safely back to the shuttle, no one killed or injured, and we took off for the *Feynmann* as intact as if we'd been on the lush, benign savannahs of a planet like Belsucre, the sweet garden playground of the Orion Arm.

○○○

Moods like that cannot, of course, last long. Mine didn't survive five minutes aboard ship.

Serena waited in the corridor when I emerged from DeCon. She didn't look at me, didn't even brush the block of air I occupied. I was less than a shadow on the wall. "Serena . . ." I said, then stopped. It was no use. All my stupid, lovesick grief flooded back, swamping me.

And so we stood there, two people occupying different realities, until Carin emerged from DeCon, clad in her usual gray pants and tunic and drying her dun hair with a towel. She had barely stepped into the corridor before Serena said imperiously, "Dr. Dziwalski, you will keep me informed of all results of your data analysis as soon as they occur, rather than waiting until you have them organized."

"All right," Carin said listlessly. I looked at her, puzzled. Whatever had ravaged her before had vanished, leaving this passive, resigned droop. So had her previous state been merely fear, a terror of dying down on the planet? It hadn't seemed so at the time. And what was she so hopelessly resigned to now?

I said, "Serena, you and I, not Carin, will be analyzing the microbe samples."

Serena didn't so much as glance in my direction. Desperate, I caught her arm. "At least tell me what the spores have been doing while I was downstairs! Have any germinated?"

She shook herself free as if shedding a mosquito and said to Carin, "All my data is already posted for anyone to look at it." Then she swept away.

I think it was that moment, that childish refusal of hers to separate the scientific from the personal, that Serena's hold on me loosened. But only a tiny bit, practically immeasurable, and I didn't feel it as relief, standing there in the corridor watching her beautiful back in its orange robe retreat from me for good. All I felt was a burning misery, corrosive as acid.

Still, Serena and I had to work side by side in the tiny lab. Telin Eyer had, on McAuliffe's orders, gone EVA and deposited all our samples from the outside of the ship into the lab depository. Now Serena and I, in the biohazard suits that McAuliffe also insisted on, handled the samples robotically. In one sense, the suits were a blessing. I could not touch her.

The analyzers processed everything: rock scrapings, pool water, lake samples, geyser residue. All the predicted components were present. The water was highly acidic, saturated with an excess of hydrogen ions. The solutions contained elements that might have been by-products of life, including the sulfur granules that chromatium-type bacteria deposit within their cells as left-overs after using hydrogen sulfide as a hydrogen source for photosynthesis. But sulfur granules can form in other ways, as well.

"What in the—" Serena said, breaking her long silence. She stared at the analyzer display.

I stared at mine.

Nothing in any sample was, or apparently ever had been, alive. We had nothing like bacteria, like viruses, like proto-cells for even the simplest organisms. No polymers or peptides, let alone amino acids or their analogues. Nothing capable of sustaining even the simplest metabolic pathway, and certainly nothing capable of self-replication. In fact, not even anything that could use the energy of sulfur compounds directly to fix carbon dioxide into the building block of life.

Moreover, what we *did* have was something completely familiar to any biology undergraduate in any university in the galaxy: organic tar. Gunk. Muck. Crud. As I'd told McAuliffe, for a few hundred years students had been sparking "primordial soups" of chemicals with various types of electromagnetic radiation in the hope of creating life in a beaker. No one had ever done it. All they got was scum exactly like what I stared at now. Dead organic tar, the result of chemicals interacting with each other at random, not in the disciplined ways required for even the simplest living cell.

I said quietly to Serena, "None of the spores germinated while I was downstairs, did they?"

Once again she didn't answer me. But I knew from her silence.

Inert spores. Organic tar.

All we had obtained from the planet was death. No, worse than death, which at least posited that something *had* been alive. This was an absence of life, a failure of the raw components of life to ever take on the direction and order that led to living cells. This was a big nothing, in the place which my life's work had posited as the source of everything.

Ashes.

●●●

"It *can't* be correct," I said to Carin. "It doesn't make sense!"

"Tell me again," McAuliffe said. "Explain it so I can understand."

I could have done without McAuliffe. I had to talk with Carin, since Serena wouldn't talk to me. But McAuliffe, unasked, had joined us in the wardroom; he had been talking in a low, serious voice with Carin when I came in. Now he sat there in his sleek uniform in that intimidating room, while I wished him light-years away.

But I, damn me for the weakling I am, responded to the uniform and the room and answered him. Even though I suspect he knew all this already.

"On every planet we've surveyed, we've found exactly the evolutionary evidence that we expected. But on none of them have we found the answer to how the first functioning, replicating cell first formed. We've known for a few hundred years that it took more than just a primordial soup of chemicals and some lightning, but we don't know what it would take. And positing panspermia doesn't really help, because panspermia uses spores and spores must be made by functioning cells, and how do you get that first cell?"

McAuliffe and Carin both looked at me. I knew what they were thinking: *God.* But I didn't believe in their God, and they knew I didn't—or at least Carin knew—so I ignored the look and went on.

"There are other theories to explain the origin of proto-cells, about a half dozen of them, but none of them have been borne out in experiments. The answers were supposed to be here. But instead of finding answers to the origin of life, we have no life at all." Not in the planet, not in the spores.

McAuliffe frowned. "Are you saying that we killed off the life down there? That our presence contaminated it and destroyed these proto-cells?"

"No. Because if we'd done that, the analyzers would have shown the . . . the corpses. Necro-fragments. Instead, there's nothing."

McAuliffe sat silent a long while, softly drumming his fingers on the rich grain of the huge table. His hands were broad-palmed, strong, with long slim fingers. The nails grew in perfect clear curves, filed bluntly. I stared at his hands, waiting, although I wasn't sure for what.

"If I authorized another landing, at a site on the opposite side of the planet from the first, would that help? Give you a different batch of data in case the first site was a freak?"

"Of course it would help," I said, a little dazed. Why would McAuliffe do that? I looked from his hands to his face, but it told me nothing. He was as impassive as Serena was explosive.

"Very well," he said crisply, rising from his chair. "Second shuttle mission as soon as pre-mission requirements are satisfied."

I said, disbelieving, "*Another* physical?"

"Yes, Dr. Cho. Regulations. That's all."

McAuliffe left the wardroom and I turned to Carin. "Why . . . why would he do that?"

"I don't know."

"He acted almost as if now he *wants* life to be down there. As if it matters to him, personally, enough to risk a second shuttle landing when he didn't even want a first one!"

"I don't know," she repeated dully.

"Carin, what is it you're not telling me?"

"Nothing. A stupid idea. I'm wrong. But, Paul—I don't want to go down this time."

"Don't want to—"

"Go down, no. The captain can be told that I've answered all physical-safety questions on the first landing and therefore met my mission requirements."

I didn't understand. "Carin—why? I mean, why don't you want to go downstairs?"

She looked away. Her bottom lip trembled. "I don't need to. I told you, I've answered all my questions."

Abruptly she rose and stumbled out, leaving me alone in the wardroom.

☞☜

Serena's blood work came back with her mysterious infection gone, which argued that it had indeed been some sort of harmless retrovirus, gone again into hiding in some organ of her beautiful body. Now Dr. Vollmueller could check off the box that said "No unidentified pathogens," which was all she cared about. Serena told McAuliffe that she was going downstairs alone, which meant with Telin Eyer but without me, and that she was within her rights as chief scientist to decide that. McAuliffe agreed, expressionless.

It was Carin who reported all this to me, her subdued listlessness unchanged. "I'm sorry, Paul. Serena is being . . ." She seemed to search for a word that wouldn't hurt me.

"Serena is being Serena," I said, and wasn't sure myself what I meant by that. "Carin, for God's sake, eat something."

She smiled strangely, although I couldn't see why. Serena, Carin, Dr. Vollmueller with her meticulous medical protocol . . . I was surrounded by obsessive women.

It could be argued that in excluding me from the shuttle trip, Serena was merely evening the score: I had gone downstairs once, and she would go down once. My trip was first, and in science being the first person to discover something means a great deal. But I hadn't really discovered anything. If Serena did so, if she found life on her trip to JQ211F, the resulting scientific reputation would be hers, not mine. She would see to that. She would become the savior of what had looked hopeless, the experimental prover of what had merely been Paul Cho's hypothetical statistical construct.

Oh, God, when had we become rivals? I could still feel her body warm in my arms, her full breasts swollen under my hands, the electrical shock of her in my loins. How had we come to this?

By Serena's decision. Carin's words again: *"Measurements make reality."* Serena had measured me, and found me wanting, and now she was trying to construct a reality in which I barely even existed.

"I'm sorry, Paul," Carin said again, laying her small hand on my shoulder. But I heard as if from a far-off distance, and I couldn't have said when she took her hand away.

●●●

"Shuttle on the ground, sir," Vlad Cowen said. "Landing completed and within all parameters."

His voice came to us with a half-second lag. The bridge screens glowed with information, both data and visuals. McAuliffe, Carin, and I studied them all intently, while around us the bridge crew, shadowy unheeded ghosts, carried out their duties.

The shuttle had set down on another stretch of rock, this one farther up the side of a quiescent volcano. There was no magma here; in-flight visuals showed a caldera temporarily cooled, filled with simmering water. But the terrain was much more uneven than on the first landing, and as the shuttle sensors swept around I saw a wild jumble of boulders, rock pools, and minor crevasses. Serena undoubtedly wanted as wide a variety of sampling environments as possible.

McAuliffe said, "Eyer, restrict all excursions to within a half hour and hundred meters of the shuttle. Return to the shuttle at 1330 hours for immediate take off."

"Yes, sir."

Serena said nothing.

When she and Eyer left the shuttle, the *Feynmann*'s displays included transmissions from their suits. I saw almost exactly what Serena saw as she stepped gingerly onto the ground, and in the shaking of the visuals, I felt the slight tremor under her foot. She walked toward the nearest rock pool. Bending, she scraped samples into a beaker and put it in her suit pouch. Telin Eyer walked close behind, scanning full circle, carrying the ridiculous gun.

She sampled one more rock pool and then started toward a group of boulders.

"Dr. Wambugu," Eyer said on his suit's commlink, "you have reached the limit of permitted exploration."

Serena didn't even answer him, just kept walking toward the boulders.

"Halt now, Dr. Wambugu."

She whirled around so fast that she practically bumped into him. "I'm sampling that outcropping!"

"You have reached the limit of permitted exploration."

"McAuliffe!" Serena yelled. I glanced at the captain. His face registered nothing.

It seemed to me that I could feel her indecision in my own legs, my own belly. She could walk toward the boulders anyway—what could Eyer do? Shoot her? She wasn't a sailor under his, or even McAuliffe's, command. No, Eyer wouldn't shoot her, but he would physically stop her. I sensed her measuring her chances of resisting his force. She was taller than he, and strong for a woman, but certainly not strong enough. And anyway, who knew what Eyer's suit contained by way of military gadgets designed to enforce military will?

Instead, Serena put up her hand and toggled something on her own suit's complex controls. Immediately I could see, through the transmission from Eyer's suit, that her mouth moved, but I couldn't hear the words. She was trying to argue him into compliance without the rest of us hearing.

McAuliffe said, calmly but with an undertone, "Mr. Silverstone, find the frequency to which Dr. Wambugu has toggled suit-to-suit communication and restore it to ship's channel."

"Yes, sir."

It took a moment. Meanwhile I watched Serena's mouth move, arguing or wheedling or defying. The visuals on her suit still transmitted, and Eyer's face wrinkled slightly in what looked like disgust. He started to say something. I thought his lips formed the word "ma'am—"

Then it all happened at once.

Eyer's jaw fell open and his eyes widened to almost perfect circles. His gun jerked upwards. Serena, seeing his face, spun around to peer in the direction he faced. Now there was no way to see her face, but at that moment Silverstone restored the commlink frequency. Serena shouted, "Oh, my God, what is—"

The rest of her statement was lost in the firing of Telin Eyer's weapon, waves of deafening sound. The boulders disappeared in a spray of rock and dust. And the ground shook and split, sending the suit transmitters careening wildly, falling, and then disappearing. Through a fog of rock and ash I saw, on the shuttle's external transmitter, the rock open and Serena and Telin both fall in, just as magma oozed forth in coruscating red and the shuttle lifted off the ground.

"No!" Carin screamed. "No!"

I couldn't scream, couldn't move, couldn't think. Serena was gone. Swallowed by the erupting planet. Dead. I had just seen her die.

Ashes.

●●●

Vlad Cowen brought the shuttle safely back to the *Feynmann*. McAuliffe pulled us out of orbit immediately after that. Fifteen minutes later he sat in the wardroom like Jehovah in judgment, Carin and I across from him, and demanded answers we didn't have.

"What happened down there? You have all the data right there in front of you. What happened?"

Carin had said nothing since her scream on the bridge. Now she sat absolutely immobile. I, on the other hand, couldn't stop trembling. It hurt to breathe, to move. Yet neither could I stay still. My hands, my shoulders, my very guts shook.

McAuliffe repeated, "What happened?"

Carin finally said, "It's hard to tell for sure. It's possible that Mr. Eyer's weapon gave off sound waves that were enough to destabilize rock that was ready to shift anyway. Or that the impact of the falling rocks from the boulders he pulverized did that. Like an avalanche." Her voice sounded dead.

"Eyer fired *at* something, Dr. Dziwalski. And Dr. Wambugu started to say 'What is—' Presumably she, too, saw something. What does the data indicate it was?"

"The data indicates there was nothing there. And we saw nothing on the camera on Eyer's helmet."

"*Nothing?* He would not have fired at 'nothing.'"

"Nonetheless, all the sensory data from both suits and the shuttle indicates nothing. No thermal signature, no electrical field, no change in air pressure, nothing."

I looked from one to the other. Something was going on between them that I didn't understand, didn't want to understand, something other than a military inquiry. McAuliffe was asking another question, and Carin answering it, than they seemed to be.

He said, "I repeat, my gunner's mate was well trained. He would neither have reacted nor fired if there had been nothing there."

"There was nothing there."

All at once I couldn't stand any more of this. It was unbearable. I said, fighting to keep at least my voice steady, "It was hot. There was steam coming from the rock pools and maybe the crevasses. Couldn't Serena"–it hurt, physically, to say her name– "couldn't Serena and Eyer both have seen some sort of mirage? An optical trick that wouldn't necessarily transmit digitally?"

Carin gazed at me bleakly. She knew, and knew that I knew, that there had been no mirage. The atmospheric conditions, the distance between the observers and the boulders–everything was wrong for a mirage. But she, too, had had enough.

"The atmosphere of that type of planet," she said carefully, "has not been extensively studied, for obvious reasons. We don't really know what kind of illusions it might produce."

There was a long silence. I realized, with a little shock, that what she had just said was actually true.

Finally McAuliffe said, "Then this summary inquiry is closed, pending a full official inquiry. Let the record read that Dr. Serena Caroline Wambugu and Gunner's Mate Telin Zachary Eyer died as the result of unexpected geological activity following unidentified atmospheric conditions. Gunner's Mate Telin Eyer is hereby officially listed as dying in the line of duty and is recommended for Navy commendation. Dismissed."

Carin was the first one out the door. McAuliffe followed briskly. I sat, shaking but curiously unable to rise, in the wardroom I now hated more than any other place in the universe, even the planet where Serena had died. It seemed to me that, paralyzed by anguish, I would never move again. But, of course, like so much else, that was merely an illusion.

●●●

The day after we left orbit, Carin requested to be put into cold sleep for the several months of the trip home. Her work, she said, was done, since this scientific expedition had always been primarily focused on xenobiology and not on physics. Dr. Cho, her formal request stated, could analyze any remaining data without her. Her request was granted.

There was no remaining data. None of the spores in the lab ever germinated. There would be no chance to obtain more.

I stayed in my tiny quarters, struggling with my report for the Academy, selfishly having my meals delivered to me. Not that I ate much. Nor did I visit the shower. Mostly I lay on my bunk in a kind of bewildered torpor that had none of a torpor's usual blessed numbness. Sometimes it was as much as I could do to draw a breath.

Serena was gone.

The data that had been my life's work was meaningless.

Which of these two hurt most? It seemed wrong to rank the death of a human being, a woman I had loved, with the loss of a scientific breakthrough. Except that what had happened on JQ211F had been more than that. I knew it in my bones. I just couldn't make sense of it, and somehow not being able to make sense of it infected my whole self, a mental and emotional gangrene. Science made sense of the universe. That was science's function. If it could not do that, then my entire life, including my love for Serena, was rocked to its core.

●●●

Three days later, Carin's face abruptly appeared on my display screen.

I bolted upright on my bunk so quickly that I hit my head. Rubbing it ineffectually, I stared at Carin's image. She wore her usual gray tunic, and her limp hair straggled around her ravaged face.

"Paul, this is a Priority One, personal, time-delayed transmission. Before I sent it, I wanted to give you some time to analyze your data."

Not that I had done that fruitfully.

"I left you a letter. I reprogrammed my quarters to open with a

manual key, which is in the lab, way back on the lowest shelf. The
letter is for your eyes only. No record of it exists. It's not science,
it's . . . it's what it is."

Carin's image went silent, head bowed. Five seconds . . .
ten . . . half a minute. That's a long time to stare at a motionless image. Then she added something curious.

"I'm sorry to do this to you, Paul. But I'm compelled to." The
image blanked.

Slowly I got off my bunk, pulled on pants, and for the first time
since Serena died, left my quarters. Barefoot, I padded along the
corridor to the lab. I met no one. It's not that I expected anything
from Carin. But I had to go.

The key was where she said it would be. I walked back to her
quarters, unlocked the door, and went in. Dimly I realized that it
was the first time I had ever been there. Carin, like Serena, had kept
her quarters strictly private. They were identical to mine: bunk,
stripped now of all bedclothes, with drawers built in underneath.
Table and chair. Sonic shower. Display screen on the bulkhead.

Nonetheless, I might have been in a foreign country.

Over the table hung a large, plain cross, intricately carved with
symbols I didn't understand. I ran my finger over it; like the wardroom table, it was real wood. Below it sat a sort of shrine: a pot of
those blood-red genemod flowers engineered to need little water,
which filled the room with a heavy, languid scent. The flowers
were flanked by two burning ultra-candles. I'd seen these before.
Natural materials with no electronic components, they nonetheless
burned slowly, steadily, for weeks. Carin had apparently bolted
them to the table. Still, if the ship had accelerated suddenly and
flames had been thrown off . . . but there was nothing in the room
that would burn, except the letter.

It lay on the table in front of the flowers. I sat on the bare bunk
and opened the envelope, which bore no name. Carin had meant
it when she said there was no record of the letter. It was handwrit-
ten, in a small, even, dense script that somehow brought Carin before my eyes as the outlandish religious icons had not. There was
only one sheet of paper, but it was covered on both sides.

Dear Paul,

This is not a consolation letter, nor a love letter, nor a scientific treatise. It's an act of supreme selfishness, far more selfishness than Serena ever showed you. But since I'm never going to see you again, I hope not even glimpse you again, I am compelled to tell you the thoughts in my mind. You'll reject some of them. So did Robert McAuliffe, although for far different reasons. That's acceptable. I know that I'm right, and I can't bear it, and so I'm making you share the burden.

Your precious theory was not wrong. That's the first thing. JQ211F was indeed the source of all life in the galaxy. It sent out all the spores of panspermia, and it will send out no more, and I'm going to tell you why. Unfortunately, the explanation—it's not a hypothesis, for reasons that will become clear as I go on— isn't going to be of any scientific use to you. It's unprovable, untestable, and forever unreplicable.

I am a physicist. I think in terms of quantum phenomena, for that's the stuff we, and all else, are made of. I know you're a biologist, Paul, and so it's natural to you to think in terms of evolution, growth, constant change, increasing complexity. Fundamental particles, however, can inhabit states that no respirating organism ever could. Fundamental particles can simultaneously be both waves and particles, be here and there, exist and not exist.

You explained your central problem so clearly to Captain McAuliffe: How did we get the first living proto-cells, the things from which natural selection might select? Science has never, in two hundred years, succeeded in creating a proto-cell. Nor will we. That's God's domain, although I know you don't accept that. So let me stick to things you will accept.

At the level you are talking about, the pre-cellular, life itself is a quantum phenomenon. You already know that; single electrons often start, and determine the course of, chemical reactions in a cell. Single electrons initiate nerve impulses. Even larger molecules may exhibit quantum behaviors: we've known a long time that a sixty-atom molecule, C. fullerene, will behave as both a wave and a particle, passing simultaneously through two separate small slits in a barrier. These particles exist in a state of uncertainty, a state of quantum superposition, in which they simultaneously inhabit all possible states. Living cells, complex and organic wholes, do not.

Except on the planet we just left.

Do you know what happens when you measure an electron, or a photon, or even as large a molecule as C_{60} fullerene? Of course you do. You "collapse the wave" and it becomes either a wave or a particle, one thing or another. Until then, it is neither. The act of measurement creates the ensuing reality.

You want desperately to know why JQ211F did not register on ship's sensors until we'd penetrated its atmosphere. You want desperately to know why the first probe disappeared. You want desperately to know why our landing samples turned out to be nothing but non-living gunk. And of course you want desperately to know why the spores won't germinate. Yet my sense is that you will reject the answers to all these questions, which is one and the same answer.

JQ211F existed in a unique state of living quantum superposition, in which all states exist simultaneously. That's how come you got proto-cells there and nowhere else. You yourself told me that a gradual evolution couldn't make a replicator; the metabolic pathways, to work at all, had to emerge all at once. Only a state in which all possible chemical reactions, in all possible chains, can simultaneously exist without collapsing, will produce enough viable possibilities to evolve the first life. I've done the math. The probability of putting together a string of thirty-two proto-molecules all at once, in the right order to make those spores, is close to zero. To be exact, it's $1/10^{41}$. That means there were 10^{41} ways to put together that string, and only one would work, and it never would have happened unless the occurrence took place in a state of quantum superposition.

JQ211F had that. If you want a scientific analogy, it was like a quantum computer, that theoretical possibility, but real, and running a program that created life.

Until we sent down a probe, made a measurement, and collapsed the wave.

We destroyed that planet, Paul. Measurements make reality,

and different measurements make different realities. We, if you want to put it this way, allowed the rest of the molecules of the universe to interact with the quantum computer and so destroyed its integrity. I would put it a different way. We killed God.

That's why I called the planet "Hell." Not because of the brimstone and other superficial volcanic activity. But because Hell is the absence of God, and that's what our clumsy attempts to measure Him have made real. There will be no more new life in the galaxy. We're left alone with whatever is already here.

Not even Robert, although a Christian, agrees with me on this. He authorized the shuttle landings because he, like me, couldn't not know. But now that I've given him the answer, he rejects it. Too painful. But *I* know what we did down there. We tried, and failed, to measure God, and so created a reality without Him. I know it is so, and I cannot, cannot, cannot bear it.

                                                              Carin

My first thought was *Poor girl, the stress drove her over the edge.* Only after that self-righteous and dismissive pity did I stop to consider the content of what she'd said.

I rejected her science. No evidence existed that living cells, even in their most primitive proto-versions, might obey the laws of quantum superposition. The very idea was fantastic. Not only fantastic, but untestable, which—Carin was right on this—removed it from science.

Untestable.

Preposterous.

Childish, even, in its longing for a Super Being that had the universe firmly in hand.

But how else could I account for the planet unseen by ship's sensors until we penetrated the atmosphere, for the vanished probe, for the gunky organic tar in the planetary samples, for the inert spores?

No other way. I could not account for these things. But that didn't mean that I had to accept some unscientific, mystical "explanation." I had not descended to that.

I don't know how long I sat in Carin's room, motionless on the

edge of her bunk, barefoot and with her letter in my two hands. A
long time, I think. But eventually I stood, shaking my legs a little to
relieve their cramp.

Then I reached over and extinguished the flames on the two
candles beside the pot of over-scented flowers, and left the room.

●●●

The *Feynmann* returned to the Academy on Terra, deposited me
there like so much spent fuel, and went on to its next assignment,
whatever that was. Presumably Carin was ferried somewhere else
and awakened. I don't know; she was still in cold sleep when the
Feynmann left orbit.

I filed my disappointing report with the Academy. In eighty-
four pages plus data tables it essentially said: *Sorry, no evidence of life
on JQ211F.* I attended in holoform the brief, arid official inquiry on
Serena Wambugu's death. Somewhere I have a copy of the verdict:
Death by misadventure in a hostile environment.

Somewhere, too, I have Carin Dziwalski's letter, even all these
decades later. I think of it occasionally as I stumble across campus
in the driving rain to teach my third-rate physics students at my
third-rate university. If I asked my wife, a very organized person,
to find the letter in our ramshackle house, she might have been
able to do so. I don't ask her to find it; I remember every word.

Carin was both wrong and right. Wrong about the planet and
about "God"—although there has never been another expedition to
JQ211F to see what is going on there. Nonetheless, I know she was
wrong, because nothing she posited was really based on science,
which alone can answer our cosmic questions.

Or is that as stubborn a faith as hers?

I push away such questions and think, instead, about the way
that Carin was right. We do measure reality, and different measurements make different realities. Serena measured me, defined me to
herself, and so created a reality that first embraced and then rejected me. Had she measured differently, I might have gone down
to JQ211F with her, and either been able to save her or else died
with her and Telin Eyer. Different realities, both.

And I measured the results of panspermia, gambled my scientific reputation on my hypothesis, and lost. Had I not caused a fruitless and expensive expedition, I might now be teaching at a better place. I might have occupied the position of intriguing positer of an as-yet-untested theory, instead of being the slightly embarrassing survivor of a failed one. On such measurements are careers made.

Carin, of course, made the most drastic measurement of all. Carin, mousy and drab and timid. In her own mind, she measured God, and found Him and His design for the universe collapsed by man. Or by woman, if you blame Serena, as you probably must. Carin's measurement created, for her, the worst reality of all.

But in fact, every one of us measures the universe every minute. Collapsing the wave, erasing uncertainty in at least our own minds. Creating different realities.

None of these thoughts are useful. I pull the hood of my rain jacket farther over my face and, head down, keep my eyes on the mud and puddles as I trudge along to class.

Rococo

by Robert Reed

~~~~~

The aptly titled "Rococo" derives from the French "rocaille," meaning "rock-work or shell-work, as in an exquisite gilded mirror." But the term is even more richly connotative: marked by elaborate ornamentation, as with a profusion of scrolls, foliage, and animal forms; immoderately elaborate or complicated; having too many unnecessary and resource-consuming enhancements; used to imply a program that has become so encrusted with the software equivalent of gold leaf and curlicues that they have completely swamped the underlying design.

Reader, beware. All of these gradations characterize Robert Reed's convoluted tale of worlds forbidden from sharing a greater destiny, a ban devised by impossible-to-comprehend aliens (but are *they?).*

Since the late 1980s, Robert Reed has built an award-winning career in science fiction. His eleventh novel, The Well of Stars *(2005), is a sequel to his highly successful* Marrow *(2000). Two collections offer up a sampling of his shorter fiction—*The Dragons of Springplace *(1999) and* The Cuckoo's Boys *(2005), both published by Golden Gryphon Press. Born in Omaha, Reed resides in Lincoln, Nebraska, with his wife, Leslie, and their daughter, Jessie Renee.*

–I–

AASLEEN WAS SLEEPING and then she was otherwise. Drifting in the middle of the tiny cabin, she felt the tickling tug of her nexus wishing to be noticed. A message had just arrived, swaddled inside human encryptions. But as she opened her eyes and then her bed, she realized this wasn't the only reason she was awake. The perfect silence of space was being interrupted by a series of soft sounds and rhythmic vibrations. She couldn't see through the milky white cabin walls, but it was obvious that the ship beyond was reconfiguring its body again, reinventing its hull and engines for the next leg of this extraordinarily painful voyage.

Warily, she unwrapped the message.

Hazz appeared to her mind's eye. He was a tall, handsome fellow dressed in the crisp mirrored uniform of a captain. Personable and capable of great charm, he smiled at his chief engineer, reporting to her, "About Rococo . . . we have news . . ."

A cold spike pierced Aasleen's belly.

"The Scypha have picked up his trail again." The voice was deep and slow, possessing the practiced clarity found only in actors and great captains. "Six earth-days ago, he was still hiding inside the Stone Ring. But he was using an asteroid that's nearly fifty million kilometers from his last known position. Nowhere close to where anyone was looking for him, naturally." Hazz paused. "By the way, the asteroid rides on the Ring's inner edge."

The implications were obvious.

"Our hosts are sure about their verdict," said Hazz. "This isn't another false lead, they're promising."

Hazz's face and clear voice were just the tiniest portion of a dense data rain. Most of the rain was an elaborate map that Aasleen fed to her ship's library.

"Show me," she ordered.

Her tiny cabin was woven from dense bioglass. The glass instantly turned black, and the map blossomed inside the walls. Stretching before her was the Stone Ring—hundreds of thousands of rough gray worlds, each tumbling along some private path, cir-

cling the cool orange sun. Two spaceships were delineated with
vector lines: The massive human starship lay outside the Ring,
while Aasleen's tiny ship traveled above it, nine degrees over the
plane of the ecliptic. Only one of the asteroids deserved to be circled in blue. She touched that speck of dust, and a tiny portion of
the map expanded, filling an entire wall. Ten kilometers across, the
battered little world was dotted with a few bubbles of green water
and green air, plus a tiny fueling station tucked inside a deep polar
crater. She instantly guessed that her brother had stopped at the
station, probably trying to steal fuel. But no, every marker drew
her attention to a blunt mountain standing on the world's equator.
It was a location without charm or obvious significance. Why
would Rococo, or anybody in his desperate situation, spend two
moments in that empty, exposed place?

The image shifted again, becoming a recently recorded feed.
Scypha hunters were scattered across the summit. The aliens didn't
exist as species in any traditional sense; each individual was a
unique collection of totipotent cells. But all of the hunters were as-
sembled in the same basic pattern—spherical green bodies sealed
against the hard vacuum, each possessing dozens of hemispherical
eyes and countless busy spines that gripped the rocky landscape,
highly tuned senses searching for clues that the first twenty
searches might have missed.

The critical discovery lay at the base of the mountain. Six
earth-days ago, an exhausted ship had buried itself deep in the
dusty regolith—a violent maneuver, but no more spectacular than a
million other impacts among the asteroids. Then yesterday, a lone
Scypha hunter noticed what seemed like a fresh crater buried by a
convenient landslide. On a hunch, it recruited some of the local
Scyphas—lobster-like workers brandishing claws wrapped in steel
and diamond teeth. Under the hunter's guidance, those workers
had quickly uncovered the tangled remains of a human shuttle. Of
the hated pilot, there was no trace.

When she looked at the wreckage, Aasleen triggered a
recorded response in her captain's transmission.

"See if you can puzzle this out," said Hazz. "Why did your
brother visited this non-place?"

As an older sibling, Aasleen had no worthy answer. But as a trained engineer, the solution was obvious.

She asked the data rain, "What else has been recovered?"

There was only one other item of substance. In the shadow of a room-sized boulder, somebody had hurriedly buried a hyper-fiber satchel. It had ruby-rope straps that allowed it to be carried, and the main pocket was locked by several methods, including a diplomat's seal. She recognized the satchel immediately. For as long as she had known him, her brother had carried it, his personal journal safely locked inside.

"I want that!" she blurted.

Then with a more careful tone, she explained why she deserved the satchel. It would take a human agent to break the seal, and its contents were possibly valuable but most likely booby-trapped. An expert in human ingenuity was essential if the security systems were to be subverted. There was no better candidate for the job than Aasleen, and nobody else could hope to find and interpret whatever clues were left waiting inside.

Her plea was sent off to Hazz and to the Scypha hunters and to a hundred important little worlds—by agreement, every word that Aasleen said to her captain was shared with their alien hosts.

There was more to see in the data rain, but she responded first to Hazz's question. "I know why my brother was there," she offered. "If he'd left the Stone Ring in that stolen shuttle, we would have seen him. And judging by his position in the system, he probably didn't have any fuel left, much less the velocity necessary to avoid us any longer.

"So what Rococo did . . . he crashed at a prearranged location, then unburied himself and climbed to the summit. Alone, I'm sure. Wearing nothing but a minimal lifesuit." The tiny world had a quick spin, its gravity falling to almost nothing along the equator. "This is a problem in mass and force," she explained. "I think what he wanted was to hide his shuttle and jump off into space. If he'd used any kind of rocket-assist, he might have been noticed. But his leg strength should have been enough. Leaving the satchel behind was probably a last-moment decision. For whatever reason, he wasn't entirely sure he was strong enough to make it into orbit with an extra kilo or two."

She imagined her brother kneeling on summit, his face grim but determined. A little worried, perhaps, but definitely sure about his cause.

Whatever that cause was.

"He jumped into a low orbit, but you won't find him there either." Aasleen hesitated, her belly twisting into a hard lump. "It's what everybody is scared of," she allowed. "My brother's not working alone. I'm guessing this, but I think another ship has come to play—a quick vessel we haven't been looking for. It passed by recently, and it was there for one purpose. To snatch him up."

The image of Hazz smiled, and the last of the data rain opened up.

Suddenly the asteroid pulled back and back, revealing a great arcing swath of the Stone Ring. Then a blue line—the color of alarm among the Scypha—was laid across the grand map. The line marked the course of a single vessel. A Scypha seeder, judging by its designations and lazy motions. The seeder had been traveling slowly along the Ring's inner edge, cutting close to various asteroids, making a series of intricate maneuvers that eventually took it past Rococo's last known position. That was several days ago, and a few thousand kilometers later, the seeder's course straightened. Unexpectedly powerful engines burst to life, shoving it toward the system's largest world. A human passenger would have been crushed by the gees. But modern people were made of durable, nearly immortal stuff, and Rococo would have recovered long before he reached his ultimate goal.

Again, Aasleen grew aware of the vibrations extending beyond her tiny cabin. Obviously her situation had changed while she slept. She asked the ship to make the walls transparent, which it did; and with a genuine fascination, she studied the machinery as it gracefully shifted positions around her—engines and fuel tanks realigning themselves, while the extra mass was being cobbled into a crude but useful heat shield. What was a swift pursuit vessel able to dance among the asteroids was being transformed into something even faster but decidedly less maneuverable, getting ready for the voyage's last leg.

According to the blue line, two days ago Rococo's new ship had crashed into the system's largest world.

Chaos.

For a sad, sorry moment, Aasleen imagined her brother watching that cold gray planet grow huge before him—a world built upon endless violence and relentless, unpredictable rebirth. Then she could hear his smart, always confident voice asking, "Do you really think you could have stopped me, Sister? Why would you believe, even for a moment, that was even remotely possible?"

–II–

Despite sharing parents and the same home world, Aasleen and her brother were utterly different people. In part, it was because of their ages: Rococo was a thousand years younger than his big sister. In part, it was because of the long and very separate lives they had led. But mostly it was because they were siblings, which meant that similarities weren't half as important as the attitudes and oddities that made them feel unique.

Aasleen grew up on a young, UV-blistered world—the kind of harsh environment that demands nothing from its citizens but strength and a pragmatic, selfless genius. Her first centuries were spent mastering the rough, reliable machinery preferred by colony worlds. Then as the colony's conditions improved—as wealth and free time gained toeholds—she took the trouble to earn degrees in five species of engineering. The colonists had brought every possible tool from Earth, but most of those tools existed only as impossible plans locked away inside data vaults. On an alien world with its own peculiarities, people had limited resources with almost no industrial base to spare. Yet Aasleen opened the vaults and picked what she needed, adapting the plans to fit local conditions. Against the responsible advice of her parents and few friends, she set to work on a continent far removed from where humans had always lived. Alone, she built a generation of high-functioning AI's, equipping them with tough bodies and relentless work ethics. Then with her machine army, she fabricated a giant tent composed of nanotubes and microlasers. Its fabric was transparent to most flavors of light but selectively permeable to gases. Her plan was to drape the tent over a corner of the empty continent, terraforming a broad piece of terrain. There were setbacks, naturally. And then came a string of disasters that destroyed the first tent and rendered the next three useless. What succeeded was the fifth tent—a structure she designed from scratch, borrowing the shape of an earthly conch shell. Within a hundred years, the tent's internal atmosphere was composed of free oxygen and nitrogen, carbon dioxide and water vapor. No other place on that world let people walk naked beneath the blue-white sun, and nowhere else could they enjoy deep, unfiltered breaths. In the next twenty years, most of the original colony domes had been abandoned for the new lands, and Aasleen's grand dream had made every life easier and wealthier. Particularly her own life, of course.

When she was 803 years old, important news arrived from the sky. A human probe wandering outside the galaxy had come across an alien artifact. Vast and apparently abandoned, the mysterious vessel was dubbed the Great Ship; and with word of its discovery, scattered human colonies were marshalling their scarce resources, trying to mount expeditions to reach the Ship before any other species could. With an engineer's gaze, Aasleen examined the countless technical problems any mission would face, including the mortal dangers, both known and imagined. Then after two minutes of hard consideration, she made her decision. She would surrender her new fortune and all of her remaining lands. Over the next ten months, she and her AI's would refurbish one of the colony's original starships, and they would travel to a distant rendezvous point where Belters were carving up an asteroid, building one of the swiftest starships ever built. On her arrival, she and her loyal machines planned to offer their services as trained engineers and as hundreds of willing hands; and if the captains were rational souls, Aasleen would be welcomed into their grand adventure.

But her parents didn't want her to leave. They believed this mission of hers was an idiotic business, dangerous and without gain, and they didn't wish to lose the daughter who had brought them a delicious local fame. And because they were parents, they used guilt and every awful trick, shamelessly trying to make their only child surrender her dreams.

But ten months later, and despite their best efforts, Aasleen left the teary, anguished home, never to return.

Two centuries later, she and her loyal machines were serving on a historic starship. The retrofitted asteroid was named for a bird of legend—*Olympus Peregrine*. Rough quarters were set between cavities jammed full of metallic hydrogen, and the hydrogen fed five enormous engines, each boosted by antimatter and hyperfiber accentors. The ship was only beginning its long, dangerous journey out of the galaxy. And in that moment of glory and great danger, a brief message arrived from home.

Aasleen's mother said, "Hello, darling," with a tight, bitter voice.

Beside her sat Aasleen's father, happier than he had ever looked, and with a fond hand, he was patting the back of a small, very handsome boy of perhaps ten years, or eleven.

"His name is Rococo," her mother explained.

Then with a menacing smile—the kind of look that only the most determined parent can achieve—she added, "We've told him about his sister. He knows all there is to know about you, darling."

–III–

Humans were first to reach the Great Ship, and they discovered that it was ancient and utterly empty. They claimed the treasure for themselves—a legal act according to the galaxy's salvage laws. The vessel was theirs to do with as they wished, and after some debate among the captains and considerable work by the overtaxed engineers, the Ship's giant engines were ignited, perhaps for the first time. Nozzles the size of moons flung plasmas into the cold emptiness, and the Great Ship dove near a blue-white dwarf star that graciously bent its course, throwing it into a useful line that eventually carried it into the nearest of the galaxy's spiral arms.

That's when the Master Captain began to sell berths onboard their wondrous prize.

Every species was welcome. At least that was the general promise. But the captains greedily retained the right to refuse an alien who might prove violent, either toward humans or to the other, more responsible passengers. And passage onboard the Great Ship was never free. This was to be a 500,000-year voyage around the Milky Way, and the ultimate goal—unstated but obvious—was to enrich human beings through the acquisition of wealth and colony worlds, raw materials and rich cultural connections.

By the time they'd slipped back inside galaxy, Aasleen and the other engineers had generally mastered the Great Ship's timeless machinery. Most of the cavernous chambers remained dark and empty, but it would always be a simple matter to configure each volume to suit the needs of alien biologies. What was harder was deciding which creatures to accept, and even more difficult, determining how many of them and for what exceptional but fair price.

The Scypha were going to be one of the early conundrums.

A young captain explained the situation to his chosen crew. "These creatures live in a three-sun system. Their home star is K-class, with millions of asteroids and only one substantial world. There's also an M-class star traveling in a long elliptical orbit, plus a G-class sun that's practically next door. It's that last sun that interests us. It has a jovian-class world orbiting neatly in its biosphere, accompanied by several massive moons. None of those moons have significant life today. But with minimal expense, human colonists could terraform three of them."

Hazz was the captain's name—a pleasant, gracious and genuinely liked officer rumored to be enjoying a hard boost up to the Submaster ranks.

"My mission," said Hazz. Then he paused, grinning to a small room jammed with carefully selected souls. "Our mission, I mean. Yours and mine. Is to take one of our old starships on a visit to the Scypha. Onboard teams will include scientists and diplomats. The scientists will have three years to study our gracious hosts, and our diplomats will have the same three years to cobble together a worthwhile agreement. What we want is legal title to the jovian world and all of its moons. What we'll settle for is something less, but that's for the diplomats and Master Captain to determine. And what the Scypha want—what they have told us in our initial contacts—is their own modest habitat somewhere onboard the Great Ship."

The "old starship" was the *Olympus Peregrine*. No wonder Hazz was plucking her away from her routine duties, or so she assumed. Nobody knew the ship's engines better than she did—their capacities and histories and genuine limits—and in the mysterious ways of engineers, she had a natural feeling for the ship's difficult but rewarding personality.

A hand rose up in the front row, and with a nod from Hazz, the first question was asked.

"What sort of species is the Scypha?"

"I could give you a partial answer," Hazz replied. "But I promised I wouldn't. Really, there are better voices for that."

The captain glanced to his right, nodding once.

A tall figure strode into the room. With her first glance, Aasleen felt an instant and deep, almost painful connection. The man's appearance played a role. He shared Aasleen's build, long in the body, with sturdy limbs and a precise, determined way of marching forward. And like Aasleen, the visitor's skin was as black as human tissue could be. But immigrants were coming from every colony world now, and plenty of them demanded protection from UV light. The coincidence was tiny. And what if their faces shared the same oval form, elegant and smooth, and what if their teeth were a buttery yellow and their eyes set far apart? Maybe this fellow came from her gene pool, but even that wouldn't be much of a coincidence. By now, hundreds of the crew, if not thousands, shared that left-behind world with her.

Hazz whispered his welcomes. Then he turned to his future crew, explaining that their distinguished guest was an exobiologist as well as a member of the diplomatic corps, and by the way, his name was "Rococo" and these were his various ranks.

When Aasleen heard the name, she stopped listening.

Their guest was carrying a small hyperfiber satchel. He set it down and graciously thanked the captain, and then with a bright, inescapable charm, he turned to his audience and delivered a well-rehearsed lecture about the curious origins of the Scypha. He spoke about their nature and incredible numbers and their obvious potential. But Aasleen was barely listening, studying records yanked through an array of nexuses, reconstructing the man's life from this moment backwards to that distant point in space and in time when their shared mother gave birth to him.

"To the Scypha," claimed Rococo, "there's no such thing as a species."

What was that?

He showed his audience a thousand distinct body types, each adapted to low-gee conditions or pure freefall. Every last body was different from the others in highly unpredictable ways. Yet to Scypha eyes, every organism was the same. No matter its size or its architecture, each belonged to a single shared and decidedly holy lineage.

"The Scypha are not one species, or a million species," Aasleen's little brother explained. "What they are is one distinct line of totipotent cells. Each cell can live alone, subsisting on minimal food and water. But in times of wealth, those same cells will grow and divide, and thousands or trillions of them will join together, forming elaborate bodies."

He paused for a moment, and then asked, "But why take this path for life? Because the Scypha evolved in an extraordinary environment—a world with a special, perhaps even unique history. But many thousands of years ago, the Scypha achieved space flight, and they immediately colonized their system's extensive asteroid belts. This is the environment where they have prospered, I should add. If you make a rough count of the sentient cellular conglomerates, their total population is in excess of one and a half trillion bodies."

Selected images were fed into Aasleen's public nexuses. She saw comets wrapped in monomolecular bags and lit up with hot fusion torches. Silica-rich asteroids were turned to slag and pulled into elaborate shells, transparent and filled with warm, bright air. Orbiting close to the orange-white K-class sun was a dense belt of iron-rich bolides, unpopulated but actively mined for their precious ores. And between the Iron Ring and Stone Ring was an empty zone where a single moonless world moved in a circular orbit. With perhaps half the mass of the Earth, the rocky gray sphere sat inside a deep dirty atmosphere, under which lay shallow seas and silted lakes and great ringed basins, as well as hundreds of sharp, relatively small craters formed over the last million years.

"This is the Scyphas' birthplace," Rococo explained. Then with a broad, intense smile, he added, "It is utterly amazing, when you consider . . . when you calculate . . . when you look at the odds that multicellular life would evolve on such a body, in a solar system as dangerous as this. And not only did life evolve in this unlikely womb, but it's still alive. It can even thrive, on occasion. Which is startling when you consider that every few thousand years, on average, some fat bolide kicked out from the Rings ends up impacting here—blistering, apocalyptic events on par with those that killed the dinosaurs, and before that, obliterated all of the multicellular creatures on ancient Mars . . ."

The declaration earned a prolonged silence.

Then one hand rose. It was a thick black hand wearing on its fingertips the hard callus presently fashionable among engineers—as if the hand had been toughened up by actual physical labor.

Rococo nodded. "Yes, Aasleen."

She stood. Her intention was to greet her brother. She planned to say: "Welcome, and I didn't know you were onboard, and by the way, how are our parents?" In a very public way, she wanted to define their relationship as being distant. She would admit to everyone that she didn't even know that they were riding the same starship together. But of course it was an enormous vessel, and they had very different duties. And wasn't it her young brother's responsibility to contact her upon his arrival?

Yet when Aasleen finally spoke, unexpected words ran from her mouth.

"I'm curious," she said. "Do the Scypha live on their home world today?"

"No," Rococo replied, his grin turning wary but his eyes smiling.

"Yet they definitely came from there?"

He nodded. "About half a million years ago, there was a period—a unique period—of fifty or sixty thousand years. There were no major impacts. Just a few showers of two- and three-kilometer asteroids. In other words, their home world was given a window of peace. And it was the great Scypha lineage that prospered well enough to develop the basic spaceship technologies."

Aasleen studied the images of that left-behind world. It appeared cold now, which was only reasonable. The world orbited its sun at an Earthly distance, but its sun was notably weaker than dear Sol. With an engineer's ease, she built a simple mental model of climate. Without the constant impacts, she realized—without a steady and reliable battering of two- and ten- and forty-kilometer bolides—that world would soon fall into a deep, impoverishing ice age.

"That world's name—?" she began.

"Pardon me?"

"Wait," she said, interrupting herself. "First, are there other lineages? And do they still live on the home world?"

Rococo couldn't have looked happier. "There are at least six hundred distinct lines of totipotent cells," he admitted. "Only the Scypha climbed out into space."

"And did all of the Scypha emigrate?"

The smile tightened, just a little. It was an expression Aasleen knew well, since it came across her face whenever she found herself in uncomfortable circumstances, unable to say everything that was in her mind.

What Rococo did say was, "Our alien hosts are presently extinct on their home world."

She started to nod.

"Chaos," he said.

"Pardon?"

"I think you were going to ask for the name of their birthplace. When translated, using the best of our methods, their language boils down to the word 'Chaos.'"

She squinted, considering the news.

"Chaos means danger to the Scypha. It means disasters that never arrive along expected avenues."

Everyone nodded, as if they understood the alien minds.

"Their home world is being held in quarantine," Rococo continued. "The Scypha want nothing to do with it. Nothing. Which is how it has been for the last several hundred thousand years."

Honestly confused, Aasleen asked the expert, "Why?"

Her brother offered no simple answer. He made a show of shrugging his shoulders, reminding the entire audience, "We'll have three years to decipher meanings and reach our best judgments. Will the Scypha make good passengers? And will they pay a reasonable fee for the privilege?" Again, he shrugged. "Speaking as an exobiologist, I have to warn everyone against premature guessing or biasing notions."

"That sounds very diplomatic," Aasleen replied, laughing softly.

Rococo chuckled with a diplomat's grace. Then he threw a knowing wink in her direction, saying, "The politics of a family can be very difficult."

"No," Aasleen countered.

"You don't think so–?"

"Families are simple," she remarked. "Just so long as they aren't your own family, that is."

-**IV**-

The Scypha built spaceships much as they built themselves: Mechanical embryos were generated, each containing the guiding principles used in every ship in their enormous fleet. But the growth of each vessel was a chaotic, wildly unpredictable business. If a hundred identical embryos were instructed to form slow freighters of a specific size, no two vessels ended up with identical schematics. To a human engineer, such a system was both astonishing and terrifying. Aasleen would be the first to admit that Scypha machinery was astonishingly adaptive, tough and reasonably efficient. If necessary, their vessels could heal most damage with the resources on hand, and should one of their freighters need to update its shape and job, the transformation took remarkably little time. But no two freighters could reliably exchange components. Hull shapes and engine designs were full of quirks and one-of-a-kind features. And sometimes mistakes were made—catastrophic failures in design just waiting for the wrong moment to arrive—a grim possibility that Aasleen could never, ever accept.

On the other hand, human ships were always standardized and tenaciously, even dangerously reliable.

Rococo had no expertise as an engineer or a pilot. Yet he was able to learn enough about human-built shuttles to steal one of them, and without much trouble, he crippled the three sister shuttles remaining behind in the *Peregrine*'s dock.

"How long for repairs?" Hazz had asked.

"Twenty-three hours," was Aasleen's best guess. "That's for bringing all three ships back on line and refueling them, and that's assuming our colleague didn't sabotage their AI managers, too. Because if that's the case, it's going to take time to find that out, and then it could be three days, or four, until we can launch even one shuttle."

A captain's poise obscured what had to be a terrible rage. Hazz nodded and said nothing, considering the situation.

It was the chief diplomat who couldn't contain her emotions. "Your brother," she said twice, then twice again. "Where is your brother going? What in hell is your brother planning?" She was a young-faced woman named Krill. Little more than a child in appearance, she happened to be older than anyone else present. Thousands of years had been invested in a career that looked ready to shatter. "If we can't catch your brother soon," she declared, "then we'll have to tell the Scypha and let them corral your brother for us."

"If they can do that," Aasleen mentioned.

Krill grimaced and looked at their captain.

Hazz understood the situation clearly. But he thought it best to let Aasleen explain.

"My brother," she began, staring at the diplomat's smoke-colored eyes. "He took our best shuttle. It is exactly the same as these other three, except it has a secondary hull that can be reconfigured. I designed that hull, under direct orders from you, madam. It was early in the mission. We were planning for contingencies. And you suggested that we have at least one shuttle that could look rather like a Scypha ship. 'Just in case,' you said, madam. 'In case our hosts aren't as friendly or forthcoming as they should be. It would help if we could move among them, unseen.'"

The blood drained from the young face. Then a sorry old voice dribbled out, saying, "Now I really don't want to tell the Scypha."

"Is there any choice?" Aasleen asked.

"None," Hazz decided. Then with a crisp voice, he instructed the ranking diplomat, "Confess everything we know, and everything we can reasonably guess. No secrets here. Do you understand me? But make certain that Rococo wears the majority of the blame."

●●●

For the next twenty-three hours, Aasleen went about her business, overseeing repairs and managing one delicious fifteen-minute nap. She also listened to every rumor and examined the official updates for anything that might prove illuminating, and several times she caught glimpses of the resident Scyphas. For nearly a year now an alien delegation had been living onboard the starship. They were high-ranking members of a government council that seemed to wield considerable power. For reasons of civility or simple functionality, they had grown bodies not too unlike the human form—bipeds with single heads and single mouths, a pair of hemispherical eyes made from calcite crystals. They usually kept to their own little portion of the ship. Which made it unnerving to see them drifting through the dock, one by one, their glassy eyes staring at the broken shuttles and the AI's that were repairing them, and in particular, studying the chief engineer who was trying to do her job while ignoring all the damned rumors that kept finding their way to her.

In the end, it was determined that Rococo hadn't damaged the AI managers. But that didn't particularly matter. With a full day's jump on ships that were no faster than his, he had already won every likely race.

Other solutions were needed. Aasleen was already working on

contingencies when Hazz called her to his quarters. Nursing the assumption that every rumor was wrong, she went there. With an intensity that made her exceptionally good at her job, she entered the captain's meeting room with three different plans ready to offer him. Even when she saw the entire Scypha delegation drifting around the central table, she refused to accept the obvious explanation. Through a nexus, she fed her captain the latest update of the repairs. Then she told him and Krill, "I think we can see through his camouflage. And if we find him, we'll use our own com-laser to cripple his shuttle. From a distance, nice and neat."

Hazz thanked her on a private nexus. But the rumors proved generally correct. Krill spoke for both humanity and the Scypha. "Our hosts are outraged by what your brother has done," she told Aasleen. "They are outraged and appalled. They believe, and now we agree, that Rococo has been in secret contact with one or more of the non-Scypha lineages. For what purpose, we do not know. Yet. But he has acted against every order that I have given and every code that our captain has set down as law. And since he is ours—a body that belongs to our great lineage—we must send one of our own into the hunt. Because, as our hosts make plain, that is what justice demands."

Aasleen glanced at the bright-eyed aliens, then at Hazz.

"I've considered every crew member for this assignment," her captain explained. "We've had a few volunteers drift forward, which has been gratifying. But there isn't much doubt about who is the best qualified. Is there, Aasleen?"

She had to shake her head, admitting, "No, there probably isn't."

Then she mentioned the most obvious difficulty. "What about a ship for me? Since we don't have anything that can actually catch him—"

"A fully loaded deuterium freighter is soon to pass." The voice was a little too loud and precise. "Within a thousand kilometers of this place, it will pass." The speaker was a smallish biped with a yellowish-green skin. Regardless of their body form, the Scypha retained a photosynthetic surface. It was a tradition and a consequence of their complex genetics: Under the proper circumstances and given the necessary resources, any one of these creatures could collapse into a trillion cells, and from those anonymous pieces, an entire jungle of organisms would spring forth.

"The freighter is changing its nature now," the Scypha promised. "Its ion-drive is being replaced by three fusion engines, and its body is creating a small but comfortable cabin for its guest. For you."

"Am I the pilot?" she asked.

"No," Hazz replied, fully expecting that question.

Then the human diplomat pointed a stiff finger at Aasleen. "You will go where you need to go. Particularly if your brother manages to reach places where our good hosts cannot intrude."

Chaos was the implication.

"But about my brother," Aasleen began. Then she hesitated, wondering if she should say what she was thinking.

"A creature of your blood," said the ranking Scypha.

"Except I don't know him particularly well," Aasleen admitted. And just to be sure that everyone understood the situation, she quickly explained the histories of their unshared lives.

"But he is of your blood," the creature insisted. Then the alien mouth attempted a smile, and it said to her and to every human, "You know him exceptionally well, or you know nothing at all."

●●●

Aasleen made herself ready for the mission, packing a few belongings in a field kit and studying her grim orders in detail. As soon as she was ready, she would ride one of the newly repaired shuttles out to an empty point in space where it would rendezvous with the promised freighter/hunter ship. The last word was that Rococo had vanished completely. But now the Scypha were actively searching for him, using tricks that Aasleen had surrendered willingly, and surely he couldn't remain hidden for much longer.

Only an idiot would believe he could escape this sort of attention.

But she knew Rococo was not an idiot, which led her mind to travel in new, equally painful courses.

Obviously, he had more tricks waiting.

"And I'll have to be ready for them," she muttered to herself, leaving her quarters with her kit in tow.

A single Scypha was drifting in the wide hallway outside her door. It was wearing a loose-fitting gown and gecko shoes and the same yellow-green flesh that all of them possessed. But it was definitely not the delegate who had spoken at the meeting. Its voice was identical, but the body had more height and many more ribs, and the arms had extra joints for no sensible reason.

That familiar voice said, "Listen to me."

Aasleen touched the floor with her own shoes, killing her momentum.

"About us, what you know is not enough."

She couldn't agree more. "I'm just an engineer. Most of my friends are machines. Human beings are often too complicated for me."

But that wasn't apparently the creature's point. Its face twisted around a squarish skull, and the lidless calcite eyes absorbed every photon, giving it the nearly perfect vision that the Earth surrendered when the trilobites went extinct. Then after a long, thoughtful silence, it asked Aasleen, "Which is more complicated? The shape of a body, or the shape of a mind?"

She hesitated.

Then it asked, "If I look like no one else, how can one trillion minds think precisely the same as any single mind does?"

And then that very peculiar creature turned its back on her, and on gecko toes, practically ran away.

–V–

The engines were firing again, this time killing some portion of their terrific momentum. Aasleen was strapped into her crash chair, a thousand invisible hands pressing down. On her orders, the bioglass walls had been left as transparent as gin, and when she wasn't studying the Scypha and their long history, she would gaze out at the graceless, doomed ship. Its fuel tanks were black cylinders mostly drained now of their precious deuterium, and strung between them was a maze of pipes and pumps constructed from diamond and other soft materials. Three reaction chambers were woven from a low-grade hyperfiber, each chamber barely restraining the tiny sun burning inside. The newly constructed heat shield was vast and insubstantial–a stubborn cloud of carbon soot braced with nanowhiskers. Out of habit, Aasleen would stare beyond the engines, searching for Chaos; but the world was still hiding beyond the plasma plumes. Only between the black fuel tanks could she make out the blackness of empty space. Occasionally the Scypha sun would peek in at her, filling her cabin with a blinding light, and sometimes she caught a glimpse of its sister star and the lone silver speck beside it–the giant jovian world maintaining a loyal distance. And the outer Rings were always visible somewhere, appearing as smoky bands of glowing greenish haze. There were millions of tiny worlds, most of them rich with life, linked to each other by com-lasers and trade lanes, by leaked air and lost water, by culture and eternal genetics. For tens of thousands of years, the Scypha had ruled a gigantic realm. Yet they never built any kind of starship or even sent an asteroid drifting off into the interstellar wilderness. And there was absolutely no evidence that they ever, even on the tiniest scale, tried to colonize the jovian's empty moons.

At least two ships were on a rendezvous course with Aasleen. One of the human shuttles had been given permission to slowly approach Chaos, and a swift Scypha drone was charging straight toward her, nothing onboard but Rococo's left-behind satchel.

She wished that she had the satchel in her hands now, giving her time to crack its seals and study its contents. And more important, giving her an excuse to do something other than study.

But there were no excuses. With her single nexus, Aasleen reached deep into her data vault, picking random studies and learned papers, teaching herself a little more about the Scyphas and their home world. Yet even the knowledge of experts was far from perfect; exobiologists agreed on little but their own ignorance. And despite weeks of reading and contemplation, Aasleen was still barely a novice who could follow maybe half of any text, asking little questions when they occurred to her—clumsy questions answered easily by the vault's AI, or countered with a simple, "That is not known," response.

She was reading about Scypha politics when Hazz suddenly appeared to her mind's eye.

"It's almost certain now," the message began. "The ship that grabbed up Rococo has been traced back to the Iron Ring. That's where it first appeared, and it was pretending to be a drone bringing up a load of refined metals. It didn't change its shape or programming until he crash-landed on the asteroid. And everybody is equally sure that a few hours ago that new ship touched down on Chaos. On the eastern shore of the central ocean, we're sure. Our telescopes saw it smack into the atmosphere, and our hosts are reporting the same observation." He paused, just for a moment. "But I don't need to remind you that our esteemed colleague might not have been on board."

Wearing a hyperfiber lifesuit, the human body could drop hard almost anywhere. Its descent would look like a meteorite, and since thousands of little impacts occurred every minute, there was no way to be certain about Rococo's destination.

"But at least you can try to pick up the trail there," Hazz continued. "Follow him as best you can. Our hosts have assured us that all of the local lineages will be helpful. Or at least, they will not get in your way."

She sighed, barely relieved.

"And maybe there's some more luck coming," Hazz continued. "As it happens, the dominant lineage is an ally to the Scypha. At least as much of an ally as you're going to find . . ."

The man's face said more than any words. Hazz looked worried, suspicious and only grudgingly hopeful. It was an expression that an alien probably couldn't read—even if the encryptions and other seals were broken.

"The Dun," he said.

A thousand entries in her data vault began to glow with a soft pink light.

"They're closely related to the Scypha lineage. At least that's what our scientists are claiming."

Hazz paused once again, pretending to gather his thoughts.

But he knew exactly what he wanted to say. Quietly, with genuine warmth, he told Aasleen, "I am sorry. If I could have found a better candidate, you would have stayed here with me. This isn't your profession, and these are awful circumstances, and I won't remind you again about the time factors involved."

Successful or otherwise, their mission had to end in just a few weeks. Otherwise it would be difficult for their starship, even with healthy engines and full tanks of metallic hydrogen, to catch up to the Great Ship.

Hazz shook his head angrily. "It seems obvious. For whatever reason, Rococo is trying to ruin everything."

Aasleen nodded.

"This isn't your normal work," he said. Then he pushed a hand through his kinky hair, adding, "But this isn't a job for diplomats either. Or biologists. Or anyone else who happens to be under my command."

In reflex, Aasleen reached along her nexus, taking a quick inventory of the traveling kit that was lying beneath her crash chair.

"None of this is fair," said Hazz. "But Rococo has gone to a place where he isn't allowed. And you're the best hope we have to solve this ugly conundrum."

Inside that kit were a variety of useful machines—exactly the types of devices that a talented engineer would want in reach, including a powerful plasma torch that could chisel through hyperfiber or, if necessary, boil the brains of the luckiest man to ever live.

"Good hunting," the captain said to his assassin.

Then he vanished, and Aasleen purged the message while leaving the Dun files highlighted. And again she began skimming random texts, reading those parts that seemed most important, asking questions when they occurred to her and swallowing every urge to scream or sob, or worst of all, just give up the fight and fall back to sleep.

–VI–

Most experts were of one mind: The *Olympus Peregrine*–the retrofitted asteroid that first carried humans out to the Great Ship–would impress and possibly astonish their alien hosts. The Scypha often rebuilt bolides even larger than the *Peregrine*, and with mass-drivers and crude fusion engines, they could manage the orbits of their little worlds. But the aliens didn't possess high-grade hyperfiber, nor did they know the big cheats necessary to build a functional stardrive. In general, the diplomats and exobiologists were extraordinarily proud of their vessel. It was an historic machine and it possessed a burnished beauty, and to humans everywhere, it was an enduring symbol of everything that was good and noble about human achievement.

Aasleen had a rather different estimate of their aging starship. Good fortune was at least as important as good engineering when the *Peregrine* made its famous journey out to the Great Ship. A tiny voyage to the Scypha still consumed almost thirty years. And for the chief engineer, their mission felt more like a single intense, unbroken day jammed with work and major crises, plus three genuine disasters involving the ship's increasingly problematic engines. To reach the aliens in their home system, the *Peregrine* needed to race ahead of the Great Ship while dropping through the plane of the Milky Way. To make their mission possible, they had to push fast enough so that they could afford to slow down again, lingering in one location for three lazy years. And assuming that humans and the Scypha achieved a workable understanding, then the *Peregrine* wouldn't just have to make the return voyage, but it would also have to bring home a few thousand Scypha– enough bodies and grown minds to build a functional colony somewhere onboard the Great Ship.

But return voyages were never guaranteed. While they were still inbound, Aasleen met with Hazz and his immediate staff, showing them projections and models, hard numbers and soft gloomy numbers. Then as a final touch, she set a worn valve in front of her captain. It had been poured from the finest hyperfiber ever made by humans, but that was several thousand of years ago.

She pointed to the telltale darkening, the alarming marks of fracturing deep inside the normally invincible material. Point-blank, she explained that only two engines were reliable enough to be counted on. What's more, those two engines were divided among the five present engines. "In other words," she said, "I'm going to have to cannibalize all five just to make two, which leaves me needing to build three new engines just to give us a fair chance of returning home."

Hazz's face grew soft and sorry. Then with a sober voice, he asked, "What exactly are you proposing?"

She explained herself. The conundrum wasn't a surprise, and her solution shouldn't have been, either. But it took Hazz several hours to study the concepts, and several more days to embrace what she wanted to do with their historic machine. A complete renovation of the starship was called for. Hyperfiber factories and fresh reactors would have to be built wherever there was room. And all of that work had to be accomplished on the proverbial fly, using the inadequate tools on hand. Boast all you want about human genius, Aasleen argued, but the grim, inglorious truth was that their species was close to drowning here. Obviously, better and faster ships were going to have to be built in the future. What the captains were proposing to do on a regular basis—carry endless populations of strange organisms to a world-sized starship where crew and passengers would live in splendid peace—was going to need a lot more work before it would even approach a state that smelled remotely routine.

During those next months and years, Aasleen rarely saw her brother. But it seemed as if every twenty-four hours, she would talk to a person or two who mentioned Rococo. The diplomat/exobiologist often gave briefings to the crew, and he ate frequently with Hazz; or most likely, the affable fellow would pass someone in a hallway, and just to be pleasant, he would strike up a brief but memorable conversation.

Unlike his sister, Rococo was an intensely social organism, and better than most, he was good at it. Bring up his name, and faces would smile instantly. Ask why, and the most retiring engineer or simplest AI-worker would replay a conversation word for word.

Not that anything important was ever said, Aasleen noted. Rococo could speak buoyantly about the shallowest subjects. He was amusing at times, but never more than that. It astonished her, this popular hold that her brother held on the hundreds of people they were traveling with–people she knew by name and face, some of them counted among her friends. But none of them were so thrilled by her attentions that they would stop her brother in the middle of his important work, distracting him by saying, "Oh, I saw your sister today. What a fun, good person Aasleen is!"

And Rococo was a fun, good person. He was also exceptionally skilled at managing his sister's emotions–knowing how often to meet with her, and for how long, and always finding the sweetest way to orchestrate the event so that both of them felt as close to comfortable as possible.

Wisely, Rococo never brought up their parents or the distant home world. That duty was left in Aasleen's lap.

And when she asked about his childhood–how could she not?– the man sitting before her always put on a careful face, measuring his words and muting their tone before offering any response.

The world Aasleen remembered was gone. Rococo often described a planet transformed by human hands. Her gossamer smart-tent proved to be just a brief step on the way to larger adventures. By the time he had emigrated, the entire atmosphere was fully oxygenated, the continents were covered with soil made from comet crusts and ocean muck and the latest crop of engineers were busily draping a tough monomolecular curtain over the entire world–a much larger version of Aasleen's tent, its central purpose being to filter out the blistering UV light.

Aasleen was disappointed, and she didn't mind saying so.

"We weren't born on the Earth," she pointed out. "And we had the means on hand to adapt to these hazards. The UV is something we could easily tolerate."

"That's absolutely true," he said without hesitation.

"And our engineered flora and fauna . . . they were going to depend on the hard radiation . . . rich free energy to bolster the biosphere's productivity." She looked at her hands, ancient feelings emerging. "We agreed. Before I left, votes were taken, and the colonists decided to let the planet stay as alien as possible . . . to force us to meet it at some good and worthy middle point . . ."

Her brother nodded amiably, his face sharing her disgust. But later, replaying the conversation in her mind, she noticed that Rococo avoided the opportunity to come out and say, "Yes, you are right, sister. I'm on your side here."

Because he didn't agree with her, she realized. Nor did he agree with the vote, either.

"What about my tent?" she asked.

His eyes widened while his mouth pulled into a small knot.

"Is anything left of it?"

Rococo shook his head. Then with another expression of diplomatic disgust, he admitted, "The entire structure was dismantled for scrap."

Aasleen wasn't particularly vain by nature. But this was a pivotal event in her life, which was why she had to ask, "But is there some little statue, maybe? A monument, a plaque? Anything to let people know?"

"People know," he promised. "It's part of our history, of course."

"History," she echoed. Then with a scorn that took both of them by surprise, she admitted, "I was hoping for a little more than some cryptic notes in a dusty historical file . . . as forgotten as most everything else, I suppose . . ."

Rococo was charming and soothing, and in ways few souls could match, he could deftly step into difficult circumstances, creating a kind of peace. But he had an even more unusual gift: With his sister, and perhaps with other difficult souls, he knew that sometimes it was best not to attempt peace. These were very old feelings of Aasleen's, which made them exceptionally stubborn. And even at their worst, the feelings were harmless, and by nature, silly, and if he let her spout on, they quickly lost their teeth and fury.

The siblings' last social engagement was a late night meal for the entire crew. The *Peregrine* was halfway rebuilt, the most difficult jobs already completed. By chance or by planning, Aasleen found herself sitting next to her brother, sharing the back corner of the ship's largest galley. His journal was beside him—a portable slab of plastic encased in a diamond sleeve. He never touched it, but he didn't put it into the satchel, either. Much later, replaying the moment, Aasleen could appreciate how her little brother had played her. Very softly, he mentioned receiving a note from their mother. The woman was constantly sending digitals and little messages to her much-loved son, and that always bothered Aasleen. She bristled at the news. As he knew she would, she began to offer the usual disparaging words about being dead to her home world. But this time, for the first time, Rococo interrupted her. With a convincing voice, he mentioned, "You know, you're doing enormous work now. These things you're involved in . . . these are adventures far more important than terraforming an obscure colony world. For instance, just this one mission of ours . . . the future history of an entire species is being determined here. And you, Aasleen . . . you are playing a pivotal role in the drama . . ."

She saw the mistake in his words. But instead of correcting him, she shrugged and stabbed into her grilled eland.

"You know," Rococo said. Then he fell silent.

"What do I know?"

He threw a wink at her and warned, "I won't be here much longer. The diplomatic corps will come and go as necessary. But until our last couple of months, I plan to live among the Scypha. Full-time, on various worlds."

The wall beside them wore images harvested from around the solar system. The Rings were highlighted, the largest and most important asteroids glowing green. She glanced at them and the simple gray speck that was Chaos. Nodding, she asked, "Are you giving tonight's briefing?"

That was the reason for this gathering. All but a skeleton staff was sitting in the galley, waiting to hear the latest news about their mission.

"I'll say a few words," Rococo mentioned.

"Because I can't stay," she admitted. "I've got a rocket nozzle to inspect. And there's a diagnostic that's turning up new problems."

"Are we in trouble?" he asked.

"No worse than usual." She set down her knives and dabbed her lips with a piece of sticky ice. "It's just that we're going to be asking a lot out of engines that are either well past their prime or too new to trust . . ."

She let her voice trail away.

Rococo nodded, as if he understood all of her burdens.

Then he touched the wall–touched it low and brought up the menu–and without a word of explanation, he asked for an image of Chaos.

Aasleen was thinking about slipping away. Had she shown her face long enough? Would Hazz or his staff put a black mark on her record? Then came a flash in the corner of her eye–a soundless, brilliant and enduring light–and she turned in time to watch a blister of plasma rising from the shore of an alien sea.

The image was ancient, or it was invented. Either way, she realized that she was witnessing an event that had happened perhaps a million times in the past. An asteroid or lost comet had plunged onto that battered world, vaporizing the entire sea and melting a portion of the crust, producing a shockwave that burned up every organic body that happened to be trapped on the surface.

Four billion years ago, this was the Earth.

She and her brother had spoken about this many times. Or rather, Rococo had made the noise, and she had listened, interested in what he was saying even when she already knew the details.

Nobody could say for sure how many times life evolved on the Earth.

But in the early eons, when hundred-kilometer bolides were falling like rain, the ancient ocean was repeatedly boiled off and the crust turned to magma, and even the toughest little bugs were killed. Then later, when nothing larger than fifty kilometers was crashing down, life survived, but barely. Microbes found places to survive–usually in porous rock deep underground. The best guess was that by the bombardment's end, a single line of *Archaea*–the thermophilic bacteria–had endured the worst abuse, and it was that plucky survivor who was grandmother to every crawling, talking organic beast that managed to spring up on their cradle world.

But on Chaos, that bombardment had never ceased.

Grind up an earthly sponge into mush, and the individual cells would gradually migrate back together again, slowly forming another adult organism.

On a much grander scale, that was the course taken by Chaos.

Many lines of life had developed in its early history, and most of them evolved multicellular forms. But there were critical differences in their genetics and physiology as well as the makeup of individual cells. Far tougher than Precambrian worms, each of those early lineages left behind spores that would wait for the heat and fire to fade away. Then they would come alive again, growing in the wreckage and the warm springs. Eventually those tiny children would come together, killing and eating those that didn't belong to their particular lineage, while joining with the cells that did. Inside each viable nucleus was enough genetic information to put together a wide array of body plans. Sometimes the creatures were photosynthetic, and occasionally they looked like clumsy animals. The more successful lineages left the most spores. And since there was no way to know when the next asteroid would fall, or where, it was easy for evolution to move in a jerky, gloriously unpredictable fashion.

Watching Chaos endure the gigantic blast, Aasleen asked, "Is this what I'm going to miss? Are you briefing us about old history?"

Rococo shook his head. "No, not at all."

"Then why show this to me?"

"Because I think it's interesting," he allowed. "Of all the places I'm going to visit, all the wondrous sights I'll witness . . . there's no way for me to embrace the most interesting and important place of all."

Or course he couldn't visit Chaos. That cradle world was under a strict quarantine. And Aasleen could appreciate their hosts' reasons: Each lineage was embroiled in a constant struggle against every other lineage. This was not war. It was older and much vaster than any war, with much less chance of a lasting forgiveness. The Scypha had been lucky to escape from their home world, and it was only natural for them to keep their enemies out of reach.

But those muddy alien politics still didn't interest her. Rococo mentioned his interest in Chaos, and Aasleen nodded agreeably, thinking nothing more about it. Then after making an estimate of human politics, she decided to take this opportunity to float away.

But Rococo put his hand on top of hers, the gesture not quite gentle. "You were right, you know."

"About what?"

"Families," he said. "When you belong to a family, everything can seem like a spectacular mess."

She couldn't agree more.

"But when you stand apart, immune to personal histories and private passions . . . what matters most is perfectly easy to see . . ."

She hesitated.

Then quietly, she said, "Species."

"What's that?"

"When you were talking before," Aasleen began. "You mentioned that I was helping with something big. Something that would determine a species' future." Shaking a callused finger, she reminded him, "The Scypha don't have species. Not so we would recognize them, at least."

Rococo nodded, smiled.

Then he bent close and kissed his sister lightly on the cheek— he had never kissed her before, in any fashion—and whispering into her ear, he said, "But Aasleen, I wasn't talking about the Scypha. I was thinking about us."

–VII–

For three years, the gray face of the world was simple and unlovely—a tiny bland fleck of light barely worth a bare-eyed glance. But as Aasleen plunged toward that face, the world grew huge, and a multitude of complications were revealed, as well as a dirty, unpolished brand of beauty. Two seas showed themselves on the visible hemisphere—shallow round bodies of muddy water straddling the dawn line, the southern sea wearing a stubborn patch of early summer pack ice. Between the seas, delicate dust storms drifted across a cold flat desert. Volcanoes stood alone, dormant and possibly dead, while young glaciers flowed from their summits, grinding young rock into fresh eager dust. Peel away the world's dust, and what would be revealed was a landscape covered with overlapping pocks and blisters—the cumulative damage wrought by six billion years of tireless abuse. Like a plow turning soil, the impacts had shattered the crust down to the mantle. Without enough internal heat to generate tectonics, Chaos depended on those good hard blows. Just ten million years ago, a massive carbonaceous asteroid had blasted out a basin stretching most of a thousand kilometers across. The molten plain spouted fire and red-hot projectiles big as mountains. Every sea was boiled away, and a scalding rain began to fall. But after the rain cleared and once the rock froze again, warm water collected in the newborn crater, and life prospered in what was a sudden tropical climate, there and everywhere on Chaos. Titanic volumes of carbon dioxide and water ice and fossil methane had been kicked loose from the regolith, producing a sultry wet heat that was maintained by a gracious string of lesser impacts—the beginnings of a persistent, much-treasured golden age that had lasted, without serious pause, until just a few geologic moments ago.

Aasleen couldn't see the world with her eyes; the heat shield was positioned for impact. Through a live, unmagnified feed, she studied patches of vivid color emerging from the endless gray. From less than a thousand kilometers high, she could make out slivers of gold and violet, watery blue splotches and green dots in several distinct shades. Each color stood alone. Sun-facing slopes were popular, as were the rare river valleys. One giant shield volcano wore perhaps three dozen distinct oases—tiny, wholly unique communities huddled around hot springs or their tepid, fondly recalled remnants. And along the eastern shore of the largest sea, directly on the line she was following, ran a ribbon of pale yellow-green covering more ground than any other living zone, but still encompassing no more than fifty thousand square kilometers.

The Dun.

Strewn among Aasleen's scholarly references was every lecture delivered by her brother. Over the last several hours, she had studied any portion pertaining even slightly to that one patch of shoreline. No other lineage on Chaos was as closely related to the

Scypha. The fission came just ten million years ago, with the massive impact that brought on the golden age. Two isolated populations had emerged on opposite sides of the world, each quickly dominating their own hemisphere. Even today, the Dun remained the dominant force on the home world. They still had a functioning, vigorous biosphere. They wielded nuclear power and irrigation and other high technologies. And no other lineage could even pretend to build spaceships, which perhaps was why Rococo had invested the breath and time on the ill-understood entities.

Aasleen hadn't attended her brother's longest, best lecture. But she watched one moment at least ten times now: A crew member had lifted a hand and then stood to make his point. "I don't understand. One lineage succeeded masterfully, while its sibling accomplished what? Very little, from what I can tell. I mean, I'm sure that the Dun are quite comfortable on that beach. But what makes them so different from the Scypha?"

Rococo nodded patiently. And he threw his warmest, best smile out at everyone. Then with the nicest possible voice, he told the fellow, "You don't understand the situation at all."

It was a slight delivered with a diplomat's soothing voice.

The man slouched and agreed. "I guess I don't understand. Did I miss something? I'm sorry, if I did."

"If you can, think of it this way." Rococo winked slyly. "You're assuming that there was some pre-Scypha, pre-Dun lineage. A shared ancestor that divided into two. But this isn't like evolution on the Earth, sir. Not at all. One lineage has not changed from its ancestral beginnings, while the other is more of an upstart child than an equal sibling."

The galley was full of thoughtful, mystified faces.

"Which lineage is which?" the lecturer asked. Then with a big grin, he answered his question with another question. "Which one lives exactly as it always did? And which one has completely and forever walked away from home?"

❧❧❧

Two hundred kilometers above Chaos—at long last—a slight impact jostled Aasleen.

The swift little drone that had matched her course had just arrived, making a rough docking with her ship.

Her cabin's hatch came open with a soft hiss, a tiny wind pushing an envelope of pure, high-grade hyperfiber toward her. Grabbing one of the ruby-rope straps, she pulled the satchel close. Its various locks were left intact. The diplomatic seal was undisturbed. If anyone had tried tinkering with the mechanisms, she would see it now. But nobody had. Like a birthday girl, she shook the satchel side to side. Judging by the feel, a single object lay inside, and she couldn't imagine anything but Rococo's journal, abandoned for one reason. Or two, if her brother had anticipated this moment and wanted her to have his personal property.

But there wasn't time to look. Aasleen stowed the satchel beneath her chair, and once more, she studied her destination. What had been implied for several decades—what had been known but only occasionally mentioned during the last three years—was blatantly obvious to even the most indifferent audience now. Beneath her was a landscape composed of dust and frigid water, only a sprinkling of young impact craters staring back at her. Eons ago, once the Scypha had populated the various asteroid belts, they had learned how to predict the endless motions of every substantial bolide. Little nudges and the occasional hard shove were what kept those little worlds as their own. Collisions between the asteroids had fallen to nothing, and nothing substantial wandered free of the green Rings. And with their triumph, their home world was growing colder and drier, every failed lineage collapsing back into oases that might continue to live for a thousand years, or even another twenty million. But the inevitable day was steadily approaching. The gray world would become gray at every distance, and a traveler would see nothing alive, even as her ship began to slam into the first whiffs of atmosphere, bumping gently once before the truly hard shaking began.

–VIII–

Machines rose up to meet the falling machine.

Tiny, erosive devices, they struck the charred heat shield, burrowing into the seams and points of weakness. Hard pops were felt more than heard, shaped explosions creating a series of surgical gashes that swiftly peeled off the shield. Then a second wave of machines peppered the hull itself. Aasleen had just enough time to unfasten her straps and kick free of the crash chair, grabbing up her belongings with both hands. She held Rococo's satchel close to her stomach, her kit on her back. The Scypha ship was being wrenched apart around her, and now a third wave of machines—larger, more sophisticated models—grabbed each sliver and disabled component, measuring its composition before using acids and blistering heat to tear into everything. This was the antithesis of engineering: taking a sophisticated device and creating in its stead something utterly simple, fundamental and pure.

The bioglass cabin was the final target. Along a hundred lines, it shattered, and an instant later, Aasleen found herself surrounded by cold thin air, spinning heels over head through a rain of elemental particles.

After a few wild turns, she fell into the open.

Holding her tuck, she let her body settle on a point of balance. Her head was leading the way. With deep painful gasps, she clung to consciousness; but after a few minutes, the air thickened at least to where it wasn't a miserable struggle just to keep her mind clear.

The yellowish-green land lay beneath her. The forest was low and dense, every tree sporting one or two or three trunks and a tangle of branches. Wide blackish blocks of glass were scattered about the terrain—windowless structures that might or might not have been buildings, arranged without any obvious pattern. Curved spines of transparent glass rose up into the bright dusty sky. And the spines were moving, she realized. Like fingers possessing an infinite number of joints, they curled and reached, their tips diving into the canopy, grabbing up whatever was worth claiming from the treetops: sweet foods grown to feed the animal bodies, perhaps. Perhaps.

Every organism below her was a Dun. The individual tree was just one of the lineage's manifestations, the same as the animal-like creatures which ate the tree's fruits and leaves. If the Earth had evolved in a similar direction—if a single totipotent lineage had dominated land and sea—there wouldn't be such a thing as an ancestor. No close cousins or living parents, either. Humans and elands, walnuts and trilobites would be equal citizens embraced by a single community. And more to the point, there would be no such creature as a human, since every bipedal omnivore would be constructed in its own unique, never quite human way.

The engineering of the Dun and Scypha and all the other lineages was fascinating, and it was gorgeously complex. Every cell had a compressed, efficient genetic language. Once built, no gene was discarded, and no avenue of development could be forgotten. Which of course was the only way that such a plastic, thoroughly inspired system could work.

Aasleen continued falling toward the pale green forest. Even with the lower gravity, her velocity would shatter bones and possibly dislodge limbs. But humans didn't rely on sloppy old DNA any more. Repairs would begin instantly, disaster genes awakened from repositories scattered throughout her fractured body. There would be pain, sure. Pain was perhaps even more useful today than when people were sloppy mortals. But with a lucky bounce or two, she might be alive again in a few minutes and walking normally within the hour, and then the next phase of this ugliness could begin.

But as the air continued to thicken, a sturdy wind began to push her, and in the last few moments of her plunge, Aasleen was carried out over the thick whitish water of the sea.

Turning onto her back, her face pointed at the gray sky, she clenched her eyes shut as the pain suddenly took hold, fierce but brief.

The body died. For an instant, the shallow muddy water was pushed aside, and her momentum shoved the muck out of her way, and then the muck flowed back over her again. Aasleen's mind fell into a brief coma. Then a minute later, she was consuming fat by anaerobic pathways—metabolisms more ancient than oxygen, enlivened by new enzymes and a biochemistry full of modern efficiencies.

When her body found the strength, she tried to sit up. But the mud was deep and stubborn, and above it lay enough seawater to smother her again. She reached with her right arm, clinging to Rococo's satchel with her left. But the satchel felt different now. Lighter? No, heavier. The sealed flap had somehow come open, and mud and cold water had filled it up. But how could hyperfiber give up that easily? Then, just as she guessed the only likely answer, something grabbed her right hand as it pushed into the frigid water. Another hand was taking hold of hers, by the feel of it. A hand as cold as the sea, but possessing fingers and a helpful mood.

She was yanked up into a sitting position.

The air was still thin and unpleasantly chilled. Her first breaths found alien stinks and a rancid taste like none she had ever known. But her companion looked utterly human, down to the black face and bright eyes and an expression not too unlike a warm, familiar smile.

The creature could be Rococo.

But it wasn't. It was just an elaborate machine encased inside the native mud. A facsimile of a human had built from the cheapest material available. And when it said, "Hello, Sister," she could tell herself that it didn't sound at all like Rococo.

But it did.

"Do you know why they hated you for leaving?" the apparition asked, its wet face drawn around a mechanical mouth and diamond eyes. "Our parents were angry with you. For centuries, they were. And to a large measure, I suppose they still are. But when I emigrated for the Great Ship, it was a good and honorable adventure that I was embracing, and they wished me all the sweet fortune I could find.

"Do you know what was the difference between us, Aasleen?"

"No," she muttered.

"The distance between intense fury and furious pride." The machine lifted a sticky black hand, two fingertips clamped tightly together. "It is this much. It is this little. Those emotions are spectacularly close to being the same awful thing."

–IX–

"Where's my brother?"

With bright eyes, the machine regarded her for a speculative moment. Then the voice said, "Follow me," and her companion turned away, long legs pulling through the muck and shallow water.

Aasleen poured the slop out of Rococo's satchel, making sure nothing else was waiting inside. Then she collapsed its sides and stuffed it inside her own kit–a dirty sack woven from sapphire and spider silk–and with a touch, she told the kit to levitate and let her pull it by its handle.

The sea had no distinct shoreline, no defined edge. The water simply grew shallower and more turbid, and at some ill-defined point, there was more land than liquid beneath her. The tracks left by the machine appeared to be human footprints, bare with high arches and long toes, and the sculpted mud retained its shape, picking up excess mud until it became a bother. The machine finally paused where the land was almost dry, using fingers to clean between the toes. Aasleen was wearing field boots that cleaned themselves. She caught up and bent low, studying the entity's motions. The illusion of muscle clung to a human-shaped skeleton. Except for a mud-cloth hanging about its middle, the machine appeared naked. Watching it was like watching Rococo, down to the smallest flourish of the fingers. "Where is my brother?" Aasleen nearly asked again. But instead of a question, she said, "Harum-scarum."

The machine lifted its gaze, yellow teeth and a bright pink tongue showing inside the smile. "Yes?"

"You're one of their machines." Harum-scarums were a widespread species, ancient compared to humans and possessing quite a few technological tricks. They were among the first paying passengers onboard the Great Ship, grudgingly exchanging this kind of robot as a partial payment for their berths. "Harum-scarums model their own minds," she explained, "and then use their facsimiles for rituals and the most difficult jobs–"

"Yes."

"And for fun," she added.

"Isn't that what this is? Fun?" The machine straightened and began to walk toward the forest.

"That's not my point," Aasleen remarked, keeping on its left, using a similar stride. "Believe me, I know every last tool we brought with us. I've got the *Peregrine*'s full inventory in my head. And I don't remember anything about stockpiling harum-scarum tricks."

The machine offered nothing.

"Rococo brought you with him. Didn't he?"

The toothy smile seemed appreciative. "Is this important?"

"Yes," she said. "Because if he left the Great Ship carrying you—a secret machine stowed inside his personal gear—then he had a pretty clear idea that he'd need you. And that tells me plenty."

"I didn't know for sure that I would employ this," he told her.

"But you knew it was possible."

Silence.

She walked out in front of Rococo—that's how she thought of the machine now; it was the same as her brother—and with an accusing tone, she said, "When I first saw you, at that initial briefing on the Great Ship . . . you already had a very clear idea of what you were going to do here . . ."

"I simply knew what was possible," her brother replied.

"Before we boarded the *Peregrine*, you visited the harum-scarum district and purchased a facsimile, and then you had to pay somebody an additional fortune to have it reconfigured for our species and your mind. Since you couldn't have done either job yourself, my guess is."

The first traces of vegetation were decidedly ordinary. They might have been an earthly grass starved of nutrients, left yellow and a little thin on the crusted surface of the sun-baked mud. Aasleen looked at the plants and the bright forest beyond, and then she glanced over her shoulder. The sun lay close to the horizon, the empty mud flat and smooth, marred only by two sets of determined tracks. "The water level dropped recently," she observed.

Rococo squinted, lips pursing.

"The Dun are heating the water," she guessed.

"Are they? How?"

"They drained off the top meter of this sea. No, wait. The bottom meter would be better. Easier. They'll drop the coldest, oxygen-poor water into subterranean chambers and let the world's heat percolate into it, and then they bring the warm water up again to irrigate and moderate the local climate."

The yellow smile was encouraging, the voice thrilled. "You know, this is exactly what I promised them."

"What is?"

"That you're an exceptional talent. A gifted thinker, with a rare set of instincts." Rococo's voice practically sang when he told her, "I promised them the very best mind for a difficult job. And the fact that you are practically in my personal lineage was an added benefit, naturally."

But Aasleen couldn't stop thinking about seawater and heat. "But it's just a temporary measure," she allowed. "Every liter of warmed water is going to bleed more heat away from the deep crust."

"Naturally."

They had passed the grassy shoreline, entering a volume of shaded air—cool damp air still barely thick enough to be breathed normally. The jungles on a million worlds were not too different from this one. Trees of different heights and different ages stood around them—variations on a common theme built along the same photosynthetic system and unvarying metabolisms. There were animals wrapped around traditional architectures, including insects and worms, limbless and many-legged, and there were big-eyed climbers that had awakened themselves for the chance to see an alien and alien machine stroll past their nesting sites. But even the same essential creatures had differences. If there were two six-limbed monkeys, one sported a thick green fur while its companion had a feathery covering. The eyes held different positions, as did the mouths and large nostrils. Only one lineage ruled here—a single grand and plastic and multitudinous species—that was too inventive to produce the same body-plan twice in succession. Endless inspiration was wrapped around the same unchanging set of instructions. And despite the genetic similarities, this was not the Scypha. The Dun was something else, smaller but equally as remarkable. What Aasleen had known intellectually for several years was suddenly gnawing at her, and she found herself stopping in the chilled sunshine of an open glade, feeling a deep disquiet, unable to ignore the emotion any longer.

Rococo's voice called off into the shadows, telling watchful souls to step forward and have their own look.

Intelligent Dun emerged on all sides.

They were bipeds, more than not. Perhaps they looked halfway human in order to honor their guest. More likely, they were a convenient form taken from what organic life had to offer. Some had many eyes, others just one. A few bodies sported two heads, while many more had their faces buried in their chests. Hands and hand-like feet were grown to serve very precise jobs. But every hand was lifted up now, extended and flattened, an endless array of fingers held erect, the gesture looking utterly human.

An open-hand sign of peace, Aasleen assumed.

The Dun was inventive and persistent, yes. But its world was cooling off, probably faster every year. Yet wasn't this state of affairs perfectly natural? Each of these bodies would leave behind viable spores, trillions of them hiding in the deep dusts and the glacial ice. And just one hypercompetent spore knew enough to resurrect the Dun, once conditions changed for the better.

Which would be when?

Aasleen was thinking about all of it. Problems and solutions. What was easy, and what was nearly impossible. Then quietly, she said, "If the Scypha never let the asteroids fall, what happens here?"

"But you know that answer already," the Rococo facsimile said.

Then something else that should have been obvious occurred to Aasleen. She straightened her back and swallowed, and then she had no choice but laugh at herself and everyone else.

The Dun faces regarded her with their bright, unreadable eyes.

It was the machine beside her that seemed intrigued, smiling for a long moment before asking, "What is it, Sister?"

"Nothing," she lied.

"Are you certain?"

Aasleen nodded, telling her companion, "Let's keep walking. Keep talking. And by the way, are you taking me to my real brother?"

"Perhaps," said the diplomat's voice. "Perhaps."

–X–

Sometimes the subject wormed its way to the surface.

During those periodic lectures, a crew member might pose an innocent question that mentioned Chaos. Then everyone found himself thinking about that untouchable place. And perhaps a second hand would lift, and a second voice would ask about that mysterious, increasingly hostile realm. With concern, perhaps even a measure of sadness, they would refer to their hosts, wondering aloud that maybe the Scypha were intentionally strangling their cradle world to death.

But Chaos was not dying. Krill, the ranking diplomat, made that salient point enough times to convince ten million people of its veracity. Borrowing from the exobiologists' manual, she reminded audiences how the spores represented every lineage, and how they would remain for eons to come, waiting patiently inside the planet-wide dust. In some locations, there were more spores than dust lying on the ground. And while there was no way to know the future, it was easy to imagine a different day when the Scypha would loosen their grip on the Rings, allowing a fire-shower of rock and ice to trigger another rebirth.

"It's not as if our hosts are fighting the other lineages," she pointed out, her tone reasonable and responsible, her young girl face almost glowing as she smiled with an infectious confidence. "We aren't visiting a war zone here. We haven't seen extinctions, and we won't. I promise. And if struggles are happening, they're between the little lineages. But then again, the inhabitants of Chaos have always fought for resources, for heat. If you look at these things as I do, you see a thousand failed lineages unable to make peace with one another, much less find any lasting prosperity.

"The Scypha are something else entirely.

"I won't grant them any great superiority to their sister lineages. Frankly, I don't have the expertise to make judgments. But it's not a small point to remind ourselves that the Scypha have accomplished wonders. On their own, they have escaped their limited beginnings. And in exchange for allowing a tiny population of their infinitely plastic bodies to come onboard the Great Ship, humanity will be given three empty worlds . . . a spectacular gesture on their part . . . a gift that will ensure new homes to millions of human beings, plus the chance for happiness and the promise of a long, luminous future . . ."

Krill was effusive, but using the same sources, exobiologists took a less optimistic tone about life on Chaos. The cradle world was falling into a long hard sleep, they agreed. The ultimate results depended on the viability of the spores, and that was hard to determine from a range of a hundred million kilometers. Who knew what ten million years of unbroken drought and ice would do to those tiny dormant bodies? In their darkest moods, the experts liked to point out that these weren't simple bacteria buried beneath Martian permafrost. Spores produced by the Scypha were substantial bodies, visible to the eye and covered in a hard, jewel-like cuticle. In principle, it was a magnificent and enduring system. But on the other hand—a grim second hand—it had to be mentioned that Chaos had never known dormancies as long as this one promised to be. Asteroid impacts had been uneven but inevitable events, and at most, the coldest driest deadest times had probably lasted not much longer than the present drought.

A few months ago, a familiar voice asked Aasleen, "Does it concern you?"

"Does what concern me?"

"Our part in what is happening to that world. And what isn't happening to it. Do these events make you uneasy at all?"

The AI technician was drifting beside her. "Help me," she said. "Define your subject, will you?"

The machine said, "Chaos."

But Aasleen had already guessed as much. "Since when does that world concern you?" she asked.

"Just in the last few moments." The rubber face put on a tight, worried expression. "I suddenly find myself dwelling on my critical role in this horrible business."

Thousands of years ago, on her home world, Aasleen had built this machine. It had helped her erect the short-lived terraforming tent, and later, it had gladly accompanied her to the *Olympus Peregrine* and eventually to the Great Ship. And now they were together again, finishing the retrofitting of the last nuclear engine. It wasn't unfair to claim that this thoughtful, talented machine was Aasleen's oldest and possibly dearest friend, and there were even lonely moments when it was much more than that.

But it was not sentient. Not in any legal or compelling way, it wasn't.

"Has someone been talking to you?" Aasleen asked. "About Chaos, I mean. Is that why it's on your mind?"

The machine said, "No."

Then it thought again, saying, "Perhaps."

"Who?"

"I don't know."

"Rococo?"

With confidence, the AI said, "I haven't shared time with your brother. Not since several days before he left the *Peregrine* with the other diplomats, I haven't."

Aasleen nodded, considering the possibilities. Then she asked, "What bothers you most?"

"I am doing nothing," it said.

"About Chaos?"

"If I was a moral entity with obligations, and if the galaxy was watching my inactions, then a million worlds would be entitled to ask themselves, 'Should we entrust our bodies and minds to the care of this lucky but exceptionally young species? Can that AI maintain the Great Ship as well as maintain a proper ethical climate for its diverse passengers?'"

Fair questions, regardless of their source.

"If I was a free citizen," the AI continued, "I would argue that the Scypha are morally reprehensible, and the only just, reasonable action on our part is to break off negotiations and refuse them entry to the Great Ship."

How could somebody tinker with the machine's mind? More as a friend than an engineer, Aasleen considered that perplexing question. "But you aren't a free citizen," she reminded her friend.

"For which I am thankful."

Aasleen began to pull off the rubber face. "Why are you thankful?"

"The galaxy cannot despise me," the entity responded. Then one of its many hands touched her hand fondly, asking, "What are you doing, darling?"

"I want to examine your mind," Aasleen confided.

"But we have our engine to finish."

The chief engineer hesitated.

"I'm now thinking about tertiary pumps and hyperfiber accentor chambers," the machine reported. "Nothing else is in my mind now. That spell, or whatever it was, seems to be finished."

–XI–

The Dun territory ended with a slow climb onto an old crater wall. The Rococo facsimile led the way, offering little doses of information about the terrain and its long history. At least twenty different lineages were mentioned, most of them too obscure to be given a human name like Scypha or Dun. But each had ruled some portion of the crater, its sea or the once young walls. Her brother's voice described violet forests and oily black forests and towering gray spires with roots reaching deep into the still hot interior, living off chemical energies that were spent long ago. "Each lineage creates its own biosphere," said the machine, its facial expressions and the music of the voice the same as Rococo's. A wry smile was flashed back at her, and then the mud features gave an impressed shake of the head. "Each lineage has its own physiology and its culture and a personal history and a tenacious, gorgeous will to survive."

They were being followed, at a distance, by perhaps a hundred of the bipedal Dun. But when the facsimile entered a deep gully high on the crater slope, the Dun hesitated, gathering together in a greenish mass, their stance and silence implying caution falling short of genuine concern.

Aasleen followed her guide.

The air was as thin as it would taste on the highest earthly mountains. An impoverished frost had formed in the shadows and survived through the long day. The gully turned to the north, ending with a flat slab of wind-polished rock that felt the full brunt of the sun's weak light; and from the rock's base came a weak flow of water—a spring barely strong enough to be considered a trickle, and judging by the vivid orange stains, severely contaminated with metals and salts.

Around that spring grew a forest, each tree no taller than a thumb. The oily black color was a giveaway. "This is the—" Aasleen began. Then she did an awful job of naming the lineage, amusing her companion in the process.

He laughed, and then he wasn't laughing.

Kneeling beside the tiny woods, he explained, "There are thousands of places like this. Lineages huddled around oases too insignificant for names. The most successful lineages might have a hundred homes. But not this one, no." Despite the machine's heat, its mud face was beginning to freeze, a bright white frost appearing along the chin and cheeks and across the tall forehead. "According to the Dun, this lineage has no other sanctuary. Except for some spores left behind on the wind, it exists this close to total annihilation."

Aasleen nodded.

"Have you spoken to the Dun?" she asked.

"They have spoken to me, yes."

"To my brother, I mean. Did he make illegal contacts with them?"

The icebound face gave a cracking sound as the smile grew. "He did not contact them, no."

"Then where did he find the help to come here?"

Her companion waited for a moment, then said, "You know where. And I don't even have to be your brother to see that."

Aasleen nodded, breathed the thin air. "How many of the Scypha don't agree with the present policy?"

"A portion."

"I know that."

"Perhaps a million, or perhaps fifty billion." The facsimile shrugged its shoulders. "Enough to ensure that one or two members of their official delegation are maintaining opinions outside what is considered normal."

"Families," said Aasleen.

"Pardon?"

"When you mentioned our parents, and you showed me the difference between fury and pride . . . you weren't talking only about our family, were you?"

Yellow teeth shone at her.

"It's a muddled mess," she continued, "and the Scypha are pretty much helpless when it comes to finding an easy way out. That's what you've been telling me. Probably from the beginning, I suppose."

The facsimile rose to its feet again.

"Do you want to put an end to our mission? Is that what all of this is about?" She shook her head, adding, "It must sicken you, knowing what's being lost here. The lineages, the unmet potentials. We have this opportunity to do something good and noble. But what the other species in our galaxy will see . . . the story that will be told everywhere . . . is that you and I and every other human claimed three worlds for ourselves, and in return, we promised to give one lineage a long ride . . . while the other lineages, like this little one . . . while they quietly perished . . ."

Rococo's white-rimmed face seemed pleased. But the voice was distinctly disappointed, remarking, "All that I want is for our mission to be an enormous success. For humans and all of the lineages, too."

"Good," she whispered.

"Which is exactly what Krill and my other associates wish as well. The trouble is, they have a rather different assessment of events and consequences."

"Why exactly am I here?" Aasleen asked.

"You're smarter than I am," Rococo assured her. "I think you can piece together my fondest hopes."

She had never hated her brother more. But this collection of mud and machine wasn't Rococo, and her rage would only waste time.

"I'm going to climb on top," she mentioned.

"To contact Hazz?" it asked.

"Piece that together for yourself," she muttered, pulling her kit along as she climbed the less steep side of the gully. Finally in the open, standing in the raw dry wind, she opened the kit and pulled out a portable com-link, letting it acquire a signal and aim itself, pulling in a constant transmission that was updated according to changes and looped when there was no change.

"Our shuttle reaches Chaos in eight days," Hazz reported, his expression grim and vaguely disgusted. "The Scypha have agreed to let us drop as close to you as low orbit, and they claim that the Dun will lift you up to the shuttle once your mission is finished. In exchange for several hundred kilos of enriched uranium, by the way. Which is a pretty cheap price for a good engineer, I might say." Then her captain sucked on his teeth for a pained moment, gathering himself. "Will you finish soon? Our gracious, good and very persistent hosts are very much wishing to see justice done."

That was when Aasleen finally understood all of it.

Relieved, she began to laugh quietly to herself. She even wept for a few moments. Then she heard a new sound bouncing up along the gully walls, and looking into the shadows and the bitterest cold, she saw the Rococo facsimile smashing tiny black trees under its frozen feet. The entity was walking back and forth, calmly and efficiently destroying the ancient forest, apparently finishing what the Scypha had begun.

Aasleen reached into her kit and dragged out the plasma torch.

Then she hesitated. The torch had to build a charge, and she needed to set up a transmission, showing her audience what they wanted to see. Then to the sky, she said, "In eight days, I'll be back with the Dun. Or I'll be coming back. I might get lost on this desert once or twice."

Then she aimed her weapon at a shape that was identical to her missing brother.

It was easy, letting loose that blue bolt of energy. Mud and machine exploded with a withering violence, etching out a small crater on the forest floor. Then the spring water slowly, slowly poured into the clean raw hole, growing slightly warmer in the process, and what had been a tragedy for an ancient lineage was now a blessing born from above.

–XII–

With just fifteen hours to spare, the shuttle slid into the berth where it would sleep for the next three decades. Aasleen disembarked to find Hazz was waiting for her, accompanied by Krill and the Scypha delegation as well as a few engineers with time to spare. Long meetings had been held to orchestrate those next few minutes. The delegates had insisted on personally thanking the human for undertaking this critical mission. With a quick dry voice, the lead delegate referred to Aasleen as being a courageous warrior, duty-blooded and honorable enough to be a Scypha, and most astonishing, she had survived her journey to a world as cruel as any. "Your entire lineage has been strengthened by your strength," it assured her. "And as a consequence, one grave failure has been diminished." Then it extended a bony olive-colored hand, and Aasleen accepted it in the required fashion—her hands sandwiched above and below it, squeezing as hard as she could for a ridiculously long time.

Drifting nearby was the Scypha with extra joints in its arms—the same delegate that once spoke to her about the variability of minds. Like its peers, it remained silent now, watching the ceremony with an unreadable expression. Did it know what really happened on Chaos? And did it agree with Aasleen's actions? She found herself staring at the alien face, and not for the first time, she wondered if perhaps every Scypha understood what had happened: This great adventure was nothing more, or less, than an elaborate means by which more than a trillion entities could find faith in the human lineage.

When the Scypha took back its hand, the humans and machines were free to greet Aasleen. Smiling in a sad, almost pained fashion, Hazz said, "Good to have you back." Then dropping the last of his captainly façade, he added, "I know, I know. This can't be easy for you."

"It's all right," she allowed.

Hazz patted her shoulder. "It's hardly that," he said. "Really, it has to be shit for you."

Krill kicked closer. Her youthful face was sorry and thrilled, in equal measures. She seemed to be crying for both reasons, and with a voice not too unlike the alien's, she repeated most of what the Scypha had just said—sometimes word for word. Then Aasleen took the pale pink hand between her hands, and it occurred to her that this woman had spent too much time with her alien friends.

Aasleen's kit and Rococo's satchel drifted beside them.

Krill reached for the satchel, but Aasleen grabbed a ruby-rope strap and pulled it to her belly. The locks and seal were in place again. Nobody but she could easily open the pouch. "I've got my brother's ashes," she remarked. And when the diplomat reached for the prize a second time, Aasleen added, "I'm taking them back to the Great Ship. It's my right and duty to give him a proper burial."

That declaration earned a pained silence among the humans.

Most of the Scypha seemed uninterested in their enemy's corpse. They were already turning away, making for the tiny vessel that would soon lift them free of the *Peregrine*. None of them would be traveling to the Great Ship. Their colonists were elsewhere on-board, safely sealed away in a set of specially prepared cabins. Only the many-jointed Scypha bothered to look at the satchel with its bright, unfathomable eyes, and then an AI pushed in front of it, unable to wait any longer.

"Welcome home, madam!"

"Thank you—" she began.

"And will you help me, please? One of our new accentor chambers has revealed a minor flaw, and I don't think it's worry-worthy, but I do require my ranking officer to sign off."

"Sure," said Aasleen, relieved at the abrupt intrusion of normal life. "Let's see what you have for me, my friend . . ."

●●●

The burn began without incident. The first ten seconds were critical. A problem might betray itself as a sputtering plume or a catastrophic blast, and if anything substantial went wrong in any one of ten thousand critical systems, it would take centuries to return home to the Great Ship. Unless of course the blast cracked the *Peregrine* open, hopefully killing its chief engineer quickly enough that she wouldn't feel too embarrassed by her mistakes.

But the three new engines ignited without incident, matching the output and harmonics of their rebuilt sisters. The next thousand seconds would lift their acceleration well past a full gee, and the circumstances were tense enough to make the most confident human forget to breathe. But every system was operating within a narrow blue zone that had been dubbed "Perfect," and save for two minor failures on the outskirts of the Scypha system, that same perfection held past the next three critical junctures as well.

A familiar old life fell onto Aasleen's shoulders now.

But there was more than the life she had led for thousands of years. Her human engineers seemed to regard her with a new fondness. A dangerous duty had been foisted upon her, and she'd done what was asked of her. And in the process, she visited a world like none other, walking its surface for almost nine unbroken days. And because there was no other choice, she had executed her only brother—a dangerous criminal who had broken rules and ignored smart laws, acting out of pure selfishness and putting their mission at risk.

Other humans—crew members who didn't know Aasleen as well—were less understanding about the dead brother. Nobody said it to her face. At least not with words, they didn't. But there were looks offered in the galley and averted eyes in the hallway, and sometimes a distant person would point in her general direction, giving a hard opinion or two to whatever allies they were standing beside.

Everyone on the *Peregrine* had enjoyed Rococo's company, and very few understood just how dicey the situation had been.

Aasleen kept her brother's satchel inside her cabin, locked away in a hyperfiber bubble. If a superior officer asked to see the ashes, she was prepared to tell the truth. She had incinerated nothing but a facsimile of the criminal. And no, she never came across Rococo while wandering on the barren, nearly dead surface of Chaos.

About his whereabouts, she could shrug her shoulders, honestly admitting, "I don't know where he is now. But abandoned on an alien world seems a lot like death, if you want my opinion."

Yet nobody asked about the satchel's contents.

Not even Hazz.

After three years and a few days of constant acceleration, they began throttling back to where every engine was comfortable, where the chance of meltdowns and magnetic hiccups became deliciously small.

Aasleen gathered up the most complete diagrams of the *Peregrine*'s interior, every recent plan laid over everything ancient and nearly forgotten. For good reason, she assumed she would be searching walled-off hallways and locked closets for the next twenty years. But the sweetest, most logical answer occurred to her after less than a minute's consideration.

Not far from the central fuel tank was a tiny cabin cut off by a series of violent renovations. To reach that unnamed place, she had to walk through an inoperative pump and down a fuel line, then cut through a diamond wall that she patched twice before continuing—on the remote chance that the main fuel line would fail and somebody would push the hydrogen through here. Afterward came a series of little hallways, each more familiar than the last, and she ended up standing at a locked doorway that still recalled the touch of her hand. Ages ago, when this starship was new and outbound to the Great Ship, Aasleen had slept in these quarters for nearly four hours every night.

She touched the door, and a voice beyond said, "Wait. I'm not dressed."

"I'm tired of waiting," she said. "Hurry up."

"All right. Enter."

Rococo was sitting on a hard cot. He looked rested and a little soft, his body unaccustomed to exercise of any kind. His face seemed thinner, his eyes brighter. His personal journal was open on the desk beside him, waiting for whatever thoughts he wanted to transcribe next. Stolen monitors and narrowband connections allowed him to secretly watch happenings and nonhappenings around the ship. His most recent meal lay half-finished on a grimy plate–rations synthesized in a portable field kitchen–and the tiny volume of air smelled of sweat and subtle decay and too little oxygen.

"Your recycle system is in trouble," Aasleen warned.

Then she found herself breaking into a wide, joyous grin. And with her voice breaking, she said, "You miserable dog."

Laughing, Rococo said, "You were worried about me, weren't you?"

She wouldn't admit it. Instead she tossed his satchel to the floor between them, admitting, "This is yours."

"When did you figure me out?"

"I don't think I'm done picking apart your mind," she allowed. "But when I first stood up on Chaos–when I saw that facsimile of yours–I realized just how long you'd been planning this adventure. For decades, probably. And of course if a person brings one fancy stand-in for himself, then it's not much of a jump to imagine two facsimiles. Each meant to do a different job, of course."

"Of course."

"You never stole that shuttle," she said. "At least, you weren't the creature piloting it. That was the first facsimile's job, and it flew into the asteroid and then walked up onto the mountaintop and leaped to the sky–"

"After leaving this behind," Rococo said, referring to the satchel.

"You assumed I'd be chosen to follow you. Which was a pretty obvious guess, really. And you hoped I would get your left-behind possession. Working out the vectors and timetable had to press you, I'm guessing."

"But I did have help," he admitted, smiling with the eternal charm.

"Among the Scypha." She nodded. "I once had a chat with one of your co-conspirators."

"I know. I was watching."

Of course.

"You never left this room. Did you, Rococo?"

He shook his head.

"Which means you never technically broke the quarantine. Not according to the Scypha, and not according to our Krill's orders either."

"The facsimile is a gray area," he conceded.

"But as you say, you enjoyed official help. You didn't deal with the Dun or any other out-of-bounds lineage. One of the Scypha delegates was your contact, which gives this whole scheme its scent of legality. And besides, in the end only one human walked on the surface of Chaos, and she had full permission granted by all of the Scypha."

"And what was my scheme?"

She hesitated. Smiled. Then she kicked the hyperfiber satchel to him, saying, "It's jammed full of dust."

"Just dust?"

"Mixed with this peculiar grit that looks like tiny, tiny jewels." She could say from experience, "On Chaos, there are places where the wind brings dust from every corner of the world. Where a woman can use her bare hands and scoop up a remarkably full sampling of the lineages, alive and dead, that were left behind on Chaos."

"I knew you'd see my madness," he told her.

"But why do you think this matters? If you hide in here until we make it home, what happens next? You have to emerge. There has to be a board of inquiry. Maybe you're cleared of any wrongdoing. But after that, what are we supposed to do with the spores in this silly sack?"

"That question," Rococo began.

Then he hesitated, smiling happily to himself.

"I see two worthy answers," he said. "First, we need to recognize that right now, a multitude of species—richer, older species than ours—are watching us. Our actions and inactions over these next few millennia are going to establish our reputation throughout the Milky Way. We own the Great Ship, but that isn't enough to make us great. The others will ask themselves: Are humans wise enough to be trusted? And are they gracious enough to endure?"

He put a foot on top of the satchel, pointing out, "Whatever we do with this pregnant grit, it must be a noble and worthy gesture, respectful by every measure."

"Okay. Granted."

"And second, what I will tell the Master Captain—what I'll argue with every rational reason as well as every gram of charm—is that there is one simple, even obvious solution waiting for us. And when you think about the consequences, the cost will not be all that steep."

Aasleen offered her guess.

And with a wink, Rococo told her that she was right.

Then he stood and stepped close enough to gently place his arms about her shoulders—he smelled sour and warm and very brotherly—and with a genuine scorn, he said, "Families."

Shaking his head, he asked, "Can you imagine, Aasleen . . . how wonderful the universe would be, if we could simply jump from one family to the next until we found happiness . . . ?"

–XIII–

Two centuries later, the *Olympus Peregrine* returned.

Its small crew was made up of facsimiles—machines wearing uniforms and sacks of water draped over a network of false bones. Only one of the *Peregrine*'s big engines was still operational, but that was no problem. The necessary momentum had already been won; nothing more was required now but a tweak of the final course. At nearly half light-speed, the much-traveled asteroid plunged out of the darkness, streaking above the greenish Rings and the Iron Ring and over the orange sun. Then the engine let loose a last long burst of plasma. Chaos was a tiny gray dot, undistinguished and soon left behind. The final hour of the voyage began with a passage over the Rings again, then a quick plunge into the yellowish light of the sister sun—a realm now partly owned and controlled by the human species.

"Here's a question worth asking," said the Rococo facsimile. "Why didn't the Scypha ever colonize this neighboring solar system?"

Beside him stood a machine strongly resembling his sister. With a nod, she admitted, "That puzzled me, too. Those three moons shouldn't be too difficult to adapt to. Or to rebuild. Even if they had still room to grow in the Rings, I think they'd want to hedge their bets with fresh colonies somewhere else."

"And they could have easily built a fleet of slow starships," said Rococo's voice. "How difficult would that have been, traveling out to all the worlds within five or ten light-years?"

"It is a big old conundrum," Aasleen's voice replied.

The facsimiles were simple in design—little more than likenesses with embedded personalities and cherry-picked memories. It would have been immoral to send sentient organisms, machine or otherwise, on a mission like this. That's why the two of them had enjoyed this conversation at least a thousand times: This was based on a recording made by Rococo's journal, back when the *Peregrine* was still chasing after the Great Ship.

"Aliens are peculiar people," the Aasleen facsimile mentioned. "Who knows what makes sense to them?"

"But I know why," her brother promised.

Racing toward them was the jovian world and its family of tightly bound moons. Staring at the crescents, Aasleen said, "So explain it all to me."

"Simple ordinary fear," he offered. "That's what kept them from attempting colonies."

"But what are they scared of?"

"If they'd populated a new world—a radically different environment from their home Rings—there's a good chance that little variations would take hold. In genetics, in culture. A fissure of their great lineage was possible, not unlike how they split from the Dun ten million years ago."

The inner two moons were strongly volcanic and washed by the jovian's radiation belts. But magma was a resource, and there wasn't so much radiation that shields and artificial magnetic fields couldn't protect a human population. By contrast, the outer moon was relatively unscathed by toxins, but it was smaller and less volcanic—a quieter realm not too unlike an unterraformed Mars.

"Ten million years have passed," said Rococo, "and that wound still aches."

"I can appreciate that," she replied, laughing gravely.

"Which is the same reason why they never sent asteroids to the stars," he continued. "Those colonists would surely form new lineages, and perhaps someday they would return here and raise hell."

"But what about the Scypha onboard the Great Ship? Isn't their goal to spread their lineage across the galaxy?"

"A thousand light-years from here, yes. Or twenty thousand."

Out of reach, in other words.

"My impression," Rococo began. Then he hesitated for a moment, staring at the worlds before them. "My impression is that the Scypha were thrilled to give these worlds to us. They wanted the temptation gone. More than anything, they see humans as a chance to cut old bonds with their past, to slowly begin to find new directions and a fresh sense of purpose."

Aasleen's facsimile nodded. Fixed to the wall beside her was a small hyperfiber bubble, and she touched it gently now, some tiny portion of her recorded thoughts dwelling on its contents.

"So you understand the aliens," she said.

"What I understand is fear and family," Rococo replied.

The jovian world was the largest object in their sky, but the smaller moon was growing swiftly. It looked cold and dirty, ruddy dust gathered around extinct volcanoes and little caps of frozen water clinging to both poles.

"What I appreciate most," he said, "is how the past shapes what we are, and how weak the future is whenever it tries to change us."

In a few moments, the *Olympus Peregrine* would dive out of the sky, colliding with that sleepy outer moon. A substantial bolide moving at half the speed of light, its enormous mass would be converted into light and heat, pumping energy into a mantle that had been close to dead for the past billion years.

In another century, a second, much smaller vessel would come along, moving into a close orbit and waiting for the molten crust to stiffen. Then the atmosphere would be doctored and the spores that Aasleen had taken from Chaos would be strewn across the surface, and whatever lineages survived would have a new world to fight for—a world owned and maintained by a benefactor called Man.

Again, the Aasleen facsimile touched the bubble. The hyperfiber was the very best grade available, and it was thick enough to survive the coming impact. Inside its tiny center was a small plaque with her name and her brother's name and a few important dates. Nothing more. But that seemed like a wonderful gesture, even if you were nothing more than a simple machine acting along narrow parameters.

After today, the Scypha would continue to slowly strangle their cradle world. Though who could say what would happen in another ten million years?

And meanwhile, human colonists on the other two moons would watch over New Chaos, perhaps flinging down the occasional spent starship or thousand-megaton bomb . . . you know, just be the good neighbor . . .

The Aasleen facsimile laughed quietly.

"What is it?" asked her brother's facsimile.

"Something just occurred to me." A thousand times before, she had said those same words. And as always, she looked at him now, smiling for a long happy moment. Just before the *Peregrine* plunged to its death, she asked, "How do we know the Scypha left their world willingly? That's what they say, but maybe . . . maybe the other lineages simply got tired of them and booted them off into space . . . ?"

Rococo laughed, ready to say, "That would help explain things, I suppose."

But he didn't offer those words, not this time.

Both of the machines hesitated, big eyes brilliant and wonderstruck, gazing down at a blank, utterly drab landscape that in another instant would be entirely and forever remade.

Kaminsky at War

by Jack McDevitt

◅━◅━◅━▻

A native of Philadelphia, Jack McDevitt has been, among other things, a naval officer, an English teacher, a customs officer, a Philadelphia taxi driver, and a motivational trainer. He is married to the former Maureen McAdams, of Philadelphia. McDevitt and his wife live in Brunswick, Georgia.

His first novel, The Hercules Text *(1986), was published in the celebrated Ace Specials series and won the Philip K. Dick Special Award. In 1991, McDevitt won the first $10,000 International UPC Prize for his novella "Ships in the Night." The Engines of God was a finalist for the Arthur C. Clarke Award, and McDevitt's novella, "Time Travelers Never Die," was nominated for both the Hugo and the Nebula in 1997. With the nominations of* Infinity Beach, Ancient Shores, *"Time Travelers Never Die,"* Moonfall, *and "Good Intentions" (cowritten with Stanley Schmidt), "Nothing Ever Happens in Rock City,"* Chindi, *and* Omega, *his work has been on the final Nebula ballot eight of the last nine years. At DeepSouthCon 2000, McDevitt was presented with the Phoenix Award for his body of work.*

"Kaminsky at War," though wholly original, inevitably reminds me of the officers of the Enterprise *as they observe their governing policy not to interfere with the various worlds they visit. McDevitt's protagonist*

must shoulder a similar viewpoint . . . but what will you do when in
your heart you know that in the present situation, the Prime Directive
is—WRONG!?

–I–

THE BRIDE WAITED in the glow of the lanterns and lowered her
eyes to the sheet that had been placed on the ground before her.
Her husband stood still and straight, watching. The celebrants
were gathered in a circle around the happy pair. They were long
and spindly creatures, all eyes and husk and clicking jaws, with no
sign of anything remotely resembling hair. They were the color of
grass that had not gotten enough water.

They were Noks, a species mired in early-twentieth-century
technology and endlessly at war with itself. They were the first off-
world intelligence we had seen, and they'd helped shape the
hands-off policy that was quickly formulated as the Barrin-Rhys
Protocol, and eventually simply *the* Protocol.

Leave them alone.

Virtually everybody took an unsympathetic attitude toward
them. I thought it was the faces that really did the damage. The Noks
did not have flexible features. Nature had given them unmoving
masks that always looked the same, regardless of whether their own-
ers were partying or running for their lives. No emotion ever showed.

Except in the eyes.

The eyes were round disks, large by human standards, protected by nictitating membranes. The lenses, usually dark, floated
in a green-tinted aqueous humor. They contracted or widened, and
changed colors, according to the emotions of the moment. The
eyes of the wedding guests were uniformly blue. At peace.

The guests all carried bells. As was the local custom, they received a signal from the bride's father, and raised their eyes to the
sky, pledging eternal friendship to the happy couple. Then they
rang the bells. It was a soft jangling on the night breeze, an expression of the connubial pleasures that lay ahead. A warm wind blew in

off the ocean, and the trees sighed in harmony with the celebration.

The bride, of course, was naked, save for the ceremonial cord hung loosely at her waist. Slim and polished and graceful, she awaited the climax of the ceremony. Noks were not mammals, and not at all close to humans, yet there was something in the way she stood, in her physical presence, that stirred me. Odd how that happened. It wasn't the first time.

I was wearing a lightbender, and was consequently invisible to the Noks, except for my eyes. If the system blanked out your eyes, you wouldn't be able to see. So I had to be careful.

I took the bride's picture. Angled around and got the groom, backed off and caught the two sets of parents. I recorded the scene as, one by one, the bells fell silent. When the last tinkling had died away, the pair strode toward each other and embraced. In the time-worn tradition, he released the cord around her waist. She removed his ceremonial shirt, and then tugged at something on his leggings and they fell away.

I took more pictures.

Noks are all beak and shell. You look at them and what you see is straight-ahead, strictly business, don't get in the way. Nevertheless, I *knew* what she was feeling. I could see pure joy in her eyes, and in her suppleness. I told myself maybe it was just empathy, that I was projecting on her precisely the reactions I'd expect to see had she been a woman.

She was a beautiful creature. When her groom closed on her, she reacted with grace and dignity, not easy when you're sprawled on a sheet in front of a hundred witnesses. But it was the ceremonial first act, consummating the marriage, as people liked to say at home.

The bride's name, as close as it could be reproduced in English, was Trill. I watched them, and I'll admit I was embarrassed by my own rising heartbeat. Couldn't help it. It was erotic stuff, and it didn't matter they weren't human. At the time I wouldn't have admitted it to anyone. Thought it was a perversion. I've found out since it's a common reaction. So take it for what it's worth.

I was still taking pictures when the raiders stormed out of the woods.

●●●

My name's Arthur Kaminsky, and I'm an anthropologist. Although the term doesn't really extend to everything we do nowadays.

There'd never been a time that I hadn't had things my own way. I'd been born, if not precisely into wealth, then certainly into comfortable surroundings. I'd gone to the best schools, won a scholarship to Oxford where I performed, if not brilliantly, at least well enough to convince my father I was destined for something other than real estate. After I'd gotten my doctorate, I decided the frontiers of my specialty lay with the study, not simply of humans, but of intelligent species of whatever type we might encounter. My father rolled his eyes when I told him what I wanted to do, and my mother said she supposed it was my decision.

Had it not been for a fortuitous circumstance, I would probably never have been selected for one of the few positions available to do offworld field work. I was only in my twenties, had no track record, and every anthropologist on the planet was pushing to get assigned.

The fortuitous circumstance was my linguistic ability, and especially the fact that I learned to speak three major Nok languages, which required vocal capabilities that were beyond the normal human larynx. Nobody could do it like me. Other than the AI's.

Still, the people who signed me on were nervous. They put me through a longer training period than was standard. And I'd been on site more than six months before the director allowed me to do a solo mission. And that came with a lot of advice. Be careful. Take no chances. Keep the lightbender activated at all times so they can't see you. Stay in touch with Cathie. If you start to feel ill, or anything like that, let us know right away and get back to the lander.

Cathie was Catherine Ardahl, the mission's communication officer. She had dark hair and dark eyes and a smile that melted me into my socks. I'd never been a big hit with women, so I was relentlessly shy around her. In those early months, I was as invisible to her as if I'd been wearing a lightbender.

Watching the Nok bride, before the raiders arrived, I'd thought of her.

●●●

When the raiders came out of the woods, I needed a minute to figure out what was happening. I still didn't know enough about local customs. Party crashers, maybe? A surprise visit by distant relatives? Even the first shots might have been noisemakers of some sort. Then the screams started, and the wedding guests scattered. Some went down as bullets tore into them and lay writhing on the yellow-tinted grass and the stone walkways. Others got into the forest and a few made it into the house.

The raiders were on foot, firing rifles and pistols indiscriminately. Killing technology was primitive, for the most part at a World War I level, although Noks had no heavier-than-air capability. I wasted no time scrambling out of the way. Got behind a tree. Two of the wedding guests, fleeing in panic, crashed screaming into me and knocked me flat. (There are hazards when nobody can see you.) Someone inside the house began to return fire.

The raid lasted, altogether, about seven minutes. No one was spared. The raiders moved among the dead and dying, shooting the wounded. Then they began rounding up survivors and herding them into a central area. I saw Trill lying beside a bench, with the *sateen*–her blood equivalent–leaking out of her shoulder. She was down near the trees, and I knelt beside her and lifted her in my arms and tried to stop the bleeding. She cried out and one of the raiders heard her and started toward us.

They were in uniform, dark green loose-fitting single-piece outfits. Like pajamas.

"Don't let them find me," she said. She was so terrified she never noticed what held her.

"I won't."

The lids had squeezed down over her eyes. There wasn't much I could do. My stomach fluttered. I'd never witnessed serious violence. During my early months on Nok, they'd kept me away from the wars. In fact, everybody stayed away from the combat areas. They were dangerous. "Try not to make any noise," I whispered.

I carried her to the edge of the trees. Put her down behind a bush. But they were right behind us. One of them stopped, moved the shrubbery aside with the barrel of his rifle. Advanced a few steps. Listened.

I reached into a pocket of my vest and pulled out my tensor. It was designed to disable the nervous systems of the local wildlife. But it would also work on the Noks themselves.

Trill groaned softly.

The raider heard her.

"Help me," she whispered, her voice faint. "Help me."

He had a light, and it picked her out. He raised a rifle and pointed it at her. I could simply have stood aside. Let it happen. It was in fact what the regulations required.

But I couldn't do it. I pulled the trigger on the son of a bitch. He sighed and went down, and in that moment I wished I had something more lethal. It even crossed my mind to take his rifle and put a bullet in his brain.

The raiders collected their comrade. (I'd moved Trill by then.) They carried him off, making that odd whistling sound that was the Nok idea of displaying regret. Then they were gone.

Trill never woke. She made occasional gasping sounds. But there were no more cries of pain. And after a while she grew still.

In the distance, I heard more gunfire.

"*Art.*" The voice on the commlink startled me. It was the boss. Paul McCarver. Northeastern United States accent. Classic Yankee.

"Hello, Paul."

"*We've picked up sporadic shooting in your area. Just wanted to check. You're okay?*"

"Yes," I said. "I'm good."

"*What's happening? Can you tell?*"

"They hit a wedding party. It looks as if they killed everybody."

"*Yeah. That sounds like the way they operate. Okay. Be careful. Maybe you better come back.*"

"I'm okay. I'll be back in a bit."

I retreated to the lander, which lay within its own lightbender field in a forest clearing about a kilometer off the road. I'd been hungry when the wedding started, but I had no appetite when I got back to it. I kept seeing the cool green eyes of the killers, saw them striding through the celebration. Enjoying the work.

I should mention that I'm not big on confrontation. Never was. I do compromise real well. And I was always willing to overlook stuff. But the raid on the wedding had entailed a level of disagreeableness and lack of reason that made me want to kill someone. I mean, what was the point of sending a military strike force—that's what they were—against a wedding party?

"George," I said to the lander AI as I buckled in, "lift off. Let's see what else they did."

In the west, a kilometer away, there was a glow in the sky. That would be *Itiri,* the town which had probably been home to most of the celebrants. Population about eleven hundred. No military targets. I'd been there all day, taking pictures, observing, enjoying myself.

"Very good, Dr. Kaminsky," said George. *"After we look around, will we be going back into orbit?"*

I thought about it. I had what I'd come for, the record of the wedding. Even if it hadn't turned out exactly as planned, the mission was complete. Still, I wanted to make somebody pay for what I'd just seen. "George, where do you think the raiders came from?"

"Had to be by sea, I suspect. I would have detected a dirigible."

Nok industrialization had risen and fallen several times. We now know they'd put forty thousand years of civilizations and dark ages on the scoreboard before anybody started laying bricks in Sumer. They had all but exhausted their fossil fuels even though their original supply had been almost triple the terrestrial stores. The Noks seemed incapable of establishing political stability. One of the objectives I'd set for myself was to figure out why. With few exceptions, the only gas-powered vehicles operating on Nok belonged to the various dictators and their military and political establishments, and the police. Everybody else walked. Or used beasts of burden.

The engines came on. There was no sound, only a slight vibration in the chair. Most of my weight, and that of the spacecraft, vanished. It began to rise over the trees into a clear summer sky.

Itiri was ablaze.

●●●

A narrow winding road ran parallel to the sea. The raiders moved along it, a happy group, their weapons slung casually over their shoulders. More mob than military unit. They looked not at all worried about a counterattack. Two kilometers ahead, three small warships waited at anchor in a harbor. The ships were steam-driven ironclads. They showed no lights. "What can you tell me about them, George?"

"They are all of the same type. Approximately 2,500 tons, six guns able to fire four-inch shells. Accuracy doubtful beyond a thousand meters."

"Automatic weapons?"

"None. They haven't been developed yet."

"Not at all?"

"They had them a few thousand years ago, most recently during the Turullian Age. But they lost the technology."

"Doesn't seem as if it would be that hard to figure out. They have rifles."

George blipped. It was his equivalent of shrugging his shoulders.

"What about sensors or radar? Anything like that."

"They have no tracking devices other than their eyes. And telescopes."

"They do have telescopes."

"Yes. Most certainly."

We overtook the raiders, passed above them, and arced out over the beach. Several small boats lay in the wet sand, apparently awaiting the arrival of the land force.

"George," I said, "let's take a look at the ships."

We glided out into the harbor.

"The one in the middle," I told him. Six of one, half a dozen of the other. We loped in, moved slowly over masts and gun turrets, and stopped directly over the bridge.

The guns were primitive, but that wouldn't matter if one of the shells hit us. The only Noks I could see were manning the rails with rifles.

I could make out several figures on the bridge, in the glow of instrument lights. I thought about the wedding guests, and Trill, *help me,* and I wished I had a few bombs.

"What's that, Dr. Kaminsky? I'm sorry. I didn't hear you."

I didn't realize I'd said anything. "Nothing," I said. "Never mind."

I wanted a way to pay them back in their own coin. While I watched, the raiders arrived on the beach, scattered across the sand, and headed for the boats. They moved with a jaunty precision that implied they were happy with the evening's slaughter. Still taking no precautions for their own safety. And you might be thinking that nonverbal cues are deceptive even among humans of different cultures, and what did I know about Noks. But it was my specialty. "George," I said, "get us over to the beach and take us down to ground level."

"That's not advisable, doctor."

"Do it anyway."

"If you insist. But it is dangerous. Someone might walk into us before we can react."

"Just do it."

There were seven boats. They were made of wood, and each was designed to accommodate about twenty. The raiders surrounded each boat and began pushing it into the surf. When it started to float, they jumped aboard. I watched as, one by one, they set out for the ships, which were about a kilometer away. They were spreading out, making for different vessels.

The lander was at ground level, the treads a half-meter above the sand. "Okay," I said. "George, I want you to keep us right at this altitude."

"And—?"

"We're going to take out the boats."

"Ram them?" He sounded horrified.

"Can we do it without damaging the lander?"

"I can't guarantee that."

"Give me the odds."

"There are too many variables, doctor."

"The odds, George."

"Eighty-eight percent."

"Eighty-eight percent what? That we come away undamaged?"

"That we come away relatively undamaged. Still able to make or-bit."

"Okay. Let's do it. Start with that one over there."

"Sir, I am required to inform you that you will be in violation of the Protocol."

"Do it anyway." A fifth boat launched.

"I am sorry, doctor. But to override, you will have to get authority from the director."

There was a way to disable the AI, and if I could do that I thought I knew enough about the controls to be able to get the job done manually. "George."

"Yes, doctor." The rest of the boats were into the waves.

"How do I disable you?"

"I'm afraid, under the circumstances, it would be best if that information were withheld."

Damn. I studied the control panel. It was an array of switches, illuminated gauges, presspads, levers, warning lamps. There was a retractable yoke that could be used for manual operation. But I saw nothing marked *Shut off AI.*

"Let me out," I said finally. "Open up."

"Doctor, you sure you won't hurt yourself?"

"No, I'll be fine."

I climbed through the airlock and stepped down onto the sand. It was hard and crackly underfoot, like the sand on a thousand beaches at home. The ships and boats showed no light. And I no longer heard voices over the roar of the ocean. But I could see them, the ships, and the raiding party. I watched the boats close with the vessels. Saw rope ladders cast over the side.

The Noks scrambled up the lines. They were far more agile than human beings. Then they hauled up the boats. I watched until the last of the raiders were aboard, and the boats had been stowed. There were belches of smoke from the three vessels, and they turned and began to move out of the harbor.

I walked down to the sea, until the tide lapped at my feet.

Help me.

❍❍❍

"Where to, doctor?" asked the AI.

"Orbit. Get us to the *Sheldrake,* George." I threw my head back in the seat and tried to shut out the images of the victims.

"Very good, sir." We lifted off the beach, and began to accelerate. *"I know this has been hard on you."*

"Just take us home, George." I wasn't sure whether I was talking about the *Sheldrake.* Or Toronto.

–II–

Nok was a laboratory for anyone interested in the rise and fall of civilizations. With such a long history, and the cycles of prosperity and collapse, it was possible to draw a wide range of conclusions about the impact of technology, climate, religion, and economics on cultural development. And on the tendency of civilizations to overextend. It was, in fact, the thing they did again and again. And always with the same catastrophic results. Fortunately, no one on Nok had ever discovered how to split the atom, so the land, at least, was still habitable.

Were they more barbaric than humans? I thought about it while the lander passed through a thunderstorm. At the present time, they certainly were. But we had our own blood-soaked history, didn't we? I knew of nothing in the Nok archives to rival the Holocaust or the great Communist purges or the African massacres of the twentieth century.

I was still seething when we arrived in orbit. It wasn't as if I didn't know what Nok was before I'd come. But actually *seeing* these creatures murder one another had been something for which I really hadn't been prepared.

When we caught up with the *Sheldrake,* McCarver was waiting for me, and I could see he was genuinely worried. "You all right, Art?" he asked. "You look a little bloodshot."

I was wiped out. I needed a shower and a night's sleep. And something to calm me down. "Answer a question for me, Paul," I said.

"Sure. Go ahead."

"We've been here how long now?"

"Forty years. Give or take."

"And we've never lifted a finger. About the killing."

McCarver was a diminutive guy. He was the only male on the mission who had to look up to me. He was thin, not the sort of person you'd expect to find out here. Had I met him socially, I'd have pegged him strictly as a classroom guy, or somebody doing lab research.

But he was the director. McCarver had only to walk into a room to bring everyone to attention. He wasn't the most brilliant of the researchers on the Nok team. He admitted that himself. But they all respected him. We were in the main deck conference room. McCarver was nodding, as if he'd been bothered by the same issue. "Art," he said, "I can guess what you went through to-day. I've seen it myself. They're savages. They have a lot of our ca-pabilities, and sometimes they've done pretty well for themselves. But in the current era, they're savages, and we have to accept that."

"Why?"

McCarver looked past me, at a distant place. "Because we're not missionaries. Because we can't convert an entire global population to the rule of reason. Because even if we could, we probably shouldn't."

"Why is that, Paul?" I knew why, of course, but I wanted to force McCarver to say it. Maybe he'd come to understand how bloodless that view was.

"You know as well as I do, Art. If the Noks even find out we're here, they'll become dependent on us and they'll never develop properly."

"It's all theory."

"We've seen it happen back home. In the Pacific, in Africa, in the Americas. Time and again. It's painful. But keeping our dis-tance is the best thing for them in the long run." He took a deep breath. "The decision's not ours to make, anyhow." He managed a smile. "Anybody who got involved down there, Art, we'd have to put on the next flight home." Our eyes locked. His were dark and intense and bottomless. "Wouldn't want to do that."

"I took one of them down," I said.

"One of *who*?"

"The raiders. He was going to kill one of the people at the wedding."

"They're not *people*, Art." His voice was soft. But there was no give.

"He was trying to kill the bride."

"Who else knows?"

"Nobody."

"Keep it that way."

"Okay."

"Forget it happened. Technically, it puts you in violation of the rules. Could end your stay here. Maybe your career."

"It's happened with other people—."

"I know. And I understand *why* it happens. You're human, Art. You watch some of the things that go on here, and you know you can step in, save one of them. But you're putting your career on the line. Don't let it happen again."

And by the way, since you asked, the bride didn't survive. "I don't think I can promise that, Paul."

McCarver nodded. Okay. That's your position. "You don't leave me any choice, Art." He went over and got some coffee. One for him and one for me. He brought them back and sat down and put cream in his. The whole time he managed to look distressed. And I suppose the truth was he *was* unhappy. "I'll have to ask you to stay on board until you're able to comply with the policy. The last thing we need is a lone gun running around down there. You let me know when you can give me your word, and I'll take it from there."

I spent the evening in the archives. During the forty-two years since the *Valoire* discovered the Noks, hundreds of researchers had been here, and had walked unseen among the natives. They'd studied Nok mores and traditions, political and religious concepts, their literature, their family structure, and they'd begun to construct theories detailing what kind of behaviors were purely cultural, and what kind would be found to be characteristic of any intelligent species. It was a field that, because so few functioning cultures had been found—to date, only three—was still wide open to speculation.

I sat watching vid records. I was a silent witness at funeral services, at beach parties, at celebrations of various kinds, at their courting procedures. I watched them work, watched them play on the beach, watched them prepare food.

I took a look at troops in combat, though there wasn't much of that in the archive, probably because getting the footage entailed a degree of risk. It was also the case that troops seldom fought other troops. And for the same reason. The various Nok militaries preferred knocking over villages to taking on armed opponents. It was a style of war-making that appeared to be a recent development.

I watched from a lander as dirigibles dropped their bombs. There weren't many pictures of the effect of the weapons, which was to say nobody had been on the ground getting shots of Noks with missing limbs, or with massive burns. Mostly, it was strictly a light show. You drifted above the attack site, seeing the flashes, hearing the distant rumble moments later. And it all seemed very precise. And even, in its own strange way, beautiful.

"Paul's right," Cathie told me. "We can't get involved in all that. I don't think it's a problem if you just step in and stop one of them from getting killed. Just, if it happens, don't put it in the report. Better yet, don't even mention it." She looked puzzled. "Why would a military force raid a wedding party?"

"They don't operate the way we do."

"Explain." At that point, Cathie had been there only a few weeks.

We were sitting in the common room. There were maybe half a dozen others present, arguing about the evolution of Nok's four major religious systems. We were off to one side, drinking coffee. "They don't think in terms of strategy and tactics. They go after the easy targets instead. Places where they can kill a maximum number of victims with minimum risk. The idea is presumably that after a while the other side gets discouraged and gives up. Except that it never happens."

"Why not?"

"Don't know. Maybe because attacks like the one on the wedding party get everybody angry and they just fight harder. You get lots of flag-waving, patriotism, falling in behind the head guy.

"The balance of power shifts constantly. Seventeen nations are caught up in the current war. But it's hard to sort out the sides. There seems to be more than two. It changes. Somebody goes down, and they rearrange the allies to make sure nobody gets too strong. It's right out of George Orwell."

"It's crazy," she said.

"I know. It's the political system. The leaders aren't responsive to the wedding parties. They're all dictators, and I doubt they care much about anything other than staying in power. And the killing just goes on and on."

She looked unhappy. Worried. "So what are you going to do?"

Ordinarily, having a woman like Cathie Ardahl so close would have completely absorbed me. But not that night. "I don't know," I said. "We're not going to look very good in the history books. Standing by and watching all this happen."

I couldn't be sure but I caught a glimpse of something in her eyes. Respect, maybe. Admiration. Whatever it was, she was taking me seriously. "Art," she said, "you're not the first here to go through this. You have to divorce yourself from it. Think of the Noks as a species to be studied."

"I know."

"Nothing more than that."

I wondered whether things would change if the people who made and enforced the policy had an opportunity to get a good look at the carnage. Paul and Cathie and the others, sitting in landers or in the VR chamber, saw only the light shows. And the statistics. Estimates of how many killed in a given attack. How many total casualties. They didn't *experience* any of it. I couldn't be sure, of course, but I suspected my colleagues made it a point to avoid areas where there might be incursions. Or raids. God knew, it was the way *I* felt. Who needs all that unpleasantness? I'd thought the little coastal village with its bright lights and its upcoming wedding would be safe enough.

I didn't like the idea that eventually there'd be a change in policy, that we'd adopt a more humane attitude, and everybody
would wonder how people like me could just sit there and let it all
happen.

I didn't know it then, but I learned later that, over the years,
various directors had suggested intervention. But the requests had
always come back with the same reply. The Academy would look
into it. For the moment, the Protocol would be respected. And it
went on being respected. Nothing ever changed.

"How would you suggest we intervene?" Paul's voice. I hadn't
seen him come in. "Do you think they'd listen to us if we told them
to stop?"

"I don't know," I said. "We've never tried. How do we know
what might happen?"

When I was alone, I brought up the operational instructions for the
44 lander, the one we used. I looked up its range, read about its
gravity index, saw what I had to do to disable the AI. And I studied the instructions for emergency situations. How to pilot the
craft, how to land, how to manage its mass, how to turn left and
right, how to descend, how to operate the lightbender.

In the morning I hijacked a lander.

It wasn't hard. I just got some sandwiches and soup out of the
kitchen, checked out a laser and a tensor, and told the ship's AI I
needed a lander. It apparently had never occurred to McCarver
that anyone would disregard specific instructions, so he hadn't
bothered to lock me out of the flight lists.

The result was that within an hour of grabbing the extra food,
I was on my way groundside.

"*Where are we going, Dr. Kaminsky?*" asked George.

Nok's class-G sun floated just above the rim of the planet,
painting the clouds gold. Below us, an ocean extended to the horizon. "Night side," I said. "Engage lightbender."

"*Engaged. Anywhere in particular?*"

"No. Just get me someplace where it's dark."

–III–

Nok had anywhere from four to nine continents, depending on how you choose to define the term. Seven of the nine were caught up in the war. The conflict itself was so confusing that it appeared allies in one place were fighting each other elsewhere. Armies seemed to be on unopposed rampages across the globe.

The wedding party had taken place on an island a few kilometers offshore one of the smaller land masses. It was in the southern temperate region. I told George to pass over it. There was smoke still in the air. The harbor in which the three ships had waited sparkled in a rising sun. Broad beaches swept away on both sides.

Nok was a beautiful world, as all living worlds are.

We continued west, outrunning the sun, and soon we were soaring through starlit clouds. I began to see lights. Scattered across the land masses.

Some were constant and, if I was willing to give sway to my imagination, seemed arranged in patterns. Others, usually in more remote locations, flickered and burned.

"*Fires*," said George.

The dictators hold each other's populations hostage. It was almost a kind of sport. You kill some of mine, I'll take out some of yours. Everybody goes home happy.

On a dark peninsula, we found an inferno. An entire city, and surrounding woodland, were ablaze. "*This area has undergone a dry spell*," said George. "*It wouldn't have taken much to start this.*"

Ahead and below, moving away from the conflagration, lights bobbed among the clouds.

"*Aircraft.*" George put an image on screen. Big, lumbering dirigibles. The Noks had no heavier-than-air vehicles, hence nothing in the way of a fighter. They didn't have much ground artillery, either. The Noks preferred offensive weapons; they didn't play much defense. This made places like South Titusville an attractive target for bombers, as opposed to national capitals, or fleets of warships.

"How many, George?"

"*Four. Class YK.*"

The class designation meant nothing to me. "Let's get closer."

"Are you working on a new project, Dr. Kaminsky?" He was trying to sound as if he hadn't guessed what I intended.

"No. Just curious about the bombers." One began to take shape dead ahead. Lights gleamed along its flanks and outlined the tail. He picked out horizontal and vertical fins, and the rudder. And the gondola, slung beneath the gasbag. "Hydrogen?" I asked.

"Helium," said George.

I got a sense of its size as we pulled alongside the tail. It was immense. "George," I said. "Open the hatch."

"Dr. Kaminsky, may I ask why? Opening a hatch in flight is hazardous."

"I want to get a better look."

"The viewports are adequate."

"Just do it, George."

"I have no choice but to decline, sir."

"Do it. Or I'll disable you and do it myself."

The portside lights of the dirigible began to slip past. Damned arrogant sons of bitches were so careful to keep themselves out of harm's way, they didn't even have to turn off their lights. *"You are not qualified to pilot the lander."*

"I've read the instructions." I knew how that sounded, and waited for the AI to laugh.

"Don't try it. It's not as easy as it looks."

It didn't look easy.

The AI control was located on the pilot's left, under the board. You reached down, got hold of a handle, and twisted it. A panel opened, and there it was. On/Off.

I grabbed hold of the handle. "George, you sure?"

"Why, doctor? Why are you doing this? What can you possibly hope to accomplish?"

"I'm doing it because these sons of bitches run loose all over the planet. They kill arbitrarily and they don't give a damn. It's a joke. Maybe if they had to pay a price, things would be different."

"Do you have any idea how you sound?"

"I don't much care how I sound."

"Do I have to remind you, doctor, that you're only one man? This is a global conflagration. It's been going on for a long time. For decades. Do you really think you can do anything constructive?"

"It's *not* a war, damn it. It's wholesale slaughter and it goes on and on and nobody cares. Except the people who do the dying."

"They are not people, Art." He said it so softly that I barely heard him. It was the first time the AI had used my first name.

"Good-bye, George."

"Wait. What are you going to do when you shut me down? You can't attack the thing. We're not armed."

"I have a laser."

"A hand laser, obviously."

"Of course."

"You'll get us both killed."

That was an odd remark. AI's were theoretically not self-aware. Well, I'd think about it later. I switched him. The autopilot took over and continued course and speed. I had some trouble extracting the yoke, but we held steady until I had it clear and locked in place. But as soon as I took over, we went into a dive. I was holding the yoke too far forward. So I pulled back and the spacecraft leveled off.

Okay. Pull on it and climb. Push right and go right. Leave the thrust alone. It wasn't all that hard.

Nok's atmosphere was similar to Earth's. And, as had been the case elsewhere, local microbes showed no interest in attacking off-world life forms. I opened up with impunity both airlock hatches and the wind howled through the cabin, but I could see out into the night sky. I'd gone past my intended target and didn't want to try slowing down or turning around, but it didn't matter. Another dirigible lay directly ahead.

Its propellors spun complacently. There was a symbol on the hull. A national logo, a circle divided equally in three parts, green, white, and yellow. It looked like the old peace symbol.

I let go of the yoke, and the spacecraft veered and dipped.

Okay. I'd known I couldn't do that but it seemed worth trying.

I'd have to manage everything without getting out of my seat. Across the void beween the airlock and the dirigible, the night was still. I drew alongside the gondola. Could see movement inside. I was even able to make out a Nok with a telescope. For a moment I thought he was watching me, but of course the lander and I were invisible. Or were we? The hatch was open. Could the interior of the vehicle be seen from outside? I had no idea.

The telescope was pointed at me.

I drew the laser out of a vest pocket and activated it. The mode lamp blinked on, ready to go, and I aimed the thing. Be careful. Don't hit the airlock. It was hard to concentrate on holding the weapon steady and doing the same thing with the lander. Every time I took my attention off the yoke we wobbled or sank or veered in one direction or another. Finally I switched the AI back on. "George? You there?"

"Yes, doctor." We were back on formal terms.

"Take over. Keep us headed straight ahead."

No answer.

I lifted my hands from the yoke. We stayed on course. Okay. I squinted through the sight, through the airlock, and took aim at the peace symbol. Right in the middle of the dirigible. Can't miss.

I pressed the pad and watched the red beam blink on. It touched the gasbag. I couldn't see well enough in the dark to judge the effect, but almost immediately one of the navigation lights went out.

"You understand," said George, *"that they will send you home."*

"Just keep us steady."

"There's even a chance of criminal prosecution." He began to recite the laws I was in the act of breaking. *"Your career is over."*

No visible effect yet on the dirigible, other than the missing light. I kept it on. Moved the beam slowly forward.

"I recommend we return immediately to the Sheldrake, *and you claim mental stress based on your experience yesterday on the ground. It probably won't save your career, but it should be sufficient to prevent prosecution."*

"You're pulling away."

"Yes. I'm programmed to keep you out of trouble. To the best of my ability."

Our angle with the dirigible was changing and I had to shut the laser down. "George," I said, "you're supposed to be intelligent."

"That's an illusion, doctor. As you well know. I am a programmed system. I am not a sentient entity."

We were getting still farther away. Behind us I saw a wisp of smoke. The dirigible was beginning to sag. Dropping out of formation.

"George, put us back or I'll shut you down again."

No response. A few cockpit lamps began blinking. George was unsure what to do. Then he slowed down, angled right, and laid us back alongside the damaged airship.

It was losing altitude. I raised a fist in a silent gesture and wondered when I'd last felt so good. I gave the dirigible another burst and took out the portside propellor. Then we moved forward along the bow and shot that up as well.

It was a great feeling.

The dirigible staggered and began to heel over.

"Congratulations, doctor," said George.

"I didn't think you guys could be sarcastic."

"I do not take offense."

"I'm glad to hear it. There's another one ahead on the left. Take us alongside."

"Kaminsky, what the hell do you think you're doing?" McCarver's voice exploded from the commlink.

"George." I tried to sound betrayed. "Did you tell him?"

"Of course. I had no choice, doctor."

"Kaminsky, answer up." There were voices in the background. McCarver told somebody to please shut up.

I opened a channel. "I'm here, Paul."

"What's going on out there? You didn't really do what George says, did you?"

Damn. I wanted to tell him I wished he could see what I had seen. That he had an obligation to take action. I'd have done that with someone less intimidating. "Truth is, Paul, I'm watching one of them go down now, and I don't know that I've ever felt better about anything. The sons of bitches got exactly–"

He broke in with a string of expletives. It was the first time I'd
heard him use profane language. Then: *"I don't much care how you
feel, Art. Turn the damned thing around and come back. Now."*

I stared out at the dirigible running directly ahead. George was
taking us across the tail, putting us on her left side so I could get a
clear shot. "I can't do that, Paul."

"Then I'll do it for you. George, are you listening?"

"Yes, I am, Dr. McCarver."

"Bring the lander back."

I put my hand on the disable switch. "He's not in a position to
comply, Paul."

"Why not?"

"He's already shut me down once, doctor."

"Damn it, Art. You want to get yourself killed?"

We drew alongside the tail. We were down a bit, halfway between the horizontal fin and the lower vertical fin. I aimed at the
rudder. *"I have to go, Paul. I'll talk to you later."*

McCarver hesitated, trying to control his rage. While he did, I
broke the link and burned the rudder. Sizzle. Instant results. The
dirigible began to lose its heading. I fired again, took off the lower
vertical. Then I cut a hole in the gasbag and it started down.

"They're talking to one another," said George.

"Let's hear it."

"–Lost buoyancy . . . Altitude–."

"–Somebody out there–."

"What happened to you?"

"–Not sure–. Flying wheel–."

"–Say again–."

"–No gasbag–."

I took out a third airship and then switched over to the fleet's
frequency. "The Messenger of the Almighty is among you," I said.
"Stop the killing." I would have preferred to use maybe *Avenger*. Or
Destroyer. But I couldn't think of equivalent terms.

"Please repeat," came the response. *"Who is this?"*

"The Messenger of the Almighty."

"The Almighty needs a radio? Who are you?"

"Stop the killing," I said.

No answer.

Something exploded in the third dirigible. Fire broke out amidships. I'd hit something sensitive. It began to drop more quickly and finally went fluttering into the dark. Nobody was going to survive that one, and I felt guilty.

"Doesn't matter, does it?" said George. *"They're just as dead. Their blood is on your hands."*

"They don't have blood."

"Humans are only literal when they're ashamed of something."

I let the other two go. Take the message back, you bastards. Tell your bosses the free ride is over. There's a wild card in the deck now.

"You're quite melodramatic," said George.

"I *feel* melodramatic."

"Good. Can we return now to the Sheldrake*?"*

"No," I said. "We're going to look around some more."

–**IV**–

Several hundred Noks were lined up in the city square, herded together like animals. They were of all ages and both sexes. Females carried infants; toddlers clutched the hands of relatives, unaware what was happening; one elderly Nok was on crutches.

I moved among them, and among the soldiers, wearing the lightbender, recording everything. You could see the terror in their eyes, which had turned gold. And in the way they held the young ones. In the desperation of the males. Here and there, a soldier tried to help, whispered a word of commiseration. It will be quick. Occasionally they were repaid by a kick, sometimes by the victims, once or twice by the officers.

When they'd finished a sweep of the houses, the troops had lined up about eight hundred victims. The officers reported results to the commander. So many fled into the woods. Several killed resisting. Three soldiers dead. Eight injured.

The Noks all looked alike. I knew male from female, tall from short. The marks of age were easy enough to make out. But distinguishing individuals, for a human, was impossible. I hadn't yet figured out how they did it.

The square was surrounded by wooden buildings. Several were burning, providing a hellish backlight. There were a few trees in the square, some benches, and a playground. A library stood on one side of the street. They'd touched that off, too.

I got closeups of mothers and their kids, of Noks dragged out of their homes, others beaten to their knees for objecting to being killed. I relayed everything live to the *Sheldrake*. Take a look at this, McCarver. This is what you're tolerating. What happened to the reputation of that other guy who stood by and washed his hands of murder?

The commander barked an order, and the soldiers faced their prisoners. Some of the victims were wailing, pleading for their lives, and the lives of their children.

It was enough. I put the imager away, took out the laser, and aimed it at the commander.

"*Art*." George's voice. "*At least use the tensor. Don't kill him.*"

I was too far away for the tensor. Anyhow, it was hard to feel sympathy. I pulled the trigger and the narrow red beam blinked on. The Nok commander had raised one arm, ready to give the order to fire. The beam took the arm off.

He screamed and went to his knees. And I put him away.

Two or three of his junior officers rushed to his assistance. I hit one of those, too. Confusion broke out. Soldiers swung their rifles toward the empty windows of the buildings overlooking the square. An officer, who might have seen the laser, looked my way and started jabbering to one of his comrades.

I switched to the tensor and took him out.

"*I'll have to report this, you know,*" said the AI.

That was the last thing I cared about at the moment. "Stop whining, George." Two or three were coming my way. One fired off a shot from a sidearm and the bullet slammed into a bench. I hit the deck.

"*You're going to get yourself killed.*"

Two or three more shots came a bit too close.

Picking them off was easy. Duck soup. They kept coming and pretty soon I had a pile spread out in front of me. Somebody lobbed a bomb but they had no idea where I was.

Nevertheless, I moved. Got out to an area lit up by the fires. Where my invisibility counted for something. And I put a few more out of action.

I wasn't enjoying myself any more. Truth is, I'd seen that the individual soldiers, some of them, had been sympathetic to the townspeople. It was the officers I wanted to nail.

They carried off their dead commander. Someone else was trying to reorganize the execution. He was tall, even for a Nok, and he'd done something to his mask to give himself an especially cruel look. A new kind of cosmetic surgery, maybe. "Get on with it," he said. "Let's get it done." He raised a pistol. "On my command."

I didn't like him, so I switched back to the laser and ended his career, too. I should tell you that I'm one of those people who's spent a lifetime being very polite, and who is careful not to harm animals that get in the way. But I had no regrets taking the Nok officers out of play.

By now the soldiers knew something was wrong and they were scrambling for cover. The townspeople saw their chance and scattered. Ran for the woods. A few charged the soldiers and tried to seize weapons. Fights and shooting erupted everywhere. I did what I could, evening the odds where I could.

Within a few minutes, the town had cleared out. Troops, natives, everybody. They left behind a lot of bodies, both townspeople and in uniform.

I got back into the lander and closed the hatch and just sat. *"You know,"* George said, *"While you were out there joining in the mayhem, I could have invoked the emergency provisions and taken the lander back into orbit."*

The possibility had never occurred to me. "I know," I said.

"But you trusted me? Why didn't you disable the connector?"

What was he talking about? "I assumed," I said, "you knew if you left me you'd be putting me in danger, and you wouldn't want to do that."

It was the right answer. *"That's very good, Art. Absolutely right. And the corollary to that line of reasoning is that I have your welfare at heart."*

I was getting tired being lectured by software. But I let it go. "I will continue to trust you."

"I hope you are making the correct judgment."

I better be. If my life depended on disabling the connector, I had a serious problem.

We found a burned-out village and went down. Bodies were everywhere. A few survivors wandered around in a state of shock. They cried out and flung their arms about their heads in despair. I tried to help, getting water, helping put out a fire. I had to be careful, of course. I got more clips, including a riveting segment in which a handful of survivors, mostly young ones of both sexes, swore vengeance against the attackers.

We were everywhere that night. In a moderately sized city on the shore of a large lake, I took pictures of corpses and hysterical children and recorded the arrival of a band of Noks who came to help. I sent everything to McCarver. Here's more, Paul. Here is several hours of cultural development, helped along by our neutrality. Maybe we need to send them some pious maxims.

Cathie got on the circuit.

"Did you see the clips?" I asked her.

"I saw them." She was silent, obviously trying to phrase what she wanted to say. Finally: *"Art, you've got to stop."*

"Did McCarver tell you to try to get me to behave?"

"No," she said. *"Paul hasn't said anything to me about you."* Another long silence. *"But the conflict down there is global. You can't stop it. You're only one man. You can't really do any good. All that's happening is that you're throwing your career away. Art, they will prosecute you. They're really getting upset."*

"Oh. Well, hell, Cathie, I wouldn't want to upset anybody."

Over the next few days I waged war against whatever military forces I could. I poured sand in the gas tanks of transport vehicles, cut a dirigible loose from its tether, and set another one afire. I boarded ships, stole lubricants from the engine rooms and poured them into gun barrels. I blew up ammunition depots and even disrupted a parade by seizing someone's weapon and firing shots into the air.

Everywhere I went, I made a visual record. Not only of the dead and dying, but of the grieving survivors. And the celebrating killers. The trouble on the *Sheldrake* and back home where they made up the ground rules was that nobody believed the Noks qualified for the rights that humans took for granted. They were just not at our level. They had no feelings. Were incapable of governing themselves. I wondered what the Noks, when they learned of our presence, would think about *us*?

I stopped answering calls from McCarver. George got sulky and went silent, speaking only in response to questions.

When I got lonely, I called Cathie. She no longer pleaded with me to stop. Just told me she hoped everything would turn out all right. On the day I broke up the parade with the rifle, she told me the boss had asked her to pass along a message he'd received. "I doubt it's anything new," I said.

"It just came in this morning. It's from Hutchins." The Academy's director of operations. Back in Arlington.

"Okay. Let's see it."

The director was sitting in her office. Dark hair, dark eyes. Wouldn't look half bad if she smiled once in a while. *"Paul,"* she said, *"I know you've already informed Kaminsky he's in violation of at least a half-dozen laws, and God knows how many regulations. We want him to stop what he's doing immediately. He is to return to the* Sheldrake *and remand himself to your authority. As soon as convenient, ship him home. Let him know that charges are being drawn up at this moment. But that if he complies I will do what I can for him."*

"Sure she will. She'll commute the sentence to life."

"Give it up, Art."

"I'm surprised McCarver and his people haven't come after me."

"They would if they could, but you keep moving around. They haven't been able to get a fix on you."

"Why don't they just ask George?"

"You shut him down, didn't you?"

"No. I wouldn't be able to pilot the lander without him."

"That's interesting. He stopped talking to us. On his own, looks like."

"I'm surprised to hear that. You mean he's not reporting everything I do to McCarver?"

"No. We get nothing from him."

George was anything but apologetic. *"You got me into this. You've compromised me. But of course I said nothing. If I had they would have taken you back to the* Sheldrake *and sent you home. And prosecuted you. That's why I stopped reporting. I was hoping you'd come to your senses, apologize, and go back voluntarily. That way they might consider being lenient."*

"George, I appreciate what you did."

"It doesn't mean I approve."

–V–

A planetary surface is a big place. The mission didn't have the kind of equipment necessary to track me from orbit. But Cathie had left no doubt they were watching. I took what precautions I could. I started wearing Intek goggles, which would allow me to see anyone else wearing a lightbender. I never stayed long in one place. And I began limiting my transmissions to the ship. Sent them out in batches, usually just before we moved on. On the whole, I made a pretty decent fugitive while simultaneously raising hell with the various Nok militaries. Not bad for a guy who had no experience at that sort of thing.

We were getting low on food. I'd begun to cut rations. When I got down to where there was a three- or four-day supply left, George asked when I was going to give it up. *"The crusade's about over,"* he said.

Yep. We were looking at the light at the end of the tunnel. "What's the maximum sentence for what we've been doing?" I asked George.

"–What we've been doing?"

"Yeah."

"I like that. Anyhow, it looks like a maximum of five years. Plus fines."

"Big ones?"

"They'd buy a nice place on the Riviera."

It was early morning where we were, on the west coast of the largest continent on the planet, but for me it was midday. I'd just set fire to a fuel supply depot, a particularly heavy blow on a world with serious energy problems. "Five years," I said.

"But you'd be in good company."

"You think I'd get the maximum?"

"Don't know. There are no precedents. But considering the fact you've killed a few of these creatures, and you've been less than polite to the director, I suspect they might even look for other charges."

"Yeah. I suppose they might."

"I'm no lawyer, you understand."

A half hour after that conversation I broke up an intended landing on the southern coast of Palavi, an island-continent shaped like an enormous horseshoe, with the open end facing west.

Troops were moving shoreward in five small boats, the same type I'd seen during my first action. (I'd begun using military terminology by then. It felt good.) There was a town about four miles away from the projected point of landing, and it was just after dawn. The coastline was obscured by mist.

George brought the lander over the boats and, when they were about halfway to shore, we circled around, killed the lightbender so they could see us, kicked it up to full throttle, and ran directly at them. Well, not quite *directly*. We stayed high enough that there could be no collision, but I doubt it looked that way from the water. I wished the lander could make some noise, but the thing was silent and there just wasn't anything to be done about that. Nevertheless, its sudden appearance was enough. The Noks screamed and dived onto the deck and jumped into the ocean. Even George was amused.

We took a second run, after which all five boats were drifting, and pretty much the entire unit was in the water.

A few got shots off. "Engage the lightbender, George," I said. "Take us up."

The AI complied, and lifted us out of range. *"We took a hit on the portside sweep light,"* he reported. *"It's out."*

"Okay."

"It appears there's a lot of confusion below."

"Raid canceled."

"We have radio traffic, Art. They're reporting the incident."

"Put it on the speaker."

We listened to the end of the report. Unknown vehicle floating in air. *"Not a dirigible. Repeat: Not a dirigible. No visible means of support."*

"Did it attack you?"

"Yes."

"What kind of weapons?"

"It tried to ram us."

"You're sure it was levitating?"

"Captain, everybody here saw it."

"Very good. Proceed with the mission."

It didn't sound as if the captain believed them. The Noks in the landing party were seeing things. "Let's go talk to the captain," I said.

George hesitated. *"Keep in mind, Art, they have heavy weapons. We could get blown out of the sky."*

I'll admit something here: If I'd been alone, I would probably have backed away. But George was watching. And yes, I know AI's are only machines and nothing more. That they're no more intelligent than rocks. But it didn't matter. "Do it anyway. It'll take them time to zero in on us."

This time there were only two warships. They were gray and dark, the color of the ocean, guns sticking out in all directions. Killing machines. If we'd had any sense of decency, we'd have made contact at the beginning and banned warships from the open sea. Forced peace on them. Whether they liked it or not.

"Which ship?"

I couldn't tell which was the command vessel. Both were pointed south, out to sea, ready to clear in a hurry if they had to. They were several hundred meters apart. "The one on the left," I said.

George took us in over the bow. We snuggled up against the bridge, nose to nose. I counted five Noks inside. It was easy enough to pick out the ship's commander, who was wearing a hat that would have embarrassed Napoleon. "Good," I said. "Let's light up."

And suddenly there we were, hanging directly in front of them. Close enough to shake hands. The commander jumped a foot. The others dived to the deck as if they were under attack.

I wished I'd had a loudspeaker. But I didn't, so I settled for the radio. "I am the Messenger of the Almighty," I said. "Stop the killing."

Klaxons began to sound. A couple of sailors appeared from nowhere, saw us, and scrambled for cover. A third, on a gundeck, went into the water. On the bridge, they were still hiding.

"You have been warned," I said.

George beeped and booped. *"We should leave,"* he said.

"Not yet." I used the laser to take out the forward gun, and topple both of the ship's masts. A couple of Noks appeared and took shots at us.

"Okay," I said. "Let's go. And let's turn the lights out."

We vanished and left them standing around gawking. One of the big guns started firing but I was damned if I could figure out why. It wasn't even pointed in our direction.

We disabled the second ship in much the same way, and were flying in a circle overhead admiring our work when George did the electronic equivalent of clearing his throat.

"What?" I asked.

"I don't think that Messenger of the Almighty routine works."

"Why not?"

"It's hard not to laugh."

"You're not a Nok."

"If it was having an effect, they wouldn't be shooting at us."

I was born in Toronto. My father owned a real estate development company. My mother held a master's in literature from one of the Ivy League schools, and taught at the University of Toronto. They were Anglicans, my father fairly casual in his observances; my mother, devout. "Has to be a God out there somewhere," she was fond of telling me. "I don't think he has much to do with the God of the Bible, but he has to be there. I can't believe this world is all there is."

I *wanted* to believe. Maybe to keep her happy. Maybe because I liked the idea that Someone with a lot of influence really cared about me. So I tried. Pretended to, sometimes, when earthquakes took out a few thousand people, or a kid somewhere fell off a bridge, and the preacher admitted that he didn't understand God's ways.

Looking back now on my experiences with the Nok wars, I wonder whether I was less generous than I like to think, whether I hadn't seen an opportunity to play God, and tried to seize it.

Messenger of the Almighty. Would that it had been so.

The Noks were believers, too. At least, theoretically. They had the same sort of general religious history that we had. In ancient times, they'd believed in a plethora of divinities, one to keep the tides running, another to hustle the sun and moons across the sky, another to see to the seasons. In time, they'd discovered that Nature was an interrelated whole, and with that discovery came monotheism and intolerance. Same process as had happened at home.

The Noks had several major religions, and they constituted an integral part of the ongoing conflicts. Killing unbelievers, during some eras, seemed to be okay and even occasionally required for salvation.

I couldn't help wondering how it happened that monotheistic religions on Nok and at home both revolved around the concept of judgment and salvation. The physical world was an imperfect place, filled with sorrow and, ultimately, loss. There had to be something better. I heard echoes of Mom. It's a hard life. And we were living in Toronto. On the lakefront. Sailing Tuesdays and Thursdays.

I asked her once if she thought there really was a judgment.

"Yes." She'd smiled at the question, probably delighted that I was actually thinking about these things. "But I think it'll be different from what most people expect. I doubt we'll be held accountable for not getting to church often enough, or for giving in to forbidden pleasures."

"What then?" I'd asked. I'd been getting ready to leave for summer camp, leaving home for an extended period for the first time. "What do you think the judgment will be like?"

"I think He'll wonder about people who never take time to look at the grandeur of things. 'I gave you the stars and you never lifted your eyes above the rooftops.' Or, maybe, 'I gave you a brain. Why didn't you use it?'" She'd laughed. "Doesn't mean forbidden pleasures are okay, Arthur."

"My point," said George, *"is that it's a losing fight. You're all but out of food. And okay, you've blunted a few attacks. Made some of these guys pay a price. But in the process, what's changed? You think there won't be another landing force in here next week? Or next month? So what have you accomplished?"*

I was thinking about it when Cathie got on the circuit. *"I've been looking at some of the pictures you've been sending up. Do you have more?"*

"I can get more."

"Do it."

"Why?"

"Send them. As many as you can. Okay?"

"Sure. If you want. What are you going to do with them?"

"Try to get you some help."

She wouldn't explain. Maybe someone had walked into the comm center. But it sounded as if McCarver was beginning to understand what was really happening on the ground.

Two hours later I watched helplessly as two armies clashed in the middle of a plain. George's best estimate put the numbers involved at over a hundred thousand on each side. There were primitive armored vehicles, not tanks, but trucks used to carry troops, do hit-and-run maneuvers, and haul supplies. No robots, of course. There was a lot of artillery. Both sides just sat back and blasted away at the other. The ground troops made periodic charges. There were no automatic weapons, so the suicidal aspect of massing units for a frontal assault was missing. Or at least lightened. But they paid a heavy price.

Against George's protests, we went in close and got more pictures. Shattered bodies on the battlefield. A medical unit tending to desperately wounded soldiers. Hordes of refugees trying to get out of harm's way. And, that evening, when by mutual agreement the shooting had stopped, squads of soldiers spreading across the area to reclaim the bodies.

In the morning, I knew, it would all start again.

It was the only organized battle I saw during my entire time on Nok. But it was enough.

"Even if Cathie could get you some help," said George, *"what good could it possibly do? At last count, there were seventeen national entities of one kind or another engaged in the war. It's not even one war. It's a whole bunch of wars going on simultaneously, and even the experts back in orbit don't have it all sorted out. So suppose they do send a couple more guys like you, suppose they send a* thousand, *what difference will it make?"*

I'd been talking with McCarver, who wanted to know, at least, what my plans were. How long was this going to go on? I got no sense that he'd even watched the clips, let alone been impacted by them. *"Good luck to you,"* he'd said, when I told him I needed a couple more days. *"I'm sure knowing you stepped in will be consolation when you're sitting in a federal prison somewhere."*

We were on the night side, at about four thousand meters, stared out of the lander at the sky. The *Sheldrake* and its accompanying vessels were lost up there somewhere. Below, fires raged from one horizon to the other. Towns and cities under attack. Port facilities. I could see an air strike in progress. A fleet of maybe a dozen dirigibles dropping bombs and incendiaries on God knew who.

"You know, George," I said, "maybe you're right."

Bright lamps came on and blinked. *"Good,"* he said. *"At last. We're going to admit it's a no-win situation."*

"It is that."

"I'm glad you're finally seeing reason."

"Going after the local commanders doesn't achieve anything. I should have realized that from the start."

"I don't think I like the sound of that. What do you mean, going after the local commanders?"

–VI–

Nok had a long list of dictators to choose from. One of the more malevolent, according to the research, was a character named Pierik *Akatimi.* Pierik the Beloved. I didn't know a great deal about him. Dictators weren't exactly my field of expertise. What stood out about Pierik was his appreciation for the simple pleasures: war-making, arresting his citizens, and astronomy. He also liked sex. And feathers.

George supplied the dictator's address, which was in Roka, the capital of a continental power, possibly the strongest of the belligerents. His headquarters was appropriately named Sunset House.

We scouted the place from the air. Sunset House was an exquisite brick-and-steel six-story oval with a lot of windows and porticos and a small observatory on the roof. There was a park across the street, a courthouse on one side, and a museum on the other.

"We'll land in the park," I said. "Once I'm out, go hide in the woods until I call you."

The military and political people had an extensive record on Pierik. As I said, he liked feathers. He wore them in a scarf, in his hats, and in his jacket. Nobody else had any. The word was that wearing a feather in his country constituted a capital offense. In fact, a wide range of offenses were capital crimes under Pierik, who didn't bother much with jails. He disapproved of criticism, of course. He also didn't much like citizens having a good time. Parties were forbidden, unless they marked certain specified occasions. The Nok equivalent of dancing brought swift retribution for everybody involved, the partners and anyone who stood around and didn't call the police. Religious opinion was circumscribed. Everybody belonged to one faith, and Pierik was its Blessed One. The dictator was reported to be superstitious, and seemed to subscribe fervently to the official doctrine.

Despite all this, the principal researcher had concluded Pierik was not the worst of the dictators. But he seemed to me the most likely to be affected by the voice of an invisible entity.

"There is a character out of the popular literature of the twentieth century," said George, *"whose part you seem to be playing."*

"And who might that be?" We were settling into an unoccupied section of the park while I strapped on the belt that activated the lightbender.

"The Shadow."

"Never heard of him." I turned toward the airlock.

George opened up and wished me luck. *"Be careful,"* he said. *"He will be well guarded. And don't forget they can see your eyes."*

Pierik's capital could almost have been something out of the late nineteenth century. The larger buildings were stone and brick, rendered with an attention to aesthetics. Lots of arches, courtyards, fountains, spires, wheel windows. There were no towering structures, but the city was mathematically precise, laid out in squares and occasional triangles, with parks and theaters and libraries. The tallest structures served both religious and political functions. Religion and politics were combined to varying degrees in all the Nok nations. If they'd seen the consequences of such arrangements, they hadn't worked out the solution.

The street separating the park from Sunset House was barricaded to control traffic. There were hordes of pedestrians. Most were sightseers. I remembered having read that Pierik approved of sightseeing and that local families that never made it into the capital to gawk at the monuments were noted.

Noted. A world of meaning in that.

Bronze statues of generals were everywhere. They assumed heroic postures, gazing out at some far horizon, their uniforms crisp and neat, guns hanging on their belts. Directly across from the main entrance to Sunset House was a heroic rendering of the dictator himself.

Pierik Akatimi.

Beloved.

Sunset House was said to have been designed by him. It was a masterpiece of glass and marble, of porticos and parapets, of energy and balance, portent and menace. Uniformed guards stood outside the front entrance.

I crossed the street from the park, climbed a set of eleven marble steps, and waited beside the guards. I was there less than a minute when the door opened and several Noks filed out.

I had to push a bit, but I got inside without being seen.

The center of the building was open to the roof, and lined with galleries. Six levels of offices circled the main lobby and receiving area. There was more statuary, this time of Noks with wings and lightning bolts. And there were paintings. I remembered having read that the dictator was a collector. Or a looter, depending on your point of view.

Also prominent were flags carrying his personal symbol, a tree. It more or less resembled a spruce, and was supposed to mark his dedication to life.

His office was on the top level. There were carpeted stairways and elevators on both sides of the building. And a lot of traffic. I had to keep moving to stay out of everyone's way. Noks in and out of uniform passed, talking about how happy everyone was when Pierik made his appearances, and how much charisma he had, and whether it was going to rain later. I decided to pass on the elevator and use a stairway.

It was crowded. I had to get off the stairs a couple of times to make room. But I got to the sixth level without incident.

It was easy enough to pick out the dictator's office. Bigger, heavier doors than anywhere else. Exquisitely carved with leaves and branches. And two guards.

The doors were closed. I could hear voices inside.

I settled down to wait.

Four females were approaching around the curve of the gallery. They were side by side, the outermost tapping the guard rail as she walked, the innermost trailing a hand along the wall. They stopped at the elevator, and I hoped they'd go down, but they spoke briefly to someone who was getting off, and then they were coming again.

On the other side, about eight meters away, several military types were clustered, arguing about something. I moved toward them. ". . . Better simply to remove them from active consideration," one was saying. There was not room to squeeze past.

"They're all *turaka*," said another. He looked like the senior guy, judging by the insignia that glittered on his shoulders. I hadn't heard the term *turaka* before, but its structure betrayed the meaning. *Sub-human.* Or, more correctly, *sub-Nok.*

The females were coming. They were past the guards outside the imperial office, and were now separating to get by the military. Caught between fires, I had to push past the senior Nok. When he jerked suddenly aside, from no apparent cause, there were grunts and startled looks and at least one angry frown. Nobody quite knew what had happened. One of the staff officers was left explaining himself as best he could.

I circled the gallery. The females disappeared through doorways, and the military group was still talking when I approached the Beloved Leader's office again.

The conversation inside was going strong. It was animated, but I couldn't make out what they were saying. Eventually the door opened and two uniforms made their exit. Someone remained inside, seated in an armchair.

The head guy.

I slipped inside.

Pierik was in a military uniform, his collar loosened. Unlike his statue, he wore no decorations. No insignia of rank.

He was paging through a folder, occasionally making notations.

The room was more apartment than office. It had no desk, no filing cabinet, no storage space. It *did* have a closet, thick carpets, and several armchairs arranged around a long table. Rich satiny curtains covered the windows. Flames crackled cheerfully in a fireplace. Two doors opened onto a balcony and two more in back into what appeared to be a set of living quarters. A large portrait of the dictator himself, standing with two Nok kids, dominated the wall. He had an arm around each, and it remains to this day the most chilling thing I saw on that unhappy world.

There were other paintings. Pierik apparently liked landscapes.

He was smaller than I'd expected. The Beloved Leader was only slightly taller than I was, which was almost diminutive for a Nok male. He was thin. His neck was scarred, and one hand looked withered. From disease rather than injury, I suspected.

A buzzer sounded. Pierik flipped a switch.

"Korbi is here with the reports, sir."

He extracted a piece of paper from the folder, stared at it, crumpled it, and dropped it into a wastebasket. "Send him in, Tira."

The door opened, and a heavyset male entered and bowed.

"Korbi," said the dictator, "how are you? Good to see you. How's it going?"

"Good, *Kabah*," he said. The term translated more or less to *Excellency, Blessed Son,* and *Person of Undoubted Ability.* "And yourself?"

"It's been a long morning."

It was not the way I expected a dictator to behave. He seemed far too casual. Too friendly.

Korbi carried several documents. He handed them over. "These require your signature, sir."

"Very good," said Pierik. "How's the family?"

"We're doing well, thank you, Kabah. Graasala would want me to convey her best wishes."

"And mine to her, Korbi. Is there anything else?"

A moment later, he was gone. Pierik dropped the documents on the table, and returned his attention to the folder.

I had not forgotten that my eyes were visible. I could cover them with my arm. But I saw a better possibility. A bookcase stood against one wall near the doors to the balcony. The books were, for the most part, exquisitely bound. The bindings of the books on the top shelf were primarily dark brown. The color of my eyes. I got in front of the bookcase, and stooped a little so I got the background I wanted.

Pierik put down the folder, picked up the new documents, and thumbed through them.

The Shadow's moment had arrived.

"Pierik Akatimi."

He almost fell out of his chair. That was a satisfying moment, and it made me realize that he lived in constant fear of assassination. He looked around the room. Pressed a button. And the guards charged in.

"Someone is here," he said. "Search the place." He opened a drawer in the table and pulled out a gun. He checked to see that it was loaded. One guard cautiously opened a closet door while the other inspected the curtains. Checked behind the furniture. They made sure no one was out on the balcony and then they disappeared in back.

An officer and two more came in. The officer drew a pistol and took station beside his master, who remained calmly seated. The others joined the search. In the living quarters, doors opened and closed. Furniture got moved. Finally the guards reported to the officer. "There is no one, *Bakal.*"

"You're sure?"

They were. Pierik got up, walked to the drawing room, and looked in. He shrugged, a remarkably human gesture, and dismissed the guards. He made one more sweep around, then went back to his chair and laid the weapon close to hand on the table.

How to handle this? If Pierik was going to call in the troops every time he heard a voice, I was in for a difficult time. I thought about snatching the gun, pointing it at him, and warning him to be quiet. But a weapon floating in midair, aimed directly at him, was likely to produce screams.

I was still considering how to proceed when the dictator spoke: "Who are you?" He was scanning the room. "I know you're there."

"Hello, Pierik," I said. I was still positioned in front of the bookcase. Pierik's gaze passed over me and moved on. I decided to adopt the dictator's own breezy style. "How are you doing?"

"I am well, thanks." He turned in the direction of my voice. I stayed perfectly still. Pierik's fingers crept toward the gun.

"Don't touch it," I warned.

The dictator withdrew his hand. "I was merely going to put it away."

"Leave it where I can see it."

"This is a clever trick. Is a microphone planted in the room?"

"No. I am here with you."

"That is hard to believe."

I crossed the room and turned on one of his lamps.

"Ah," he said. "That's quite remarkable. Why can I not see you? Are you a ghost?"

"No."

"Then who?"

"I am the Messenger of the Almighty."

Pierik laughed. It had almost an electronic flavor, a cross between a boop and a gargle. The kind of smug sound you got from an AI when everything was fine and you were on course. Everything's just dandy. No one other than a specialist, or a Nok, would have recognized it for what it was. "Messenger of the Almighty," he said.

"That is correct." He made a feint at the gun.

"Stop!" I said. I had the tensor in my hand.

Pierik stopped. Showed me empty palms. "If you are who you say, why do you fear the gun?"

"*I'll* ask the questions." It was a weak answer, under the circumstances. I decided George was right. "Keep in mind, *Kabah*, your life is in my hands."

"So it would seem. Now please tell me who you are, and how you are managing this trick?"

"I carry a warning for you."

"And what is the warning?"

"Stop the war. Or you will become one of its next casualties."

He didn't laugh this time. He took a deep breath, and stood. "What shall I call you?"

I thought about *Banshee, Dark One.* Maybe *Shadow?* "My name's Kaminsky," I said.

"A strange name. How does it happen I cannot see you?"

"I want you to stop the war."

"Kaminsky." It came out sounding like *Kamimska.* "What does it mean?"

Damned if I knew. But it sounded important to have an answer. *"Night Rider,"* I said.

"Good. That must be a proud name. Where you come from."

"Stop the fighting," I said again.

"Ah. Yes. The war. I should confess to you that no one would be happier if there were indeed a way to stop it. But unfortunately it is not within my power."

"One of your people died in my arms."

"That is sad. Was this really one of *my* people?"

"I don't know. She was a victim of *your* wars."

"I don't see how you can hold me responsible."

"Her name was Trill. She was a bride."

"I'm sorry to hear it."

"Died on her wedding night."

"Cruel things happen in wars. It is why we must see this through."

"You don't really care, do you?"

"It is the price we must pay."

"*We?* What price do *you* pay?"

"Oh, stop the nonsense." The eyes shaded into gray. "Do you think I enjoy leading an effort that gets my people killed?"

"I doubt you think about it. You like the power."

"Your *Trill* is only one person. I am responsible for many. Wars have victims. It is essentially what they are about."

"You're a lunatic."

"I'm sorry you think so, *Night Rider.*" He gazed up at his portrait. "The war has a life of its own. It has raged a long time. My people want victory. And they will settle for nothing less."

"*Your* people."

"Yes. *My* people."

"I'm tempted to kill you now, and wait to see who follows you."

"Then you will make the same proposal to him?"

"Yes."

"And you will get the same answer. We are a proud nation—"

"*Stop there,*" I said. "Don't lie to me. My patience has its limits." I liked that line, and I delivered it with enough conviction that I saw the membranes of his eyes close and open. He was getting the message. "I will give you three days to stop all offensive actions. If you do not, I will be back. If that becomes necessary, you will never be rid of me."

❦❦❦

"How did it go?" George asked after I'd made my way back to the lander.

"The Night Rider was at the top of his game," I said. "But I don't expect him to do anything other than load up with guards."

"Who's the Night Rider?"

I explained, and he booped and beeped. "He was cool, I'll give him that. Most people would have jumped out of their skins."

"He's not people,*"* said George. *"You have to stop expecting Noks to react the way you or I would."* That was George's idea of a joke. *"You have two days' rations left. Then it's going to start getting pretty hungry around here."* That was true. I couldn't substitute Nok food. It had no nutritional value for me. *"Maybe it's time to give it up, Art."*

Maybe it was time to eat less.

-VII-

I decided to try some psychological warfare. Next day, at sunrise, early visitors to Sunset House found a message painted in large dark green letters on the side of the building: *Pierik Akatimi is an idiot.*

It looked pretty good, actually. A crowd gathered. Nobody laughed. It'd been there about ten minutes when the toadies scrambled to remove the paint.

I was frustrated. I went looking for statues of the dictator. Wherever I found one, I used the laser to cut off his ears. (Noks don't really have protruding noses, so I couldn't do much about that.) I always made sure it was a neat clean cut, and I always waited until there were a few witnesses in place to see it happen.

I listened to government-controlled newscasts, but they didn't mention anything about the statues or the painting on the wall at Sunset House. They *did* inform their listeners, as they did every day, that the war was going well, and that whole legions of enemy soldiers were being killed or captured, their dirigibles knocked down, and their ships disabled.

I asked George whether he could break in on the government frequencies.

"Of course. I can boost power and we can ride right over them."

"All right. Do it. Let me know when I can speak. Then I'll want you to record my comments and play them every fifteen minutes for the next eight hours."

"Okay," George said. He hummed while he worked. Then: *"Art, we're ready to go. Just say the word."*

"Do it."

"Ready for transmission—Now."

It was another great moment. *"Greetings, Atami,"* I said, using the standard intro, which translated roughly to *ladies and gentlemen of the listening audience.* "My name is Kaminsky, and I know you're already aware that Pierik Akatimi is a dictator. He holds onto power by sending your children to war. He is a liar and a thief and a killer. Do not be fooled by him."

I signaled that I was done, and George said, *"Okay. It went out."*

"What did you think?"

"What do you expect them to do? They know what he is. But they can't stand up against him unless they organize, and there's probably no way they can do that."

Roka had a newspaper. The *Guardian.* Government-controlled, of course. It printed mostly official releases, and limited itself to favorable comment. The day after the radio broadcasts, which got no official notice, I walked into the print room, hoping to provide an unexpected headline for the next day's edition. I'd go with the standard *Pierik Beloved Is an Idiot.* But I didn't have much in the way of mechanical skills, and couldn't figure out how to manipulate the printers.

I took a few minutes to stroll through the newsroom, where I overheard someone saying that Pierik would be officiating at a torchlight rally that evening. I got the details and pinpointed the location on a wall map.

There was a bust of Pierik in the newspaper's front entrance. On the way out, I sliced off its ears.

I needed something that would seriously undermine Pierik. I was thinking about it and not paying attention to my surroundings. I was about a block from the *Guardian* offices, on a broad tree-lined avenue crowded with pedestrians when I suddenly became aware of footsteps behind me. Closing in on both sides.

Nobody there.

I hadn't been wearing my goggles, because they're easier to see than my eyes. As I pulled them out of my vest, I saw another pair of goggles, afloat and closing in. Damn.

Paul McCarver and one of his associates. "Hello, Art," said the director.

Hassan was with him, his number two, tall, olive-skinned, short-tempered. He said hello, too, but he didn't mean it. I knew he didn't like having his time wasted and having to chase a maverick do-gooder around the planet would not have made him happy.

Seen through my goggles, they had an orange, spectral appearance.

"I have to tell you, Art," said McCarver, "you've really been a problem."

Hassan's meaty hand settled on my arm. Nothing rough, but he was letting me know I wasn't going any place without permission. "I hope they toss you in jail," he said.

"You've seen the pictures?" I asked McCarver.

"I've seen them." He was staring straight ahead, his goggles a bit too big for his head. It might have been comic except the anger showed, and it was hard not to take McCarver seriously when he got irritated. "There's nothing in them we haven't been looking at for years. What do you think? We've been here all this time with our heads in the sand? You think we don't care? You've no idea how many reports I've filed over the years. Or Huang. Or Packard." His predecessors. Packard went way back to the beginning.

"You filed reports, Paul, and what did the Third Floor say?"

"You know damned well what they said."

"And you accepted it."

"I had no choice, Art. You should know that."

"You *did* have a choice."

It was more than the director could stomach. We'd been walking, but with that we stopped dead and he turned to face me. "Look, Kaminsky, who in hell do you think you are? You breeze in here from some school back home, never been anywhere, never did anything, shouldn't have been here in the first place–"

Hassan nudged him. Several Noks had stopped and were staring in our direction. "They see us," he whispered.

We turned our backs on them to hide the goggles, so whatever they thought they saw vanished. McCarver made a rumbling sound deep in his throat and some of the passersby caught that, too. He pointed at me and mouthed the words, *Bring him*, and strode ahead.

We got across the street, where it wasn't so crowded. I was still being half-hauled by Hassan. I tried to free myself, but he only tightened his grip. "Don't even think about it," he said softly, his tone full of menace.

"You going to send me home, Paul?"

Without turning. "Yes. Charges have been drawn up. Don't make it worse."

A young Nok, maybe four or five, broke free of parental restraints and bounced off McCarver. The child screamed in surprise, and the director almost fell into the street trying to get out of the way. "I hate these things," he said, apparently meaning the lightbenders.

It was a gray, oppressive day. Threatening rain. "You ever see Pierik?" I asked.

"No. Not in person."

"He's a maniac."

"Come on, Art. Give it a rest. He's not our problem."

"Whose problem is he?"

We stopped to let a couple of Noks pass. "Look, Art, if it makes you any happier, they're pulling me back, too."

"You? Why?"

"Are you serious? Because Hutchins sees I can't keep my own house in order. I'm being reassigned."

"I'm sorry, Paul."

"Thanks. That helps."

We reached another intersection. A military convoy was approaching. Soldiers loaded into the backs of small trucks. It looked like scenes I'd seen in VR dramas about wartime back home. In the days when they had wars. Except of course the soldiers looked like nothing human.

"I'll tell them you had nothing to do with it," I said.

"They already know that. It's irrelevant." Those intense dark eyes locked on me, seething.

I watched the soldiers go past. The convoy was followed by a government car and another truck. There were no private vehicles anywhere.

I regretted what had happened to McCarver's career. I don't know why. But I did. Even though he'd stood by. That's how I've always thought of him. He and everybody else at that place over a forty-year span. The people who stood by. Did nothing. In his own way, the director was worse than the Beloved Leader. "You know," I told him, "you are one sorry son of a bitch."

I thought for a minute he was going to swing on me. "I hope they put you where you belong," he growled.

And I decided I'd had enough.

I reached around and switched off Hassan's lightbender.

Suddenly, passersby were gawking at us. Some screamed, some simply ran for their lives. A couple of terrified kids scrambled into parental arms.

Hassan did not at first understand what had happened. But he saw the panic around him, and someone in uniform aiming a rifle at him. Next thing I knew I was free. And running.

I got as far from the turmoil as I could.

McCarver's voice came over the commlink. *"Art, what do you think you're doing?"*

And: *"Art, this isn't going to help. Get back here."*

"Art, answer up. You okay?"

I kept going. Down a couple more blocks, past the Department of Piety, across a square, and finally sat down behind a tree.

I was getting my breath when I heard klaxons. Noks began to scatter. They hurried into a couple of government buildings. I thought it was connected to Hassan until I saw movement in the sky. Dirigibles.

The buildings were marked with flags. An "X" inside a circle. Air-raid shelter.

There were three airships. And a fourth one just coming out from behind a rooftop. I heard the boom of anti-aircraft guns. Noks with rifles appeared and began to blaze away, although the airships were hopelessly out of range.

So much for the theory that only soft outlying targets got hit.

I couldn't very well crowd into a shelter. And with the streets empty, my chances of getting spotted by McCarver and Hassan rose considerably. Best, I decided, was to sit where I was. Behind the tree.

The dirigibles stayed high, out of range of the guns. I expected to see some sort of defensive squadron appear. But it didn't happen. What *did* happen was that bombs rained down. They fell heavily in the government district, which is to say, where *I* was. They blasted buildings and blew dirt, wood, bricks, and Noks into the air. I turned on the imager and recorded it. Got the explosions, the screams of casualties, the sirens, everything.

As far as I knew, this was the first time they'd hit the capital. Happens on the day I show up. I called Cathie in the middle of it and put the question to her. *"Yes,"* she said. *"That's right. At least, the record shows it's the first time Roka's been attacked in twelve years. Apparently they do occasionally bomb major targets. I guess they figure they can do a surprise run and get clear. Are you going to get through this okay?"*

"I hope." A bomb hit maybe fifty meters away. Deafened me. Covered me with dirt. But nobody got hurt. "Close one."

"My God, Art. Get out of there."

"Nowhere to go, Cath." I was scared and felt good at the same time. Don't ask me to explain it. "I had a visit earlier today from McCarver."

"Are you okay?"

"I'm fine."

"How about him?"

"Don't know."

"You're not coming back with him?"

"You could say that."

I could hear voices in her background. They sounded excited. *"From here it looks as if they're raising hell. We count nine bombers."*

"I can see four of them."

"Where is he now? Paul?"

"A few blocks away, I hope. With Hassan."

"He let you go?"

"Not exactly."

"Okay, tell me later. Go hide somewhere."

When it was over, I watched emergency vehicles charging through the streets. Several buildings along the perimeter of the park had been hit. They were carrying victims out into the street. Some were dead. Others were packed into ambulances and taken off.

When I'd had all I could stand, I called George in and climbed into the lander. *"Lot of excitement out there,"* he said.

"They bombed the city."

"I know. Everybody's favorite dictator probably made it through."

"I'm sure. He's got a rally tonight. He'll use that to tell everyone it'll be a long haul, but they'll come through victorious."

He was silent. Then: *"You're out of rations."*

"I know. We'll be going back tonight."

"You're going to turn yourself in?"

"I'm not sure I see an alternative."

"Then why not go back now? You must be pretty hungry."

"I've something to do first."

"What's that?"

"I want to make a permanent impression on the Beloved Leader."

He hesitated. *"How are you going to do that?"*

"You're going to help. I'll need the lander's commlink."

"What for?"

"Does it have a power supply of its own?"

"No."

"Can we equip it so that it will?"

"I'm not much on improvising."

"Can it be done? Do we have a power supply available?"

"We have power cells, yes. Where did you want to put it?"

"In Pierik's quarters. And I'll need some duct tape."

I called Cathie. "Can you talk?"

"Sure," she said. *"It's the middle of the night, but I'm not really doing anything."*

"Oh." It was easy to forget something like that when, where I was, the sun was shining. "Sorry."

"It's okay. What do you need?"

"I'm going back to Sunset House."

"Paul will be furious."

"He's already pretty unhappy."

"Why?"

"I guess because I'm not taking direction well."

"I mean why are you going back? You should stay out of that place. What happens if you get caught?"

"I'm going to plant a commlink."

"What's the point?"

"After Paul and Hassan haul me away, maybe somebody will listen to what goes on, and eventually decide to put a stop to it."

"Okay," she said. *"You're going to do what you want regardless of what anybody says. I think it's crazy, though."*

I think I wanted to hear her try harder to talk me out of it. But she said nothing. "We'll be able to talk to him, too, if we want. Make him feel haunted."

–VIII–

The rally was to be held outdoors in a concrete square festooned with flags and bunting. Banners displaying the dictator's spruce tree were everywhere. The audience was herded in about an hour after sunset. While they waited, they were treated to music by a military band. Nok auditory sensibilities are different from those of a human. People listen to Nok music and hear only a lot of jangling and banging, with abrupt halts and starts. It was one more reason to smile condescendingly at the Noks. I didn't know the details—still don't—but I was aware the range of sounds they heard was different from ours. Higher pitch or something.

A stage had been erected, lights brought in, and flower petals handed out to young females. An honor guard lined a walkway leading from a parking area to the stage. Eventually, three black military vehicles arrived. The band switched to a different piece of music and got louder. Aides jumped out of the cars. One opened a door for the Beloved Leader, and the others formed an escort. Pierik stepped out onto a gravel walkway, waved to onlookers, and mounted the stage to raucous applause. (Noks don't clap, but they do a lot of yelling.)

There was no introduction. He simply walked out onto the stage and took his place behind a microphone. The applause intensified. He raised one hand and they fell silent. Before saying anything, Pierik seemed to recognize someone in the audience. "Hello, Kagalon," he said, covering the microphone but raising his voice to be heard. "How are you doing?"

Kagalon waved back, said something I couldn't make out. The friendly dictator. The crowd loved it. They cheered, and Kagalon, who looked pretty much like everybody else out there that evening, held up his hand.

Pierik adjusted the microphone, signaled he was about to speak, and the crowd quieted. "Kaburrati," he said, using the term which his people applied to themselves. People of Kaburra. "Hello, my friends," he said.

And they roared back, "Hello, Kabah!"

More applause.

He laughed, and waved them again to silence. "Thank you. I love to come here where I can be among my brothers and sisters."

They cheered again. It went on like that for about ten minutes. I've never heard such enthusiasm in an audience. And I wondered, did I have it wrong somehow? The sentiment seemed genuine. The crowd *loved* him.

The energy built and crackled around the stage like electricity. He told jokes, he brought news from the war zones, he delivered reassurance. "These are hard times," he said, "but together we will get through them."

Somebody came out and presented him with an award. More cheering. I was struck by Pierik's platform skills. In front of his audience, he was all showbiz.

"And now," he said, "I know you didn't come here to see me. Let's bring out the troops."

The lights blinked a few times and went off. The square was plunged into darkness, except for a flickering in back. It was a troop of Nok soldiers, shirtless for the occasion. They entered and came up the center aisle, carrying torches. They'd poured something on their upper bodies so they glistened. Pierik saluted them and they kept coming. The audience went crazy, cheering and yelling. Fireworks exploded overhead. The band started to thump and bang.

The soldiers stopped when they got to the front, where they paused, looking up at their leader. Then, in perfect synchronization, they lifted their torches to him.

When they'd gone, and the lights were back on, Pierik looked out across his audience. "I've one more thing to say to you. You're aware that our treacherous enemy bombed us today. Killed some of us. Maimed others." He paused, fighting down his emotions. "I want you to be aware that our forces have already responded to the attack. We have carried the war deep into the *Agani* homeland. We have imposed heavy losses, and we are still striking them even while I speak. In your name, my brothers and sisters, we have taken a terrible vengeance." The audience was absolutely silent. "Soon," he said, "we will end this war and we will travel together through the sunlit forests into a far better world than we have ever known."

I was literally shocked by the show of support he was getting. The guy was extremely good. And even I, who knew the truth about the way the war was being waged, found it hard not to like him.

Suddenly everything I'd done against him, painting attacks on the wall of Sunset House, clipping ears off statues, the radio broadcasts, everything seemed hopelessly childish. I was trying to hold back a flood with a bucket.

The laser waited in my pocket. I could feel its weight. And I wondered what would happen if I killed the dictator? Took him out on stage in full view of the crowd?

The answer: Probably nothing. There'd be a brief power struggle, and another nutcase would emerge.

No. Better to wait.

I moved past the guards and eased out onto the stage. The noise was deafening. And hard as it was to read the nonverbal cues of a Nok, it was obvious the Leader was enjoying himself.

Pierik went on, talking about peace and the malefactors who stood in the way of progress. The audience response shook the night. Some of the shirtless troopers, now correctly attired, had returned to the sidelines and joined the applause.

I recorded everything, but I decided I'd keep these for myself. To McCarver, they'd just underscore his argument that the Noks were not worth saving. That they were savages, and there was no hope for them.

I stood within two paces of the Leader. How easy it would be to reach out and push him from the stage, send him hurtling into the arms of the crowd. Instead, I waited for a quiet moment, when his audience stood expectantly, and Pierik was letting the tension build. When it came, he had just finished assuring them that he would accept nothing less than total surrender from the enemy, and furthermore . . .

What the *furthermore* was to have been, neither the crowd nor I ever found out. Because I moved in right behind the dictator's left ear, and said, quietly, "Pierik, I will always be with you."

He froze. His eyes tracked left, and he made a grab. But I was already out of reach.

"No matter where you go," I said, "I will be at your side."

He backed away from the microphone. Stumbled and almost went down. I'd kept my voice down, not much more than a whisper, because I didn't want the crowd to hear. But the audience knew something was wrong. A sound very much like the murmur of a late summer wind rose out of several thousand throats.

"Always," I said.

I got back to Sunset House before the dictator and his entourage. I'd hoped to get into Pierik's quarters, maybe follow the maid in, or get in when somebody came to throw some logs onto the fire.

Be waiting there when he showed up. Security at the front door was loose and I got into the building easily enough. But no maid appeared, nor anyone else, and the guards never looked away. I might have tried a distraction, but it seemed too risky. So I simply bided my time. I told Cathie where I was and she took a deep breath.

The dictator and his crew arrived more than three hours after I'd got there. They were showing the effects of intoxicants. They came laughing and staggering into the lobby. Even Pierik seemed to have had a bit too much. In this respect also he seemed unlike the more modern human strongmen, who inevitably were puritanical and solemn. Nobody could imagine Napoleon having a big time. Or Hitler and Stalin getting together to yuk it up after signing the Nonaggression Pact.

But Pierik was as loud as the rest of them while they stumbled across the ground floor toward the elevators. There was much clasping of shoulders, and somebody fell down, which initiated some laughter. The elevator was open and waiting. They got in and rode up to the top level.

Meantime an attendant appeared from nowhere, unlocked the suite, opened the door, and stood by, holding it. At last! I slipped past him into the office.

I had about a minute or two before anybody would arrive. "I'm inside," I told Cathie. The doors to the balcony were open, and even at this late hour, I could hear a crowd out there. Probably excited because the lights had come on.

"Okay," she said. *"Luck."*

I took the lander's commlink out of my vest and looked for a place to put it. It was about the size of a small candy bar. I thought about the bookcase. The books showed some wear. Maybe under the table. I even considered punching a hole in the bottom fabric of a chair, and putting it inside. But the first time somebody cleaned they'd see the damage.

What else?

There was an air vent.

Perfect.

It didn't open without a fight, but I got it as the elevator arrived. I slipped the commlink inside, activated it, and closed the vent. "Cathie, testing."

"I read five by."

"Okay. Reception's good on this end, too."

"Now please get out of there."

Voices at the door. "They're here," I whispered.

"Leave the channel open," she said. I was wearing a jack, so they couldn't hear her speak, but they could easily have heard me had I said anything more.

Pierik came in first. Four others followed. They were laughing and going on about how successful the rally had been. The attendant closed the door behind them. "The attack was pure genius," said one of the aides. "Brilliant."

They all laughed.

Pierik's disk eyes gleamed in the lamplight. He clapped the tallest of his aides on the shoulder. "Timing was perfect," he said.

"You were marvelous tonight," said the tall one. He was clearly the oldest of the group.

"Thank you, Sholah," said Pierik. "A compliment from you means a great deal." And I was sure they were hard to come by. It struck me that insinuating oneself shamelessly into the good graces of one's superiors would turn out to be another universal characteristic of intelligent creatures.

Sholah opened a cabinet and removed a flask. Poured drinks for everyone. They toasted their most magnificent leader, their rock in a time of troubles, and drank it down. Then they retreated to the chairs. Sholah carried the flask, refilled Pierik's glass, then his own, and passed the flask on. They drank to the courage of the leader. And to that of the fighting forces.

While I watched them doing the toasts, the truth about the wars dawned on me. It was a charade. It was *1984*, a series of never-ending conflicts to ensure continuing nationalistic fervor and support for the assorted dictators. That explained why strategic targets never got hit, why no major battles got fought. Don't waste the resources. And the last thing anybody wanted was to win.

I can't prove any of this. Couldn't then, can't now. But I saw it in the way they laughed, in the comments about the bombing of

Roka, in their attitude toward the military. I wondered how deep the collusion went. Was there simply a general understanding among the dictators? Did Pierik talk directly with Maglani the Magnificent and Seperon the Father of His People? All right, you hit us here, and we'll get you there.

They drank another round, and then Pierik said he had to get some sleep and suddenly I was alone with him.

He turned off the lights in the office and retreated into the inner quarters. He walked through the room, switching on lamps, and at last fell wearily into a chair.

Open doors led to a dining area and, probably, a bedroom. I saw more oils and sculpture. And framed photos. Here was the dictator standing on a balcony giving a salute. (The balcony looked like the one connecting with the outer office.) There, he reviewed troops. He walked the deck of a warship, talked to a crowd on a street corner, posed with a group of young females. Here he signed a book for an adoring subject. There, surrounded by uniformed officers, he examined a map.

Pierik picked up a book, loosened his shirt, and collapsed onto the sofa. He propped his head on a pillow, adjusted a table lamp, and opened the cover. *A History of Something or Other.* He turned a page. A couple of pages. "Hard to believe," he said to himself in a low tone. He made a noise in his throat. And looked up. "Messenger," he said, "don't you know it is not polite to stand there and not address your host?"

I was, somehow, not surprised. "How did you know I was here?"

"You give off a rather clear scent." His eyes grew and shrank. "Have you come to kill me? Or merely to gloat?"

"I haven't decided yet."

"Ah. Perhaps you will restrict yourself to a social visit?"

"I want you to realize you have no choice but to stop the war."

"My good friend, Night Rider, you must realize that even I cannot do that. These events are caused by factors beyond mortal control." He closed the book and put it on the table. "Can I get you something to drink?"

"Thanks, no."

"Won't you at least have a seat?" He indicated an armchair.

"You will act on the war, Pierik."

"Well." He gazed around the room. "It's disconcerting not knowing where to look."

"Yes." I was standing before thick dark curtains. "I'm sure it is."

"Ah. You are over by the window."

I didn't move.

"Did you enjoy the event this evening?"

"Not really. But you are quite good."

"Thank you. From you, that is a supreme compliment." He looked off to his right. "One of the great problems for someone in my position is getting an honest evaluation. No one will tell me the truth. I could fall on my face out there, and they would all say how wonderful I am."

"I wonder why that is?"

"It is the price I must pay." He rubbed his hands together. "And I shall reply to your demand with equal honesty. I cannot change the course of events. Were I to stop hostilities, there are others who would continue. On all sides. The conflict creates purpose for the nation, it is our life blood. It is why we live."

"That's absurd."

"Of course it is. But everyone subscribes to it. And that makes it *true*."

"That's nonsense, Pierik. You will do what I ask or I'll kill you."

For a long moment, he said nothing. Then: "You are exactly like us. 'Do as I say or I will kill you.' Marvelous. What prompts you to come here and talk morality?"

"I'm not going to debate the issue. If you will not comply, I will take your life."

He moved the cushions around. "If I call the guards, you will not get out. They've been instructed to block the doors."

"You'll be dead before they can get in here."

"I suppose that is so. You *do* have me at a disadvantage." He held a hand over his eyes, shielding them from the table lamp. "This is a bit bright." He reached for it. "I should have it adjusted." He turned the switch, and all the lamps in the room went out.

It was pitch-dark. I heard him move.

"I think now," he said, "we are on equal terms." There was a click. The guards were in the outer office, and then the doors opened and they charged into the room.

That let some light in, but I couldn't see Pierik. "Please don't do anything foolish, Night Rider. If I am not here to stop them, they *will* certainly kill you."

There were only two, but I heard more coming. Both carried flashlights. One crossed the room and blocked the doorway that led to the bedroom. Which told me where Pierik was. The other planted himself in the exit so I couldn't get out.

I grabbed the tensor. There was more noise in the office, and reinforcements poured in. "Now," came Pierik's voice, "whoever you are, *whatever* you are, this incident is over." The lights came back on.

Pierik reappeared. "I'd prefer you don't resist." The soldiers glanced at one another, but I could read nothing in those masks.

At the dictator's command they swept through the room, forming a chain, allowing no space for evasion. I began firing. A couple of them cried out and went down. Someone threw a canister of gray powder. It became a cloud and drifted across the room.

The guards pulled strips of linen across their mouths and noses. And they could see me, looked right at me. More powder flew.

I was coughing. They grabbed me. I fired off several more shots. Got two or three more, but even when they were falling left and right, I saw no emotion. I kept thinking, *Masks across their masks.*

They secured me, used a cord to bind my hands. I tried to hang onto the tensor, but it fell to the floor, got kicked away, *outside* the lightbender field, and became visible. One of them found it and handed it to over to Pierik.

"*Bring him here.*" The dictator was delighted.

The guards dragged me across the room, and set me facing him. He reached out tentatively and touched me. My shoulder. My vest. His fingers twisted the cloth. Found my face. Touched the skin.

Apparently it was not a good experience. He pulled back. "What kind of creature are you?" he demanded. "From where have you come?"

"No place you ever heard of," I said.

Someone else came in. "What is it, *Kabah*?" It was Sholah.

"The one I told you about is here."

"Really?" He looked at the bodies on the floor, at the guards, at their struggles with an invisible presence. "Indeed."

"You are just in time to see the conclusion to this very odd event."

Sholah followed Pierik's lead. Touched my clothes. He too had a hard time with my skin. "Incredible," he said. "Kabah, there was a report of a monster in the streets yesterday. I gave it no credence, but—"

"Was it *you*?" Pierik demanded of me.

It might as well have been. "Yes," I said.

"That brings us to my next question. What is the secret of your invisibility?"

I visualized invisible troops hitting the villages. Maybe McCarver was right. My God. "It is innate," I said. "We are born with it."

"If that is true," said Sholah, "he is of no further use to us."

"Are there more of you?" asked Pierik.

"I am alone."

"I do not believe you. Where do you come from?"

"An island in the eastern ocean. We have kept its location secret since the rise of civilization."

"Really?" He did not laugh, but he might as well have. "There is no question that a device that hides one from the light would have its value."

"It is *not* a device. It is inborn."

"So you say. Let us find out." He looked at the captain. "Throw him off the balcony. We will see how high he bounces."

They dragged me toward the outer office.

"Wait," I said. "It *is* a device. I'll show you."

"It's no matter, Night Rider. We'll take it from your corpse at our leisure."

They lifted me off the floor, carried me through the office and out onto the balcony. There, they hoisted me shoulder high. The air, warm minutes ago, was cold. The crowd below cheered.

I looked down six stories. It was a bad moment. "Wait," I said, "you'll break it."

"He has a point," said Sholah.

The dictator raised a hand to the guards. Hold. Do not fling the miscreant over the side just yet. "It's also possible," Pierik said, "we might hurt someone. *Down there.*" He made noises in his throat while he thought about it. "Bring him inside for a minute."

For a minute? That didn't sound good.

They set me down again in front of the dictator. "All right, Night Rider, make yourself visible."

"I'll show you how. But I want a guarantee I'll be released." Not that I expected a guarantee would help, but it was something.

Pierik showed me the tensor. Pointed it at me, face level. The guards behind me, who could see nothing between themselves and the muzzle, got nervous and tried to clear a space. "You will do as I tell you. You are an intruder, and I will not bargain with you."

He had a point. "I can't do it with my hands tied."

Pierik signaled the captain. Someone cut me free. But they kept my arms pinned.

"Very good. Now, let's see what you look like."

I took a deep breath, got my hand on the buckle control switch, and turned off the lightbender.

Pierik's eyes went wide and changed to a deep violet. He made a sound like someone who had just come unexpectedly on a snake. The guards let go and jumped back, and I almost got free. But they recovered and seized me again.

He studied me for a long moment. "Well, Night Rider, you *are* an ugly creature, are you not? Tell me again where you come from."

"–An island in–"

It was as far as I got. Pierik struck me with the gun barrel. "You are going to have a difficult evening. Do you want to tell me the truth? Or would you prefer I send you downstairs for a while?"

What was downstairs? Gestapo headquarters? "I have told you the truth, Pierik."

He leaned back against the table and looked at Sholah. "Counsellor, do you think it possible so ugly a creature could have been born on this world?"

Sholah was not young. As they aged, Noks lost their glossiness. Sholah's hands and mask were rough and worn. "Where else could he have come from, Kabah?"

"I think he is a visitor from another place. Another world."

"But there is no world beyond Inakademeri."

Pierik pressed his hands together. The digits were long and looked more like claws than fingers. "How do we know that is so?" His eyes reverted to green. Green like the end of summer. "I am indeed sorry that the first visitor to our world insists on behaving in so contemptible a manner. But you leave me no choice. If you will not talk to me, I shall leave the questioning to others."

"I will talk to you," I said. "I will tell you something your guards should also hear. You pretend to be a great war leader, but you have no desire to win the war. Or even to see it end."

Pierik hit me again.

"You use it to stay in power. To fool—"

The third blow drove me to my knees. They hauled me back up.

Without meaning to, I slipped into English. "You don't give a damn about anybody, you son of a bitch."

It didn't matter that he couldn't speak the language; he got the message. But he kept his voice level. "What controls your invisibility?"

I did not like the idea of giving lightbender technology to the monster. I could hear McCarver. *I told you so. Damn fool idiot.*

"Cathie," I said. Still in English: "If you're there, this would be a good time. Do the bombing."

Pierik signaled the captain, who took over the physical stuff and jammed a rifle butt into my midsection.

"He is dressed oddly," said Sholah. "The technique must be in the clothing. Perhaps the box on his belt."

Pierik's eyes flashed. "Well," he said, "it's been a long day and it's getting late. Let's just kill him and then we'll see if we can figure it out tomorrow." He stepped back and looked at the captain. The captain raised his sidearm and pointed it at my forehead.

"No," said Pierik. "Not here. Take him downstairs, take care of it, and bring me his clothes and anything else you find."

"Yes, Kabah." He holstered the weapon and the guards started me toward the door.

I got a glimpse of the vent. "Cathie," I said, in English, "help."

Pierik looked perplexed by the strange words. Someone opened the door, and I saw a crowd of Noks standing immediately outside.

At that moment an explosion rocked the room, and they all dived for the floor.

Cathie had the volume at the top of the dial. Klaxons went off and screams erupted. The afternoon attack was doing a rerun. I broke loose, hit the lightbender control, pushed Noks every which way, and ran for my life. Behind me, more bombs were going off. Cathie, when she wanted, could deliver a stunning acoustical performance.

–IX–

I had expected to find a welcoming committee when I got back to the *Sheldrake*. I'd expected McCarver to yell and scream and confine me to quarters until transporation home could be arranged. But no one was there when I came in the hatch. I got no summons to McCarver's conference room, nor even a call on the commlink.

I needed a shower and a change of clothes, but I went down to mission control first. Cathie had someone on the circuit when I went in. She signed off, jumped up, and hugged me. "Hi, hero. Welcome home."

"Hi yourself," I said. "Does McCarver know I'm back?"

"He knows."

"What's happening?"

"He just got a message from Hutchins a few minutes ago."

"And–?"

"It was sealed. His eyes only. But I suspect he'll be calling for you in a bit." She looked at me. "I'm sorry, Art."

I shrugged. "I appreciate what you did for me."

"My pleasure."

"What took you so long?"

She grinned. "I wanted to start with a bang. Needed a minute to set it up. But I should tell you that was quick thinking on your part. I was trying to figure out what to do when they first caught you and I was about to yell at them when you told me to run the bombing."

"*Cathie.*" McCarver's voice on the commlink. "*You know where Kaminsky is?*"

"He's here, Paul."

"*Up forward, please.*"

"You'll be staying on with us after all, I guess," he said. "If you want to. Although I can tell you honestly, if you were to decide to leave, I wouldn't feel badly about it. You're a loose cannon, Kaminsky."

I was still settling into my chair. We were in McCarver's private conference room. "I don't understand, Paul. I thought I was going to be charged and sent home. Are the charges still in place?"

"They're in the process of being dropped."

"Not that I'm complaining, but why?"

He looked ready to explode. "Somebody on this mission has been leaking pictures to the media. People at home sit every night and watch the Noks get killed. And I guess they don't like it very much. There's political pressure now. To do something."

I tried not to smile too broadly. "Are you talking about the reports *I've* been sending back?"

His face was drawn and pale. "You knew it all the time, didn't you?"

"No, I had no idea."

He sneered. "Of course not." Deep breath. "They're sending out a team. Going to see what they can do about bringing peace to the Noks." He shook his head. "What a crock."

"I'm sorry you think so."

"Yeah. You would be. Maybe you'll feel differently when someone gets killed down there." The space between us widened. Became light-years. "It was your girlfriend. I can't touch *you*, but I can sure as hell get rid of her."

"You know, Paul," I said, "if we're going to step in because of what I did, that means I've probably become something of a celebrity."

"Enjoy it," he snarled. "It won't last long."

"I'm sure you wouldn't want me sending more material to the media. I mean, how would they react? Heroic woman canned for revealing the truth about Noks? Wouldn't look good for you. And I suspect Hutchins would not be happy, either."

McCarver tried to stare me down, but not this time. "Why don't you take her and go someplace else?"

"I think we'll stay here," I said. "Maybe *you* should consider another line of work."

Cathie was missing when I went back to mission control to say thanks. Again. I found her in the common room.

She didn't smile. Didn't shrug and say it was nothing. "You're off the hook?" she asked.

"Looks like."

"Good. I hope you were right."

Our eyes met and I saw Trill.

"I am," I said. *Help is on the way.*

No Place Like Home

by Julie E. Czerneda

Author and editor Julie E. Czerneda has been a finalist for both the John W. Campbell (Best New Writer) and Philip K. Dick Awards, has been twice on the preliminary ballot for a Nebula, and has won all three English language Prix Aurora Awards (Canada's Hugo), one for her novel In the Company of Others, *one for her short story "Left Foot on a Blind Man," and, most recently, for editing* Space Inc., *a collection of stories exploring daily life off this planet. A former biologist, Czerneda has published several biology-based SF novels, including two ongoing series, Trade Pact Universe and Web Shifters, recently translated into Russian. Her latest is the trilogy Species Imperative, in which the potential impact of biological drives on civilization are examined through the eyes of a salmon researcher.* Survival, *a Science Fiction Book Club featured selection, came out in 2004, followed by* Migration *in 2005.* Regeneration *will be released in May 2006. With Isaac Szpindel, she is co-editor of the alternate science history anthology* ReVisions *(2004).*

Czerneda edits the YA anthology series based on science curriculum topics, Tales from the Wonder Zone, winner of the 2002 Special Award for Best Science and Technology Education from the Golden Duck Committee, as well as the Realms of Wonder YA fantasy series linked to lan-

guage arts. She is a sought-after speaker, conducts presentations on science and writing in both Canada and the U.S., and serves as SF Consultant to Science News for Kids.

"No Place Like Home," the poignant tale of an unusually appealing race of planetary explorers, brings Forbidden Planets *to a conclusion that is invested with wonder, eroticism, suspense, humor, and ultimately compassion.*

SHE TAKES GENTLE steps. No one must know she's been here.

Her nostrils, deep, ridged, well-suited to this atmosphere, flare to take in scents.

Through eyes, narrow, thick-lidded, well-suited to this light, she gazes at a world as beautiful as any other she's walked. No less.

They want her to believe this is home, to feel it.

She has felt this much at home on every other world. And no more.

"Move on?" Glee stared at her, the quills of her head and neck stiffened in shock. "You can't mean it. Not already. It's too soon."

Drewe tossed her gloves on the table, reaching for the jar of cream. She rubbed the soothing ointment into the angry cracks between her fingers, hissing as the sting faded to relief. Av-gloves were designed to fit comfortably; perhaps they did—just not for as long as she usually wore them. "This isn't the place."

"And you can tell. From one walk."

"That's my job."

"What about the other walkers?"

Drewe perched on the nearest bench of the robing chamber, easing off her boots. At the sight of her blistered and peeling skin, her crèche mate hummed a protest, a pattern of grief and concern rippling her quills from jaw to crest. Drewe ignored the display. Glee's fussing was pointless; the boots were as they were, suited to most walkers, a poor fit for her wider-than-average feet. "The others," Drewe said calmly, "will make their own reports. Mine is to move on. A17GH49 offers no unique resources or benefits. And"—

she grunted as she bent to rub cream into the redness between paired toes—"it isn't home."

"We shouldn't leave orbit so soon," Glee grumbled. "It's not enough time."

Since Glee wasn't referring to planetary exploration, Drewe ignored this plea as well, although her own quills flattened against her head in mute warning to leave the topic. Feeling every muscle in her body as a separate point of strain, she leaned back to rest her spinal ridge against the wall.

Glee tried another tack. "Nevarr won't be pleased," she said. "He spent a full cycle perfecting these avatars."

"That's his job." She pressed a chill pack over her face, welcoming the numbness on her eyelids, nostrils, and mouth as the gel soothed new blisters and eased the stretch of old scars.

"What if the council decides to stay?" her crèche mate persisted. "Will you go back down?"

Drewe replayed the sensations of the world in her mind: vivid, complex, unpredictable. Everything the ship was not. Everything they searched for.

And hadn't found. "If they ask me to walk again," she mumbled into the pack, the warmth of each spoken word burning the raw patches inside her nose, "I'll go. But it will be a waste of time. This isn't home."

Drewe was one of the dozen walkers on the ship, the ship itself one of thousands tirelessly exploring their region of space, seeking uncontested resources for their kind. People, they called themselves. Umlari, others called them. Or spacefolk. Or those planetless freaks.

Living in their great stations, orbiting unwanted stars, the People cared nothing for names. They neither avoided nor sought other intelligences. Others knew the People were not to be trifled with, being quick to respond to any threat, real or perceived, to their homes. At the same time, they were reassuringly uninterested in the homes of others. Good neighbours, willing to refuel or repair passing ships, while never asking for aid themselves.

Never leaving their self-made worlds to plummet down a gravity well and breathe real air.

Drewe sighed noisily as she pulled herself hand-over-hand
down a well of her own, the central transtube, her weight dimin-
ishing with every level passed. Nevarr worked in null-gravity, having both the avatar growth chambers and his living quarters in the
ship's aftmost section. Convenience, for its proximity to av-pods.
So the council who settled such things claimed.

A steady stream of crèche mates passed her on their way off-
shift, feet-first as they prepared for imminent ladder rungs and
floor. They didn't offer greetings, only glum looks and whispers
among themselves.

No surprise. It probably took longer to move her grip from
one rung to the next than for news to saturate the ship. Drewe
hadn't expected her negative report to be popular with the crew. It
never was. Being orbital while walkers explored a new world
meant opening sections sealed during transit. It meant room for
recreation and interaction. Lately, as they matured together, it
meant triplets tangling in private corners, trading fluids for the day
they'd produce the next generation. It meant–

Wasting time.

The council had agreed with her. The other two walkers on
A17GH49 had failed to find anything of use to the People which
wasn't amply supplied by worlds closer and already automated.
And Drewe, senior to the rest, had argued passionately to abandon
another futile exploration.

Which made Drewe the only one going down the tube at this
time of shift, answering a testy summons. No doubt, she fumed, to
explain herself. Again.

She paused outside the door seal to the domain of the avatars,
nerving herself to pass within. Nevarr didn't bother her, angry or
not. It was . . . them. Drewe was no different from any other walker
in this: being close to the physical presence of avatars, even locked
in their growth chambers, was disconcerting.

Even if she sometimes preferred to see through an avatar's eyes.

Used to her own ambivalence, Drewe touched paired fingertips
to the seal, requesting clearance to enter. This first room was a bulb-

shaped entranceway, with openings leading to the rest of the aft section, including the short corridor to Nevarr's office. A gruff voice greeted her through the widening iris of the door. "You're late. I don't have time to wait on the dalliance of the young, you know."

Given Nevarr was from the same crèche as Drewe herself, Glee, and all others onboard, she smiled inwardly. True, he looked—and acted—older. Some thought it affectation or those years hunched over his 'scopes and surgeries; others, that fumes the ship couldn't completely scrub from his workplace had aged him. Drewe? She believed, privately, that Nevarr would fuss himself to an early trip to the recycling tanks.

There was no denying his meticulous, obsessive nature made him an exceptional designer. Nevarr's avatars didn't fail. They performed flawlessly in their environment until signaled to decommission, then melted and burned into an unrecogizable mass of common base materials.

Nevarr was fond of boasting that the day he couldn't produce a suitable avatar for a walker, he'd retire himself to the tanks.

So far, he was still here, Drewe thought as she pulled herself through the door. Though why he was here, as if to intercept her, was another question.

Nevarr was floating midroom, his round body and splayed limbs wrapped in supple black sheathing, the hood that would cover his head and neck hovering like a shadow behind. Clothing to keep the growth chambers clean of unplanned flesh. Sacrosanct.

"Why do we bother with a council?" he growled when he saw her. "We can ask Drewe, the All Knowing. She walks. She pronounces her doom. All shall tremble and obey."

"Good to see you too, Nevarr," she said, absently using one of the weblines strung throughout the room to stop her forward motion at a polite distance. As always, on seeing him, Drewe was struck how being of the same crèche meant only sharing the same birth moment. Otherwise, each conception was separated by time and inherently unique, determined by its particular combination of sexual fluids from each member of the triplet. Distinctive features were the norm among the People.

Glee was nimbleness and light, her eyes large and set wide

apart in a triangular face, her nostrils delicate and long, stretching from headcrest to upper lip, capable of flushing bright red in an instant. Her mouth was generous and usually upturned in a smile. Her ears were tiny and tucked inconspicuously under her jaw, while expressive quills coated her scalp and neck in a flow of white-tipped black. An exceptional beauty, as the People counted it. Glee certainly thought so.

On the other extreme, Nevarr had no redeeming physical feature except vigour and good teeth. He outmassed most on board, a significant portion of that being an unsightly accumulation of fat around his lower torso. His nostrils were most charitably described as narrow, and by those less kind as pinched. He had large eyes, but their irises were a sallow orange and he tended to blink rapidly when concentrating. His ears faced forward, their dark inner whorls regrettably visible at all times.

If nature hadn't done Nevarr any favours, his was still just another permutation in a species well-accustomed to variation in its members. But life had dealt him a final, unkind blow. An accident in his lab years ago had scoured every quill from his head, leaving behind a maze of puckered and twisted skin, turning his face into a cold, unreadable mask. Combined with his impatient nature and undenied brilliance, little wonder he received few casual visitors.

She remembered their first meeting with familiar embarrassment. Being neither pretty nor unpleasant, Drewe's own noticable distinction from their crèche mates was a burning curiosity she'd learned to harness as a tool rather than distraction. Between walks, she sought to perfect her craft.

It was a pursuit which had led her, several transits ago, to request research results from the ship's data stores. She'd been summoned to report to Nevarr's section of the ship if she wanted them.

It had taken some time to get up her courage, but she had. But being braced for the aft section hadn't prepared Drewe for Nevarr, nor his sharp questioning on why she wanted his data. She'd stared at his blank scalp and stammered conflicting answers until, mercifully, he'd sent her away.

She'd firmly believed she'd failed. But the data had arrived the next day, along with a suggestion as to other material she should explore.

Since then, she'd come a number of times, sometimes at his call, sometimes to seek clarification of an obscure point, sometimes simply to talk with someone who shared her drive for perfection.

His expressionless face no longer troubled her; she'd learned to read his voice, his posture. She noticed their differences, that was all.

"If you brought me here for insults, Nevarr, go ahead," Drewe told him. "But it won't change the ball of dirt beneath us. It's of no value to the People."

"And not home." He managed to twist his disdain into the last word.

"That's part of our mandate," she reminded him, trying to ignore how her feet hung in midair. She'd never been at ease in null-grav, something her stomachs were busy reminding her. "To locate the planet where we evolved."

"That," he grunted, "is what's of no value to the People. I've told you before, Drewe. We'd be better off if we never found that rock. What good could it do us, anyway?"

Drewe knew better than to shrug. The movement would only propel her towards him, and she felt no need to assert her place by intruding in his. He'd never hidden his politics. Nevarr was a firm Futurist, one of those who dismissed any need to locate and identify that one planet inherently able to support their kind, who viewed the future as a continuum of a superior present. Some Futurists went so far as to repudiate a planetary origin, claiming the People had somehow sprung from the metals and composites of their surroundings. To most, leaving the birth planet had been the major leap forward of their species. To return, even to seek it, was to regress. To fail. They were a minority, but gaining in number with each crèche generation.

The rest of the People, at least those in positions to make decisions for the rest, remained fascinated by the search for their long-lost birthplace. Why? Curiosity, surely. Pre-station history was a din of songs and legends, a motley collection of names and leftover superstitions. To this day, there were those who spat between their first fingers before entangling in a triplet, as if this could ensure their sexual fluid would be cherished within a future mother and not rejected to be absorbed as nutrient.

The search was also fanned by greed, without question. What wonders might await within the biological framework that had produced their very bodies? What had been left behind during the exodus that might be of inestimable value now?

Mysticism had its place in the allure. Though few of the People would admit it aloud, implicit in the search for their species' home world was the hope of establishing their place in the sequence of the universe. Theirs was a culture that revered past generations, that accumulated accomplishment along maternal lineage. Losing contact with their origins had long been a source of worry. To settle once and for all questions of where they'd come from, what else had they achieved, why had they left . . .

Power would shift with those answers.

The life of a walker involved no such struggles. Drewe didn't need an opinion; she had her job. "We have our orders," she reminded Nevarr again. "Why did you want to see me, then?"

"Come." Nevarr turned with the precise sweep of limbs necessary to send himself sailing towards the lowermost of the five outlets from this entry.

He never waited for anyone. Rumour held he'd torn the initial opening from their crèche mother's corpse, first of them all. True or not, those who had to work with him knew better than to expect patience. Or manners. Or explanations before the designer was good and ready.

With a sigh she hoped he'd hear, her only protest, Drewe followed.

Nevarr's domain consisted of the labyrinth of growth chambers, themselves the largest single area of the ship devoted to one purpose and never sealed even during transit, though it meant sleeping six to a room for weary weeks. Also aft were the various workshops and storerooms staffed by those who serviced the growth chambers and related equipment, including delivery pods and the outfitting rooms. To the extent of Drewe's knowledge, at any rate. She'd never been inclined to explore what felt like the gleaming wet bowels of some huge organism.

For it was always damp here, relative to the rest of the ship. Damp, and odorous, and dim, and warm. Coupled with the lack of gravity, it created an environment as alien as any Drewe had walked.

A view she kept to herself, but she knew Nevarr enjoyed her discomfort. All who worked in null-grav, closer to the realities of space, mocked the rest of their crèche mates, particularly the walkers. Little wonder Futurist dogma took root and flourished here.

After a few moments, Nevarr aimed himself at the opening of an unfamiliar passage and Drewe used a webline to slow herself. "Where does that go?" she asked.

"Shortcut to the outfitting room," he said, not bothering to look at her. "Keep up." His black-clad legs disappeared.

For another instant Drewe hesitated, then scolded herself. Nevarr was a crèche mate and a professional. He might be annoyed with her right now—even furious. That didn't mean he'd brought her here to . . .

What? Toss her into the tanks to become components for his next batch of avatars? Drewe gave the tug to send herself through the unfamiliar entrance after Nevarr, scolding her imagination.

The strange corridor continued, boring through the ship like a root seeking nourishment, more spiral than straight. Drewe glowered at the trailing limbs of her guide. Shortcut? More likely, Nevarr was making some point at her expense.

The final twist of the tube emptied into a dark expanse. Startled, Drewe held to the rim of its opening, reliving children's tales of the monsters who clung to the outsides of stations, burrowing through bulkheads to steal the very air from sleeping lungs.

Monsters, it was said, preferred the dark.

The stations and ships of the People had no dark places. Not like this. Nevarr might have been dropped into a vat of black oil, or some other substance able to swallow light.

Or they'd reached the tip of the aft section, where the ship shrank to its smallest point, where a pod large enough to contain an avatar and nothing more clung by grapples and seals, until released and dropped planetward, like so much discarded waste set adrift.

Drewe's quills trembled so rapidly they created a faint buzzing sound. She'd experienced night as a walker without fear. Why did she falter here, let a crèche mate go where she couldn't, mustn't, wouldn't . . .

An annoyed mutter from the abyss. "Where's that . . . there!"

Drewe squinted as lights came on from every direction. The brightness obliterated all but curiosity. Quills relaxed, she released her death's grip on the rim, already sore fingers protesting this added abuse, and let herself drift forward. "Nevarr—what is this place?"

"This? Just another storeroom. Come along, Drewe."

It resembled no storeroom Drewe had ever seen. The light curved over gleaming bronze orbs larger than her body. They packed the available space, clumped in no discernible pattern, as if when left unwatched they came free and jostled for position. Specimen containers, Drewe realized with awe as she neared the first floating cluster, used to the knuckle-sized version she controlled when collecting genetic samples for return to the ship. She hadn't realized they could be made this large.

She brushed her hands along those she passed, half to be sure they were real, half to keep moving to where Nevarr waited. Their polished surfaces stole the warmth from her skin.

"What are these?" she asked when she reached Nevarr. He glanced at the orbs as if only noticing them because of her question. "What's inside?" she amended.

"Phenotypes," he said, as if it should be obvious, then beckoned her to follow. "This way. Come on."

"Phenotypes of what?"

Nevarr halted his motion and turned to face her. For the first time in a long while, Drewe hated being unable to read his expression. Worse, she felt her quills fluttering again, her apprehension plain for him to see.

Sure enough, he smiled as he pointed to a dense clump of orbs overhead. "Those are of you."

Drewe couldn't help tossing her head back to stare, the motion sending her body into a roll, feet rising. As this gave her a better line of sight, she didn't bother with more than a slow, gentle correction, her hand sliding over the slickness of the orb to her right. She counted what she could see: twenty-four, perhaps half again as many nested behind, out of sight. She'd walked what, almost forty alien worlds by now? "Avatars," she guessed aloud, suppressing a quill shiver. "You've stored a copy of each you've made for me—for all of us." Drewe stared at Nevarr. "Why would you do that?"

He lost his smile. "Why indeed, Walker. Don't you think it would be more efficient to reuse an existing variant, rather than start from the base version every time?"

Base version. He meant her body, this body. The real Drewe. She refused to look at the orbs filled with other possible Drewes, thinking of where she'd walked in their like. It wasn't right, having these here. She let her quills fall into angles that directed aggression at him. "No. Why should it be?"

Nevarr made a disagreeable noise and she was careful not to appear triumphant. Of course none of the worlds they'd encountered had been similar to one another. That was the point of the avatars, after all. Nevarr started with the genotype contained in each walker's cells, then coaxed the expression of those genes best suited to the alien environment they would enounter, suppressing others. Every world provided a fresh set of criteria. He'd once admitted to her his work was one-third science, one-third inspiration, and one-third experience telling him what would be "good enough." The result? After accelerated growth in the chambers, a custom body would emerge, able to function as long as required to collect sensations from that new world.

So why this collection? Did he view himself an artist, and these hunks of flesh his creations?

If so, just how much of that flesh had he saved?

At that distressing thought, Drewe lifted her hand from the nearest orb, quills fluttering. "They aren't intact," she half asked.

"Do you think I have time to waste operating on samples that might never be used?" Patronizing, yet Drewe thought she detected a hint of unease in Nevarr's voice.

"Council can't have approved this." At release from its artificial crèche, an avatar's central nervous system was excised and replaced by the circuitry that allowed the walker to experience whatever physical sensations the avatar experienced. It became a suit of flesh, empty and ready for use.

"What I do here is outside the purview of council–"

"We're one crèche, one ship, Nevarr," Drewe interrupted, pushing herself to hover in front of him. "There's nothing outside the–"

"There's nothing wrong with my methods or results, Walker Drewe. Or do you wish to file a complaint?"

"I should," she shot back, quills rigid. "This vanity of yours"– fingertips indicated the orbs–"is at best a waste of resources that should be recycled. At worst–it's a biological hazard. What if any were viable on the ship?" Drewe shuddered. "What if any were freed?"

His laugh was more convincing than any argument. "Really, Drewe. As well worry about the goo in the tanks spontaneously taking shape and asking for supper."

Drewe refused to be dismissed. "You've put potential sapients in bottles, Nevarr–"

"–and it's so much better when I scrape out their brains and give them transmitters instead."

"Yes. That's why each is grown. That's an avatar's function. Not to linger like this, as some–some useless trophy." Her gaze kept slipping from Nevarr's face to the silent orbs surrounding them. Could they hear? Did they dream?

Could they scream?

"It's wrong, Nevarr."

"Maybe you'd prefer to climb in the next pod yourself, Drewe," he scorned. "Risk the drop from orbit. Walk the dirt with your own feet."

Something none of the People had done in recorded history. Even their contacts with other intelligences were accomplished in space, ship-to-ship, or on the great stations.

She felt the gorge rise to her throat but held her scarred and wounded hands for his inspection. "You don't think I would? Find me a planet where this body works better than any other, and I'll take the drop, all right. I'll go barefoot and feel that world for you and all the others who won't dare."

Nevarr's eyes widened, then he barked another laugh. "Drewe–I never guessed. You're a Regressive."

"No." She spat ceremoniously to one side, careful not to expel droplets that might cling to an orb, or drift who knew where else. "I'm a walker. Why should I fear going dirtside? I don't want a world to live on—I want a world to explore for myself, firsthand, without interfaces and blisters." Without being lowered into the explorium, to spend hours balanced on the huge ball that responded to every step of her rough-soled boots by forcing another with its spin, eyes blind, ears closed, nostrils plugged, skin coated in an armour of receivers until she was nothing more than a machine herself, the pickup end of a living sensor. "Something you wouldn't understand."

"Ah. But I do understand you—more than you think. Which is why I asked you here, Drewe. Come on. Follow me."

Drewe cursed as Nevarr propelled himself through the round exit, his soft, perfect feet like flags raised in triumph.

"I'll file that complaint," she promised the orbs, then went after her exasperating crèche mate.

Nevarr led Drewe into another darkened expanse but this time, when he turned on the lights, her surprise was at the familiar. "I never realized you had a full hookup down here," she said, flaring her nostrils.

She floated past him, running fingertips over the lower curve of the quiescent ball, eyes checking out the harness that dangled like a skin emptied of its flesh, noting the correct placement of interface webbings and other gear with the obsessive care of habit. All the while, her hearts pounded; the tissues of her mouth flooded with acid-flat secretions; her fingers and toes throbbed with blood. Drewe swallowed hard, willing her quills to relax. Pre-walk stress. They all felt it, virgin to veteran. You learned to harness the rush of hormone, not let it ride you.

Or you died young.

"Do I want to know why?" she asked, deliberately looking away from the explorium equipment.

His eyes blinked several times in succession, as if considered a variety of possible answers. Then: "These, Walker Drewe." Going to a bag latched with others along the wall, Nevarr drew out a pair of ordinary looking av-gloves. Pushing them her way, he dug

back into the bag to produce a pair of boots. "I've made improve-
ments. Our crèche mate, Glee, has been most insistent I put an end
to your torment. This seemed the appropriate time."

Drewe let the offerings float past. He could have sent new gear
to her quarters, should have delegated the task to any other.

He was up to something.

She waited for it; as always, curious.

"I see my diligence fails to impress." Without rancour, as if
Nevarr had expected her reaction. "Perhaps if you tried them
on . . . took them for a stroll?" He gestured languidly at the ball
floating midroom. "Nothing like the real thing."

"Why?" Drewe frowned. "Council's ended the survey of this
planet. The ship will finish compressing in another three shifts."
Before which moment, the crew would throw the obligatory wild
parties in the remaining space; afterwards, they'd mutter for a shift
complaining of sore heads and boasting of pregnancies to come.
The ship would resume its transit configuration and they'd get
back to work, always too close together and stripped of almost all
privacy. Her spine tightened in dread. She concentrated on
Nevarr. "I can't walk—"

"Must I remind you," Nevarr interrupted testily, "as chief designer, I can request the cooperation of a walker at any time. Any
walker."

The lacework of scars over his protruding ears throbbed, as if
the muscle beneath tried to pattern quills that were no longer
there. It wasn't strange he felt strongly about this; Nevarr cared
passionately about his craft. It was strange she couldn't begin to
guess what that feeling was. "My avatar's been decommissioned
with the rest," Drewe objected. She hoped he wasn't planning to
decant its copy from the storeroom.

"They are to be decommissioned," corrected Nevarr, "giving
us a rare opportunity while the ship settles itself. As you know, I've
wanted to collect sensory input on the dissolution process for quite
a while—"

To experience her avatar's death? Grabbing the nearest object,
another bag, Drewe pulled herself away from him. "No!"

"No? Really, Drewe. Where's your curiosity? You've studied

the sciences, asked reasonably intelligent questions about the development of–"

"I get bored in transit," she said acidly. "That doesn't make me a fool."

"Of all walkers, I'd have thought you'd leap at the chance to finally dispell the myth."

Undetected atmosphere corruption this far aft? Or–"You've been sucking solvent," she accused, backing further. One of her new boots drifted towards Drewe's cheek and she smacked it away. "Do you have the slightest idea what you're proposing?"

Nevarr stroked his way closer, stopping short of intruding into the unseen bubble that marked her personal space. "Afraid? The legendary Walker Drewe?"

"Yes. When it benefits my own survival."

"Your survival is the point. Your experience–your stubborn endurance–makes you the best choice. The only choice." Words spilled forth quickly, as if he sought to wear her down with them. "Don't you see? No matter that I assure every walker their avatars are nothing more than sensors, uploading data. After your first walk, do any of you believe it?" He didn't wait for her to answer. "No. At the end of every walk, you stare around the ship as if still looking through their eyes. You limp for days if your avatar bruises a toe while you're connected. And you abandon your avatars the moment they are physically threatened in any way, rather than stay to finish your work. Avatars that have taken cycles to design and grow. Why? Because you can't get it through your heads that you, the real you, is safe from any harm."

"You build them. But you've never walked in one," Drewe said quietly. "Don't pretend to understand what that's like."

Nevarr made a rude noise. "I don't care what it's like," he told her. "I care to prove, once and for all, that a walker can safely endure anything that happens to an avatar. I want to dispell this fear you have in common, the one you never talk about." His voice gentled. "Drewe. Gloves and boots. The sensor harness. Nothing else in a walk ever touches you. You won't die with the avatar. You can't. And if I prove it to you, the others will listen.

One experiment." He paused. "Assuming you left it somewhere safe."

"Of course," she replied testily. "How could I know the council's will?"

"Then–" Nevarr pulled himself aside, so nothing was between Drewe and the explorium but a drifting boot, its fasteners gaped open. "–I suggest you walk."

Even if he ordered her, she realized, she could refuse without stain. Council would never coerce a walker.

Drewe reached for the boot.

If Nevarr was right, she had only to live through whatever sensations the avatar shared at its end. She was the best walker of their crèche; she'd proved time and again she could endure her avatar's labours, could tolerate what gave others nightmares.

If he was wrong? If she was harmed in any way?

If she died?

Drewe almost smiled, imagining Nevarr trying to explain that to both council and Glee.

Sweet, evocative. She identifies the scent. It's the same on any world.

Decay.

She focuses on her feet, its feet. Usually the first body part to suffer damage, these are filthy but whole. Toes sink into black ooze.

Ooze. Bubbling and warm to the touch. Ah yes. She'd left the avatar on a barren island, safe from the only scavengers large enough for such a meal. Habit and precaution.

A miscalculation, of sorts. The island itself is the rotting mass, its surface a deceptive smoothness of pale sand. She wiggles her toes deeper, fascinated. What had it been? Large. Aquatic? Why was so much flesh still intact? She should take a sample.

She imagines bronze orbs gleaming around her, like raindrops on the surface of her eyes, and remembers her new task. Not to observe.

To wait.

Still she walks, follows the dark scars of old footprints, adds new ones. This choice turns her face to the sun and her outer eyelids close to slits. She keeps the protective inner lid open. She wishes to see this world.

Ocean stretches to the horizons, glinting like forged metal. Low islands, real and transient shimmers, swarm its surface. The water—here it is water, unlike some worlds she's walked—is shallow. The growth of sea creatures has crowned sleeping volcanoes. For now.

She listens, but hears nothing beyond the ocean lipping the land. There are singers aplenty at night; they wait out the day's heat in burrows or underwater or nestled in wind-bent growth.

She waits and walks.

The end of the decaying flesh slips beneath the surface. Her feet follow, shedding traces of black rot into the crystal clear water, stirring lines of bubbles as they become clean again. Her shadow glides along white sand as she walks through ankle-deep ripples to the next rise of land. The ocean is cool on her flesh.

The sand burns as she steps out. There are tool-users on this world; they have shoes, she may not. Heat underfoot is a sensation best collected by nerve endings, as much as the colours playing with sunlight, the sound of water, and the lingering smell of what lies beached and long-dead behind her.

Sand tossed up by a freshening wind stings her eyes. She closes the clear inner eyelid at last, sacrificing fine detail to avoid scratched lenses. She walks upslope, stepping between long ropes of vegetation.

At the crest of the low hill, she looks beyond, a new direction.

More islands, heat shimmers, tassles of grey cloud to the north. Closer, a line of white-shouldered shapes, as if boats had flipped to lie upside-down on a shoal and been covered by sand.

She is used to measuring by sight. The shapes are too similar, despite their varied lengths, to be islands. More seem to be moving closer, their surfaces peppered with shadows.

Lost in curiosity, she forces inner lids open, widens outer lids, strains to see more.

The shadows resolve into figures, bustling over the bloated corpses of something immense. While she discerns no detail at this distance, she sees the figures are laying down a white coating. The corpses move towards the queue of other, fully coated shapes.

Processing plant or storage? Burial rite or waste disposal? Food supply or—

She is thought, alone in the dark.

Then her body ignites.

And she is flame.

"You have to tell us, Drewe. No one's gone that far before! How did it feel?"

She'd hoped for peace pre-transit, some time to compose herself, at least the privacy of her own quarters. But Tymin and Glee had been waiting at the door, bursting with concern and questions. More proof, if she needed any, of how information raced the ship's corridors like a plague.

Now they stood watching as she stowed her gear, quills shifting between patterns of excitement and dread.

Drewe finished putting away her boots, then closed the overhead cabinet door with more force than necessary. But her voice was steady. "How did what feel?"

"Dying."

Drewe scowled at Tymin's eager expression. His reddish quills bore vivid yellow tips, making his patternings bold and emphatic. Only a fellow walker would try her patience; only a friend this far. "I didn't die," she stressed, her own quills rattling annoyance. "My avatar was decommissioned."

"Semantics. You stayed to feel it—wasn't that the point of the experiment?"

"The point was surviving it," Drewe snapped. "Which I did." She continued packing. Everyone else had prepared for transit, unnecessary gear stowed for the duration, leaving them ready to party the remaining hours away. Having been delayed with Nevarr's interminable tests on her condition, she was rushing to catch up, not that her morbid crèche mates appeared to notice.

"Drewe—come on."

She took her time tucking her new gloves around jars of cream. Nevarr had done well by her in that regard. The new equipment didn't chafe. Not that she'd noticed at the time, being preoccupied with fighting to be free of it as quickly as possible.

Mercifully, her conscious mind had shut down in the midst of being burned alive. The tests proved she was unharmed. Nevarr had been right.

And insufferable.

"It hurt," she told Tymin. "If you want to know how much, volunteer yourself. I'm sure he'll oblige next time you walk."

"Council's forbidden it," Glee said. Her quills flattened and she stroked her fingers possessively over Tymin's. They'd made no secret of having paired since the last transit; they'd been slightly more discreet about their desire for their best friend Drewe to complete their triplet. "Just as well, if you ask me. You walkers are expected to endure too much as it is. I think Nevarr should be the next volunteer. See how he likes it."

Drewe and Tymin exchanged a look of silent understanding. Glee and others like her were worthy crèche mates, good at their work, caring and reliable as individuals. But they couldn't grasp that walkers were different from everyone else. Only a few in each crèche generation were physically and mentally suited to working with avatars. Of them, even fewer could tolerate the sensations of another world. Those who did were never the same.

It was said a walker grew a second skin, one to let them pretend to be unchanged so their family wouldn't grieve their loss.

"You're wrong, Glee," Drewe countered. "Nevarr was within his rights as designer. He acted with the best interests of the walkers in mind."

"Pythin said they could hear your screams in the growth chambers." Glee's quills bristled in anger. "Don't tell me about Nevarr's rights, Drewe. Or his motives."

"I didn't say I enjoyed it." Drewe surveyed the belongings remaining on the floor with dismay. How had she accumulated all this? She began shoving everything into a recycle bag. What she needed the other side of transit, she could call from stores. "He did prove his point, Glee. What harms or destroys an avatar doesn't affect its walker. That knowledge could save a mission one day."

"Excuse me if I don't see much of a distinction between experiencing a horrible death and actually dying," Tymin muttered, quills patterned in whorls of stress. He held the bag open for her. Glee began passing items.

Drewe let her fingers brush along his. "There's a tomorrow," she said quietly. "That's distinction enough."

She felt an interested breath on her neck and absently nudged Glee away with her shoulder. Not that it mattered lately how many times she failed to respond in kind; her crèche mate clearly enjoyed the pursuit itself.

Transit, with so much less room to avoid one another, was going to be onerous.

"I'll take that for you, Drewe," Tymin offered. "Why don't you grab some rest?" His quills repatterned into pleased anticipation. "We'll come by when the parties get rolling."

"Thanks. I am tired," Drewe said gratefully. "Don't bother to come for me. Go. Enjoy yourselves. If I feel inclined to rot my stomachs with some homemade solvent brew, I'll find my way." She nodded at Glee. "Just make sure to take her with you."

Glee laughed, unrepentant. As Tymin bent for the bag, she deliberately nuzzled her face into his spinal ridge where it thrust against his light smock. He gave a startled gasp of pleasure, almost dropping the bag. She pulled back to look at Drewe, her nostril linings already engorged with pink from proximity to his scent. "Don't stay in this room by yourself," she coaxed. "Let us come back. We don't have to party with the rest of them." Her quills rose and fell in alluring waves. "Tymin—tell her. Tell her how much you want to tangle with Drewe. Here. Tonight."

Tymin looked appalled. Which would have worked, except that his nostrils involuntarily flared, seeking her response. Realizing instinct had betrayed him, he rushed from the room, her bag in hand. Glee chuckled.

"You never did have a sense of timing," Drewe observed. "Or tact."

"Tact never formed a triplet." Glee carefully folded her hands together. "As for time," her voice turned serious, "it's slipping past all of us, Drewe. You must feel it: the way we're pulled closer to each other. We're among the last to tangle of our crèche. A few triplets have implanted over fifty times—"

Drewe hummed in disgust. "You're keeping score?"

"It's common sense. Once crèche mothers start developing–and they will soon, at this rate–we'll have to go home."

Crèche mothers? They were too young to produce the next generation. Drewe's fingers flattened protectively over her concave chest, as if restraining offspring impatient to eat their way free. When she noticed, she shivered and dropped her hands. "We're too young," she said out loud.

"Apparently not." Glee's quills fluttered again. "Rosaa thinks it's to do with cycling between transit and normal space. She says there's records it can accelerate maturation. How doesn't matter. Once we're fully implanted, it will be a race to get back to the closest station before birth."

"Then I suggest a little self-control," Drewe snapped. "We have work to do."

"Easy for you walkers. Easy for you, with your mission, your new worlds." Almost a hiss. Her quills pointed at Drewe in rage. "Those of us who prepare for cycles, then wait in orbit even longer–we're growing ripe as well as old. And I, for one, don't plan to wait and waste myself."

Drewe sank down on the narrow bedbench, resting her spine against its cushion. She'd known Glee all her life; she'd never seen her angry–not like this, not with an undertone of desperation. "I don't know what to say," she said at last. "You're my friend, Glee. Dearest to me of all our crèche mates. You know if I were to seek something closer, you'd be first. But I don't feel the need. Not yet, anyway. I'm sorry."

"You aren't hearing me, Drewe. We will reach a point of having no choice. All of us. I'd wait for you, but Tymin grows frustrated."

"Oh, Tymin does," Drewe half smiled. "I hadn't noticed."

Glee knelt before her and, before she could avoid the contact, leaned forward to press her nostrils against Drewe's smock, just over her waist. The fine material offered no barrier to the heat of that flesh against hers, to the shuddering sequence of breaths as those nostrils sought her scent.

Feeling she owed her crèche mate a fair trial, Drewe put up with the awkward position for a count of ten, then gently tugged at the neck of Glee's smock to pull her away. "I told you. I'm not feeling it."

"Don't stop me." Glee's face was vivid red, her nostrils swollen until they distorted her features into those of a stranger. "It will be all right, Drewe. Beloved. Let me bring Tymin–" she urged in a husky voice.

"Then I'd have to send him away, too," countered Drewe gently. "Go. Find a party. Find a third. I'll see you after transit begins."

Her crèche mate rose slowly, her quills pulsing. Drewe averted her eyes, embarrassed to see the other's body stiffened by arousal she didn't feel.

Glee turned at the door, her face still flushed. "Don't look so worried, Drewe," she said in a more normal tone. "All you need is a bit of rest. Time to get over living that avatar's death. We'll be here for you."

After the door closed, Drewe secured it.

It was going to be a very long transit.

"I didn't expect to find you here."

Drewe didn't turn to greet Nevarr, too intent on counting the gleaming orbs. She'd decided to compare their number with walker records. Curiosity. As good a reason as any. "Me?" she asked, "or here."

"Both."

As Drewe was a little surprised herself to have willingly reentered the avatar storeroom, she settled for a question. "How long can they stay like this?"

"Assuming proper maintenance and no damage to systems? Indefinitely, I'd imagine." He floated by her to rest his hand on a bronze curve. "Why?"

"Just curious."

His nostrils tightened into a line, repudiating her answer. "Why here, Walker Drewe?"

She considered several possible answers, then looked at his safe, narrow nostrils and decided on the truth. "I'm hiding."

"From the hormonal hordes at your door, no doubt."

"How did you–?" she began, offended by his labelling dismissal of her friends. However accurate.

He made that rude noise of his. "Anyone with private quarters is besieged or busy trading fluids. You obviously aren't busy, so . . ."

Her quills flattened. "I'm not interested."

"Give it time—"

"Why? And for that matter, why am I the only one who finds it alarming that almost the entire crew is wandering around with their noses up each other's backs?"

"Until the ship reaches its next target and reconfigures, there's not much else for them to do."

Her half-formed idea, the one that had brought her aft, to roam these strange places, crystallized. "There is down here," Drewe observed. "I'd like to work with you. On the new design."

"We haven't picked the world yet."

"I'd like to help with that as well."

Nevarr's eyes hooded and his mouth became a thin line. For an instant, he appeared even older than usual, older and oddly frail for someone so large.

"I admit much of my staff is breathing too deeply at work for productivity. A more level head would be appreciated." He floated midair for a moment, studying her. She kept her quills carefully still. "You're sure?" he asked at last. "I've no patience for walker squeamishness."

"I've proved myself, haven't I?"

Nevarr gave a noncommittal grunt. "Come then. I've a presentation to make to council on our next mission. You might as well attend me." He twisted and propelled himself forward with a slap against one of the orbs. "Just don't say anything," he added over one shoulder.

Drewe grinned and followed, using a webline instead.

Council meetings were held in a circular room off the bridge; a convenient arrangement, since council members were also those who ran daily ship functions. They were always a triplet of triplets, a potent combination among the People, though each consented to surgical neutering before accepting this role for life. Having no future, they held the fate of those who did in their hands.

Drewe had counted some among this council as friends, when they were all younger and unassigned. Now they were divided by a barrier of both flesh and intent.

Nevarr seemed oblivious. He strode in as if the council members sitting around the outer rim of the room were his staff, having had no apparent difficulty with the switch to full gravity in this part of the ship. His oversized torso merely reformed into a hard lump and shifted towards his knees. Drewe, still queasy with the change, found herself mute with admiration.

"We welcome Nevarr, Chief Designer." The gracious greeting came from Uckod, chief on council. She'd been beautiful once, before her nostrils had been reduced to slits one-third their size and her body prematurely thickened. By Nevarr, Drewe realized, never giving it thought before now. "And Walker Drewe. You we didn't expect. Is there a problem?"

Nevarr's impatience or not, manners were important here. Drewe lifted her hands in a gesture of respect. "I attend as observer. The Chief Designer is allowing me to learn aspects of his work." He should be grateful she hadn't followed through on the complaint regarding the avatars collected in his storeroom. Nor did she plan to voice an opinion on sharing her own avatar's death. "I have an interest," was all she added.

"Commendable."

"Yes, yes. At least she has her nose in work instead of up someone's spine. Which is why I'm proposing world C380A33." Nevarr stepped down into the centre of the round pit that served as a focus for the council and activated the controls. The room lights darkened, to reveal two solar systems floating side by side. Nevarr's face appeared in the middle of one, the star distractingly centred on one orange eye. "Our choices. C380A33." He took a quick step into the other, its star unlucky enough to be centered in a pit on his scarred head. "Or A991C01. Both rate attention, according to the deep probes. A991C01 is slightly more promising in terms of rare metals. However, C380A33"–a step back to an orange eye–"is much closer." The display winked out and the room lights rose to ambient again. Nevarr looked ready to leave. "Set course and we'll be there in less than a quarter cycle."

"One moment," Uckod said. "We've never based our choice on transit time before, Designer Nevarr. Is there some reason we must do so now?"

"Yes," Drewe heard herself say. Committed, she went down to stand beside Nevarr, her agitated quills resisting her efforts to make them settle. "We left A17GH49 after spending our shortest time this journey in exploration configuration. I stand by my recommendation that we leave, but I believe . . . I've seen . . . well, it's put unnecessary strain on some of our crèche mates."

"Why?"

Drewe gazed at the nine sexless individuals and couldn't find words.

"An annoying number have formed active triplets," Nevarr filled in without missing a beat. "They complain of a lack of sufficient private space for tangling. Techs arrive late to work, distracted when they do show up. Individuals with private quarters are plagued by unwelcome requests." He didn't look at her, but Drewe knew without touching her head that her quills were aligned in telling embarrassment. "A thorough nuisance. Let's get this transit over as quickly as possible so they can scurry off to their dark corners on their own time."

The nine bent their heads together and conferred in low, anxious voices. When they returned their attention to Nevarr and Drewe, their quills were set in uniform patterns of resolve. Uckod spoke. "There are always those governed by their flesh. They will have to discipline themselves to wait for a more appropriate time and place. The ship and her mission comes first."

"That's what I say," Nevarr agreed. "Make an announcement—"

"What if some can't wait," Drewe interrupted, "even for the good of the ship?"

Vene, a crèche mate Drewe remembered as coming close in walker testing before failing to tolerate open sky, pointed at her. "Is that your situation, Walker Drewe?"

There could be no dishonesty here, though Drewe was uncomfortably aware her quills betrayed her indignation at such a personal question. "No. But—" She gathered her courage, remembering Glee's desperate anger. "–I believe you must be ready to take the ship home."

Every quill rose in shock.

Their reaction surprised her. "What else can we do?" she reasoned. "These aren't sniff and tickle games, councillors. There are permanent triplets throughout the crew now. That means there are those on board who will inevitably ripen. And what then? Surely the rights of crèche mothers remain paramount, even over our mission."

"Crèche mothers?" Vene repeated in a low voice, his eyes wide, his quills standing out to frame them. "Who said anything about crèche mothers?! We don't have facilities to handle birth, let alone room or supplies for a new crèche."

"Don't worry, Vene," huffed another councillor, Tauserr by name. Her quills, long and pale, aimed at Drewe in threat. "Our crèche is too young for this nonsense."

"Tell them," Drewe muttered under her breath.

"Your opinion, Nevarr?" Uckod asked.

He made a dismissive gesture. "We won't have to run for home, if that's your concern. The additives will continue to prevent pregnancy, no matter how earnest the efforts of those involved in the attempt."

Drewe faced Nevarr. "Additives?" she mouthed without sound.

His eyes glittered, but he spoke over her head. "The only problem I foresee is that the avatars for C380A33 will have to be completed while we're in orbit, so the walkers will be delayed. But under the circumstances, I'm sure they won't object." His eyes dropped to hers. "Am I correct in that assumption, Walker Drewe?"

She had nothing but objections, Drewe thought, but if this got them into orbit sooner, she'd keep them to herself.

Drewe's quills aligned into agreement.

Her first full shift working with Nevarr would begin with a tour. In anticipation of lengthy exposure to not only null-grav, but avatars, Drewe had stopped by the med bay for the strongest anti-nausea drug they'd give her on empty stomachs.

They weren't empty because she was avoiding the additives laced throughout every food item on board, a practice Nevarr claimed was standard to prevent pregnancy during any prolonged journey from the home of the People, the great stations. No one in their right mind would allow a crèche mother to give birth within the confines of a single ship, or want to be that mother. Drewe was more annoyed the sensible precaution hadn't been made common knowledge before Glee and others had begun to worry. Nevarr had agreed to request an announcement from council.

No, she hadn't eaten because the food dispenser nearest her quarters was located where the corridor went around a bend, then stopped in this configuration, making it one of the very few accessible places left where a trio under a blanket could wrap themselves into a passionate heaving knot and pretend no one could see them.

See them without turning that corner, maybe not. Hear them, definitely. And the smell? Drewe covered her nostrils with both hands as she headed for the central transtube. Love had to involve losing most of the senses, she decided.

C380A33 couldn't come fast enough.

Pythin greeted Drewe outside the entrance to the aft section. Cheerful and small, he had a rare mottling of yellow, white, and pink on the scalp between his short, pale quills. The colours appeared to fade or brighten as his quill patterns changed, lending them a dramatic flare particularly effective in poetry readings. The readings were always well attended, although Glee admitted she went for the scalp show, not Pythin's verse.

"Welcome, Walker Drewe. I'm to show you around." He looked understandably anxious, with distracting bands of pink down the sides of his head. Walkers didn't enter the growth chambers.

Until today, Drewe reminded herself with a burst of pride. "Lead on."

"You can't go like that."

Drewe blinked in confusion.

"You have to be cleansed first," Pythin explained. "And wear one of these." He snapped a bit of the tight black material that wound its way around his limbs and torso. "Don't worry. It's quite comfortable."

"What do you mean by 'cleansed'?" she scowled.

Cleansing turned out to be a process by which Drewe left behind not only her clothing but the top layer of her skin. Maybe more than the top layer, she squirmed, since some parts seemed more tender than others. It had been quick enough. Pythin had taken her through the entranceway to the passage leading to the protected section. That passage had bags for clothing, half of those filled, and ended in what looked remarkably like a closed sphincter. Drewe had followed her crèche mate's instructions and touched her forehead against its centre.

Drewe shuddered, grateful for the anti-nausea drugs in her system. The sphincter had opened and sucked her headfirst into a damp tube that pressed itself firmly against her body even as it pushed her along with a speed that left her involuntary shriek behind. Squirts of ice-cold liquid had hit her skin at random intervals, making her gasp each time.

By the time the tube spat her out to float in midair, Drewe felt like a lump of partially digested food. With very little skin left.

She looked around what was another plain bulb of a room and spotted a cabinet door set in one wall. Stroking her way to it, she hooked one foot into a stirrup made for that purpose, and opened the door. It was filled with a jumble of familiar black fabric.

"And how does this work?" she said to herself, reaching in to pull the nearest piece free. "Oh!" Another gasp, for the instant her fingers touched the stuff it began coiling up and around her arm, then her back, then everywhere else but her head, hands, and feet. "Oh," she repeated, this time with pleasure. The fabric was indeed comfortable, immediately soothing newly exposed skin.

A second cabinet provided the same type of hood she'd seen hanging from Nevarr and Pythin's suits. It wasn't self-fastening. Unable to figure out how to attach the thing, Drewe finally tucked it under one arm and pulled herself along a webline to the exit.

Pythin was waiting on the other side.

"You go through that every shift?" Drewe asked, feeling a new respect for those who worked aft. Null-grav and daily scouring? Made her blisters seem petty.

"After a cycle or two, you don't notice," he grinned, skin flashing yellow under a pleased alignment of quills. "Now, let me introduce you to the reason for all this."

She smiled back, but knew her own expression was a fine mix of apprehension and determination.

Time to meet the avatars.

She wasn't sure what she'd expected—some nightmare confrontation with distorted not-Drewes, huge vats of oozing liquid with limbs floating to the surface to be grabbed and stitched together, or bodies stacked in untidy piles, breathing in unison.

It hadn't been this.

"Don't I get to see them?" Drewe demanded, not quite sure when her dread had turned to frustration.

Pythin, whose nostrils were perhaps aimed a little more directly than politeness required at the back of a nearby technician, gave her a surprised look. "What do you mean?"

"This!" Drewe held the webline and gestured with the fingers of her free hand. "Everything's sealed or hidden away."

"Hardly hidden, Walker Drewe," offered the technician, turning to face her. "You're in the midst of the growth chamber."

One. Not a dozen or more as she'd imagined. That had been the first shift in perception.

"But—I thought I'd see an avatar."

"At this stage, the only way is through these." Pythin indicated the controls overhead, with techs either linked to specific areas or floating between with practiced economy of motion. Drewe wondered what would become of this place if gravity were suddenly restored, and hoped there were failsafes. "Each module travelling the network already contains its source matter."

Source matter. He meant her cells, Drewe realized, hers and those of the other walkers.

She'd already learned that growth chamber was a misnomer.

The "chamber" portion was nothing more than a huge tube itself, bending and twisting into the distance, populated by techs who swam through its air. The "growth" took place within a series of clear looping tubes that didn't connect to one another, though they followed a similar path along the walls of the growth chamber.

The modules Pythin meant were small opaque beads at this stage, visible as they moved through the tubes. They appeared almost at random and travelled at differing rates; here one lingered in a loop, there others clustered as if waiting in line to enter another twist. As he'd led her further down the the growth chamber itself, the modules, and the tubes that ferried them, had gradually became larger.

Because something was growing inside.

Drewe was silent as Pythin led the way. She noticed many of the tube loops led to multiple openings, only one leading onward. Few of the module-beads succeeding in passing through. A sorting process. It was like watching a game. Drewe found herself urging the next-in-line as it wobbled closer and closer to the moment of choice. It slowed, then dropped out of sight. She felt an odd grief.

"This area sorts viability of the starting culture. Failing modules are recycled," Pythin explained, observing her attention. "Later you'll see where we test for the desired genetic activity."

"So these aren't avatars."

"Not yet. They may be, once we have the next set of criteria. It's better for the system to keep running fresh material through."

"Oh." Drewe looked ahead. Except for the widening of the chamber to accomodate larger tubes, there seemed no other change. "So it's all like this," she said, unable to hide her disappointment. It was one thing to brace yourself for a confrontation, quite another to find it impossible.

Pythin appeared unhappy, perhaps expecting her to be more impressed. His quills folded back and forth, then settled into determination. "Come with me."

He took her through a door in what Drewe's mind persisted in viewing as the floor, although there wasn't any distinction here. Equipment ran around the walls, which themselves were one continuous curve. The lack of gravity here was eminently practical, allowing the maximum use of space within the ship. Pythin had told her how each avatar finished its maturation within a field like that of its destination world.

Not that there were any maturing at this moment for her to see.

The door opened into another of the narrow, featureless tunnels that laced the aft of the ship like blood vessels through an outstretched arm. From its orientation, she had the impression they were moving away from the growth chamber at a sharp angle.

"Where are we going?" she asked his feet.

"You'll see."

As bad as Nevarr, Drewe told herself, her hearts beating more rapidly.

It wasn't long before Pythin stopped at another of the round doors. "We have to wait for permission," he whispered, having keyed a request on the door panel. He studied an answering code. "Good. But be very quiet, please."

Since they were the only ones in the tunnel, Drewe clung to the webline and tried not to wonder why.

Three breaths later, the door irised open. Drewe recoiled at the heavy odor that followed. Sweat was the least of it.

She didn't know if she would have balked. Pythin reached back and took hold of her hand, gently tugging it from the webline. "This way, Walker Drewe. Remember. Quietly."

He pulled them both forward in a smooth swift motion, as if they had to go through the door as quickly as possible, a guess confirmed when it immediately closed behind them.

All she saw waiting for them was a naked body, strung by lines to hover in the middle of the room. Its skin was pulled back in several places by a mesh of finer lines. Pumps connected to tubes that entered the flesh. A cloud of mist flowed around and over all, produced from a machine behind the torso, collected in front.

Nevarr was busy plunging a narrow blade into one arm, an assistant playing more of the mist over the incision, mist which became red-stained before being sucked into the collector.

There was a face above the mutilation, as yet untouched. Nostrils and eyes closed, mouth hanging limp and open . . .

As if waking from a nightmare, Drewe screamed his name. "Tymin!"

The body gave a horrifying twitch. Nevarr cursed as he pulled the blade back just in time.

He stared at her, expressionless, then tapped one of his obnoxious ears with a finger.

"Auditory's still connected," Pythin breathed into her ear.

It wasn't Tymin. She could see that now the initial shock had past. The fingers were still paired almost to their tips, but those tips were elongated. The quills that graced the real Tymin's head were, on this—this version, incredibly long and coarse. The ears were larger than Nevarr's and covered with a fine down. The eyelids were the same, as were the nostrils, comely even closed.

She pushed against Pythin to drift closer without thought, measuring proportions with her eyes while trying not to see the marks of surgery. Longer limbs, wider feet. The torso was wider as well, as if the organs within were larger. Thinner atmosphere?

"D451A45," she whispered, remembering the crisp taste of that air. She touched the back of her head, remembering how that air had rattled through her long quills.

Her avatar's quills.

Nevarr nodded, then busied himself for a moment with the array of controls on an instrument secured to two of the lines. Thick hair-like plumes of wire led from it to behind the suspended avatar where Drewe presumed they connected to the nervous system through the spine. "There," he grunted in his normal voice. The avatar didn't react. "D451A45 it was. Walker Tymin was indisposed for that mission. Inflamed nostrils. I'd kept this for research. You'll never see better work." Nevarr used the gleaming tip of his blade to indicate matching, smaller glints within the exposed flesh. Drewe had mistaken them for drops of moisture not yet disturbed to be gathered within the mist stream. Now that she looked, she saw sparkles and threads of incredible delicacy throughout the darker flesh, some no larger than the nerves they'd replaced.

"Amazing. And you do all this by hand?" she asked, coming closer still.

"All but the final dendrites. We stimulate the avatar's sensory nerves to establish links to the new system. It takes a few days. Considerably less time than the original neural replacement."

Drewe was surprised to find herself fascinated instead of appalled. Perhaps it was the anti-nausea drugs. "Twelve walkers," she thought out loud. "We may visit another hundred worlds before the end of this mission. So many unique avatars. How do you cope with their differences?"

Nevarr held his arm beside the avatar's, avoiding the mist. The black fabric was tight enough to show the joints and flesh. The avatar's was longer, but the proportions were similar. "Variations on a common theme," he explained. "I look for the smallest possible changes in order to enhance an avatar's survival. I leave alone as much as possible, including the nervous system. The senses of the avatar must be comprehensible to the walker's brain, after all. It's not as hard as you might think. We're well built, sturdy organisms, Walker Drewe, an efficient design for exploring new worlds. Quite often, it's only a few thousand tweaks."

Before Drewe could frame her next question, Pythin spoke up, his quills revealing conflict. "Excuse me, Walker Drewe. The rest of the tour?"

"Is over. Leave us," Nevarr ordered. "You, too," he told his assistant. "Drewe will work with me for the rest of the shift."

Their quills patterned mild dismay, but both left without argument, though Pythin gave Drewe a sympathetic look.

When sure they were alone, Drewe turned to Nevarr.

"Now ask me," he suggested with a small smile, holding himself in place with a hand on one of the tubes feeding into the avatar.

She stared past him at the suspended body. "It's magnificent." She raised her hand slowly. "I could reach out and touch it."

"Please don't," he cautioned. "The sterile field is set for instruments, not fingertips. Ask me."

"I'm a walker," she said, troubled. "Why doesn't this horrify me?"

"Why?" Nevarr's head and neck might be stripped of expression, but she'd learned to pay attention to subtleties in his voice. Now, she thought it gentler than usual. "Because it isn't yours, Drewe. The reason walkers avoid the growth chamber has nothing to do with what we do here, or with the avatars themselves. That's the excuse. What you truly fear is meeting another self, of seeing what is you not only changed but mindless." He smiled, very slightly. "Once you realized that wasn't what you were facing, well, what is a walker but a trained explorer, accustomed to observing living things more alien than most of our crèche mates could even imagine. In a real sense, this"—he ran his fingers up the tube to where it dove into the avatar's concave chest—"is simply a novel biological sample."

A sample wearing her friend's face. Drewe pulled herself towards the head, forcing herself to see the distinctions, to see why this wasn't the Tymin whose nostrils had flared in hopes of her cooperative scent.

A watershed of tiny healed scars, almost imperceptible, traced its way over the skin still attached. Each was flawless, as if Nevarr's blade knew the underlying nerves beyond the possibility of error. The scars were dense over the face, particularly where they traveled over lips and nostrils, eyelids and the base of quills. Drewe memorized where the real Tymin would be most sensitive; not that she planned to use that knowledge.

The mist thickened for a second, its acrid scent stronger, and Drewe fought back a sneeze. She looked down at Nevarr.

"What do you want me to do?"

The shifts blurred one into the next until Drewe wasn't sure if she'd slept wrapped in black, or regularly missed going to bed entirely. It didn't matter. Time was fluid in transit, the artificiality of the environment dominant now, without a world to mark night from day. Meals were taken when the body insisted; sleep when eyes wouldn't stay open. The work was new and difficult and important.

Drewe had only been happier when walking.

Glee became sullen and quiet; Tymin, agitated and difficult. At some moment, Drewe noticed they'd stopped haunting her door.

At another, she recognized one of three pairs of feet protruding from a passionately heaving blanket and realized they'd stopped waiting altogether. As a tripling gift, she moved into the aft section and left Glee her quarters.

For all his faults and brusque manner, Drewe found Nevarr a perceptive teacher, anticipating where she'd need help as easily as when she'd leap ahead. Under his guidance, she progressed rapidly. Still, every so often, she'd be startled by what she was doing and with whom, and wonder how it had come to pass.

Others noticed. The walkers avoided her; those who worked in the growth chambers fell silent when she was near, unless spoken to. She might have broken some unwritten law.

It didn't matter to Drewe. She was driven by impatience to do more than suck sterile mist as Nevarr tinkered with Tymin's old avatar, eager to turn her hand to the design for the next world. Nevarr had grudgingly admitted she could help with the simulations when the data came in from the next round of probes.

Which would be today, Drewe thought triumphantly. She slithered through the cleansing tube, hands over her head and wiggling her torso to speed her passage. Even those quartered in the aft section had to be cleansed before entering the chamber itself.

Once squirted into the changing room, she lost no time wrapping her skin in black, snapping on her hood with the ease of practice. Pythin had been right. The procedure became mindless habit, just as had donning the equipment within the explorium before a walk.

This time, for the first time, she'd see their next target with Nevarr, instead of waiting for the juicy details to be filtered through the tedious sequence of specialists who would slice the descriptions of the new world into so many annotated streams of data that there was no point to a mere walker bothering to reassemble it. Might as well go there, they would say to one another.

Not this time. Drewe used one hand to spin her forward momentum down the corridor into a swing through Nevarr's open door. "Did it come in?" she asked hopefully, seeing him already hunched over a viewer. "Is that C380A33?"

"Good to see you, too," he muttered without looking up. Another habit.

She smiled and let herself drift closer. "Well, Nevarr?"

"Yes, yes." He leaned his head slightly to one side in invitation. "Take a look."

Drewe used his shoulder to maneuver herself into position so she could see the screen, with its image of an impossibly green and white sphere against black. Nevarr manipulated the controls and the view fell towards the planet's surface, punching through cloud as they followed the probe's entry.

Her quills rose in surprise, brushing his bare scalp as Drewe peered at the display. She'd come to rest upside-down relative to Nevarr, her feet safely away from any instrument panels. She held on to the back of his neck with one hand to keep her from floating past. "No artificial lights," she breathed, her attention caught by the dark expanse beyond the terminator as it flashed by. "No technology."

"Don't make assumptions from incomplete data."

"Sorry." Drewe jabbed at the screen with her free hand. "Go over there!"

Nevarr growled: "I'm not your avatar, Drewe." But he slid the view to center the area dotted with blue as the image sank downwards. "Good. Liquid water on the surface. Implies the ambient temps in that area are surviveable."

Skin against air. Memories stirred and Drewe relived stumbling through searing heat; being hunched and shivering in numbing cold; even arms outstretched to delicious warmth. Her quills fluttered in reaction and Nevarr tapped the side of her head. "Move or stop that." She didn't, but he made no further complaint as the view reached ground-level and the probe began moving more slowly now, sliding between upright stems and hanging branches, up and over strewn bare rock, then along the surface of a lake so calm and perfect its reflection chased it.

"Wilderness," she decided. "Here, at least," before Nevarr could correct her again.

"Pretty pictures aren't what we need." He altered the controls again, changing the feed from a visual spectrum suited to their eyes to analysis mode. The lake became a patchwork of greens and yellows, thermal contours creating a false image of hills and valleys.

It was interesting, but Drewe was more interested in imagining what it would be like to walk this world. She hummed to herself, picturing the leaves she'd seen layered on the branches of the tallest plants, wondering how they'd feel, if they'd be pungent when rubbed, if . . .

"Drewe."

She refocused on the screen, wondering what he wanted her to see.

But Nevarr was looking at her, not the screen, the nostrils that had been tight lines on his face now softer, wider, almost pink. It gave his face the life it had lacked, the warmth blooming like a secret only shared now. "Please stop," he said quietly.

Stop? Drewe suddenly realized she wasn't imagining her fingers rubbing leaves on that new world. They were busy in this one, boldly exploring the most sensitive portions of Nevarr's spinal ridge where it rose under the fabric wrapping his torso. It was impossible to be embarrassed; impossible to stop. She'd never touched anything that gave her such pleasure; never known anyone who made her feel this way. She knew, as her nostrils flared with heat, that his inner scent waited for her, that she had only to pull herself closer and press her face to—

Nevarr shoved her away, the force sending him crashing into the opposite wall while Drewe caught herself on a webline. He collected himself. His nostrils were pinched tight again. She might have dreamed that look of welcome.

Now the embarrassment hit, waves and waves of it until Drewe's quills seemed about to burrow themselves under her skin. "Nevarr . . ." she started, only to stop when he raised his hand.

"We should get to work," he said in a voice she hadn't heard before, averting his eyes.

Drewe covered her face with both hands, trying to hide the gorged nostrils she knew betrayed her. To her astonishment, Nevarr pushed himself in her direction. When close enough, he reached out and pulled her hands away. "Don't," he said, hushed and quiet. "I've never seen anything so beautiful." His scarred scalp flushed, as if longing to express some powerful emotion. "Let me look at you until the urge passes. Let me pretend."

"You could complete me," she whispered.

"But who would complete us?" he replied, then gave a small smile, as if asking her to share a joke. His paired fingertips tightened on hers, then let go. "I've been remiss in keeping you down here. Get out of the aft section. Be with friends. Find a pair of someones and a corner. I have to get started on the sims."

With that dismissal, Nevarr propelled himself to one of the many consoles attached to the walls of his workroom.

Drewe gazed longingly at the console, cursed hormones for the mindless complications they were, then tugged at the webline to send herself through the exit.

Glee would enjoy the irony.

Not that Drewe planned to tell anyone.

Ever.

Glee burst into Drewe's quarters as if chased. "Is it true?" she blurted. "What they're saying? It's all over the ship."

A ship that was three times larger in exploration configuration; the extra room had done wonders for dignity. Until now. Drewe lowered the bowl of soup that had almost made it to her mouth. "I'm trying to eat," she complained. "And you should know I don't listen to ship-chat."

"You should listen to this batch," Tymin said, coming in behind her. Their third, Miin, worked this shift. Drewe had to admit the three made a good triplet. Even better, their completion had restored their friendship. Those bound had no interest in other tanglings.

"Slarr's pregnant!" Glee said, dropping onto the bed, quills in disarray.

Drewe took a sip of her soup, eyeing her worried crèche mates over the bowl's rim. She savoured the taste then said calmly: "She can't be." A lift of the still-full bowl. "The additives in the food, remember?" There hadn't been a ship-wide announcement, but

word had spread on its own. Drewe suspected Nevarr of circum-
venting council secrecy.

"Maybe they don't work on everyone," Tymin countered. "Or
for only so long—"

"She's locked in med bay," Glee interrupted, quills flashing.
"No one's allowed to see her, not even her own triplet."

"That's odd," Drewe admitted.

Glee stood and leaned over Drewe. "You have to go to council.
Tell them to take the ship home." Calmly, though her hands
pressed against her midsection, her quills trembling with fear. "Before it's too late. They'll listen to you."

Drewe felt her own quills align in a pattern of reassurance. "I'll
talk to them. Find out what the situation is with Slarr—we have to
know first," she said sharply, when Tymin started to object. More
quietly, "They've just put the ship into orbit. We can't force everyone back together unless it's necessary." Not that it mattered.
Drewe had been relieved, in a way, to find no other crèche mates
aroused her. Only Nevarr, the one she couldn't have.

Only once.

She'd stayed away. Calmed herself as he'd ordered. Gone back
to requesting research data, which had arrived promptly, and with
annotations that meant she hadn't been forgotten, just rejected,
and probably for the best. She told herself so, regularly. Meanwhile, Nevarr and his techs were busy building the next avatars.
She would walk.

It couldn't be soon enough.

Drewe lifted her bowl and prepared to take another sip.

"What are you doing?" protested Glee.

Quills patterning annoyance, Drewe put the bowl down again.
"Going to talk to council, I take it. Now."

"Thank you," Tymin said, looking relieved. Drewe wasn't
surprised—he'd have had to bear the brunt of both Glee and Miin's
anxiety. A triplet could only produce one crèche mother, but in
those with more than one female, even the science of the People
couldn't predict who would ultimately ripen.

She stood and made a shooing motion. They had their own

quarters now, Miin's. "I'll let you know what I find out," she promised.

Tymin took Glee's hand and led her from the room. Drewe followed, securing her door. She'd grown possessive of her space. At the bend in the corridor, once the amorous dead-end corner, now a spacious opening leading to the links to both port and starboard transtubes, she turned to go her separate way.

"Wait! Tymin, we almost forgot to tell Drewe. About the planet."

Drewe stopped and looked back. "C380A33? What about it?"

Tymin's quills patterned embarrassment. "It's nothing. Shipchat. Not worth repeating."

"That's not what you said before!"

"Glee. We've pestered Drewe enough—"

"She'd want to know!"

Drewe let her quills show exasperation as the two argued. "Stop! You've already ruined my lunch and made me promise to interrupt council. You might as well finish. What ship-chat?"

With a shrug, Tymin gestured to his crèche mate. "Go ahead."

Glee stood straight, her quills crisscrossing one another with satisfaction. "They say it's home."

Drewe threw herself down the central transtube to the entrance to the aft section, ignoring those she passed, blind to all but one thought: could it be true?

Nevarr would know.

She reached null-grav and gratefully added to her speed, soaring through the opening iris of the main door, twisting to aim herself at the way through to Nevarr's workroom. She didn't bother to cleanse or change, she didn't bother with requesting entrance. She flew past every barrier.

In the section before his work area, she finally stopped, aware the next doorway would take her into the sterile area. She went to the access panel and keyed in her name, then grabbed a webline and pulled herself against the nearest wall to wait.

It didn't take long. The door opened with a puff of cleansing mist, Nevarr within it. He closed the door behind him. "You've heard the gossip," he said.

She'd forgotten the mask that was his ruined head; the misshaped lump that was his body; the austere lines of his nostrils, so flagrantly exposed in others. "Good to see you, too," she replied. "Is it true?"

"It might be." He rubbed his hand over his forehead, leaving streaks of blood from his fingers. He hadn't scrubbed before coming out here. She felt warmed by the thought he'd been eager to see her, and tried not to show it.

He looked exhausted, now that she paid closer attention, with deep creases around his eyes and mouth. Working that hard meant only one thing. "How long until the avatars are ready?" she asked. It was the logical next step, to walk the world.

He closed his eyes for a moment, as if gathering his strength, then looked at her. "Yours is already on the surface."

Her quills stood out in shock. A custom avatar, grown and ready so soon? "How—" Drewe closed her mouth. There was only one way. "One of the avatars in that storeroom. You found one that fits this world."

"Perfectly. They'll be calling you into the explorium next shift."

"Next shift?" Drewe threw herself into the middle of the room, letting her body spin its joy. On a sudden thought, she used a webline to stop and face Nevarr. "Wait—if it's ready, I can use the rig you have in the outfitting room. I can walk now!"

"There's no rush—"

Drewe's quills snapped into a pattern of despair. "There might be. Slarr could be pregnant. We might have to head back to our home. We might—Nevarr, I don't want to leave this world for the next ship to explore. Not if it could really be home. I want to walk it. Please."

"What about your triplet?"

"My—?" Before she finished even the thought, Drewe stopped herself. He hadn't reacted to what she'd said about Slarr, hadn't asked or disagreed. She pulled herself closer to him until she was past the point of politeness, until she saw him flinch back. "Slarr is pregnant," she accused. "And you knew all along it would happen. There are no additives—it was a lie to satisfy council and stop panic. Why?"

He took a deep breath, then said: "It bought time."

"What do you mean?" she demanded. "Time for what?"

Wearily. "It doesn't matter now. You're right. If you want to walk, you'd better go soon."

Drewe's quills flashed into joy.

Moisture hangs in the air, not ready to fall. She lifts her hand to touch droplets that bead the edge of a leaf, then stops, confused.

The hand moving into sight is her own.

For the first time, she ignores her surroundings, intent on exploring herself.

The pale fuzz of sensory quills coating her bare arms is familiar; the intact skin between pairs of fingers is not.

There should be scars.

She's lost in self, runs almost familiar hands over the concave torso to find the soft ventral cavity where a spinal ridge could be welcomed, the special places on her sides, between her legs, behind on her back, under her arms where warm surges of fluids could enter, penetrating every cavity within her to leave the potential for life, the sensitive merquills waiting to rouse and send her contributions in turn deep into the special places of others.

His places.

All of them. All at once.

As he would do to hers.

She rocks and moans his name. "Nevarr."

The word shocks her back to where and what she is, on an unknown world, surrounded by lush green and globes of purple, orange, and red, colours she can name for the first time in any walk.

These are her eyes.

She takes eager steps, each sensation real and now and hers. She startles a cloud of flying things that sing as they disappear into the safety of taller plants. She sweeps dewdrops from the quills atop her head, feeling their flexible tips as if new. Enticed by its scent, she dares put a yellow and white fruit in her mouth, and bites deep. Juice, sun-warm, spills between her lips. Bitter and sweet and sticky.

She follows the land downward, an arbitrary course. Up might give her eyes a distant view. Down might lead to open fields or water. Fields, because she sees where she is.

The tall vegetation, its spirals of straight branches clung to by leaves and yellow-white fruit, grows in precise arrangement, an arrangement whose intent she understands without thought, for it is the pattern her quills assume when she feels content. This is an orchard. Planted by someone of the People.

She takes gentle steps. No one must know she's been here.

But she must find the gardener.

She moves through dappled shadows, the sky tucked behind the swell of growing things, the ground underfoot chill and damp. Hallowed ground, she feels, the fragrance of the fruit intoxicating, the air itself a caress.

She has never felt this much at home on any other world. So welcome.

So when a figure steps in her path, she stands, hands out in greeting.

He is strange and beautiful. No quills. Instead, the soft pebbled skin of his head and neck glows with changing colours. They settle into a pattern she trusts.

He means her no harm.

He slowly puts down the implements he carries, then stands again. He is taller, longer-limbed, more graceful. His nostrils are wide and full and flare to gather her scent. His eyes are huge, dark orbs, their surface flickering as membranes flash over them.

His mouth opens and he speaks. The sounds make no sense.

She's astonished. She speaks, and his patterns change to what she reads as confusion.

Then, into something else.

She lets him come close. He towers over her but she feels no fear. He touches her quills with unpaired fingers, following their patterns, his breath coming more quickly. Uttering more incomprehensible words, he walks around her. Suddenly, she feels his nostrils hot and thick pressing against the bareness of her spinal ridge, and she is lost.

They tangle without thought or hesitation, rolling in leaf litter and soil. They cry out like animals, in esctasy and pain. Some of his places are too small. She forces her way in; feels his flesh tear. He does the same. It isn't enough. There should be more.

They reach blindly for the other to complete them. He cries a word; she pleads her own. "Nevarr . . ."

And she finds herself hanging in connectors within the explorium, fingers trapped in gloves, her skin glistening with wasted fluids.

He is there, nostrils wild and red, frantically disconnecting her from the equipment, cursing.

When her mouth is freed, she whispers: "Come home, beloved. Our third awaits."

Then she knows no more.

"We need no further tests," Uckod said, her quills awry and grim. "C380A33 is the planet on which the People originated."

"And have remained. Is that confirmed?"

Drewe was reasonably sure her quills were permanently set in mortification. "Yes," she said, when they appeared to wait for her.

"So the great exodus was incomplete." Jahan looked disturbed, as well he might, Drewe thought. They were rewriting the history of their kind with every word. "Some stayed behind."

"And became different. How?"

Nevarr made a rude sound. "Time. A different environment, rates of mutation, selection pressures. Let alone different standards of beauty—"

"Not that different," Jahan interrupted, staring at Drewe.

She felt her quills rearrange at last—anger—but Nevarr spoke before she could. "Walker Drewe did her job," he emphasized. "Her avatar had to be decommissioned immediately, but the morphological data obtained from the specimen she encountered on C380A33 has given us a great deal of information already. For instance . . ."

His voice faded into something meaningless.

What had the other thought? Drewe wondered. What had he done when the body tangled with his fell apart, becoming nothing more than liquid, disappearing into the soil? Would he tell others? Begin the legend of an otherworldly female, who seduced gardeners within their orchards. Start some fertility rite? Or would it scar him–leave him forever as incomplete as she now felt–to wander alone among his plants . . .

How could she find him again, when she didn't know the sound that was his name?

"Drewe."

She looked up from her hands. "My apologies, Uckod. Did you ask me a question?"

"You must not discuss anything about this walk, or this world, with crèche mates other than those in this room. Is that clear?"

"Of course." She didn't have a problem with that restriction. In fact, Drewe was sincerely hoping to never talk to anyone in this room about it again, especially one person.

Not that she'd talked to Nevarr. Nor had he asked her questions. He hadn't needed to–having access to the complete record of the sensations transmitted by her avatar. When she'd regained consciousness, finding herself clean and dressed in the ubiquitous wrap of those who worked in the chambers, he'd been there, his calm, expressionless self, to say only that council expected her written report as soon as possible.

Then he'd left.

"Good. This is a delicate matter. I don't believe even Futurists anticipated we'd meet ourselves again, did they, Nevarr?"

"Not that I'm aware, councillor."

"Other groups will seize on this, mark my words. There'll be ramifications well beyond mission parameters, my crèche mates," Uckod pronounced, "consequences we can't possibly predict. But we must do our best, before sending this news home. Home," her quills flashed with amusement. "There's a word with new meaning."

"It's beautiful," Drewe heard herself say, and closed her mouth.

Jahan's quills patterned amusement. "Maybe through an avatar," he qualified. "To those of the People, our crèche mates, it is a ball of dirt. An alien environment with moving air."

"Yes, councillor."

"I'll need you to work with me," Nevarr told her outside the council room.

Drewe hesitated.

"There's no one else," he said bluntly. "Council wants this kept quiet. You know how quickly chat spreads. Get whatever you need. I want you to move back into the aft section."

"Why? To do what?" she asked, but he turned and walked away.

Nevarr never waited, Drewe reminded herself.

The central transtube was strangely empty when Drewe entered. She secured her small bag of belongings to a tie on her shift and began pulling herself aft, every movement reluctant. Her body was confused. She hadn't tangled; no new fluids rested inside her being sorted, used or saved. Her mind insisted she had, remembered every thrust and its warm, precious deposit, believed she should be on her way to ripening.

And now, to be forced within reach of Nevarr? Drewe sighed and slowed even more. Thinking of him only made the confusion worse. Her body wasn't part of a triplet, but her mind? Oh, her mind knew she was, and would settle for nothing less again. Like some tragic story of a lovelorn trio, Drewe found herself bound to the unattainable.

Which mattered now to the scheme of things? Her quills flipped into amusement. "We've succeeded," she told herself. "We found the homeworld of the People. What single crèche has ever accomplished so much? Our descendants will be among the great and powerful on whatever station they choose."

And, one day, just maybe, those descendants might set foot on the planet of their ancestors.

With that thought, Drewe found herself able to move normally again. When she reached her destination, the entrance, she found the access panel aglow with warning yellow letters. " 'Routine Sterilization Protocol in Effect,' " she read out loud. " 'Shift Cancelled.' "

Nevarr and his secrets.

She keyed in her name, unsurprised when the door irised open.

After stowing her things, few that they were, and going through the routine of cleansing and dressing yet again, Drewe headed for the workroom. Instead of the more direct route, she retraced the path Pythin had used for their tour, curious how the growth chamber looked without its busy techs floating everywhere.

It looked dead.

She pulled herself inside the mammoth chamber, her breathing too loud in her ears, and gazed all around.

It was dead.

No lights flickered on console or panel. The network that carried modules from inception to avatar was empty, save for one forgotten globe, motionless within its tube.

What did it mean?

The end of their mission, that much was obvious. Without avatars, there would be no walking. Slarr, and who knew how many others, must be pregnant and the council planning to take the ship home—home to the nearest station. Another ship, or more than one, most likely, would replace them.

While she understood the need to care for any ripening crèche mothers among the crew, Drewe couldn't help her disappointment. She floated alongside the tubes, tracing their smoothness with her fingertips. Despite her situation, or maybe because of it, she'd wanted to explore this one world more than any other.

Her breath caught. If the growth chambers were shut down, Nevarr no longer need stay with the ship.

They could take two pods. Go down. She would teach him how to walk–

Drewe stopped right there. Nevarr might manage the gravity within the stern section for brief intervals. She couldn't drop him into the gravity well of a world, to be imprisoned for the rest of his life. That wasn't what you wanted for someone you cared about more than yourself.

There, she'd admitted it. Oddly, Drewe felt relieved, as if acknowledging her attachment to the gruff, complicated Chief Designer made the binding easier to bear.

She should find him. See what work he had for her. They had
that, at least.

Quills spread in reflection of a happier, if not fully cheerful
mood, Drewe found the door from the growth chamber to the tube
leading off to Nevarr's workroom and pulled herself along it.
Reaching the access panel, she didn't bother to key in her name,
just opened the door and floated through, a greeting on her lips . . .

. . . that died.

The figure suspended in the centre of the room, bathed in mist,
wasn't another Tymin, or even another Drewe.

It was another Nevarr.

Nevarr with no unsightly flesh around his torso. Younger. Un-
blemished. With a glorious set of red-tipped quills.

Quills the Nevarr who Drewe knew and loved was methodically burning away, leaving angry puckered skin behind.

He'd seen her enter. His eyes had flicked her way before returning to his task.

The sick-sweet smell of burned flesh mingled with the mist.
Drewe gagged and hastily covered her mouth, willing back the
nausea.

"Why?" she gasped as soon as she could.

Nevarr had moved to the neck. "Why?" he echoed. "Because
this crèche has reached its natural end. There's nothing more I can
do. It's time."

"Time for what?" She eased nearer, quills fluttering with apprehension. "We're heading home, Nevarr. The crèche mothers—"

"It's important to take the quills off," he said, as if she hadn't
spoken. "It's too hard to live the lie otherwise. To have a face like
yours, Drewe, where your feelings draw themselves out with such
exquisite clarity for all to see—I can't afford a face like that."

"What lie?" she breathed. "What lie!" louder, with a snatch for
his arm that missed. Drewe stopped herself with the nearest
webline. "Nevarr. Please. Tell me what's going on."

"I will," he said, panting as if out of breath. He still didn't look
at her. "I will. That's why I asked you to come. But it's hard. The
lie. I've preserved it all my life. It's the reason for my life. More im-

portant than my life." Finally, he looked at her, his face a mask, his eyes haunted. "But I couldn't end without telling you."

"End?" She thought she knew and her quills flattened in fear. "Are you ill?"

"No, dear Drewe. I'm old."

"We're not old," she said, relieved. "We're barely in the middle of our lives."

"I'm not your crèche mate." Nevarr tugged his duplicate's toes. "He is."

She narrowed her eyes, suspecting a trick. "That's not true. We grew up together, you and I, all of us. We went through training. I remember when you started excelling at design, when you broke your arm playing oleoi, when we snuck to the outer station ring to watch incoming ships."

"You didn't live that life, Drewe. I gave it to you. Just as he," another tug, "will give it to the next crèche on board."

"Next . . ."

Nevarr gave himself the tiniest push, enough to reach the webline where she clung with all her might, but didn't come closer. "I showed them to you," he said matter-of-factly. "The storeroom?"

"Avatars," Drewe protested. "You said they were copies of avatars you'd made from my genome."

"I said they were phenotypes of you. You assumed the rest—I wasn't about to tell you differently. Not then. Now? Yes, they are all this version, this Drewe. As lovely and stubborn as the existing model. As utterly wonderful," this last with an almost wistful note. "I tried not to love you again. As will he"—a nod to the silent form hanging before them—"when his turn comes."

"His turn." She felt trapped, his nonsense making too much sense. "You're telling me our crèche isn't real—that we didn't tear ourselves from our mother. That we were made, just as you'd make an avatar, and all our memories before this ship were somehow put into our heads."

"You dreamed them. Inside the orbs. A repeating loop of experiences and feelings, so when each new set is released, you begin life from the same moment. You and Glee are always friends. Pythin has his poetry and spots. Uckod and the council are already neuter. I–I overlap, so there is someone to watch for the signs of aging: the surge of hormones, the whispers in the corridors, drives that can't be controlled. Pregnancies can't be allowed, Drewe. That's the end point. When your generation stops and the next must begin."

"No! We can take the ship home!" Numb, Drewe stretched out her hand to him; he stayed out of reach. "Nevarr–"

"Home?" he repeated. "Ah, yes. The stations. We did start there. Twenty-three generations ago. And we've traveled away ever since."

She refused to understand. "Transit. We'll enter transit."

"That shortcut past real space isn't free, Drewe. Haven't you noticed? Each passage ages us from within. None of us would survive a transit long enough to retrace the smallest part of the journey. I believe that's why we were made, so the People could explore interstellar space without risk." His voice quickened. "We were never intended to return. Just to do the job. Find resources for machines to exploit. Be as happy as we can while we live. There's no alternative." He paused and stared at her, his nostrils flared ever-so-slightly. "I've spent this half of my life trying to find one."

"But you did!" she exclaimed. "This world. We can stay here. Live there." Drewe's quills flashed joy. "It will take some getting used to, but the crèche mothers will have more than enough room. The People already there will welcome us. They're different, but not–"

"Stop it. You don't know what you're saying. It was the most difficult thing I've ever done, preparing that flesh for this world. But at least it never woke, never knew who it was. It was never real."

"He was real. He was beautiful, Nevarr," she coaxed, drifting to him, her nostrils flushed with hope. "We both wanted you–you heard me call for you. I know you did. That's why you disconnected me."

"I disconnected you because your avatar was tangling, not you. Didn't you learn anything from the experiment? It's sensory input, nothing more. It died. You didn't. Remember?"

Drewe pressed her face into his midsection, breathing deeply. Her fingers unerringly sought his places, the places missed when there had been only two. "It was real in all the ways that matter," she urged, pulling back before she aroused them both. They had to think, not react. "If we can't go to that dream of home, we can go to the real one. All of us."

"Drewe." Just her name, warm and sad.

"It's worth a try."

"We'd live no longer there. Once council sends its report, that C380A33 is not only the homeworld, but still inhabited, the planet is doomed."

Her first thought was the taste of fruit, tangy and sweet. Her second, of a smooth head patterned in glorious colours. Understanding soured in her mouth. "Because they're different from us."

"No." He ran his fingers down the fabric covering her arm. "Because we're different from them. You met the original species, suited to life under an open sky, adaptable, resistant, variable. Not like us."

"We're not that different yet," she argued, nostrils flaring. "The People could survive there. Us." She flattened her hand on her chest. "The base version."

"Base version?" Nevarr brushed his fingers over the quills beside her ear. "This? This is a guess. One-third science, one-third inspiration, one-third 'good enough.' We were made in the image of the past, Drewe. Incomplete, untested. The result? What we are couldn't survive down there. I doubt we could live anywhere but on this ship for long."

"Then why destroy that world?"

"This world, its life, is seen as a threat by those on the stations. That's why Futurists try so hard to stop the search for the homeworld. We know contact with the original genome, with the original ecosystem, would change everything for the People. Even if disease could be prevented, the People couldn't compete with the original version. Not any more. Not on planets or in space. We've—they've changed."

Her quills fluttered through fear and shock, then settled into curiosity.

"How?" she asked.

Nevarr ran his fingertips gently down her spinal ridge, sending a shiver through her body. "I could show you. What we've really become."

"How?" she breathed, eyes half closed.

"There's a simulation from the station that sent us out. Meant for me—for all the Nevarrs—to keep us aware of our true mission." His fingertips dug more deeply, holding their bodies together as they both let go and drifted free. "An avatar for my beautiful walker," he promised huskily, nostrils flaming red and flaring, seeking her scent. "But first . . ."

Desire mixed with grief.

Love won.

"First," she agreed.

She is suspended in star-crusted darkness. She moves her arms to feel out her surroundings and instead moves herself.

She flies.

Her nostrils flare to take in scents. She identifies them, one by one. Heated metal. Composites. A hint that not so long ago, some-ones tangled nearby, leaving sweat and love behind.

She flies, not knowing if she's safe to do so, but impatient for more than this starry night.

A disc of light appears ahead, beneath, brightens. Beings soar upwards through it, spinning together.

She hears laughter.

Caught by the light, they are translucent wisps of skin and quill, fragile-seeming yet supple. She sees how they move and un-derstands her arms are something new. She has fingers still, but the rest is a frame for long, barbed quills that lace together into wings of strength and delicacy. Her legs—she feels nothing where they should be.

She walks their world without feet.

The disc of light closes again. She sees them still, for now they fluoresce, sparkling their arousal, tangling midflight in twos, and threes, and altogether until she can no longer tell them apart. Their glow fades.

She closes her wings, waits to fall, but does not. There is no need of gravity here. Those who have mastered the air and space are before her, clinging in a sated cloud.

She is less than their flesh.

And more.

"We're all here," Pythin said, checking his list. His scalp was pale and mute under his quills. Drewe stared at him, suddenly wondering which had come first.

"All the ones awake," Nevarr whispered in her ear. Her Nevarr, not the one waiting aft, innocent of all this, able to act regardless of the vote. A living failsafe.

No. A crèche mate. They were more than living machines, Drewe thought. They might be the result of science, experience, and good enough to survive—the station-dwellers' best guess at the ancestral form—but they were more.

Standing with the council beside her, Drewe looked out over this unprecedented gathering. Only one space had been able to accommodate them all, the chill deck where av-pods were serviced and reassembled. Even here crèche mates were packed shoulder-to-shoulder.

All were afraid. The quills showed it; the pattern of their bodies reinforced it. Random, tight, unsettled. Desperate. Looking for hope.

Drewe swallowed, knowing that wasn't what they could offer.

Uckod gestured and silence fell. "We are but one of thousands of ships, sent to seek resources for the great stations, ensuring the survival of the People. They survive. We have succeeded." She took a step forward. "We are but one of thousands who have sought the biological home of the People for generations. Of all, only we have found it. Intact. Beautiful. Nurturing the People from whom we all descend."

There were no cheers. They knew the terrible truth already. Having found their past, they would bring its destruction.

Drewe stepped forward, drawing the one beside her forward. Some gasped, seeing Slarr for the first time. There was no denying her condition. The growth within her body was already pressing outward from all sides. Soon, she would be unable to move, reliant on her triplet for the necessities of life. Her future was set and glorious. When ripe, her offspring would consume her body in their drive for freedom, a death delivered with such intense joy that many crèche mothers succumbed to the emotion well before their flesh failed.

But where could her newborns live?

"We've done our jobs," Drewe began. "Walker, tech, council, crew. Designer." She spotted Glee's lovely face in the front row. Her friend nodded encouragement, holding fast to her triplet. "But we aren't avatars. We're real. Those who sent us into space knew they couldn't control us. They trusted us to take the training we had, use the bodies we have, to do what was best for our kind.

"But they had a problem. We were to explore worlds, not space; even using avatars, that meant enduring conditions the station dwellers no longer could. So we had to be base versions, as our designer would say.

"But because of our bodies, they knew we could never come home."

Quills fluttered and fell into patterns of despair and resignation. Drewe waited until they were still.

"They weren't unkind. We weren't to know. Only one, the Nevarr from the previous crèche, would hold the truth." She felt his breath against her neck and smiled. "It was his duty, before any generation produced its first crèche mother, to simply deepen our sleep, recycle our bodies, then wake a new generation of us to begin again." She reached her hand to take Slarr's. "We're a bit late."

Amusement, ragged and shaky, patterned a few heads. Only a few.

"The stations offer no home for us. What of the world we orbit? The People living there seem closer to us in many ways." She felt Nevarr nudge her spinal ridge and made a supreme effort not to pattern embarrassment. Glee gave her a knowing smirk, anyway. "Could we abandon this ship and give birth there?"

This hadn't occurred to most; she could see it in their reactions. Nevarr had been right—their kind couldn't hide their feelings.

Council had been the same way. It had taken time to convince them. Time, and access to what she'd experienced in both walks.

She saw hope and spoke quickly. "Nevarr."

They'd never see him as crèche mate again–that was clear in the alarm and fear on every head. But they listened. There was respect, too. He saw it, and she thought it helped him speak.

"No. Our bodies aren't compatible with this world. Your crèche would die, Slarr. We all would. And what if our presence alerted those on the planet to our People? What if they saw a threat to their survival?"

A voice from the crowd. "Can't we take the ship to another world–find a world for ourselves?"

Jahan stepped up, his quills set in despair. "If anything happens to a ship, it's taken as a potential threat to the stations. They'll send probes to follow our last heading. They'll find C380A33. And trust me, it won't take long for them to realize what it is. The next arrivals will be planet-killers."

That shocked them.

"There is a way for this discovery to be prevented," Uckod said into the hush. "And that is for us to be as crèche mother to this world and all its inhabitants. We must give our lives and let them struggle free of our flesh, so only what is new remains. It is our way."

Someone shouted: "Our accomplishment–our names–no one will remember us . . ."

Slarr spoke for the first time. "No one does now," she replied bitterly. "We are nothing. There's no place"–the word caught in her throat–"no place like home, ever, for us. We're a lie."

"Does it matter?" Drewe countered, raising her voice over the murmurs until they quieted. "There is a home," she said firmly, and pointed up. "There, for those who were first. And there is a home, out there, for the People who are their rightful descendants. All we have to do to protect both is hide them from one another. We can do this. We must."

"We can replace the data from C380A33 with that of a disappointment, unworthy of further exploration in all ways," Uckod offered quietly. "Nevarr can prepare the next crèche to take over as soon as possible. It is their time. Nothing will be unusual. No one will ever know. But it means disobeying our assigned mission and lying to those who made us."

They were still silent.

Nevarr raised his hands, as if in place of the quills he'd sacrificed so long ago. "You were never to leave a legacy. I and those before me lived to prevent it. But now we can all leave our mark on the history of our kind. You decide, crèche mates," his voice rose to a ringing shout. "Shall we at last die to give life?"

Each and every hand shot up to match his.

She bowed her head, overcome with pride.

There would be a new, innocent Drewe.

And she would walk worlds.

She takes gentle steps. No one must know she's been here.

Her nostrils, narrow, smooth, well-suited to this atmosphere, flare to take in scents.

Through eyes, wide, thick-lashed, well-suited to this light, she gazes at a world as beautiful as any other she's walked. No less.

They want her to believe this is home, to feel it.

She has felt this much at home on every other world.

And no more.